# The Last Shiksa

# The Last Shiksa

## B.H. Litwack

G. P. Putnam's Sons, New York

SBN: 399–12065–3

**Library of Congress Cataloging in Publication Data**

Litwack, B H
    The last shiksa.

    I. Title.
PZ4.L7823Las    [PS3562.I789]    813″ .5′ 4    77–23900

*For Ruth, a kind of Moabite;*

*and*

*For the sloppiest soldier in World War II*

# The Last Shiksa

*He goeth after her straightway,*
*As an ox goeth to slaughter*

Proverbs 7:22

# Book I

# Chapter 1

---

*Arnold Goff begins his most sensational day in his great
spring of '69*

Christine. Goff woke with her, with the touch and taste and scent of
her. In his head. Not in his bed.

Christine. She of the long slim legs and the golden hair and endless
bright blue eyes of arctic summer; she whose shimmering northern lights
would shine on him before another day dawned.

Christine. He would be faithful to her forever. After they got started,
that is.

Goff squinted his eyes at the sun shining in on his Park Avenue bedroom. He had the delicious sensation of being at the peak of his powers.
Yahoodie! He bounced out of bed, gave his balls a hearty good morning
scratching and, barefoot, toes buried in deep fleece carpeting, hurried into
his ornate marble bathroom to get himself started for a sensational day.

Sensational days do not exist in a vacuum. They are the consequence of
intensive, dogged and constant effort. Forgings and reforgings.

Goff had always felt he had great potential. He was sharply aware that
his many early stumblings had been caused by a recurring sense of insecurity. Although during the war all that seemed to have been effectively
suspended. He had served in the Army with rousing success, if not emi-
nent distinction. No, he hadn't received any medals; he had never even
been shipped overseas. However, he did obtain a commission as a lieutenant and fucked his brains out all over the country. He had handled

11

himself, in general, tremendously. He had gotten along great. But when he was discharged, all his military confidence had collapsed the moment he had stepped into his parents' old apartment and taken up his old room and seen his old life stretching out in front of him again. World War II, the bloodiest war in history with its cost of untold lives, untold sacrifices, hadn't been fought and won so Arnie Goff could go and resume being a schmuck again. The war had to have *some* meaning.

During those early uncertain days before Goff had established himself, his accountant, Chaim "Chuck" Addelson, having just finished his profit and loss statement on a new and shaky enterprise involving the manufacturing of phonograph records, had shrugged sympathetically at his client's despondency. He urged him to see Kummerlos, his own psychiatrist. "I'm seeing him every week. He's helped me something enormous—in all areas," Chuck assured him. "He'll give you confidence. That's all you need. The books aren't so terrible. You're holding your head above water. Go see Kummerlos."

Kummerlos! Christine's husband. The most important man he would ever meet. It was the best advice Goff ever got.

Kummerlos had proved his brilliance from the beginning. Goff obeyed his instructions to bring in a dream. It was a recurring dream.

He was in his father's old Chevie. He was back in the Army. He was with Josie McLeod. She was a WAC corporal from Pensacola. They were in the back seat. She had curly red hair and she had opened her blouse. She had beautiful breasts, huge freckled marshmallows. He was ready to bury his head in them when he looked out of the window and saw Christ on the cross at the side of the road. Christ was shaking his head, no, no. He had felt scared, but nothing was going to stop him. But when he buried his head in those marshmallow breasts, they had no substance; they were merely froth. Although that wasn't too bad because her legs were spread wide open and he was about to enter her when his pop came driving up in the very same old Chevie that he and Josie were occupying. Screeching, skidding off the road, his pop's Chevie crashed right into his Chevie, which was also, in the way of dreams, his pop's. His pop, wearing his long johns, then yanked open the door, laughing and cackling, accusing him of having caused him to have an accident, then ordering him out—sputtering that his son was going to ruin the springs. Arnie Goff obeyed. Pop then climbed into the back of the car and slammed the door shut. And Goff remained standing outside. He wasn't able to see inside, but he saw the Chevie bouncing, bouncing and he heard his father cackling, cackling.

Kummerlos told Goff that the dream furnished him with much significant raw material to process. Goff agreed excitedly. "It has plenty to do with my Jewish problem and my father, right, Doctor?"

"It has plenty to do with your father—and your mother. As for the Jewish problem, as you call it—the appearance of Christ, the redheaded gentile female figure—I would say that these are all decoys. Everyone has a Jewish problem."

"I suppose," said Goff, unconvinced.

"I am for now principally concerned with your father's crashing into you. Can you tell me your thoughts on that?"

"But, Doctor, if I dream of Jesus Christ commanding me not to have sexual relations with a beautiful red-haired gentile girl, I just can't see how that is unimportant."

Kummerlos would not be distracted. "This girl, she was an actual person, yes?"

"Yes. She was Josie McLeod. I knew her in the Army. She was a WAC, and I did have real relations with her for a while."

"Quite. So I gathered. You see, Mr. Goff, this segment of your dream was merely a transliteration of actual or literal events, and has nowhere near the value of symbolic happenings."

"But you can't say that Jesus Christ was a translation of a literal event."

"I said transliteration, not translation. There is a difference."

"Yes, of course," said Goff.

"Now, your father crashing into you—is that based on an actual occurrence?"

"No."

"Well, that's why it has so much significance. There is a secret there. A code, which if deciphered may supply us with important information. But I see you are still troubled about Christ on the cross. All right, let us deal with that. Let me ask—with this girl, did you ever sleep in a hotel room or any places that contained a picture of the crucifixion?"

"No. It was mostly back seats in back streets."

"All right. Did you ever go to church with her?"

"No. Why should I go to church with her?"

"All right. Was she religious? Did she resist your advances or create some obstacle for you based on religious beliefs, or mention Jesus, or something similar?"

"No. But wait a minute. . . . I got my first date with Josie when she stood up a big red-assed battalion sergeant-major from Texas, and he would have liked to kill me. He always went around bragging how he hated Jews."

"How did you know he had a red ass, or is that some Army or regional slang?"

"No. He had a big red ass. Not fat, mind you. Just tremendous, beefy. He was a very big man and I remember him in the shower room, and all I remember is a tremendous Texas red ass. Yeah, like a farmer might have a red neck, he had a mountain of beefy red ass."

"Do you think that has any connection with the crucifixion in your dream?"

Goff paused. "Yes," he said hesitantly. "Something . . ." and then he exploded. "Jesus Christ! You know what, Doctor? He was from Texas, from Corpus Christi, Texas! My God! My God!"

"A-ha," said Dr. Kummerlos.

Goff had been astonished at this revelation, and equally astonished at his doctor's cleverness. And Kummerlos, having cleared the way, then prepared to go further.

"Let us get back to the car crash. What did your father say when he crashed into you?"

"I think he said, 'You made me have an accident.' "

"But he was laughing, right? Or cackling, as you describe it."

"Yeah, he was cackling."

"The fact that he called it an accident—what can you comment on that?"

Goff slapped his head and his mouth flew open. "Doctor, my God! My father always jokes that I was an accident. It's almost a family joke. Oh, but it's so obvious. How did I miss it?"

"But you didn't miss it."

"Only because you led me to it," Goff said in a reverent tone.

Kummerlos lowered his eyes. He did not want to encourage any emotional display. He was satisfied that his patient understood his doctor's key role in this revelation. "Let us delve a little more. Your father charges you with being the cause of his accident. He laughs at you and orders you out of the car. And you are forced to watch ignominiously as he enters the car and takes your place with the female figure. You stand there helpless as you watch the Chevie bouncing, bouncing," he finished deadpan. He pursed his lips, clasped his hands and waited a moment for the full effect to sink in. "We must close now," he murmured.

Goff had staggered out. That hour had been a smasher. He had immediately advanced his sessions to twice a week. The next year it had been three times. Thereafter it was four, although the fourth session was in a group, Kummerlos' Thursday Night Group. Goff had thrived on this increased schedule and had maintained it for nineteen years. He owed Kummerlos plenty. He had derived so much good from him, so much comfort, so much healthy, wealthy and wise, so much everything, really.

In the following weeks Goff and Kummerlos had consolidated the lessons of the dream. It had been obvious that his designation as his father's accident had caused incalculable damage to his self-esteem. Kummerlos had gone on to explain that the Chevie represented the womb. Even the word Chevie, he suggested, might be the she-V or the female genital. Goff had been dumbfounded. What eye openers.

Kummerlos pressed further. His pop chasing him out of the car undoubtedly grew out of his Oedipal phase. His pop's long johns. The symbol was clear. And Goff standing outside helpless, looking on—classic. Had he ever witnessed the primal scene, Kummerlos wondered, his mom and pop doing it? Goff didn't think so. Kummerlos suggested that he had, but had repressed it.

Kummerlos continued to mesmerize him with his virtuoso showpiece dazzle—all with subdued, controlled assurance, a Heifetz effortlessly and with no visible emotion stupefying him with the most intricate bowings and double stops.

"What about my pop complaining that I broke his springs?"

"I would say that is a statement signifying that your having been conceived accidentally probably caused a radical curtailment in your father's sexual or procreative activity."

"Was Josie McLeod supposed to be my mother?"

"As much as any girl is your mother."

Goff nodded. New depths of understanding yawned gravely, scaring him.

Kummerlos, despite his early minimizing of the literal, had gone on to almost a whole session on Josie McLeod, eliciting minute details about Goff's knowledge of her both in the dream and in the flesh. Plenty in the flesh, thought Goff suspiciously. Well, why not? His doctor had earned a little detour.

"Was she avid?"

"In the dream?"

"In the flesh; you didn't consummate in the dream."

"Right. My pop took over. Well, she gave me great sex. She was a

beautiful redhead with a freckled face and a freckled behind. We had
some tremendous sex in the back of my car. She didn't know I was Jewish."

Again Kummerlos ignored the Jewish matter and took on a new line of
questioning. "Tell me, Mr. Goff, in conclusion, what segment of the
dream disturbed or bothered you the most?"

Goff shrugged. He didn't know.

"Was it when Christ commanded you No?"

"No. I was scared, but it didn't exactly bother me."

"Well, was it when your father crashed into you?"

"No, I don't think that bothered me the most."

"How about when he ordered you to leave Josie McLeod and get out of
the car?"

"No-o-o-o, I don't think so."

"You hesitated."

"Well, Doctor, you want to know the real truth?" Kummerlos looked
piercingly at him. "The real truth is that when my pop busted in on me
and Josie and told me to get out, what bothered me most was that he was
talking in that Jewish accent of his."

Kummerlos nodded. "We must close now."

Well, the basic thing had been uncovered quickly. Goff began to feel
much better. New confidence set in, the basis of which was not so much
the recognition of the "accident" damage, but more, the fact that he had
such a great counselor to turn to now.

Goff puzzled briefly over the doctor's avoidance of his Jewish problem.
Kummerlos' response that everyone has a Jewish problem was not a bad
answer. But it was still kind of an evasion. The question just didn't seem
to interest him.

Goff had had to conclude that Kummerlos regarded it as a minor problem. On his own, frankly, he could never decide whether it was major or
minor. It varied. Sometimes it seemed major, sometimes minor—
sometimes it didn't even seem to exist. But he could always count on its
cropping up in some form—if not as a problem, at least as a consideration
to be dealt with.

It had its own intrusive energy. Sooner or later it was always pressing
some claim on him. Always demanding something—money, time, sacrifice, devotion, courage. Who could be so constantly bothered?

"What do you *want* from my life?" Goff could picture himself pleading
with an old rabbi.

"But *is* it *your* life?" asks the rabbi with exasperating reasonableness.
"You bet your ass," replies Goff to the rabbi, who executes a sorrowful
Jewish shrug, the eternal shrug, and schlumps away.
"No disrespect," he shouts after the fading rabbi.

His old friend, Leon Finger, had once said that a man's Jewishness
should be handled like a gentleman. Like a gentleman handles his liquor.
Goff, cocking his head, thought about it for a while, savored it and was
ready to swallow it, when it suddenly turned sour on him.

"Bullshit," he said cleanly.

Goff had come to tentative terms with his Jewishness. For him, Jewishness, or his Jewish problem, was like some minor congenital disability.
Always there—you accustomed yourself to it, adjusted to it, forgot about
it as much as you could—or were allowed to.

It was like shortness of breath. You move a little too fast, push a little
too hard, and there it is. Even when it doesn't show up there's always
somebody to remind you—Hey, Goff, easy there—don't forget, fellah,
you got shortness of breath.

He always figured his nose for Jewish was his seventh sense. Yes, he
could detect Jewish a mile away.

He could drive through suburban streets and identify Jewish houses
and lawns, and he didn't have to wait for Christmas. While driving on rural roads, he would suddenly become tensely alert like a bird dog, and fee,
fi, fo, fum, there would be a quaint rural cottage with the name Kaplan on
the RFD mailbox. He could cut into a proud Viking stance and rip away
its layers of pretentious sham and ham and tear the furtive, shriveled Jewish heart out of the hollow, bronzed, blond body. He could swoop down
on a suave, slick Mike Whitfield and come up triumphantly with a
squawking, plucked Myron Weissfeld.

He regarded everything in terms of its relation to Jewish. Things were
either Gentile, Jewish or neutral. They were never constant. What might
be Gentile at one time could slip over to Jewish at another, or vice versa,
or to neutral—and from neutral in turn to either. Take, for instance, divorce. At one time implacably Gentile, he now catalogued it as neutral.
Italian was Jewish. Irish was Gentile. Arab was neutral. He was beginning
to sense some strong movement in bagel. Jewish rye had always been
Gentile; rye bread was Jewish, but not Jewish rye.

The basis for his designations was quite subtle, heavily emotional, totally subjective and often unconscious. It had to do with feelings of security, threat and hostility, strangeness and unfamiliarity. For instance, why
was Arab neutral? Why not Gentile? Arab was threat, hostility, yes—but

it also embodied a kind of kinship, not only because of ancient common ethnicity, but more important, a peculiar emotional connection growing out of their fierce hate—the hate of someone who strongly acknowledged you, proven by their maniacal insistence on nonacknowledgment. This was the deadly hate that exists only among brothers. Might he not then consider Arab as Jewish? Well, not quite—yet. The boundaries were elusive and ever shifting.

And as keen as his seventh sense was, his sixth sense was even keener. Perhaps the keenest of them all, his sixth sense was his nose for pussy.

Its alertness was constant. Its acuity was genius. He never had to strain. Once as a very young man he had visited his friend Leon Finger who was working as a waiter at a Jewish summer resort. With enormous pride, Leon confided he was laying one of the guests. When Goff asked, Who? Leon suddenly drew himself up in silent chivalry. He would rather not say.

But Goff told Finger he had guessed who his lay was and unerringly pointed her out.

Finger was incredulous. "But how could you tell? By the way she looked at me?" he demanded.

"No, Leon, by the way she looked at *me*."

And that had been child's play.


In the past year or so Goff's sessions with Kummerlos had become quite relaxing, even pleasurable—certainly free of the gnawing apprehensions of former years. Most of his big breakthroughs were behind him. But a new and tumultuous development had been taking place. He felt new exhilarating currents charging through his sturdy compact body. Ordinarily he would have poured everything out to Kummerlos, but in this instance he kept it all to himself.

He felt he was perched to soar. He was as ready as he would ever be to take on a perfect relationship. Bring it on! He was ready to tackle it; he was already racing headlong toward it—toward Christine.

He knew now that this relationship he sought—more, ached for—required a special ingredient, one which he had never been able to supply before. The missing ingredient was benignity. He conceded he had never been benign before. How could he have been? Always so pressed, always so occupied with finding himself, proving himself, securing himself.

But now higher levels beckoned. Now he was ready to take on something new, something loftier.

It all had to do with his mounting passion for Christine. Tonight he would be fucking her.

For the first time in his life he recoiled from that word. Because Christine was special; with Christine it would be making love. But by making love to Christine he'd be fucking Kummerlos—because Christine, God help him, was his psychiatrist's breathtakingly beautiful shiksa wife. There led the way to a spectacular final breakthrough! A defiance of the gods! Well, he couldn't help it. Cured or cursed, the die was cast.

It was true that in the course of all these years Goff had become deeply conditioned to Kummerlos' approval of all his conduct. He knew it was too much to expect it for this. But he was beginning to wonder. If anyone should be expected to understand, it should certainly be his own psychiatrist. Nineteen years!

It was Wednesday, a beautiful fresh April morning. Hurrying into his day, Goff entered the down-bound elevator. He felt impelled to communicate and share his sense of well-being with the other two passengers. He covered them both with a smile. One passenger, an aristocratic-looking elderly lady, returned his smile. The other, a mature, impeccably dressed man, didn't. Underneath his fading smile, Goff began to bristle.

In the silently descending elevator, Goff, hand in pocket, gathered up his genitals, swaddling them in cotton pocket cloth, and cradled the cluster comfortingly. Although he had been a millionaire for several years, he still sometimes found it unsettlingly necessary to stifle his old anxiety-ridden, aggressive, premillionaire instincts. He strove to be gracious. Of course he would allow the friendly aristocratic old lady to precede him out the elevator. But he certainly had no intention of permitting the same for that other bastard.

Taut lean with iron gray hair, he bore himself with icy dignity. The sharp crystal glistening of his rimless eyeglasses caught Goff's eye. They were the brightest polished lenses he had ever seen, like Prussian monocles. The better to see through you with, you anti-Semite prick, suddenly snap-judged the fast intuitive-thinking Arnold Goff.

Goff made other appraisals and conclusions. With a quick practiced sidelong look, he took the full sex-life measure of his lean challenger-designate for firsties out the elevator. Frustrated, repressed, bitter. Hadn't had a good piece since his early twenties. Strike that. Make it never. Not with Erich von Stroheim eyeglasses like those. He concluded that the man's lifelong efforts at sex had been at best giddily self-conscious or piddling pricklings. Sex frustration, sterile bitterness, even hints of despicable aberrations gleamed diamond-hard from the immaculately polished chilled glass around his eyes.

\* \* \*

His adoring sister once told him he should give sex lectures. He was such a mavin. He had accepted the designation with an immodest smile. Indeed, his most profound and analytical thinking was usually reserved for sex. In all other matters he managed very well with quick, shrewd or intuitive decisions. To sex he brought to bear all his accumulated knowledge of everything. What his forbears had tortuously devoted to Talmud and Torah, Goff applied to sex.

He couldn't honestly say that maturity had cooled his concentration on the subject. On the contrary, he thought about it now as much as when he was nine, twelve, seventeen, twenty-two, thirty-two. And now at forty-five, he thought about it even more. He couldn't remember when it wasn't the foremost and almost exclusive thing on his mind.

About the bigoted passenger, it served that bastard right that his sex profile had emerged so unfortunate. Too bad. Firmly convinced of the accuracy of his appraisal, Goff, with self-satisfaction, now awaited the opening of the doors and his sure triumph over the basically tormented (tough shit on him) prick.

When the elevator reached the lobby, Goff gallantly allowed the friendly aristocratic lady to precede him out. As he expected, the other passenger attempted to follow directly, but Goff adroitly body-blocked him. He got a despised look as he bested the bastard, stepping into the lobby first.

Goff took in the furnishings of the Park Avenue lobby with his customary satisfaction. It gave him a hefty lift to use his lately acquired knowledge about the value and worth of furnishings and objets d'art. He had been thoroughly immersed recently in furnishing his own six-room apartment and had engaged the help of a professional interior decorator. The closest he had ever come to art before was after the war in the late forties when he had bought several hand-painted ties of nudes, which he proudly strutted on his puffed-up chest.

Yale Printztein, his interior decorator, had curtly advised him in his surprisingly gruff Brooklyn accent to get in on the ground floor with marble sculptures. They were the coming hottest items in art.

Printztein's wife, who was reputed to be French, was a sculptress herself and could be counted on for helpful consultations. It was Dr. Sherwin Meltzer, an orthodontist in his therapy group, who had recommended Printztein to Goff.

Meltzer had encouraged Goff's reliance on the Printzteins. "I owe plenty to Printztein and Kummerlos," he said. "Kummerlos has provided me with the frame of mind and Printztein, that Brooklyn momzer, has provided the beauty. You know what's my best tranquilizer? Beauty! When I come into my beautiful living room, my dinette, that's beauty! The drapes, the paneling, the sculptures, the mirrors, even the appliances all in avocado green—those are the true tranquilizers. The natural tranquilizers. You know what I mean? It's like the difference between figs and Ex-Lax. You know what I mean?" he concluded fervently.

Goff nodded. "Day in, day out, somebody is always breaking your chops. At least you always have an inner sanctum of beauty where you can forget a little. And by the way, Doc," Goff grinned, "your example about the Ex-Lax couldn't be better timed for me now, since I'm having a little trouble with my piles." Meltzer chuckled appreciatively for a moment and then abruptly turned dead serious. "Arnie, I know a very good man."

"Thanks, Doc, I think it's under control now."

Meltzer nodded soberly and felt closer to Goff than in all the past eight years they had been co-groupers in therapy. Goff in turn still regarded him as a schmuck.

A moment later Meltzer assured him that he could rely completely on Printztein's French wife for sculpture. "She's undoubtedly a very hot piece, a very exciting woman. I doubt that he appreciates her. Isn't it amazing how his sense of art is confined only to interior decorating? In everything else he's an animal."

"Look," said Goff, "I think this applies to all of us. We all have a little part of us that is our unique specialty, our exclusive art domain. For you, Doc, it's your touch and feel for dentures and the human mouth. You are an artist of the human mouth. And as for me, I humbly submit, it's my *putz*."

Meltzer's eyes had already begun to glow excitedly seconds before Goff's punchy finale, and as Goff spit out the word "putz" Meltzer was already punching him on the shoulder, bubbling with gleeful enthusiasm. "I *knew* you were gonna say that, Arnie, I knew it!"

Several weeks later Goff did acquire a marble *Diane the Huntress* after first receiving the sworn assurance of its worth from Printztein's French wife.

With her hot Gallic breath she pressured Goff into buying the Diane. "In five years you will be able to sell this for easily double the money. It is a masterpiece!"

Goff bought, but he snickered contemptuously at Meltzer having been taken in by this woman. She was as French as his aunt Sadie. Sure, she had a French accent, but her French accent had a Russian accent, and that Russian accent was overlaid with a Yiddish accent. You didn't have to be a 'Enry 'Iggins to detect that. That schmuck Meltzer had mistaken steamy for hot. She had all that damp hair, yeasty hair pockets under her arms and between her legs, he was positive, and had the nerve to nourish the notion of Frenchness! French, his ass. Goff envisioned her performance in bed. She certainly wouldn't fuck French. She would fuck like a heavy-thighed Bronx Zionist, singing Slavic-Hebraic work-pioneer songs to activate her steamy hair pockets. Her parents by some fluke had ended up in France rather than in their natural habitat, the Bronx.

The more he thought about her passing herself off as French, the more indignant he became. "It's as if my old man would try to pass himself off as an American. You take your citizenship papers and that's it. It doesn't give you the right to go around claiming you're an American."

It really burned his ass off. That schmuck, Meltzer!

Nevertheless, Goff himself would gaze at his statue, his one hundred percent verified thing of beauty, and force himself to feel pleasure.

# Chapter 2

*Goff recalls a touching incident of his youth*

To Goff, apartment house lobbies were Jewish. His first glimpses of elegance and the finer things had been in the lobbies he was schlepped through on visits to relatives and doctors as a child. In those days, the goy found his splendor in his churches and cathedrals; the Jew found it in his lobbies and vestibules. Cavernous as castles, dimly lit, with electric fireplaces, splashing fountains and live goldfish pools, they used to awe him in spite of himself when he was a hot schmuck kid growing up in Brooklyn dating solid Jewish girls in solid Jewish apartment houses.

Not that his awe prevented him from screwing Rhoda Lewin on a velvet lobby couch in a shadowy corner.

She had avoided taking him up to her apartment because, as far as he could make out, her parents were religious and she respected that, or some such irrelevant notion. Nobody could beat *his* father for religion, and he knew for a fact how his father rejoiced whenever the news got around the family that Arnie had got himself laid. Goff figured it was rejoicing acceptable to the religion because it fell well within the traditional tenet: "I want better for my children than what I had."

He remembered he had been taken somewhat off guard when without so much as a token protest, except the gibberish about her religious parents, she had suddenly spread her legs in the quick froglike motion of a Brighton Beach Junior Lifeguard, and with her hand had floated his surprised hardon right into her. Although quite pleased with this turn of

23

events, his sense of order had been jarred. There had been the disturbing sense of something premature. His hardon, although in solid workmanlike condition, had not yet reached the point of warhead bursting brilliance. His conditioning had been programmed to a somewhat different sequence. There weren't the "no, no, no's" and then the "no, I mustn'ts" and finally the "no, we mustn'ts" which marked the critical shift from individual guilt to the less burdensome collective one.

Maybe this had been the reason for his almost immediate overpowering resurgence. His hardon hadn't diminished a whit.

In any case, he had been driven to have another quick go at it. But she had clenched up and shaken her head.

He remembered his desperation to overcome her unexpected resistance; her maddening, ritual-like insistence that on a second date passion might excuse going the limit once, but would be unthinkable twice.

But he had persevered hotly, and he *nudzhed* her so cadgingly and deftly that she finally consented to alleviate his distress, but she wanted to make it clear, it would only be with her hand this time. Goff had felt it polite to groan out an anguished protest, but actually he considered it more than fair, considering that he had just laid her. It was still a rather pleasant surprise, because in those days getting laid was a very big deal, and getting laid in Brooklyn never came easy.

He remembered clearly her bittersweet smile. Her naive, childish recourse to Brooklyn protocol. Her heart wasn't in her resistance, but neither was it in her compliance. It was mainly a gentle detachment and wistful generosity. She was a good-hearted girl with no real inner conviction, a real humanitarian. He had been amazed at her sexual dumbness. She had been otherwise a very intelligent girl and was reputed to be a gifted flutist.

He never saw her again after that.

Over twenty years later, attending a Parents' Day at his children's private school, during the talent show in which a little girl played the flute, he was suddenly transfixed with the jolting conviction that he had missed out on an obvious and tasty sex morsel. He was absolutely convinced he could have pestered Rhoda Lewin into blowing him instead of the lousy hand job. Missed sexual opportunities, even over twenty years later, rankled Goff hard. It would have been a pushover. He berated himself for having been a schmuck, and played fleetingly with the idea of looking her up to collect his back dues.

When the parents applauded at the completion of the flute solo, he did not join. Arnie Goff was a hard sex loser.

# Chapter 3

*Family sketches—*

His most irrepressible admirer was his older sister, Blanche. She looked to him, never to Murray, her husband, to provide her and the family with its sex excitement. For any poor maiden upon whom Arnie had set his appetite, Blanche showed no mercy, no trace of sisterly compassion. Her appearance, always a little pinched and dry and prim and thickly bespectacled, would change markedly when she sensed that Arnie had got inside the pants of another of his sacrificial appetizers. Like an old-time movie high priestess, Blanche would dart Goff's sacrificial virgin a venomous once-over and then smile a conspiratorial approval at him. You have done well, my lord and monster, bubie, her look would hiss. Goff, although contemptuous, ate it up anyhow. He found it fun to be idolized.

When Goff went on a date, Blanche would speed him on his quest by showering him with salacious encouragement and praise in the form of leers, winks, puns and heavy-handed one-dimensional double entendres. She would constantly contort the interrogative pronoun "who" into variations of "whore." "A whore you gonna go out with tonight, Arnie?" Blanche rarely addressed her sex allusions openly. It was always with the awkward indirection of the play on words or a well-timed leer or an expressively significant sniff or hike of eyebrows.

In her own affairs, she was prudish, snappish and virginal. When she married Murray, she quickly converted him into a worshipful admirer of Arnie, the family sex champ. Murray was an easy disciple for the full-

blooded sex operator Arnie, because in his own bed, Blanche barely
allowed him to eke out a marginal sex living. With Blanche the diggings
were very bare and rocky. Although it was easy to guess that Murray had
never had much hope that it would be otherwise, he accepted it as his natural, flinty legacy. As the eldest son of an impoverished moujik inevitably
accepts as his lot the barren patch of land handed down to him by his father.

Goff's father, Abraham Goff, was considered an elder of his *shul*. He
held himself forth as a man learned in the Talmud and Scriptures and
thereby finagled his congregation to esteem him. The congregations were
usually small, threadbare splinters of larger more affluent synagogues.
Somehow, he invariably estranged himself from the well-established,
affluent synagogues of the area and drifted into the shaky and transient
ratty storefronts and one-flight-up *shuls* that invariably sprang up to
accommodate dissidents, protestors, cranks, crackpots and cheapskates.

Goff suspected that A.G., as his children half mockingly called him,
had been uncovered, if not unfrocked, as a fraud and even worse, a *nud-
nik;* that his self-proclaimed "learning" couldn't hold up to the close scrutiny of the duly ordained, seminaried rabbi of a well-established, major-
league synagogue. He could however con the sour-stomached second-rat-
ers who usually drifted to these bush league "pickup" congregations. Or
maybe they were swindling *him*, only pretending to be taken in by his pious posturing, in order to enable themselves to obtain the mandatory
figurehead to cluster around and thereby maintain themselves as a going
congregation. After all, they had to belong somewhere. Was it not stated
that piousness is not measured by what is in a man's head, but what is in a
man's heart? And who knows what lies in a man's heart? And if you don't
know, then how can you deny him the presidency of the congregation and
its attendant duties to find a *shabbes goy*, a part-time janitor, a satisfactory cantor for the holidays and to see to arrangements too numerous to
mention. If a man's piousness leads him to accept these irksome under-
takings, then by all means it should be granted him.

And the congregation will thereby be enabled to carry on as a sanctuary
for those who, whatever their pious reasons, find the rich, smug synagogues, with their outrageous demands on a man's money, unacceptable.
These matters were usually finally settled in solemn assembly at some pi-
nochle game, where an elder might intone with sanctimonious, guttural
finality as he throws in a losing hand, "Look, if Goff wants to be a big
shot, let him, if it makes him happy. I pass."

A.G. was always in some state of stubble. Never was he wholly smooth. Never entirely clean-shaven, he used the same blade until well-advanced rust erosion practically flaked it to dust. In addition to his bristly face, he was invariably in some degree of scratchy undress, parading around in itchy-looking long johns. Summer or winter he would go through days on end, shuffling around the apartment in his scratchy, baggy-at-the-crotch long underwear, carrying a sagging *Jewish Daily Forward* to match. It was a perfect match to his droopy underwear.

Old A.G. could generally be found in his long underwear hunched at the kitchen table reading his *"Fawvitz"* spread out in front of him, eating a saucer of stewed prunes or drinking a glass of hot tea. With absent-minded unconcern he took no pains whatsoever to prevent the prune juice or tea from dripping onto his paper, as he concentrated on his article. The big-paged *"Fawvitz"* soaked it all up.

A kind of cackling laughter was his characteristic display for joy or pleasure at the discomfiture of either an enemy or a fool, or for that matter, a friend too—better yet! When he wasn't pious he was lewd. When he wasn't lewd he was canny. He was basically unsentimental and untouched except with his Arneleh. For Arneleh he wanted the best. So he rasped joyously whenever family conversations revealed that Arnie had *shtupped* his latest date or had in any way pleasurably dabbled with a choice or chance female.

Once A.G. had needed new springs for his Chevie. Around the kitchen table, Blanche had turned it into a family joke. "Arnie borrows it one time for a date, and bang, Pop needs a new set of springs." The old man, momentarily puzzled, suddenly broke into his sputtering cackle. Thereafter, whenever Arneleh borrowed the car, old A.G., in his scratchy *gatkes*, would look up and gleefully rasp that he shouldn't make a ruin of his springs this time.

Blanche would smile proudly while Murray, her husband, always caught on and winked chummy encouragement at the idolized scapegrace. Goff's older brother, Armand, grinned unenviously as he guzzled down Mom's stuffed cabbage. Armand's obese wife, Laura, smiled and shrugged. It never occurred to her in her contented simpleness that on many of these occasions it was her own kid sister Sheila that Goff was banging in Pop's Chevie. Their daughter, Carolynne, already an acknowledged genius at the age of five, squinted her eyes into a sharp knowledgeable slit, and overlapped her lips into a tight twist of comprehension. Goff could swear that not only did she understand the full meaning of the family joke, but he would bet money she was the only one who knew it was her dopey Aunt Sheila he was screwing. That two such dull ones as Armand and fat Laura could have knocked out such a star as Carolynne always struck him as astonishing. He had more respect for Carolynne than all the rest of them put together.

Contempt for his family had set in at a tender age. And no amount of adoration they heaped on him thereafter would buy him off or persuade him otherwise. His contempt was incorruptible.

Whenever he departed for a date, the family trooped to the door with him to root him on. Murray, with a heavy show of snappy winking, would press a packet of Trojans into his hand and always call him "kid." "Better safe than sorry, kid," Murray would whisper, attempting to achieve the air of well-earned bravado of a once-established hellraiser whose maturity and responsibilities now force understandable and honorable retirement from the active battlefield. Blanche always knew exactly when her husband was sneaking Goff the rubbers, and she would catch Goff's eye and smile encouraging approval.

Murray bought them by the gross. Not that his consumption warranted it, far from it, but it was cheaper and it gave him prestige with the cut-rate druggist. Goff would accept the packet with the cocky grin of a seasoned campaigner. But Murray kept pressing on him many more rubbers than he was consuming.

Goff felt he wasn't doing too bad, but didn't those schmucks realize getting laid in Brooklyn was tough enough even for the best of operators? But if they thought he was doing that great, he wasn't going to disillusion them. He would just have to give or throw away Murray's Trojans to avoid the risk of someone in the family finding a suspicious surplus in his pockets.

And as he started jauntily toward the stair landing, scratchy A.G. would cackle a last gleeful warning to spare the springs. Everyone at the doorway joined in the hilarity except his mother. She would have no part of it. She always seemed to find this the moment to get herself busy with the supper dishes or cooking or clearing off or baking a *challa*. Goff could never pinpoint whether his mother had declined to join the active family cheering section out of aloofness or disapproval or sheer indifference. He knew it wasn't unawareness. But the mere fact that she omitted herself rankled him. He resented it. If anybody should be on a guy's side, it should be his mother. He felt uncomfortably suspicious that she was probably the one who knew him best. Did she regard him as a little bastard or what? But even if she did, a mother is supposed to love a child, regardless. She was shirking her duty. Not that he needed her, but hell, he was entitled. Goff suspected that his Jewish mother simply didn't give a shit. Her "Eat, eat, eat," didn't have heart in it. She didn't exhort him so that he should grow up big and strong; she did it more as though she considered it an insult to have leftovers in the refrigerator.

It was his father who urged his Arneleh to eat, eat, with genuine heartfelt concern. So that Arneleh could grow up with a nice big *schmekeleh*. His mother's face always turned blank at A.G.'s freely expressed fundamentals, and she would busy herself in the kitchen.

And as she had merely gone through the motions, Goff, the prosperous son now, was going through the motions back. Screw her. He wasn't going to give her any more than she deserved. She hadn't broken her hump for him and he wasn't going to break his for her.

# Chapter 4

*Enter Christine*

Goff, of course, had covered this with Dr. Kummerlos. "Doctor, it's funny. Maybe the best way I can say it is that I feel guilty that I don't feel guilty."

Kummerlos broke into one of his rare smiles and even rarer chuckles. "Ha, ha, ha, you are a caution, Goff. Ha, ha, heads I win, tails you lose. Ha. Ha."

So now he was a "caution" for cryin' out loud. He had never been a fuckin' caution before in his life. Where had his doctor, an East Side boy, picked up that Main Street America word? But dammit, somehow the answer made him feel good.

Kummerlos continued, his usual severity somewhat softened by the aftermath of his chuckle. "Goff, you are guilty as charged. And I don't charge for a guilt for being without guilt. We deal here with hard-core guilts." He was turning severe again. Goff liked that. "You chose to use a frivolous turn of phrase. Fine. But my interpretation is that in your mind you are uneasy about the narrow limits you have placed on what you provide for your mother. Your question is, are you truly justified. No?" Kummerlos often adopted the German style.

Goff thrilled at Kummerlos' mastery of the heart of matters. "Yes, yes, of course, Doctor."

"Without going over areas we have already gone into in detail, let us

31

quickly try to establish whether, under the circumstances, you are provid-
ing sufficiently for your mother."

Goff folded his hands on his lap. Kummerlos was sure to let him off
fine.

"How much do you give her a week?"

"It's not by the week, it's the month."

"Well, how much do you give her a month?"

"A hundred eighty-five dollars a month."

"A hundred eighty five dollars a month. Can she manage on that?"

"No, but she gets a hundred and ten dollars a month Social Security.
And also I pay her gas, electric and phone. That hundred eighty-five is
clear. And the hundred and ten a month includes Medicare." Goff felt
beautifully unburdened.

"You don't pay her rent?"

"Hell, no, Doctor. She still lives in the same place, Flatbush. It's rent-
controlled and the neighborhood is still good. It's under a hundred a
month. She gets change from her Social Security check. It makes her feel
independent and does her good." Goff felt he had acquitted himself well.

Kummerlos smiled tightly. Shit, his own mother didn't have it that
good. Still living on the East Side, not even in one of those new com-
plexes of cooperative apartments—being choked by spics and *shvartzehs*.

Goff mistook the smile for cynical disbelief of his motives. "I'm level-
ing, Doctor, I can afford to pay her rent, but she really doesn't want me
to, and it's better for her."

"My smile was for your recognition of a basic psychological concept.
Of course she feels better paying her rent herself. But what about her
spiritual needs?"

"Terrific," said Goff. "I forgot to tell you. When I got my divorce, I
thought in case she felt bad about it (which I doubt; she was always on my
wife's side), I bought her an eight-hundred-dollar color TV. Actually,
since I'm sort of in the business I got it for three and a quarter, but it's actually an eight-hundred-dollar set. She watches it all the time. Her spirit is
great."

"And companionship?"

"Terrific. My sister Blanche and her husband still live in the same place
only two blocks away. They're always up there. They all watch that TV
together. Mom's okay for companionship."

"And your children?"

"That too. She sees them even more than I do since the divorce.
Gloria's always bringing them over. She never did it before the divorce.

But now it's strictly a bitchy way to needle me. It's typical of her. Who cares? Except I think it must be an awful drag on the kids. But at least they've got a good color TV to watch there.''

Kummerlos leaned back, silent, his face a study in severe concentration. Goff leaned back, his face a study in serene faith. His doctor would soon show him the way.

Kummerlos spoke. "Does anyone else contribute to your mother? Your sister, Blanche? Your brother, Marvin?"

"No," said Goff. "My brother is Armand."

Kummerlos ignored the correction. "Why not?"

Goff allowed himself time to absorb the delicious shock of the question. And suddenly the meaning of it rushed in full-blown and insistent. He had learned to think and analyze in the psychiatrist's style, and sometimes he was even able to anticipate Kummerlos' conclusions or train of thought.

This couldn't please Kummerlos more. It fulfilled optimum professional standards: the most effectual insights are those dredged up by the patient himself. However, Kummerlos worked at his techniques to keep Goff from getting a swelled head. By exquisite little lip pursings and precise eyelid lowerings and infinitely patient, pudgy-fingered hand foldings, he conveyed very clearly who it was that was the real father of the thought. All this with carefully selected terse comments added up to the message: *See, Goff, my good lad, because you tried hard, you were able to think of it all by yourself. See how you can work up all those wonderfully perceptive insights yourself when your Dr. Kummerlos is here to expertly tickle your gullet, so you can disgorge them. Vomit them, if you will. We are surely now well beyond the stage where we still have to hesitate calling a spade a spade. Yes?* He made it abundantly clear where the credit really lay.

For all Goff cared, Kummerlos didn't have to go to all that trouble to get his credit. He gladly gave him all the credit for all that healthy vomiting.

It was simple once you got the hang of it. You could unearth so many self-insights.

He remembered that after his pop died, he had shoved Blanche and Armand away, insisting that he be Mom's sole supporter. He could afford it. Inside, he'd wanted her completely dependent on him. He wanted to control her, keep her in her place, his debt.

But deep down it troubled him that he still sought to get even with his mother. Getting even with your mother is kid stuff. What did he still need that for?

So he would now ask Armand and Blanche to contribute nominal little amounts monthly, give Mom a little standard-of-living increase. "How's that, Doctor? Have I got it?" he beamed.

"Are *you* satisfied with it?"

Goff nodded respectfully.

Kummerlos brought to bear on Goff a laser beam of a stare to nail down once and for all who was really in charge of self-produced self-insights. "Then I am in agreement," he said.

Goff felt deep thanks once again to his indispensable doctor. That mother thing was settled.

Maybe now he would visit her a little more often to demonstrate his new healthy attitude.

At the funeral his mother had shed a few tears for old A.G. which had stopped forever when one of his seedy, bearded, semi-rabbinical cronies had made a weepy eulogy in Yiddish. It had contained far more fantasy than the usual well-meaning extravaganza. Goff had seen her look change to one of surfeit already, and her face undergo a transformation into the same kind of blank impassiveness she adopted whenever the family had gone into raptures over his sex exploits.

Goff himself had conscientiously worked himself into a mild state of tears. He had just barely made it. But he felt it was worth his effort, because not only did he owe it to his pop, but maybe more important, he owed it to the living, namely himself. He felt it would do him good. He had heard that to cry was sometimes psychologically healthy, and he was spending all that time and money on his therapy, and he did want to have facets. His laboriously induced tears had caught the eye of his genius niece Carolynne. He was chilled with the certainty that she was reading right through him with that squint of diabolically premature wisdom. But fuck her; he was giving it an honest try and he didn't have to apologize to anyone.

So he had wept in his fashion for old A.G., who in his scratchy way had loved his Arneleh, his little accident, so much. As much for his fine *keppeleh* as for his fine *schmekeleh*. Goff figured he had never had a Jewish mother. His father had been his Jewish mother.

His mother's hash had been settled. Implicitly, it remained his option to open up a new topic or terminate the session before the full alloted time.

Kummerlos knew that the best policy was to give a patient his full fifty minutes without any monkey business. But when he said, "We must close now," the door was already shut. He gave full value for value received; a customer will never resent not being shortchanged. A strictly one-price store. His patients learned fast, became conditioned to the rules and obeyed them without undue resentment.

Meltzer, the orthodontist, however, was always testing him. He talked on and on always trying to sneak beyond his fifty minutes. It was an obsession with him. To break through Kummerlos' granite hour! "What will it hurt him if he grants me a few more minutes to unburden myself?" But Kummerlos stood like a rock. When Kummerlos closed, he closed.

Goff, however, still had another few minutes. He did have something he wanted to discuss. "Doctor, I've been thinking of letting one of my men go at the plant. I think I've mentioned him before, Malcolm Feiler."

Kummerlos nodded, giving full-value attention.

"The thing is," Goff continued, "he won't be able to get another job, or anyway, it'll be very hard; and I feel I have a sort of responsibility for him. You see, he thinks he's become indispensable, but the truth is that he's become impossible."

There was a soft rap, rap at the door. Kummerlos' only acknowledgment was the barest twitch of annoyance. He uttered not a word as the door slowly opened. Goff glanced up expecting to see the plump uninteresting Hunter College girl who was Kummerlos' current part-time receptionist, hired at his unbudgeable salary, never more than the current legal minimum per hour. "Why not? No carfare. They walk from school and they do their homework and sneak telephone calls to their boyfriends."

But it wasn't the uninteresting receptionist at the door. What Goff saw took his breath away. In the doorway, not half as apologetic as her hesitant knocking, stood a dazzling slender blonde, quite tall, in black slacks, bright green blouse with deep V-neckline, and a matching green kerchief binding the long blond hair that fell below her shoulders. Leaning her head into the office, she smiled her apology for the intrusion, Goff receiving his share as she nodded toward him courteously in passing. Her open radiant smile, the sparkle of her blue eyes and her languorous grace demonstrated clearly that she had never in her life found difficulty being excused for anything.

Goff's reactions to females were never apathetic. He boasted that he had the fastest hardon in the West, but he had never before had his breath taken away. He was completely unprepared for her. It was obviously Kummerlos' new shiksa wife, about whom he had been hearing.

"I'm sorry for the interruption," said the blonde, an almost pixyish challenge in her smile. Her speech, although slightly accented, German or

Scandinavian, was pronounced in fine, rather cultivated English. "But I thought you would like to know," she said to Kummerlos, "and you, too, sir," she turned, smiling at Goff so ingratiatingly that involuntarily he nodded his participating assent to whatever she was ready to propose or divulge or indulge. "St. Louis came from defeat to score two home runs in the ninth inning, and they have won the series. It has happened just a minute ago on the TV."

"Thank you, Christine," said Kummerlos.

Goff smiled uneasily and mumbled, way off balance, something about being glad to hear the news because he had always liked the National League better than the American.

Having discharged her role as courier of such exciting news, she brightened her smile even more as she removed her willowy blond grace behind a gently closing door.

Goff saw Kummerlos now turn his solemnity back to the patient himself, but he could easily detect that the sobriety for him was far different than that for her. Goff realized that Kummerlos, the husband, had been just as enchanted as he had been. That his sober, almost annoyed mien to his wife's interruption was only a tactful put-on for the benefit of his patient. Kummerlos was nuts about that girl. That was plain. He couldn't outwardly encourage it, of course, but he probably wouldn't really mind being interrupted by her every five minutes. And Goff didn't blame him. He could ravish a girl like that every five minutes around the clock.

Goff loved the gracious, feminine way she had so charmingly acted to please her husband. So completely unlike most American and especially New York women. The exact opposite of Gloria. Kummerlos was undoubtedly a baseball fan. He had also undoubtedly tried to engender an enthusiasm on her part, and what she had just done was a thrilling and touching demonstration of spirited and loyal devotion to her man and to his happiness. It was evident to Goff that, left alone, she wouldn't devote two seconds to baseball. But for that fat little bastard she was putting on like old Jolly Happy Felton, irrepressible, gee whiz, captain of the old Brooklyn Dodgers Knothole Gang. Only with her, it was continental style, with that tantalizing, high-class Scandinavian accent. He shivered up a three-quarter speed erection, sitting there, as he thought if that was the way she gave out baseball scores, what she could serve up in bed with those long blond legs! He thought bitterly about his ex-wife Gloria who had originally been a natural fan, but who had just for spite deliberately frozen herself out from all further interest when she observed that Goff had been a moderately enthusiastic Brooklyn Dodger rooter. She had gloated when Bobby Thompson had hit that home run against Branca.

The reason he had been so unprepared for this startlingly striking girl was because of that windbag, Meltzer. Meltzer had described her as a startlingly striking girl. A beautiful, long-legged, Danish blonde, like shimmering northern lights, he had poetized rapturously. Goff, remembering Meltzer's ecstatic raving about that lumpy Bronx broad of a sculptress, Printztein's wife, whom he had called the "French girl," had contemptuously dismissed any of the man's judgments as completely incompetent and worthless. Goff had translated Meltzer's ravings of a blond Danish beauty, tall and slender, into a short, dumpy, round-faced bakery countergirl type, who was probably a thick-ankled, blond Estonian or Latvian or some other Baltic breed who didn't quite make it as Aryan, but by a dope like Meltzer were enthusiastically accepted as Nordic.

But in this case, Meltzer had surpassed himself. His damned description, "like shimmering northern lights," was beautiful. It was perfect. And by hook or crook, by the strange, new excitement he felt, Goff knew he would now be driven to work things out so that he could eventually screw her. Screw Kummerlos. He couldn't help it. And Kummerlos, who had ditched his wife of twenty years, his childhood sweetheart from the East Side (Meltzer had found out), couldn't help it either, could he? And Kummerlos was his therapist. If anyone should understand, he certainly should. Furthermore, by reason of his function as his therapist, was it really too farfetched to expect some sort of help from him? Goff was definitely a stricken man. He must stop at nothing to make this angelic, shimmering shiksa princess his.

By the time the door closed he had caught his breath again and carefully scrutinized Kummerlos' face to see whether he had noticed his reaction. Goff decided he hadn't. Kummerlos had again returned to his old Jewish buddha look. Goff still had a few minutes and decided he would return to Malcolm Feiler.

"Doctor, this man Feiler has been with me three years. He's not married," he added hastily, already beginning to cut away any grounds for mercy and laying out his *prima facie* case for obtaining Kummerlos' sanction and support to fire the man. It took the four-minute balance of the hour to try, convict and condemn the wretch.

"But don't think you don't owe him anything; you would be deluding yourself. The thing to always keep in mind is that you owe yourself more." Goff nodded thoughtfully, quickly tourniqueting his bleeding

heart. Kummerlos went on, "And the quicker the surgery, the less damaging to you, and equally important, to this man, Feiler." Goff continued
nodding, cognizant of his grave responsibility to his fellow man, Feiler.
"This is a good example of what I've been trying to convey to you about
what is at the heart of creative selfishness, of course."

"Of course," echoed Goff, maintaining a now nonstop nod. He was so
in agreement with Kummerlos. He glowed with agreement. Everybody
wins in creative selfishness.

That schmuck Feiler would eventually reap benefits, which was fine.
He didn't begrudge him. He had nothing basic against the jerk, but the
son of a bitch had gone too far when he had tried to feel up Ramona, his
spic secretary.

Feiler was the only Jew in his plant; the rest were all P.R.'s and *shvartzehs*. The two groups didn't get along, always fighting and bickering and
disrupting smooth operations. Goff couldn't understand why they always
quarreled and didn't think it worth the time to find out. He had finally
made up his mind it would be all one or the other; no mixing no more.
Fuck civil rights, he had a business to run. And since he was already
banging Ramona, and she was *truly* indispensable, not like that prick Feiler who *thought* he was, he decided to go with the P.R.'s. Thereafter
whenever he called the State Employment Service for help, he would
specify, "Spanish-speaking, please. . . . Because my foreman is Spanish-speaking. . . . No, not a word of English except *gelt*. . . . I was
joking. . . . How do I communicate with him? I don't see why I'm getting this third degree. . . . Well, if you must know, my secretary is bilin-
gual. She speaks Spanish and English, Miss Markowitz." He garbled the
next, "And she sucks in Jewish. . . . I said and her husband is Jewish . . . It's like another joke . . . Thank you, Miss Markowitz. . .
And you'll screen them a little? Like, make sure their arms and legs
add up to four. I'll appreciate it."

Feiler was a stupid wise guy. Goff didn't like his addressing him with
buddy-buddy Yiddishisms. But when he took pity on him and granted him
a few responses in kind, Feiler took advantage and presumed a familiarity
that was never there. Goff expressed it, "I didn't need the familiarity to
get my contempt for him. Feiler thought since we exchanged a few Jewish
words it made us some kind of blood brothers." It had given him the un-
mitigated balls to feel up his secretary. His true-blue loyal little spic secretary had of course told him. But before he fired Feiler, he wanted to clear
it with Kummerlos.

In absentia, Feiler's fate was settled between doctor and patient, neatly squeezed in and disposed of to round out the hour. Unknown to the two, their little matter, now tidily settled, was in turn destined to ring up hours and hours of new material and a lot of old rehashing for Feiler and *his* therapist. It was in this manner that one psychiatrist came to the aid of his fellow. One man's therapy is another man poisoned. And so, lots and lots of reciprocal business.

After Kummerlos had intoned his customary "We must close now," he changed his tone slightly and spoke anew. This was rare. He pushed his voice forward and called him Arnie. "Arnie, I was waiting till we closed before I mentioned this. I didn't think it would be quite correct otherwise." Goff felt a sudden apprehension. Had Kummerlos seen the effect his beautiful blond shiksa wife had had on him? "You mentioned having obtained a color television at a most favorable price for your mother. I have a similar situation with my mother. I mean, she is widowed and lives alone, and I was wondering, if it would be no inconvenience to you . . . "

Goff interrupted in relief, "Of course, Doctor. No trouble at all. I have these connections with a lot of these electronic firms. I'll be glad to arrange it. The one I got is a Saturata. I know the Saturata Electronics president personally."

"It's a large screen?"

"Beautiful. Tremendous screen."

"It's a well-rated set?"

"It's Saturata's showpiece. Top-quality control all the time. It's Phil Epstein's prize baby. He's the president. I know him. I guarantee the quality."

"It is eight hundred dollars retail?"

"Right, you can see it at any department store, and I'm sure I can still get it for three fifty."

"I thought you mentioned three twenty-five," murmured Kummerlos politely.

"Something like that. Three twenty-five to three fifty. Where do you want it delivered?"

Kummerlos hesitated. "Here will be all right. Shall I make out a check?"

"No, no, wait till I find out and make the arrangements. No rush."

Kummerlos nodded soberly. Goff was very happy to do this. He could see himself telling Phil Epstein, "It's for my psychiatrist. I swear by him. If you ever need a good man. I owe him everything. That's the way I feel about him."

Kummerlos was aware of the risk of involving himself with a patient outside of the strictly therapeutic level, but he felt that his beautifully controlled composure and manner minimized the danger of familiarity and if he could save over four hundred bucks, that wasn't peanuts. Every now and then he would carefully take personal advantage of information revealed by his patients. It was no conflict of interest. Nor did he regard it as a breach of ethics. Actually the last time he had done this kind of thing had been a few years ago, when Goff had revealed he was on the inside on a new stock issue. Kummerlos had discreetly realized a tidy two grand from that one. It was nothing so extravagant or flagrant.

He thought it was wiser to have the set delivered to his apartment, because he wasn't yet all that certain he would give it to his mother. He had a beautiful black-and-white set, in perfect working condition. Maybe he would give her that one and keep the color. Christine would enjoy the color. How excited she would get. Well, he would see. Better deliver it here.

Goff was anxious to attend to it right away. He wanted to do something special for Kummerlos. Was it because he was thinking of screwing his wife? An offering for guilt? Goff shrugged. It didn't matter. Sooner or later Kummerlos would take care of that for him also. As he left he looked around hoping to get another peek at Kummerlos' wife. But all he saw was the dumpy uninteresting Hunter College girl. He was disappointed because there was something specific he wanted to check on. He was pretty sure this Christine, this creature of rapturous beauty, of shimmering northern lights, had been flat-chested. He wanted to make sure, and if so, just *how* flat-chested. But he didn't see her. He fought back the incipient disappointment that, if not soon contained, might slowly seep all over him and blight this whole new wonderful excitement. He finally forced out a burst of forthright resolution, "Screw tits. Who needs 'em?"

# Chapter 5

*Goff, the Basque, remembers Pat, the doorman's*
*daughter, and other assorted recollections*

Walking through his elegant lobby that glorious and promising morning, Goff carried himself with the superior self-assurance of a man attired precisely right for his surroundings. But he aspired still higher—to the ultimate self-assurance of the man who wasn't.

The doorman opened the door. Once you were a resident of the house, you automatically earned his due respect. There was no condescension when he greeted you or opened the Park Avenue door for you.

Goff wisely allowed for the limitations of the doorman that he knew must exist. Away from his job, where he lived (he figured in the West Bronx), Goff was sure he regarded Jews as dirty and/or cheap kikes, Poles as dumb Polacks and Guineas as dirty wops. He had no ambivalence problems with niggers, Goff thought, because there were none in the building. Whenever someone new moved in, the doorman accorded him the hundred percent equal regard and respect befitting his Caucasian origins. This was living democracy and it swelled Goff's heart. Park Avenue was the great equalizer. The pot melted best on Park Avenue.

The doorman's name was Fitzsimmons. He was a fine figure of a maturing man, who staunchly held an open umbrella over you like a solid oak in full leaf. Goff addressed him as "Fitz," which he thought was exactly appropriate. Not "Fitzsimmons" or "Mr. Fitzsimmons" or "John." Choosing the right name at the right time was a delicate art. It was the name that established the exact relationship. In a friendly way, it put him

41

on discreet notice of their difference. Not that Fritzsimmons had to be reminded of the difference, but Goff felt it was imperative that he realize
that *Goff* was aware of it. It was a fine democratic way to delineate clearly
and painlessly the master-servant relationship. When he called the doorman "Fitz," he would get a tremendous assimilationist thrill and, oddly,
even a surge of patriotism.

In all, Goff approved of Fitzsimmons immensely. He was the perfect
choice for a doorman. A complete abider. Whatever required abiding, he
abided.

Fitzsimmons was tall, almost massive, devoted to his job, and serious,
almost somber. Goff, applying his usual acid test, pictured the same ten-
dencies prevailing in his fucking. He was the kind of man who would fuck
without fucking around. In with quick hard staccato energy; out with
blunt finality and right on to other matters. As romantic as a jackhammer.
With friend or foe alike.

Last summer Goff had seen Fitzsimmons' daughter talking to him. She
was a blond pink-skinned lively-eyed dolly in miniskirt, and the way Fitzsimmons looked at her, he figured she was the forbidden apple of the good
doorman's eye.

Goff had sized her up as about nineteen. The kind that works as a typist
for an oil company with offices on the Avenue of the Americas. He further conjectured that she'd been laid by bank-teller trainee types by the
names of Jim or Tim.

He figured it had happened about twice, in Jim's or Tim's married
brother's apartment. She had been scared, game, and, like a good shiksa
kid, had put the teller on that it was groovy, but had ducked the guy completely after the second time had proved as disappointing as the first.

Goff, having made all these calculations, decided he'd make a low-pow-
ered move. Nothing to lose, and these kids looked so wholesome and
appetizing in their miniskirts, he could eat them up. She was so nice and
pink and firm and blond, so completely shiksa-fresh. But with her lousy
sex episodes already, she was in danger of souring completely on the
whole activity. He would do a *mitzvah* by her and show her what first-
quality screwin' could do for a person. He would renew her healthy interest. As fresh and pink as she was, she could fade overnight if she became
sex-stifled.

"Hi, Fitz, hi, young lady," Goff had said, trying hard to produce the
natural easy cordiality consistent with his station.

Fitzsimmons, at all times the professional, had responded with his perfect doorman demeanor. Miss Forbidden Apples had smiled the dutiful, respectful smile befitting a vassal's obedient daughter to the nice lord of the manor. And Goff, in turn, injected a wholesome democratic lord-of-the-manor modesty in his tone. He was a lord that conducted tours through his castle for a nominal fee. Old-fashioned divine right behavior was passé.

"Can I drop you off somewhere, Miss Fitzsimmons? Your dad has often mentioned his pretty daughter (Fitzsimmons, puzzled, couldn't remember it), and you surely must be she," Goff said in his most resplendent grammar.

He knew he hadn't quite achieved the careless, offhand, upper-class graciousness he was striving for. But it was close enough. Fuck 'em! For a doorman and a daughter, it was good enough.

Fitzsimmons remained stolid and backed away imperceptibly. He sensed he was not in Goff's primary focus. He would not intrude.

The doorman's fetching daughter had tilted her young blond head and murmured a declination. She had plenty of time to get to the subway and get to her office on Sixth Avenue. She worked for Texsahara Oil and she was scheduled to take her late turn at the office and was in no special hurry. Goff had thought about how her cute miniskirt would hitch tight and high up her thighs sitting next to him in a taxi, and he pressed a little more.

"Fitz, I insist, since I'm heading downtown, that she spare herself the subway and ride with me."

"Anytime you have a chance to keep out of them subways is all to the good. No use looking for trouble when you don't have to."

"I've never had trouble, dad."

"Well, there's always the first time, with more and more of these hopped-up Negroes." He said "Negroes" in a tone indicating that sober, judicious restraint had preceded his opinion. But neither was he about to give them the satisfaction of calling them niggers, blacks. "You just thank Mr. Goff and go ahead, Pat."

Goff was thrilled that her name was Pat. All his life he had dreamed mostly of Pats and Kathys and Pegs. Pats and Kathys and Pegs whose brothers joined the Marines, and who themselves fucked like crazy, with Congressional Medal of Honor recklessness.

Pat, the doorman's daughter, had shrugged okay in a friendly obedient way, while her father showed undemonstrative but definite approval. Goff was delighted at the doorman's place and his remarkable grasp of it. The vassal unquestioningly surrendering his daughter to the mercies of the manor lord.

All being settled, the doorman quickly dropped further paternal traces and resumed his detached professional role. He strode out onto the street and imperiously blew his whistle. He snapped open the door of the answering cab and waited while Goff watched Miss Pat Fitzsimmons' mini hike way up as she bent her way into the cab, almost revealing her cute little kissable shiksa ass. Her dormant daddy remained stone imperturbable.

Goff followed, sat down and made sure his "Thanks, Fitz" had the right tone of rectitude and responsibility. Fitzsimmons smartly slammed shut the door, smartly snapped off a two-finger boy-scout-type salute, smartly turned and smartly paced back to the sidewalk. He concluded his daughter was safe.

Goff was sure that his final nod, containing the bonding smile of mutual fatherhood, completely camouflaged his hot nuts longing to bang the ass off the good doorman's daughter. Better me than him, he thought. Healthier all around.

And it came to pass,
   That he banged her ass,
      But he didn't bang it off.

Goff had been well aware that banging an ass off couldn't be done alone. It could be done only with a willing partner who is in sincere, feverish accord with this worthy goal.

And although he had launched a first-class campaign, in the end he had had to admit failure.

His last resort for tricky tricks was usually a certain luxurious hotel set dramatically on a picturesque bluff overlooking the Atlantic, almost at land's end at the tip of Long Island at Montauk. He had once spent a weekend there with his ex-wife Gloria. Their marriage, a constant open sore from beginning to end, had been at its usual nasty and nerve-wracking level. The hotel was located at a totally secluded stretch of majestic raw shore dominated by desertlike sand dunes and barren except for some patches of wild tough beach grass. There they had had their two finest days. They had both approached the nearest they had ever come to the fucking they had ever hoped to get from each other. It was in a room extended by an open redwood planked deck looking out at the open surf. They had never shut the doors. Goff felt that Mother Nature in the stark dramatic form of the locale had settled in on them and had briefly tranquilized their constant antagonism. The raw pounding surf had worked its old hypnotism and had set their rhyme and rhythm. And they had merged with it, gone beyond it for the best fucking of their tense, gritty marriage.

So Goff, having once experienced the salubrious results of the rugged, elemental environment, made livable by a fifty-dollar-per-day room, returned time and time again for special cases and special effects. That he would hesitate to use this place with other women out of delicacy or some sort of sentimental deference to the two best days of his marriage to Gloria never entered his mind. It had worked great with Gloria, and it should work just as well with other broads.

In retrospect he should have known that the doorman's daughter would not be one of his better pieces. She had been too lower middle class, too Catholic, too weighted down with notions which gave extreme value to a sensible commercial diploma from a Catholic high school, too much part of a society that considered the A & P the only appropriate place to buy groceries, thought the best husband would be the one who had a job with a solid utility company, and considered a German the next best catch for a girl if she somehow missed snaring a moderately sober Irishman.

But he had always been (and show him a normal guy that wasn't) crazy for shiksas. It had taken years and years for the idea to penetrate that a shiksa did other things all day and night besides constant screwing. And consequently when he finally conceded them some human frailties in the form of an occasional respite, he still insisted that man for man a shiksa could outfuck a Daughter of Israel any time.

Goff had finally had to rate his lay with Pat Fitzsimmons as piss poor. He had tried to invest her with a devil-may-care shiksa *joie de vivre*. He tried everything to get it off the ground and kept pumping capital into it to try to salvage it. He tried to talk her into it, breathe life into it—so he could recoup something, reap some benefits. Nothing.

Her sweet shiksa cunt had somehow gone dead and didn't have enough of a charge left to light and spark up her eyes into the twinkle that would signal the cool green go for frolic 'n' fuckin'. She did flash a nice grin, but it never lingered long. It was never attached to anything—like the smile of the man in the moon. It had been a sure foreshadowing of unfulfillment.

But she was a darlin' shiksa and her name was Pat, Fitzsimmons yet. He had figured on taking her out to Montauk Moorings for the sure treatment to bring out the full fuckable shiksa in her. He would plan vigorous outdoor activity. Swimming, paddleball, tennis and selected short activities designed both to impress and also to tone up the glands of a man in his trim, horny forties. Then a rest period on the sand.

They had arrived shortly before noon and Goff had knocked himself out on schedule. At about four o'clock, side by side on beach *chaises longues*, Goff was hot, disgruntled and discouraged. Everything, including his pert shiksa flower, was wilting fast. Pat was on her stomach, and Goff, on his back, his hands over his head (when he wasn't swatting sand flies), was squinting his eyes and hot bushy unibrow to shield off the still powerful sun. The face-hugging wraparound sunglasses, which he bought because they were imported from Italy and were the kind he figured were smart on the Riviera, were not dark enough to shade out sufficient sun, and were causing him to sweat around the eyes. The built-in jock strap in his new trunks, besides capturing gritty sand, was also too tight, and was squeezing and grating his crotch unmercifully. The cold Cokes the beach boy had brought were warm, and the big-as-buzzard sand flies were concentrating exclusively on him, none on the shiksa. Why not, brooded persecuted Goff. If they have a choice, why should they settle on a bland product of ham and swiss on white when they got me, organically cultivated from the finest of hot pastramis, chicken livers and boiled beef. Shit, he thought as he slapped another sand fly, I've been doing this whole thing with my balls way too much in an uproar; planning out all these fuckin' activities like some hopped-up Borscht Belt social director.

They were both quiet and that at least suited him. If he still had any chance at all, it would have to be with a very soft sell. Speak soft and carry a big dick. Don't touch her. Be quiet a while longer and then toss a little bittersweet something. He would think of something.

Ten, nine, eight, seven, six, five, four, three, two, one, zero: a test shot straight into the atmosphere—"Pat, what are you going to be when you grow up?" He had put in the bittersweet something beautiful.

"What do you mean, Mr. Goff?" This had got her up on her elbow and looking at him, the rueful muser.

"I mean, when are you going to be doing what you really want to do?"

"Oh, I see what you mean." She knew he had said something deep. "What are you going to be when *you* grow up, Mr. Goff?"

Hearing this, Goff crooned silently to himself. She had bit at the bait. He still rested his head on his hands looking straight up, but he knew he had just elicited a positive twinkle. All right, it was not cunt-generated, it was rather cerebral, but the cerebral bone is connected to the cuntee bone. He had made the first bridgehead. In another second he would give her the answer. It would be a good answer. It would plant him in more secure. It would establish their unique mutuality, their inchoate groping, their mutual vague dissatisfaction with their present lives. It would flatter this young girl that he had chosen her as a confidante for his melancholy intimacy. He would show himself to be a worldly bon vivant who ruefully senses that despite his material success life still hadn't brought true happiness. Is it really too late though? Is it, Pat? I can't really complain, I'm a rich man, but sometimes I wonder, Pat. Even as you wonder about yourself. "When I grow up, Pat . . ." he paused, and finally turned his head and looked at her directly. "I guess . . ." he paused again ever so slightly and put on an endearing, wistful, forty-five-year-old, little-boy grin beneath his naughty Italian Riviera sunglasses, "I guess," he repeated—okay, Goff, now pull over on your side, lift up these ginzo glasses, look at her with syrupy WASP schmaltz and say—"I'd like to be a little kid again." What a shot. By God, I think I hit her in the cunt this time. Direct hit amidships in the cunt. I grapple-ironed onto her cunt, Cap'n Blood. Full steam ahead! Heave to. Her eyes, finally! A flicker of cunt, by George!

Pat looked at him. Gentle, strange, deep man.

Goff knew that for this particular phase he had peaked. Too much schmaltz would make it soggy. Had to keep it crisp. So he leapt up, tossed off his *La Dolce Vita* glasses, and instantly shed all trace of tired, old-world, decadent debauchery to become wholesome, straight, vigorous American. As he started running, he playfully slapped her on the ass, and so under cover of lark began to widen his bridgehead. "Last one in is a Pyrenees donkey," he tossed back, flashing her the grin of a decent guardian who, although at times sorely tempted, will keep his trust. He dashed toward the surf and dived into the breakers.

Pat immediately sprang up to follow the good guardian Goff, and she also sliced into the breakers.

And they both swam together with silent stroke and kick. Water being a better conductor of electricity than air, was there a tiny communicating charge beginning to generate stealthily between them? A baptismal, pure electricity? Goff thought of it poetically as the same water that's touching my cock is soaking into her pussy; and he trusted that somehow it was going to communicate a little agitation. Even in its present, chilled, shriveled, jock-strapped-choked stage, he figured it was still sending out urgent impulses.

After the gritty heat of the sun on the beach, the clean rolling surf he now floated in cooled him deliciously. He stroked out now with easy wind. Again Pat followed him. He would make her follow him further. "Swim out here beyond the breakers, Pat." She grinned and swam toward him obediently. And he would make her follow him more and more and more. He drew his knees up and performed a perfect surface dive, breast-stroking and scissor-kicking deep under the surface, feeling in cool control of his slithering underwater movement.

He surfaced alongside her. No coming up and grabbing her, feeling her, goosing her or fucking around. No splashing, no ducking. He would show her dignified vigor and responsible control.

"Good girl, Pat. You followed me right out," he said, spitting out sea water. "You have a good stroke," he went on with a mild sputter.

"What kind of a donkey was that?" said Pat, a fine floater who knew the knack of keeping water out of her mouth.

"A *Pyrenees* donkey. I'm of Basque descent." Pat took the word "Basque" for another sputter. "My dad used to call me that when he was angry about my stubbornness. There's a Basque saying that a Pyrenees donkey's stubbornness is in direct proportion to his stuputteridity." Goff felt more comfortable now. He had introduced a beautiful connecting common denominator. Fathers. Good, wholesome, concerned dads. Tighten the screwings a little more. "Basques are the greatest—there aren't many in America. They don't like much to leave their mountains." Pat floated and listened, wondering mildly why he was elaborating so much on those donkeys.

Play it Basque for this one, he thought as he kept flapping away at the insistent water that sought constantly, by its deceitfully friendly lapping to probe out some momentary weakness in order to sneak up on him and suck him under in a sudden tidal gulp. He felt he had to be Basque because he couldn't take any chances. Basque, because she might be frightened off by a Jew. Her record and background were not sufficiently progressive to allay for him all the fears that were never too far from the surface. She had never even finished one year at Hunter College. Her father was a sound public doorman, but unquestionably a sulking private bigot. She had gone to a Catholic high school where he was sure no one knocks himself out to boost a Jew. She worked for Texsahara Oil, which was watched over by an Arab genie who had orders to cut the company's Protestant balls off with a scimitar if they hired a Jew. She just simply had not had enough exposure and guidance and enlightenment to bring her to the point of accepting the healthy concept of equal rights screwing. He could understand the basis of her intolerance—so if she were intolerant of him, he certainly didn't have to be of her. Two wrongs don't make a right. Let *her* be the bad one.

For her he would therefore be Basque and spare her the mental agony of making it with a Jew.

Goff slipped over onto his stomach and started to swim in. He had always been a better swimmer than floater. "Let's hit the beach, Pat, follow me," waved the frogman squad leader, encouraging his men with the confidence he had to instill in them. Without turning back, he knew Fitzsimmons, the gamest little guy of them all, would be following right behind. Goff, always the competitor, had to swim like hell to make it in ahead of the game little guy.

On solid ground now, his vanity trying to force his breathing to carry on without visible heaving, he watched his sheltered shiksa move out of the surf. The way she was built, Goff thought, she should be walking out proud and graceful like a golden-assed goddess from Atlantis or some other fuckin' comic-book place like that, but instead she was clompin' out like some cowboy girl drudge who had just forded the river with the family's ox on their way to Californy. How come he had never caught that before? Shiksa nut that he was, that's why!

He realized that as built as she was, as bikinied as she was, she still had really failed to come through to him as a wholly irresistible sex delicacy. The sum of her parts didn't add up to her whole. She hadn't really worn her bikini for getting over the message, Look at my legs, my thighs, my ass, my boobs. I'm showing them to you so you can see what lovely things I can churn up in bed for you. No: her girlish message was, I feel great. Look, I can do handsprings and splits.

When he had asked her to spend the day with him at Montauk, she told him she had rented a room at Southampton for the summer with two other girls. He had promised her he would drop her off there that night, and assured her that it was only a twenty-minute drive. Actually it was an hour. He had reserved two rooms at the Moorings at Montauk, one under her name.

When they were toweling themselves dry on the beach, Pat said, "That room wasn't really necessary. It's really a terrible extravagance, Mr. Goff."

"I guess you can call it an extravagance. It feels more of an extravagance though, if you continue to keep calling me Mr. Goff. Call me Arnie, and I promise you it'll immediately start to feel less and less expensive," he grinned, and tried a tentative exploratory leer. It was completely lost on her. She responded with a friendly smile. Not a flicker of understanding, but a nice big, healthy smile, like that of a foreigner who doesn't understand what you're telling her, but smiles at you anyway just to be agreeable.

She did stop calling him Mr. Goff, but she never did call him Arnie. She somehow managed to address him thereafter on an entirely nameless basis, always skirting the need to call him by name. By the time they were having cocktails at the driftwood-loaded bar at the Moorings, Goff had become fully aware of the evasion. She wouldn't even call him, "Arnie, pass the fuckin' peanuts" to eat with her juvenile rum and Coke. Instead it was deliberately, and gingerly, "Please pass the peanuts"— Nothing.

After three vodka martinis in a holiday atmosphere with a beautiful broad like Pat, in a sleek cocktail lounge on the sea with driftwood and net and a fruit piano player who played the prerequisite show tunes for paunchy sophisticated fuckers, Goff, who would ordinarily have felt high 'n' mellow, felt disconsolate. It was clear she wasn't ever going to call him by his Christian name. Hell, he wasn't asking her to call him Avrom, his Jewish name. And he then and there adopted the general rule that a man would be a fool to expect a good fuck from a broad that wouldn't call him by his Christian name.

However, he remembered his secretary, Ramona, who also always addressed him as Meester Goff, except *in extremis,* when she would feverishly fling off office formality and in Spanish call him the most Christian name of all, but not his, "Oh, *Jesus Cristo.*" So he modified his rule to: a man would be a fool to expect a good fuck from a broad that wouldn't call him by his Christian name except if she happened to be a member of a disadvantaged minority group.

But it wasn't all a dead loss. Goff sensed that he and Pat were being stared at. She was a striking-looking shiksa. When he was a young schmuck it was his obsessive rule that any girl he was seen with must be attractive if not downright stunning. A real kid schmuck condition he further attached was that he be taller than she, and since he was short, his public girl companions had to be neat and petite. But in later years, he and Kummerlos had disposed of the juvenile notion (it had been too restrictive; it was eliminating too much stuff; people's average heights were rising), and he had got to the point where he actually sought out taller girls. There was no question in his mind about the admiration it brought him: look at that Arnie Goff, he certainly can't be classed as a giant, but just get a load of that tall yummy blonde he's runnin' around with. Another tall beautiful shiksa; where does he get 'em all? And she really goes for him. Look how she looks down at him with respect! He must have some equalizer! Doesn't he remind you something of Billy Rose? May he rest in peace. In the end he gave so much to Israel.

As he looked around the cocktail lounge from his bar stool, he saw all the Jew boys (he knew who they were; they didn't fool him a bit) giving Pat and him the eye. He knew they were all trying to make out *not* whether he was screwin' that pretty little shiksa but whether he was a *landsman*. There was no doubt in their minds that he was screwin' the shiksa. What else? Let 'em think it. Fuck 'em. To reenforce their notion, he looked at Pat and gave her an intimate little cocktail-lounge smile and patted her hand in a way that proclaimed its confirmation to all those jealous pricks. Pat had no idea the patting was her confirmation. She thought he was a nice man. But I just can't call him Arnie, and she smiled at him, and the Jew guys in the lounge nodded their reaffirmation of their established conviction as they blew cigar smoke all around.

The women in the lounge were also looking at him, and his guess about them was that they were regarding him disapprovingly because he could have been her father. Fuck them too; he'd sign the adoption papers in a minute.

He smiled paternally at her. Here's more peanuts—Nothing wants you to eat more peanuts—eat, eat, eat—Nothing gives you more—sit up straighter—show your *tzitkalach* more—stick 'em out more—so you should look nice—so people will love you—Nothing wants to be proud of you.

But Jesus, he hadn't come here to get *naches* from his shiksa, he had come here to lay her. And the likelihood was strong for a rebuff.

If that happened, it could sink him for months. He couldn't take a rebuff well. Never could.

Could he correct that somehow?

Kummerlos had said why in God's name did he want to correct *that*. "Is your goal to make yourself amenable to rebuffs and insults, and snubs, scorn and contumely?" Goff didn't know about contumely, but he certainly couldn't argue about the rest of it. No, if he wanted to seek an accommodation with rebuffs and insults, he should go to his rabbi, by God. Kummerlos dealt with strengthening one for the present, not the hereafter. Did Goff detect the tiniest trace of disgruntled challenge in Kummerlos' tone—if you don't like my way of handling things, you are welcome to go to your rabbi? Hell, no, I'll never desert my Kummerlos— and who the hell has a rabbi anyway? Goff remembered in this session Kummerlos had reached one of his finest fifty-minute hours. He had closed with a majestically wrathful Old Testament roar, and a New Testament reference, "If you have to turn the other cheek, let it be of your ass. Show them your *tuchis, ferstehst!*" he'd commanded, reverting in the end again to Old Testament flavor. This unusually passionate outburst had somehow eliminated the need to say, "We must close now." It had been a natural curtain.

Goff ordered another martini, and made a sudden, firm resolve. Okay, Patty baby, you're going to come across the way it was always intended. You know why? Because I've got all the confidence in you, Patty baby, scared little shiksa doll. I'll bring you around, don't fret. Arnie Goff is gonna go all out now. He's puttin' all his money on his little shiksa doll, right on her pretty upturned nose. I'll have you hollerin' Arnie yet.

Goff looked into his martini and saw his dear departed pop, old A. G. His pop was looking up at him lovingly, trying to gurgle a cackle up through the vodka. And when old A.G. rose out of the martini, in his stubbled long underwear, Goff didn't feel at all threatened. Pop wasn't trying to replace him this time.

"*Geb'r a gutten schtup,* Arneleh," he rasped encouragingly.

Nobody heard him but Goff. Good old pop! And one of Goff's eyes began to moisten a bit. When Pat commented on the tear in his eye, he waved it away with a sodden smile and told her it was from the onion in the martini.

Goff had a choice of two general stratagems. He could make his strong move now or continue with the treatment, a fine dinner, a walk on the dunes and more; and then make his strong move. Although he was high, it was the high of extreme alertness, the exhilarating tipsy. One big buildup, one big assault and it's make it or break it. No second chance. He chose to continue, for good practical reasons. She wasn't ready yet, Nothing's girl.

After cocktails, Goff then planned a sumptuous shore dinner at the Moorings' dining room.

Pat was like a pretty little island who existed, emerging or submerging with the tides. He had to catch her at the favorable tide, and attach himself for the brief period she would exist for him.

His sixth martini having been downed, the isle of Pat Fitzsimmons emerged. He was ready to cast another grappling hook, one always effective on a certain type of quarry. He flung back his arm and heaved out the old trusty hook of literature.

"Ca-MOOOOO," he wafted softly over to her, a deceivingly designed hook that seemed fragile, but had the strength of steel. On hearing the softly insinuating "Ca-mooooo," Pat looked up like a startled doe who has heard her first muted mating call. He pressed on. "Ca-mooooo," he repeated.

Goff commended her for having attempted to read Camus; he was admittedly tough and deep. He himself had never read him, but was of course familiar with his name.

Pat flushed, realizing instantly that Goff's pronunciation must be correct.

Goff congratulated himself on his impeccable tact. He had milked the "moo" for all it was worth.

Pat was unquestionably impressed by this gentle, cultured Jewish millionaire who knew about Camus and about another fine writer whom she must not fail to read, Eudora Welty.

"What a beautiful name," said Pat, allowing the euphony of the name and the presence of the gentle, smiling man with his bushy single eyebrew to lull her into a mild reverie. The rum and Cokes were beginning to make her feel delightfully cozy, and the songs from *Carousel* on the piano were fitting and sweet. And best of all, Mr. Goff wouldn't be making any uncomfortable demands on her. God, certainly nothing like Jim-Tim. What a relief. Relax and enjoy it—and tell the girls at Southampton later.

In recommending Eudora Welty, Goff was passing on a recommendation he had received twenty-five years ago from a woman a few years older than he, who wrote book reviews in Lawton, Oklahoma. She had considered Eudora Welty one of the finest writers in America. Goff had been a second lieutenant stationed there, and he had gone on renewing the recommendation ever since, although he'd never read her books either. It always impressed well. Everyone had always somehow vaguely heard of Eudora Welty. The Oklahoma book reviewer had been the first literary shiksa he had ever laid, and she had been a terrifically exciting piece of classic shiksa Americana. Anyone she recommended would have made an indelible impression on the young lieutenant fresh out of Brooklyn. It is a lucky author who is the momentary favorite of an especially exciting lay, for that name once imparted to the hot appreciative lover will have a fine reputation etched out for life, carried permanently onward in gratitude.

Fitzsimmons Isle had finally emerged, and El Conquistadore de la Nada, the Bold Basque, was ready for his landing and conquest.

His patting had ceased and he was suddenly holding Pat's hand; the velvet-covered grappling hook had hooked on.

"I have a great idea," he said. "I'll reserve a table for about eight-thirty, and why don't we have another swim now. I guarantee the lobster will taste out of this world with the appetite we'll work up."

Pat, who had hoped that perhaps Mr. Goff's last pat on her hand was only an especially long one, now knew that the pat had matured into a hold. And the realization, without any drum rolls, twenty-one gun salutes or sudden crashes of thunder, came to her that Mr. Goff was going to try to screw her like Jim-Tim. Well, she supposed she'd really asked for it, coming out with him and all. Would she avoid him? She didn't know. Maybe she was wrong in her guess that Mr. Goff would try to screw her. She didn't think she was wrong. She would wait and see what happened. She wondered whether he had those rubber protection things. She smiled at Mr. Goff whom she still considered a nice man.

Goff smiled back. He knew her smile was still intended for Mister Goff, not Arnie or anything like it. For cryin' out loud, he wasn't even much thinking of her as a shiksa anymore, why couldn't she stop thinking of him as a Mr. Goff-Nothing. Anyway, it had been a good precaution that he had told her he was Basque. If he finally had to score merely as Mr. Goff-Nothing, the Basque, so be it. You can't win 'em all big.

Pat's last thought about it as she went to her room to slip into her bikini was that she also had to consider that Mr. Goff was Jewish and she wouldn't want him to think that . . . well, she wouldn't want to make him feel bad on that account. And if he did try and if she decided not to let him, she hoped she would be able to find a way to say no in a way that wouldn't hurt his feelings. But she hoped he just wouldn't try. That would be the best.

She had been in the extravagant room for only a few minutes and was just slipping out of her panties to get into her bikini when there was a knock at the door, and she knew it was Mr. Goff, and she knew he was coming to screw her. He had told her they should meet in about twenty minutes. He had to make some phone calls. So when he came to her room in three minutes, it seemed to her that she had made a reasonable supposition. And as she put on a beach robe and went to the door, she was still undecided about what position she would take.

As she opened the door, Goff hustled in with clacking clogs and tight-crotch trunks. Pat decided she didn't want Mr. Goff to screw her. But how could she avoid hurting his sensitive Jewish feelings?

"I decided to let those calls go, so I came to tell you we might start now, if you're ready."

"In just a sec. I was just getting my suit on." Turning to go to the extravagant room's dressing alcove, she knew she wasn't going to make it.

When he whirled her around and his kiss forced her on the bed and his fingers started to claw between her legs, she told him no, no, no. (It was just her luck to have been caught between pants.) It was no, no, no for his tonguing her ears. It was no, no, no for his removal of his tight-crotched elastically obstinate trunks and the jack-in-the-box explosion of his pent-up penis. It was no, no, no for his nimble-fingered attempt with the clasp on her bra. And it was especially no, no, no for his culminating attempt of insertion of prick. Her no's and throes had prevented the accomplishment of all major objectives, and, of course, the ultimate one.

In the melee, with scarcely any of the skirmishes for Goff's win column, he attempted to put his hand inside her bra. She warded him off even for this modest spoil of battle. This final denial was the straw that broke the hump. From his deepest tortured depths, somewhere in the vicinity of his bosky scrotum, came a ball-rending cry of primordial anguish, "Not even bare tit!" It was the most agonizing human cry Pat had ever heard. "All the time NO! NO! NO! Couldn't it at the very least even be NO,NO,NO, *ARNIE!* Couldn't you call me No, No, No, Arnie, once?" he choked pitifully.

Pat was deeply touched and genuinely distressed. She decided to make a supreme effort to call him Arnie. She looked at his pained face, and said, "Please don't feel bad. . . ." nothing. She realized she had failed again. She just couldn't do it. The hell with it, so she decided to let Mr. Goff screw her. That would compensate for it. If she couldn't bring herself to call him Arnie, she could at least have the decency to screw him. She just couldn't call him Arnie—it was just too damn uncomfortable or something. So if he insisted, he could go ahead. And he was still a nice Jewish man—she simply wouldn't let his sex drives prejudice her, and letting him screw her would take care of that also. God, poor man, on top of everything else, he might think I'm rejecting him because he's Jewish. Go ahead, Mr. Goff, if you still want me. I asked for it and I'm not going to squirm out of it anymore. But please don't ask me to call you Arnie. No disrespect, mind you. And lying next to Mr. Goff who was momentarily immobilized, she gritted her teeth and stiffened her body, awaiting the thrust of lust that she knew was inevitable.

As Pat had expected, Mr. Goff rallied and started his assault again, like a well-trained boxer. Goff, the old pro, sensed her loss of will to resist, and as he started to nuzzle and fuzzle her, he hurled himself once more at the most humiliating symbol of his disastrous encounter up to then, the unclasping of that maddening brassiere clasp. But Pat, trying to be helpful, told him she would unhook it. Goff nodded his lukewarm acceptance—a general whose spirited troops are champing to scale the walls suddenly sees the gates of the town opened wide in surrender. He always preferred to spring the bra himself to see those compressed breasts come tumbling out in their luscious fullness—which sometimes really happened. Pat's didn't. They were full enough but had no special bounce. His most exciting bra-springing had been with the American classic book reviewer in Oklahoma. He'd never forgotten how thrilled he'd been when, sitting on that bed in the hotel, she had summoned him from across the room and coolly requested him to "undo my bra, please." He had never before been witness to such intimate class in his life. He considered that this, in a way, had been his first introduction to upper-class style and chic. Thereafter. anyone who said anything but "undo my bra" was put down as graceless.

And although she had called him "Arnie" generally, she always resorted to "Goff" when they fucked. "Goff sounds better for fucking," she had told him with euphonic assurance. She had clarified further that "Fuck me, Arnie" sounded like somebody was lying, whereas "Fuck me, Goff" had the ring of truth. What an ear she'd had! What a wild one she had been. It had been new and dazzling. Breeding gone berserk. He had shrewdly concluded that this unleashing of wild behavior was a certain mark of good lineage. Her obscenity was a thing of beauty. The savage purity of a violent electric storm. It was a raw, flawless truth, such as no nonupper-class person could ever hope to attain and certainly no middle-class Jewish girl could ever free herself to face. Outside of bed her language was impeccable except for one time at a bar in downtown Lawton, when she had said, "Don't give me that Basque shit."

When Pat demonstrated her helpfulness by volunteering to unhook her bra, Goff's response was almost to lose his hardon which wasn't too worked up in the first place.

What a stiff for a shiksa, he thought. She's never going to call me anything. She won't even give me a little pantomime. She's a game little thing though. Got guts. Shiksas got guts. *Stug tog saskish*, as his backward Hungarian forebears would say. You had to give them credit. Pat was neither fish nor fowl. She didn't have the heart to be a real shiksa swinger and she didn't have the strictness to be a good Irish Catholic uncomplicated healthy confessin' piece of ass. She's going to go through with it—with a stiff upper lip for her, and a limp *putz* for me.

He was even thinking of calling it quits for the sake of that game Irish *shiksaleh*. He looked at her Irish shiksa face and gave himself a sharp reproach. Schmuck, what are you thinking? A beautiful shiksa is ready to lay you and you want to let her go!

And grimly he piled on her like a lineman crunches into a pileup because he's got orders to evaporate the quarterback. He zealously brought out his full repertoire of sex tricks and dirty play. He tickled her asshole and tit. Rubbed her pussy and clit. A dialogue with his homologue. And wet with a spot of spit. Peripherally and sniffily, he poked and kissed and stirred, and tweaked and twanged and twitted twat, all cunningly befurred, to get his prick interred.

As a tribute to Goff's frenetic behavior, Pat tried to look tender, but managed only to look tense. Dr. Goff then made a brilliant diagnosis. She was sinking fast. Her respiratory rate stank. And he had no more oxygen to supply her.

He would try shock treatment. He suddenly grabbed her hand and closed it around his waning wang. She clutched it in a docile, death grip. She was more rigid than his dying dick. He was tired, tired. No will to live, that girl. But Dr. Goff, his whole training and conditioning forced him to go on with the operation, regardless of the dim prognosis.

"Nurse, harder hardon, please."

"Sorry, Dr. Goff. No other available."

"I will proceed with this one then, thank you, nurse." Dr. Goff, above all, the surgeon, plunged in with what was available to him. Most operations were exciting fun. This one was a chore. The operation would be a success, but the patient was already dead.

Pat, the spunky patient, although terrified, tried to keep it from showing. She kept her eyes shut; she froze in a tense, wispy smile. Poor thing, thought Goff. Penetration had been hard. He pumped on relentlessly. When he fucked he could drive on unmercifully and simultaneously feel sorry for the girl. He had given up trying to draw her into it. He just wanted to blow his nuts now. Afterward, he promised himself, he would really show her compassion. But it would have to wait awhile. Poor kid, he kept thinking, but screw her, and he kept on. Finally, he had a third-rate spurt. I could be accused of necrophilia, Goff thought grumpily.

I think he's finished, Pat thought. She had meant to ask him to put on one of those things, but with everything else she'd had to contend with, she had lost her nerve. But he must have done something, a man of his worldliness. He was quiet now. God, what a difference between him now, and his carryings-on a few seconds ago. He had hurt, though. It had been as bad as with Jim-Tim. When was he going to get out of her? Should she start to move herself away? Better not. She didn't want to hurt his feelings now, not after all she had gone through already. But Jesus, Mary and

Joseph, she sure wouldn't have gone through it if he weren't Jewish. She
wouldn't tell the girls at Southampton after all. They wouldn't understand.

Goff, contracting fast, gave himself sour congratulations. He knew it
was only because he'd played the Basque that he'd gotten into her at all.
His old dependable role, Goff, the Basque. Another rack for Goff, the
Basque. She was a nice kid. Too bad she had to be infected with those
age-old anti-Semitic prejudices.

His usual pattern was quick postcoital quits, but now he found himself
with a fond regard for this game little *anti-Semitkeleh*. She had heart.
Hell, he knew she hadn't got any pleasure out of it. You had to give her a
lot of credit. He would take her to Southampton, deposit her with her girl-
friends. Oh, Christ, he still had to feed her, he reminded himself. The hell
with that swim, though. That was out!

They grinned at each other as the waitress tied their lobster bibs. Surprisingly, they enjoyed their lobster dinner and ate heartily. They were
both starved. Pat was a little sore, but it wasn't that bad. She thought Mr.
Goff seemed to be relieved. *She* certainly was. And he was a really charming and witty man. She gave a tremulous thought to the notion that things
might have been better had Mr. Goff waited until after their delicious dinner. She shrugged.

Goff, the old sharp-eyed Basque smuggler who could spot and elude the
must cunning of the border customs guards, caught Pat's shrug and understood it completely.

Fuck that. Christ, hadn't he learned his lesson? Cut it short now as
quickly as possible, hustle her down to Southampton and get to the city. It
was Saturday and the night was still young. To go through that scene
again—to pin some new hopes on a shrug—no. Bad, bad odds.

Deep in his cream-colored Jag XKE, Goff smoked a cigar, drove carefully within the speed limit, felt very comfortable and was in the mood to
give Pat good, safe, fatherly advice. He really couldn't care less anymore
whether she called him Mr. Goff, Arnie, Nothing or anything. Cars were
zipping past. Screw 'em, he thought. He wasn't going to race them. He
didn't have to be such a hot Basque anymore. That meal had tasted damn
good. The broiled lobster was juicy and sweet. But no matter how good it
was, he still liked his lobster best Jewish-style—Cantonese. That had
been his first breakthrough into exotic gourmet cooking when he had one
day (God, how many years ago that was) graduated from chicken chow
mein to lobster Cantonese. He had damn near come in his pants when he

had first tasted that lobster, swimming in that rich cummy, eggy sauce. If the Jews were going to extract loyalty from their people via their food, then they had to expect defections through their food too. If you live by the sword, you die by the sword. Chinese food was a subtle, gentle sacrament of modification, not heresy. Not to be compared to gross pork sausages. *That* was heresy. Chinese food somehow gently insinuated itself with soft Oriental tact and modesty. The Chinese always absorbed their invaders.

Now, of course, he ate his Chinese food in only either the highest rated places or else in unprepossessing out-of-the-way "discoveries." meltzer's excited recommendations always stank, but his accountant could be relied upon. It was a real coup to "discover" a new Chinese joint. He hadn't heard the word "Chinks" in twenty years. Why should he? In the circles he now traveled, civil rights bullshit and gold-leaf menus had just about done in that old comfortable word altogether. And when one of his circle led a skeptical, ravenous horde one flight down to a new "discovery," he waited like a tense actor at Sardi's for the weightily considered first-night reviews of the deliberating body of guzzling Chinese mavins who absolutely everybody in his circle claimed to be. And what warm inner delight it was, when the circle around the table nodded with sucking sounding approval.

And the dishes they now ate—and God forbid you should profane the food with a metal fork—no—it had to be only with wooden chopsticks to keep the flavor pure. Jesus Christ, no more like roast pork with Chinese vegetables or the number-three special with fried rice and eggroll. Now it was nothing less than pressed dong, sweet and pungent, or thousand-year testicles, hot and sour, or Taiwan Twat with black muck sauce, or sizzled balls—Szechuan style, please. And there was this irritating sharing dishes shit. Let me taste some of your pressed dong and I'll give you some of my sizzled balls. That was one polite big pain in the ass. He came to eat, not to sample. Crap! The next time he went to eat Chinks—he didn't give a shit who was with him—he was going to tell One Ball Hung Low, "Look, bring me an order of lobster Cantonese with all that nice cummy lobster sauce, and one plate only; it's all of it for me!" None of that sharing shit. "And a side order of roast pork flied lice!" Fuck them! Amelican plicks! And shove the chopsticks up your ass. Gimme clean fork.

Goff snapped a Sinatra tape cartridge into his Lear Jet stereo and turned the volume low for the touchy, torchy singer he felt epitomized him. He had been a schmuck, spending all that time and money on a kid that wasn't with it. He figured, with tips and all, it had been close to one hundred fifty bucks.

The cigar tasted delicious, and he told Pat with puffed-up two dollar cigar wisdom and contentedness to marry Jim-Tim, the teller, and become a good little Catholic shiksa with ten blond-headed kids and a large station wagon. He decided he would give her a hundred-dollar check for a marriage present.

He reached Southampton at nearly eleven, pecked Pat on the cheek good-bye, and couldn't resist accelerating his Jaguar for a rakish screeching getaway. He heard her say, "Thanks for everything, Mr. Goff." Sweet *goyisheh kop*, he thought, well impressed with her blond, Gentile deportment. To her credit, she had sense enough to realize that the ban on "Mr. Goff" had been lifted.

Cruising toward New York, he felt terribly horny. The doorman's daughter had just whetted his appetite. He also wondered whether those steamers and clam broth he had had with his shore dinner had some influence. Nah, that was bullshit. Eating straight cream cheese and jelly sandwiches for a month, and he'd still get up a hardon like a cast-iron bull. Working the stick shift with smooth synchronization into high, he zoomed past a creep. The car's response was so elegantly beautiful, and Goff, the cockpit cocksman, felt heady self-satisfaction and elan as he masterfully rode his purring Jaguar west to New York. Sinatra's voice, filling the cruising car, seemed to float around him like a friendly arm around a pal's shoulder.

# Chapter 6

### Goff and Meltzer in Israel

If it hadn't been for business, Goff would never have considered a trip to Israel. He wasn't interested in Israel. Oh, he'd allowed himself to be carried away a little during the Six Day War, and he thought Moshe Dayan was interesting mostly because he was a swinger, but other than that, Israel was a bore. He knew exactly what to expect of it. Always had.

How did he know so well? Because he knew Jews, that's why. He knew them inside out, upside down. He knew all the varieties. From the most meek to the most nervy. From the richest to the poorest. From the most honest to the most false. From the smartest to the dumbest. From the most holy to the most profane.

So they're prouder now and walk taller. He had seen them walk just as proud on Pitkin Avenue. Look, he *knew* them. No matter where, no matter how, he knew them. And they bored him. And on top of that, that awful climate. No, thanks.

"Wait, Goff. Tell me, who exactly *doesn't* bore you?"

"Ah, a very good question, rabbi. Cunts. Cunts don't bore me. Cunts are my oxygen, my stuff of life. It's the cunt that makes me sing my song. And that the shiksa cunt makes my song louder and purer, well, that's the way my balls bounce. No apologies. I can't help it, rabbi. No offense, I hope."

Goff hears hundreds of reports of people returning from visits to Israel. They try to express exaltation. Goff sees through it. They feel it's their

61

duty. He doesn't condemn them. The only negative thing they concede is about the food. It wasn't that good. But anyway, who went to Israel for food? Right? They went to every fuckin' place else for food. But Israel gets excused. Goff understands that too. But doesn't that prove what people have long been whispering? That while you have a Diaspora you keep a Jew a Jew by the food you feed him. Weren't the Protocols of the Elders of Zion a conspiracy of cuisine? It's not the Torah, it's the *tzimmis*. It's the chopped liver. So the Diaspora is over. Israel lives. The liver is finished. Food is dead. Long live Israel.

Israel, where finally a Jew can be a Jew without cuisine, without restraint, without inhibition. Stop! That's all he needed! Look, it just wasn't for him. No more discussion.

But Arnie, a fantastic phenomenon has taken place. They fuck like crazy now. He didn't want crazy fucking, thank you.

He had made this trip to Israel before his divorce, before he had become a millionaire. It was to work out a deal where he would advise a couple of Romanian Israelis how to set up the facilities for making phonograph records. Meltzer had got wind of the trip and begged Goff to be allowed to accompany him. He promised Goff he would not interfere with him in the times he had to devote to his business. But evenings, wouldn't he welcome an old friend for companionship? Meltzer expected a typical Goff boff for an answer and merrily steeled himself, but was surprised to have Goff consent straightforwardly. Goff had remembered how miserable he had been alone in Rome once.

After debarking at Lod Airport in Tel Aviv, Meltzer, just as Goff had expected, had exclaimed how exciting it was that the customs officials, the pilots and stewardesses, the police were all Jewish. How reflective of genuine Israeli sovereignty.

In the taxi pickup area, Meltzer expansively lit up the two-dollar cigar Goff had given him in New York. Meltzer had said he would save it for a suitably celebrative occasion, and felt that now, standing on Eretz Yisroel, was the appropriate time. The taxi driver they drew had a pre-Israeli Jewish face and Meltzer joyfully pointed out that even the taxi drivers were Jewish. "What other kind are there anywhere?" muttered Goff wearily.

When the taxi pulled up to them, the driver peered sourly at Meltzer and said, "I can't take you with smoking that cigar. I have asthma."

Meltzer without a moment's hesitation grandly threw down the cigar Goff had given him. "Of course," he said with exquisite good will. "See, I've thrown it away."

Goff gave them both a look of disgust. The driver nodded his acceptance of the unconditional surrender due him for his condition, and continued sitting immobile at the wheel, morose master of all he conveyed. Goff finally opened the door with an angry yank, threw his bag in, followed it and flounced down hard in his seat.

After starting out they saw some laborers and asked what they were doing. "They are Arabs working on an extension of the airport. They receive the same wages as if they are Israeli," the driver told them.

A little way farther he informed them that they were passing a factory which manufactured toilet seats, also with equally paid Arabs.

Meltzer nodded approvingly at the fairness. "Another sign of independence and sovereignty."

Goff, looking out of the window, muttered peevishly, "It would show more independence if they weren't so chicken fair." Meltzer giggled at his shrewdness. Forgetting the injunction, Goff put a cigar into his mouth and struck a match. The taxi driver immediately waggled his finger furiously.

"No, no! My asthma!" Goff angrily threw the match out the window. "Fumes from the match are not the best thing for my asthma also. It would be better you should open the window more now."

And Goff littered the land of Israel with his dead cigar. The taxi driver worked up a cough and drove on with the back of his neck bristling at him. Goff knew it was going to turn out this way. Fuck him and fuck this trip to Israel, he thought.

That evening in Tel Aviv they were having their dinner at a sidewalk cafe on noisy, crowded Dizengoff Street. It was Pitkin Avenue. Suddenly Meltzer interrupted Goff, who was picking at a turkey dinner. "Arnie! Look! That girl—my first Israeli streetwalker—there—look, look! The girl that just passed us!"

Goff looked up and saw the back of a slight, rather emaciated-looking girl, her bag almost swinging *her* down the street, dressed in the very high heels and floozy flash of an obvious streetwalker. She sensed Meltzer's attentive excitement, turned back toward them and smiled. Goff was oddly incensed. That smile wasn't the tough, brazen smile of a self-respecting street whore. First off, she looked as if she were very nearsighted and could use some eyeglasses, and second, she just fell short of shrugging her shoulders in apology.

"Look, Arnie, I know she's hardly anything to write home about, but . . ."

Goff interrupted, "This one, I wouldn't hesitate to write home about." He was glad Meltzer was sitting at the other side of the table, because he knew he had just said the kind of thing that would trigger him to jab him in the shoulder appreciatively.

Meltzer did start to reach over, but saw he couldn't make it, so he settled for a head shake of admiration and continued, "Sure she's not the greatest, but this is a new country. Don't you get the significance of it?"

The girl had been waiting for a sign, and Meltzer finally smiled her dismissal with a friendly shake of his head, as if he were turning down a girl at a sisterhood bazaar who was holding out a box for donations for the Jewish National Fund. It was the smile that meant to say, "I already gave at the office—hundreds, believe me."

"Arnie, doesn't it send a shiver of pride up your spine? You know what I mean? The police, the officials, all Jewish—great! But to also have their own prostitutes! That's what I call real independence. You know what I mean?" Meltzer bubbled.

Goff gave him an excruciating look of annoyance as he tried to go on eating his dry turkey with all the fixin's, Israeli style—gravied noodles. Goff tried to absorb Meltzer's flood of enthusiasm with an affirming nod. It was like using a sponge to try to blot up a summer cloudburst. Meltzer could not be absorbed that easily. Meltzer poured it on. "You know what I mean? This feeling of a country being born. Making its own toilet seats is great, but when they have their own whores, that's finally real self-sufficiency, you know?"

Goff was forced to acknowledge Meltzer's Israeli fervor. He wiped a clinging noodle from the side of his mouth and said with dead evenness, "I know what you mean, Doc. It's like a house is not a home until it has its own toilet you can take a comfortable crap in."

Meltzer beamed. "What a knack you have, Arnie, for the succinct. I mean it. Exactly," he finished.

"Except she was no Israeli. She was a starved, fuckin', clapped-up Arab."

"No, she wasn't," said Meltzer, still infatuated with the miraculous manifestation of the Israeli renaissance. "I'm sure I saw a Mogen David hanging around her neck."

"Shit, Max Baer used to wear it on his trunks for professional reasons, too. Israel doesn't have their own whores," said Goff. A crucifix around a broad's cleavage turned him on something terrific, but the six-pointed Jewish Star of David had the reverse effect. He had once, on a subway wall, seen the scrawled question: "Is Dracula Jewish?" He was like a Jewish Dracula. Show him the Star of David and he'd cringe in tortured frustration and slink crookedly away.

THE LAST SHIKSA 65

"If she comes back we'll ask her. I'll bet she's Israeli," said Meltzer. But she never came back and after the meal they separated. Goff said he'd go to a movie. Meltzer firmly said he was going to find a genuine Israeli whore.

Goff had gone to sleep in an irritable, disgusted mood at about one, with a *Playboy* magazine. He had gone to an Italian movie he had meant to see in New York. He forgot to realize that the subtitles would be in Hebrew. He had tried to contend with it, but finally had walked out disgusted in the middle.

In his putzy way, Goff thought, Meltzer was right. It was a sin not to try to get laid—even in Israel—and he had committed a sin. He slept fitfully and had a dream.

He was in a crowded, noisy cafe on Dizengoff Street, looking around for a broad with whom to atone for his sin, but they were all laughing at him. The Beatles were blaring out a song. They had an Israeli accent.

> Get beck, get beck,
> Get beck to vere you vunce belonked.
> Get beck, Jewjew. Go hum!

Goff turned and tossed and sweated. He would have to go home to where he belonged. But where the fuck did he belong? He panicked in his dream. He wanted Dr. Kummerlos.

At three Meltzer quietly opened the door of their shared bedroom and whispered, "Arnie, Arnie, are you awake? I got her!"

When Goff opened his eyes, he detected two figures. He turned on his reading light. Meltzer stood beaming, swelling with pioneer accomplishment. The girl was blond, peasant-stocky and heavy-legged. In contrast to the apologetic street whore, she carried herself with arrogant self-assurance. But it was not the brazen assurance of a cynical streetwalker; it was more like the arrogance of a bureaucratic female commissar. Her flat broad features made Goff think that somewhere in the past, some energetic Odessan had worked his way into her lineage. From her shoulders hung an efficient-looking leather shoulder bag. She wore a khaki shirt and a blouse with collar points overlapping her jacket. She wore no makeup; her only concession to her role was high-heeled shoes.

"Arnie, meet Miriam. We have an understanding." He could hardly contain himself. "If you want she'll take care of both of us." Meltzer smiled heartily at the chunky blond. She regarded him with stern puzzlement, so he circled a clarifying finger to encompass Goff.

"Yes," she said stolidly, finally understanding.

"See, Arnie. Okay? If you want you can take the first crack. This is a real first," he said with continued jubilation.

"No," said Goff, "I guess I'm a little tired." And again it was poor Murray whose dick he wouldn't fuck her with. He thought Meltzer was high.

"He do not want?" said the girl.

"No, he's tired," said Meltzer, trying to nullify any possible negative impression.

She shrugged and nodded. "Maybe he want later."

"Right," Meltzer agreed hastily. "Sit down, Miriam." She sat. He turned to Goff, "Arnie, look she's a real Israeli, native-born, a *Sabra*, right, bubie?" He turned to her. She nodded sternly. "She's in the Army, and she does this as a sideline. I was ready to give up when I saw her sitting at a sidewalk cafe alone. You could have knocked me over when she asked me a price. I never imagined she was one. She doesn't look it at all, does she?"

"I agree with you. I bet she has a license that lets her drive a tractor-trailer."

"Aw, Arnie, she's a real Sabra."

"My ass!"

The girl stood up. "I am business girl. I am in Israeli Army and I am a blondie Sabra. I speaking four languages. I do not come for insult. If you want pleasure, I will give to you. It cost one hundred fifty pounds for you and him—both. If gentleman is tired I will give to you pleasure alone for eighty pounds."

Goff, whose ego required that he be fascinating to all females at all times, put on a pleasant manner to win over the Sabra part-time whore. From his bed he smiled politely, "I'm sorry if I hurt your feelings, Sylvia. . . ."

Meltzer quickly corrected, "It's Miriam, Arnie."

"Miriam, but I really am very tired or I would be honored. You have a wonderful country. You should be proud. One thing though, isn't eighty pounds a little high—expensive?"

Miriam did not respond. She didn't like that little man in the bed. He was like an Arab shopkeeper ass kisser. Trying to *shnorren* her price. She looked coldly ahead.

"Aw, Miriam, " said Meltzer, "he's really tired and we woke him. Arnie, she's really a Sabra and she knows that other girl . . ."

Miriam cut in with some feeling. "Yes, I know other girl. She is Moroccan and the Army not take her. You can have her for fifty pounds and maybe less if you tell her 'no'—and later you get sickness from she. But I am blondie Sabra. I am in Israeli Army and I am healthy, blondie girl and I wish to fetch eighty pounds," she concluded.

"I'm sure you're worth every bit of it, honey," said Goff soothingly.

"Arnie," whispered Meltzer, "look, do you mind if I go ahead alone?"

"Fine, where?"

"In here," said Meltzer sheepishly. "She hasn't got her own place. She's in the Army and it's getting late. She's got to get back to her barracks or wherever she goes for reveille or something at six. I'll be very quiet. You can turn off your light and go to sleep—and if you change your mind, you know . . . you know what she said. She's a business girl. Look, if you go ahead, I'll pay the eighty and you can pay the seventy. How's that?"

"It'll never come to that. Go ahead, Doc. Enjoy yourself. And if you can keep it quiet, I'd appreciate it. I'm going to sleep. Can I turn off my light now?"

"Sure, sure, I'll just leave the bathroom door open a little. That'll give us more than enough light."

"And if you can't see where to put it, just let her whistle." Goff knew he was going to get a jab in the arm. Was his crack worth it?

Meltzer again shook his head and chuckled as he predictably came through with his shoulder-jab tribute to Goff. And then turning to earnest concern said, "I'm sorry I woke you, Arnie."

"It's okay, Doc. It's a once-in-a-lifetime thing. I understand it perfectly. Give me a report in the morning." He was glad he had restrained himself from saying something about Meltzer's hardon contributing to the Jewish national fun. He couldn't take anymore of Meltzer's demonstrative tributes anymore tonight. Goff looked at the girl and, still trying to win her over, tried a final, ingratiating, sincere smile and tone. "Good night, Miriam. Again I want to tell you, you have a wonderful country." She nodded at him icily as he snapped off his reading lamp. He looked to her as if he would sell military secrets to the Arabs.

The acoustics of the room were better than a recording studio. Goff heard every word, pant, plaint, bleat, flutter, mutter, snap, zip, sigh.

First he heard a flurried, whispered argument about the money. He heard the Israeli whisper, "You must first give me the eighty pounds before we begin the pleasure."

"I don't think it should be more than sixty. You will not remain here and give me pleasure for the whole night. You will be gone in ten minutes—and I don't have eighty Israeli pounds," he whispered in return.

"I will take American dollars, English pounds or marks—what you have—at what is correct exchange. I don't know why you argue. You rich man. How much for pleasure in New York? Is one hundred dollars, no? I know. For me is not even thirty dollar, and I am blondie Sabra Army girl. So, okay, you give me and we begin, yes?"

I'll have to give you a traveler's check, okay?" sighed Meltzer.

"Is good."

"Do you have a pen?" whispered Meltzer tightly.

"Yes." Goff heard her snap her shoulder bag open and heard her whip out a pen. He saw Meltzer in the beam of light from the bathroom signing a traveler's check. He heard the tear-off of the check, and then saw the Israeli step into the light beam and examine it. As she stepped back from the beam he heard her grunt of approval. "Good, bubie," she said, adapting the counterfeit word of endearment—now internationally accepted as a convenient negotiable—legitimized enough. Goff next heard Meltzer's clutch and grab. "Wait, bubie, I take off clothes," she whispered in a contained voice.

"Sure, sure, Miriam," was the contrite response—ardor compromised by practical realities. Goff heard male and female clothing being shed. Zippers, snaps of elastic, shoes and socks, the clunk of wallet and coin-laden pants thrown on a chair. But he could have sworn he hadn't heard the unsnapping of a brassiere. His ear was proven uncannily accurate, because after the settling creaks of the mattress and bed, he heard Meltzer complaining, "Aren't you going to take that thing off?"

"To take off is not necessary for me to give pleasure."

"But that's a big part of my pleasure—please, baby," he whined.

"No."

"Please, it's not fair."

"No." ˙

"I hate to bring this up, but do you know how many thousands I give to the United Jewish Appeal?"

Silence except for a kind of wheezing sulk from the orthodontist. Then a relenting, "You promise you not bite or pinch or squeeze. Army show us film about VD and cancer."

"Of course, bubie. My word of honor."

Snap.

"Ah-h-h."

"You careful."

"M-m-m, yeah—go slow, bubie, I'm a little tired. You be a nice girl and help."

"No worry."

"Put your head there, please, like a good girl."

"You want I suck?"

"Yes, that would be very nice."

"I suck, but you tell me before, yes?"

"Of course," whispered Meltzer virtuously. "I want to finish in you regular."

"Yes, bubie. I suck and then you fuck—but you say to me before, yes?"

"Yes. You're a good girl, bubie."

Silence except for Meltzer's breathing.

"Stop quick!"

Not to his surprise, Goff found he had a respectable hardon himself. He began to think that maybe he would change his mind.

"Oh, bubie, you have your pleasure already," she said with elaborate regret.

"What do you mean?" whispered Meltzer in alarm.

"I mean you have pleasure. Is all wet. You come."

"Now wait a minute. I didn't come. Just a little drip-out. I certainly not have pleasure yet."

"Yes, you have pleasure. Is finish. I must go now, please. No more, bubie," she said with chilly resoluteness.

"Now wait a minute! I didn't come! I not get fucked! And I not get pleasure! You have to stay till I get pleasure! I never got on top of you or nothing!"

"No. You have pleasure. And there is nothing there by you no more. I go."

Goff heard her get up from the bed and heard Meltzer muttering and thrashing angrily.

In less than a minute, Miriam, the part-time Israeli whore, blondie Sabra Army girl, had dressed and was at the door. As she left, Meltzer hollered after her, "The United Jewish Appeal is never getting another dime out of me, you bitch!"

Goff laughed till the tears came.

Meltzer was a broken man. "I don't know that I'd appreciate this coming to light with the group, Arnie. Don't say anything, huh?"

"Of course not, bubie; it'll be my pleasure!" Goff roared. He hadn't had such fun in years.

All men seek their carnal bonbons. They envision being engulfed by beautiful girls, within whom to be smothered in a heavenly crush of flesh and fury. These lush creatures are never found in their own backyards. They are, of course, exotic and distant. The swarthy Italian finds his ecstasy a thousand miles north in the big blond Swede. The Swede, in turn, reaches for the Latin. The lyrical Irishman reaches for the sensual Jewess, and the recalcitrant Jew craves the roguish broguish colleen. And they are all on the right track. For if their passion is sufficient to thrust them out of their usual orbit, it is certainly sufficient to generate an additional hot enough whoosh of trail to draw in all who restlessly approach. As in battle, somehow or other, the restless ones will be there.

Pat the doorman's daughter was one of the restless ones, and she did get married several months later. When Goff learned about it he sent her a check for a hundred dollars, which was promptly returned to him. He'd sent it when he learned that the groom was a black man.

"It figures," he thought. She couldn't find herself. What did these kids want these days? She could have remained a happy, insulated, bigoted Irish cuntee, but no—what had happened to parental discipline?

The doorman had kept up appearances. Certainly that fine April morning, with Goff on his way to the doctor, he was his old staunch self. Goff thought it was a pity that such a good predictable sort as Fitz should be subjected to such humiliation. The irony of it. Her old man had kept his hands off her just to save her for some Mau-Mau hearted, murderously resentful black panther whose act of love was pure hate. That's no way to fuck and produce a better world, thought Goff piously. Sure, Goff had learned the details from the night doorman who happened to be a relative of Fitzsimmons by marriage. His name was Hans Stahrts. The two, familiarly known as Fitz and Stahrts, were a highly reputed doorman team in the seventies on Park Avenue.

Stahrts told Goff that Pat had met the black one at her office. The office manager had phoned Fitzsimmons and had told him that Pat and the black one were spending a lot of time together. The office manager was dampt angry that the company had hired the black one for the office, but the company couldn't help itself. The company was forced, because since they couldn't hire Chews because they were doing oil business with the Arabs, so they had to settle by hiring someone else they didn't want. That's the law. So they settled on a black one. Ha, ha, America is funny. You are Basque, Mr. Goff, correct? Then I can say. I didn't want to hurt your feelings if you wuz Chewish. I didn't take you for Chewish, but I want to make *sicher,* excuse me, certain. I say between a black one and a

Chew, I'd rather work with a black one. There is never confusion. You see him right away, ja? Ha, ha, if you know what I mean. You don't forget yourself, you see? The office manager in the oil company is a Irish woman, and it broke her heart to see what was happening to a nice Irish girl, but when she called up Fitz, it was already too late. This black one was a member of the Black Phantoms or something. Anyway, one of those where they allowed to make deals with white people. Ach, what a shame. Poor Fitz. I remember he was so happy when she got that chob with that oil company because he knew there were no Chewish people there. Fitz is old-fashioned. Me, I say there's good and bad with everybody. Live and let live, that's my motto.

Goff thought he detected a more cautious note toward the end of Stahrts' statement. The Nazi prick must have thought to tone it down just in case Goff wasn't so Basque after all. He felt an uneasy hatred for Stahrts. Better a truculent out-and-out healthy anti-Semitic Irishman than a suck-ass German gas-chamber tender. He thought of telling the bastard off, but overruled himself and decided he would first talk it over with his psychiatrist. Better wait for Kummerlos to help him weigh it. He could have kicked himself in the ass for the enforced pleasant way he had answered Stahrts' final, "Haff a pleasant evening, Mr. Goff."

# Chapter 7

*Judge Rosenbeng and the Law of the Letter*

"Good morning, Mr. Goff," said the doorman.

He certainly knows how to keep his shame from showing, thought Goff. "Good morning, Fitz," he replied pleasantly, forgetting all about the anti-Semitic prick trying to catch up to him.

"Good morning, Judge Rosenbeng," said Fitz.

Goff recognized the name immediately. He knew of Judge Maurice Rosenbeng, the well-known jurist and director of many of the most impeccable Jewish and other prestigious boards. The 92nd Street Y, Mount Sinai Hospital, Temple Emanuel, the Grand Street Boys, Educational Alliance, Henry Street Settlement; Chairman of the National Council of Christians and Jews, honorary president of the Joint Moslem-Judaic Cultural League and friend of the late Cardinal Spellman.

So the prick was a Jew after all. He glanced back at him and shook his head in disgust. He knew intuitively that there walked a man who had never jerked off, and who wouldn't hesitate to hand out the death penalty for any weaklings or degenerates who did; which of course accounted to a good degree for the anti-Semitic look about him. If Hitler had won the war, Eichmann would have sought out Rosenbeng as a responsible, cooperative community leader to supply him with the lists of Jews to be sent to gas chambers set up in Staten Island.

He wondered about the name Rosenbeng. As a child he had heard stories of how insensitive, arrogant clerks at Ellis Island, through caprice, whim or boredom, had created and assigned names for the timorous immigrants passing through. According to old A.G. if the announcing clerk sneezed, the recording clerk would inscribe "Kerchoo" as the name of the poor wretch before him, and the next applicant would be dubbed Gesundheit. Or if he got tired of deciphering the names in the passports, he would arbitrarily announce, "You next twenty-five on line are Goldstein, and the next twenty-five are Steingold." The high-handed clerks lorded it over the greenhorns who couldn't read and were too intimidated to make corrections. Thousands of names were thus created. Goff's father had told about Uncle Sol Retcheck, who had claimed his name had been really Resnick, but that a drunken clerk, who was having difficulty making out the name clearly, had looked up at him, seen a large red check on the tag around his neck, and with great drunken satisfaction had gone ahead and inscribed Solomon Retcheck. It hadn't made much difference to Sol, but it had to his son Benny, who had changed his name to Barry Reade. Had old Sol remained Resnick, it might have influenced Benny toward Barry Reese, which was the name Benny's cousin Aaron changed to. Aaron Resnick changed to Aandy Reese. Aaron's father had gone through immigration with his name Resnick unmolested. So among the inner circle of the family, the genealogy experts knew that the Reades stemmed from the Retchecks and the Reeses stemmed from the Resnicks, but that they were all really Resnicks. You see, in Jewish law, you stick to the letter. You stick to the letter of the law? No, *yold,* you stick to the law of the letter. The law of the letter obliges you to choose a name with the first letter the same. So when Aaron, a real fanatic for the law of the letter, changed his name to Aandrew Reese, his meticulous regard for the law of the letter was obvious with Aandrew.

The Jewish law of the letter is quite liberal and is not practiced to the letter of the law. Perhaps the tradition is more hollowed than hallowed. Perhaps it is not even a tradition, but the offshoot of a tradition and has yet to establish its own firm roots. It would be fair to say it is more correctly a modification of tradition to meet modern needs, pressures and fashions.

The hard-core traditionalists insist strictly that the newborn be given the full exact name of the nearest dead relative. They would not permit what they derisively call "the loophole of the letter" to achieve outlandish assimilationist names. But those purists have in the main been overwhelmed by the liberal moderns. And even among the moderns there are the strict constructionists and the loose constructionists.

The development may be illustrated by the following. At one time

Great-grandpa Moishe would have turned over in his grave if his grandson had been named Morris and not Moishe. But it is more likely that now he would have to wince painfully or shrug fatalistically in his grave for Mark or Michael. And if the poor soul had the misfortune to have his grandson marry a flighty nothing who had always been enamored of the name Meredith, it would be his luck that the girl would stop at nothing to find a suitable "M." She would scour her own family tree, and finding no "M" would ruthlessly explore her husband's, and she would be sure to dig up poor Great-grandfather Moishe. "We will honor Great-grandfather Moishe and name our little girl Meredith," she would announce with sanctified delight. But a *girl* for Grandpa Moishe? "Of course, silly. It's quite common, and would you deny him the honor? After all, can you deny that your sister used him for Marcy?"

Grandpa Moishe would just have to live with it. After all, it was an honor.

And take Aunt Ida and Aunt Esther conversing in their rocking chairs on the great big porch in the sky:

> Aunt Esther (with no great elation): "I just got news my niece just gave birth and I've been honored again."
>
> Aunt Ida (with equal lack of elation): "Same with me. What name did they find for you this time?"
>
> Aunt Esther (now definitely glum): "Eileen."
>
> Aunt Ida: "Funny, it was 'Eileen' for me too."
>
> Silence for a few moments.
>
> Aunt Esther (resigned): "I guess sounds have become good now. They don't have to stick exactly to the letter anymore."
>
> Aunt Ida (equally resigned): "Yes, it must be they can now go by the sound. I'll tell you the truth, letter or no letter, I like it better than the last one, Illona. Iris was nice, though."
>
> Aunt Esther: "Eileen isn't bad. The name that was really *feh* was—let me see—three names ago, I think. There was Eunice, Ellery—yes—Eudora, *feh!* What an honor."
>
> Aunt Ida: "You know that old cigarmaker Baruch? He still can't get over the honor his granddaughter gave him when she named her boy William. How does William come to Baruch? Simple, because they not gonna call him William. They gonna call him Billy—such a cute blond little boy. Looks just like a *shaygets*, a regular Billy. You're right, Esther, I can live with Eileen."

So it was for Aunt Ida and Aunt Esther. For the latter there is the letter, and for the former the alliteration. The loose constructionists are in the ascendancy. Thank God, they haven't yet got to the point where they will find another loophole so that you can begin to name a child after a living one. But we'll live to see that one too.

The way those Ellis Island clerks played around with the names of those scared Jews was probably how Rosenbeng got his name. Rosenbeng's father was undoubtedly Rosenberg. But the clerk misread it or miswrote it as Rosenbeng. Judge Rosenbeng's father must have been a fawning, boot-licking, collaborating, incipient snob, who accepted the distortion without a qualm. "Thank you, your excellency. Come, Bessie."

"But, Max, he made a mistake. He wrote Rosenbeng," his wife protested.

"Bessie, please, we are now Rosenbeng."

This eventually made a world of difference. No longer would they automatically be lumped as eastern European greaseballs. One day someone would question "Rosenbeng? Is that Swedish or something?" The father executed a slight, tricky movement of the head, so that it could be taken either way.

"It is not bad to have ourselves thought of as Swedish."

With this identification encouraged, a subtle difference in outlook began to take place. Old man Rosenbeng began to regard his fellow greenhorns with snobbish condescension. After all, he was taken for Swedish. This gave him a higher standing and consequently a higher self-regard. And so gradually he adopted a different tone and style and taste in accordance with the identity that was suggested him and which, in fact, he encouraged. And after a while his wife's heavily garlicked, lumpy Jewish meatballs gave way to stylish, little gracefully parsleyed Swedish meatballs, and his accent and inflection changed from a ghetto gutteral to a kind of lopsided Swedish swell.

And when a son was born to this couple with their furtive vanity, it was understood between them that he not be named as a commonplace street variety crack-o'-the-walk weed of a Morris, but as an elegantly potted Maurice.

So, Maurice Rosenbeng, Jewish Scandinavian, embarked on life with a decided and deceitful edge over Morris Rosenberg, ghetto snotball.

Goff considered the advantages gained. Rosenbeng would thereby walk and carry himself differently. He would walk straight like a Scandinavian. Oh, a ghetto *shlump* could also walk straight, but think of the effort he had to put in it. He would have to lift weights or become proficient at the parallel bars—and always, he would have to be conscious of his posture. And the straightness wouldn't be the same of course. The strained, muscle-bound artificial straightness against the natural Scandinavian stride which was directly related to the open show-down amble of cowpokes without circumspection or circumcision. Jews play the Indians and Scandinavians play the cowboys. Hadn't Metro-Goldwyn-Mayer or some big Hollywood prick said that very thing or close to it? You could account for Goldwyn and Mayer, but who was Metro? Was Metro another product of the law of the letter—somebody named after Great-grandpa Moishe? Thank God, at last, for Kirk Douglas. And the Lord split his fuzzy red chin and allowed a thousand Jewish cowboys to escape their bondage as Indians. Whaddya mean there were no Jewish cowboys? What about Barry Goldwater's grandpa? What about all those guys called Dutch? Ah, the West! When a guy had a Jewish name and spoke with a Yiddish accent, those good-natured, give-their-sweat-stiff-shirts-off-their-backs guys chawed their tobacco, spit in the spittoon, asked him for a grubstake and called him "Dutch." What a fine, friendly name for a man—and for a Jewish man—none better. "And, Bessie, you know what they call me? Dutch. Truthfully I like it better *wie* Jacob."

With arched little body, Maurice dived into the pool of America and climbed out clean-limbed, glistening, and speaking clear, inland American. "Rosenbeng, I swear, I would never guess you're from New York, more like Midwest, Iowa, Illinois. I guess Slaughter, Owens, Pritchard and Crowe can find a spot for you. You can start Monday." So it was with Maurice Rosenbeng who never quite achieved the complete, easy erectness of a Swede, but settled for the cold stiffness of a fuckin' Prussian.

Actually a Jew, could you really label him anti-Semitic? Admittedly there were examples every now and then—renegades and turncoats and warped ones, poetic Arab lovers, and plain *meshugge* ones, but they were so rare. And also the self-haters, which is very big nowadays.

As far as Goff's conclusions about Judge Rosenbeng were concerned he had been right in regarding him as an anti-Semite prick, regardless of his formal affiliations.

"Sir, I challenge you to prove that I am an anti-Semitic pejorative. I demand that you substantiate."

Goff: "Your honor, the charge against the defendant Maurice Rosenbeng is that he is an anti-Semitic prick at heart. I intend to prove that charge."

Rosenbeng's attorney: "I object. I move that the charge be dismissed as too vague and totally incapable of measurement against any objective standard."

Goff: "If you want to hide behind bloodless technicalities, I have no recourse but to drop the whole thing, but that will not alter my contention."

Rosenbeng's attorney: "My client has reconsidered and will waive the so-called technicalities."

Goff: "Then take the stand, Judge Rosenbeng."

Q.–"Have you ever masturbated?"

A.–"Never."

Q.–"How do you regard those that do?"

A.–"I hold them in the lowest esteem."

Q.–"Did you ever vote for Franklin D. Roosevelt?"

A.–"Never."

Q.–"Whom did you vote for?"

A.–"In consecutive order: Hoover, Landon, Dewey."

Q.–"What about Willkie?"

A.–"I went fishing."

Q.–"Were you aware that Mussolini made the trains run on time?"

A.–"Indeed."

Q.–"Do you know what Max Lerner thinks?"

A.–"Don't know the gentleman."

Q.–"Have you ever gone to a Catskill mountain resort?"

A.–"Never."

Q.–"Where do you spend your summers?"

A.–"Maine."

Q.–"Is it true you once lived in Brooklyn and moved because you feared your children might catch an inflection?"

A.–"It was a contributing cause."

Q.–"Did you consider the late Cardinal Spellman as one of your best friends?"

A.–"I did and I trust he regarded me in like manner."

Q.–"Are you being correctly quoted when reportedly at your daughter's marriage you said, 'I'm not losing a daughter, I'm gaining a son?' "

A.–"Correct."

Q.–"Is it true your son-in-law is Presbyterian?"

A.–"Yes, of course."

Q.–"Is it true your relations cooled with your son when he chose to become a druggist, after you had arranged to have a West Point appointment available to him?"

A.–"I wouldn't say that."

Q.–"Well, sir, is it correct that you did not attend his wedding to one Helen Lefkowitz, daughter of a prominent scrap-metal dealer in Youngstown, Ohio?"

A.–"I couldn't get away. I had been urgently requested to remain in New York pending the assignment of a judge to a case of national importance."

Q.–"There is absolutely no evidence that you made a like statement at the instance of your son's marriage, to wit: 'I am not losing a son. I am gaining a daughter.' "

A.–"Correct. I never made such a statement."

Q.–"The case you were awaiting. Were you not most anxious to obtain the assignment?"

A.–"That is correct."

Q.–"Were you not in fact deeply disappointed when it went to another?"

A.–"In the sense that I would have deemed it a high honor to sit on that case—yes."

Q.–"Was this case, in fact, not the Julius and Ethel Rosenberg case?"

A.–"Yes."

Q.–"Is it possible you were not chosen because you may have been related to them?"

A.–"Indeed not. I must point out the difference in names. Mine is Rosen-BENG."

Q.–"Did you agree with the verdict and sentencing?"

A.–"Assuredly."

Q.–"Do you travel, sir?"

A.–"Quite extensively."

Q.–"Have you ever been to Israel?"

A.–"No, sir."

Q.–"No more questions."

# Book II

# Chapter 1

---

*Ramona*

Goff stepped into the street with crisp assurance. He smoothly declined Fitzsimmons' offer to hail him a cab. "Thanks, Fitz, I'm walking."

"It is a beautiful day, Mr. Goff." Goff nodded with sunny agreement and began to stride down Park Avenue. He was on his way to Dr. Levine's office for a checkup. He was in perfect shape, which was the right time to get a checkup, to confirm his top condition. But what had really triggered his decision to go for a checkup had been his accountant's suddenly dropping dead of a heart attack last Sunday.

In the manner of accountants, he had served Goff with measured and balanced servility. He had loved his work and had always joyously pointed to his name, Chaim Pincus Addelson, as evidence of some divine predeterminism. "Chaim Pincus Addelson, C.P.A., but my friends call me Chuck."

For an accountant he was a fine figure of a man and that was undoubtedly attributable to his devotion to body building and handball. It was handball that finally closed his books. For it was among the heavy-fleshed, T-shirted, over-thirty, Sunday schoolyard sports on the handball court where he had breathed his last. He had just executed that most satisfying of Brooklyn athletic skills, a black hardball dead killer hit smack at the precise point where the gray concrete handball wall meets the ground. His elated follow-through pirouetted into his collapse and there he died amid the concerned "Are-you-all-right-Chucks" of the Marvs, Hys and

Howies, lying at the base of the up-reaching, free-standing, gray tabular concrete wall—as fine a monument for an accountant handball player as any monument works boss could conceive.

At his funeral the mourners' buzz in the chapel room assigned to C. P. Addelson hummed out like a low-key congregational kazoo: never sick a day in his life while playing handball never knew what hit him a coronary that's the way I'd like to go wouldn't call him overweight did he smoke no don't remember for sure never got excited probably the reason kept it all inside that's no good either such a young man was making a very comfortable living three beautiful children everything to live for forty-one years old go know wife is still a young woman still has her teacher's license just put a binder on a house must have had nice insurance and she'll get Social Security such a good family man she didn't deserve him he was too good it's not too good to be too good we should meet on happier occasions how's the market treating you?

The funeral had been on Monday. On Tuesday Goff had told his secretary to get him an appointment with a cardiologist as soon as possible for a complete checkup. He didn't know of any himself. His first thought had been to call Meltzer, but he abruptly restrained himself. He had to start keeping away from that guy. He inquired of Dr. Kummerlos at his regularly scheduled Monday afternoon appointment right after Addelson's funeral. Addelson's widow, Cookie, had tearfully begged Goff to accompany the hearse and the mourners to the cemetery; Chuck's cousin, Julie, the bachelor, had plenty of room in his car. "Chaim" (she had stopped calling him Chuck) "considered you not a client but a dear friend. *Kim mit, Arneleh bubie—es ist a mitzvah*—and for me, too, bubie," she wept. Goff hadn't intended to go in the first place, and with her "bubie" babbling and with her lapsing more and more into tearful Yiddish, it stiffened his resolve beyond any wavering; and shit, he didn't want to take any chances missing his appointment with Kummerlos. Christ, he didn't miss his appointment when his old man died. This funeral had already cost him a lunch date with Christine. He had sacrificed enough for an accountant. But the weeping widow was so insistent that he finally had to submit to the compromise that he come up to the apartment that evening to visit her while she was sitting *shivah*. Goff figured the place would be loaded with jabbering relatives, boxes of candy, fruit baskets and honey cake—and in the commotion he could make a quick getaway.

On hearing the news, Kummerlos was sympathetic in a noncommittal way. He knew of no cardiologist personally except an old medical school friend of his in Brooklyn. Goff couldn't see going to a specialist in Brooklyn. When he'd lived in Brooklyn he was always drag-assing to Manhattan—why should he drag-ass back now?—he would find one himself, on the upper East Side. He knew how to go about it.

Goff had spelled out his requirements for a doctor to his secretary. He remembered the trick that Gloria used. She would call up a good hospital and request a list of the specialists on their staff. He had complete faith that Ramona would find him a doctor worth ten of Meltzer's recommendations.

It was amazing how this simple Puerto Rican girl could accomplish for him the most sophisticated and intricate feats. For him she could weave her way with the most modern techniques through myriad telephone circuits to the right remote muck-a-muck pusher in a department store so that Mr. Goff could have a rug delivered to his apartment weeks before the "earliest possible" scheduled date. For him, she could tame mad-with-power civil service clerks and have them docilely murmuring comprehensible explanations about their diabolical forms and impossible regulations. She could persuade computer-directed office managers to admit their computer figured billings wrong, and nulevar all the other impossible daily tangles and stonk that confront a man in these complicated times.

But she collapsed into Spanish-speaking helplessness if her own telephone bill had an error and the phone company sweet-talkers were threatening to cut off her Puerto Rican-ass service; or if she had to contend with a Jewish school principal to request a change of class for her daughter, and it was even more paralyzing after the Jewish principal was pushed out in favor of a black one. (Wasn't it for her benefit? So as to enable the black and Puerto Rican community to identify with their own authority figure?) "The black is for the Puerto Rican? *Mierda!* It is only the Puerto Rican who is for the Puerto Rican—*maybe.* It is all bullsheet, excuse my expression, Mr. Goff."

The reason for her disparate levels of effectiveness seemed quite clear to Goff. She performed so excellently on his behalf because he inspired her with his own dynamism, and because he always remembered to praise her when she did well. He had learned that in leadership school in the Army.

Her name was Ramona Ramirez. He had hired her six years ago soon after he had taken over a destitute, near-abandoned synagogue in a once heavily Jewish-populated lower East Side street, and converted it into his "plant."

She had a six-year-old child and a husband who had scurried back to Puerto Rico with his hands over his ears to keep out the noise of New

York. She was cute. Small, beautifully shaped in miniature, big black eyes and a strong smile that fell short of captivating because it lacked that necessary quality of careless grace achieved only by people without troubles, or those who don't know they have troubles. But as far as Goff was concerned (and undoubtedly as far as she was also) her biggest drawback was her complexion. She wasn't quite light enough, despite the often-expressed astonishment of business acquaintances who said they just couldn't believe she was a P.R. At times, though, he was so carried away that he began to think that maybe she could pass. And he would start to think about expanding their relationship, but his enthusiasm was always finally contained. And he thought that all those pricks who oohed and ahed and were so surprised that she was Puerto Rican would to a man start snickering "spic" if he ever made her his official girlfriend or better.

Her grasp of the job, her anticipation of his needs, thoughts and requirements, and her quick, deft execution of duties were astonishing to Goff. He was well aware of her uniqueness and value.

Once he was screwing her on a desk in the once Hebrew classroom that now served as his office. She had shed her secretarial demeanor for the occasion and was at a point where she was rhythmically moaning *Jésu Cristo*—as in all moments when her disciplines were adrift, she had reverted to Spanish. Goff had caught the spirit and was approaching his own shuddering ecstasy. His excitement was intensified by a dainty gold crucifix which lay in effulgent repose amid the surrounding heaving turbulence of her small sweet breasts. In his half-frenzied, half-reverent kissing of nipples and breast, he also kissed the quietly nestled gold crucifix. So it's a sin—fuck it! I'll confess tomorrow to Father Kummerlos. The cross was beautiful against her honey-colored skin. At times like these Goff felt amenable to instant conversion.

He would never forget what his loyal secretary had done when, just at the peak of their crescendo, the phone rang. Ramona started to moan a deep shivering protest, but as a born secretary, quickly stifled it and signaled Goff not to be disturbed. Goff was everlastingly grateful to her thoughtful murmur "Querido, finish, querido." Goff in his inflamed gratitude knew that for her it was dead and over, as she deftly managed to stretch for the phone, while maintaining an uninterrupted rhythm to ensure the completion of her employer's delicately critical moment. Goff made a hot mental note to reward her adequately, as he continued with hard grunts to try to wrest a little pleasure for himself on that hard uncomfortable desk.

"Phonotronics. Thank you for calling. May I help you?" Goff never allowed his ecstasies to blur out his realities, and in the midst of it all, he noted approvingly that Ramona had not forgotten the "Thank you for calling." He had instructed her to use this as a classy greeting. He had been greatly impressed by its use by airline reservation clerks. What a joke it would have been to try to teach Mrs. Solomon, his former girl, to say it. What a wrinkled-up Jew nose of sarcastic distaste she would have given him. He would never have tried.

Ramona, what a wonderful girl, thought Goff as he ground himself to a halt with a final metallic grunt denoting the end of his production run. Ramona, with her extremely sensitive response, had begun to slow down and ease off her rhythmic pace, as her bottom half began to phase out, and her top half began to assert its businesslike functioning. Goff sprawled spent and bent in his remarkable secretary, listening with pure admiration as she conducted her top-half telephone conversation.

"No, Mr. Schindler," said Ramona's upper half in crisp tones, "your mother has not been shipped. Mr. Goff has given strict instructions that nothing gets shipped until we receive payment for the outstanding balance. As soon as we receive your check, I'll see to it that your mother is shipped immediately. That's a promise."

Goff, still inside his secretary, had now turned his thoughts completely to business. Shoestring Sam Schindler's master die had already been shipped, thanks to the awfully irretrievable efficiency of his energetic but spittling shipping clerk, Malcolm Feiler. Someday he was going to kick him out on his ass, *rachmones* or not.

Goff quickly realized what his secretary was doing. Fully aware of its mistaken shipment, she was trying to con Schindler into mailing out a check. And a wave of tenderness engulfed him and again he fleetingly felt the pity of it. If only Ramona were just a little lighter. What a team they might have made—with her passing and him kind of passing. Together—touchdown combo—it would have been so smooth if she were only a little lighter.

Ramona continued negotiating with Shoestring Sam Schindler, "But you are interrupting, Mr. Schindler. I can't make it clearer.. The moment we get the check, the mother goes out." Ramona hung up and fell back with an ancient doloroso smile at Goff. She lay there awaiting his pleasure with subservience—she would fiercely impose her subservience on all her men—and her ancient ingrained instinct would force her men to accept her subservience. She would fight to the death to retain that subservience. With Goff the arrangement was fine. He would not embark on any enlightened program of liberation. If her submission didn't get out of hand, it was great. She lay there awaiting Goff's ascension.

Refreshed, Goff arose out of Ramona and pulled up his pants. His businesslike manner was now plain to her and she was clearly now inappropriately positioned. With rapid, unobtrusive movements she quickly slipped on her panties. When Goff briskly embraced her, she was aware he was expressing appreciation for having been well served and nothing more. She knew his mind was already way beyond their love making, if it had ever been on it at all.

The quick, hard kiss of duty over, Goff concluded, "You handled it so beautifully, Ramona. It was my fault letting Schindler's mother ship out. Feiler's efficiency was too quick for me. He's like a fast waiter who grabs your plate away the minute you put your fork down, finished or not."

With a secretary like Ramona, Goff had full confidence that she would find him the best doctor for his checkup.

He had told her to call Mount Sinai Hospital and get a list of their cardiologists.

He also left instructions that the doctor had to have his office on the upper East Side or roughly bounded on the west by Fifth Avenue, on the east by Park, on the north by 96th Street and on the south by 70th Street. He would thereby be within a twenty-minute walk of any location. This was the heart of Mount Sinai territory and contained the best men. As his father would have regarded them: "Not just plain doctors, but all professors."

It gratified him that all his medical business was conducted in this high-density district of best men. For his piles operation, the surgeon, a Mount Sinai man, was on East 79th. A blunt orthopedist on Park and 80th who told him after examining him for backache, "It's not from fucking. It's from fucking in a draft." His ex-wife's obstetrician was on 94th Street. When he needed the proctologist—East 82nd Street between Park and Madison. His children's pediatrician on East 87th off Fifth—right by the Metropolitan Museum of Natural History—or was it Art? And every single one a Mount Sinai man, a top man, a professor. Residentially even his psychiatrist qualified—Park and 73rd. His practice made it excusable for him not to be affiliated with Mount Sinai. And although not of Mount Sinai, his word was more law than any of the others.

What a sense of comfort and well-being it was to him living there on Park Avenue in the heart of the best medical territory in the country. To be able to stroll from your apartment to the best top medical men in the world.

There wasn't that much difference with dentists, however. They were like Chinese restaurants. With a little luck you could just as well find a good one right in any neighborhood.

Goff walked with the easy confidence of one who belonged; he didn't have to apologize to anyone for living on Park Avenue. Park Avenue, of course, was a clear symbol of success. When had the wild possibility of living there occurred to him? He wasn't sure. But it was certainly well after he had maneuvered his partner out of the business.

"Doctor, I don't know if I feel adequate to it, but I think I want to live on Park Avenue."

"What do you mean, you don't feel adequate to it?"

"I don't think I have the confidence to take it on and be comfortable with it. I don't think I'm ready, Doc."

"Maybe you aren't."

Perfect answer, thought Goff.

Perfect answer, thought Kummerlos.

Dr. Kummerlos had mastered the essential concept of a successful medical practitioner: to tell his patient what he wanted to hear. Goff had wanted to hear that he was not yet ready for Park Avenue.

"Doc, you've been helpful." Kummerlos remained cool and impassive, unafraid to hit straight from the shoulder. Goff appreciated the truth. "See you Thursday."

"Right," said Doc, clipped and cool. They both understood the cold realities. Goff simply was not yet ready for Park Avenue.

Goff had known this was the beginning of a program. Doc would help him attain his goal. Doc always came through. Built him up and prepared him for new challenges.

Before Kummerlos, he had already been operating his business and was almost drowning in doubts and uncertainties. It had been a shaky and doubtful venture. He had been in bad shape when he had first become Kummerlos' patient.

It had taken all of Goff's scared guts to buy into the business in the first place. He had had to scare up the initial money from his father and his brother, Armand. How they had put him through the wringer with their doubts and fears! Armand had been dispatched to look at the books.

His sister Blanche had also gone along. Her husband, Murray, also schlepped along. It had been all he could do to persuade his father, old A.G., to please, please stay the fuck away. Armand and Blanche were very reliable. They would give him a full report.

In the Army he had been a looie and had worked up a polish and confidence mostly from having got laid all over the U.S.A. This polish and sophistication were completely beyond the comprehension of his family and had been wiped away with practically one swipe a few days after his separation, when one morning old A.G. in his long johns looked up from his "Fawvitz" and said, "Nu, so what do you think you'll do now, Arneleh?"

Arneleh? Arneleh, *sir!* You impossible old bastard! It was incredible how devastating that inevitable question had been. His three years of fantastic living away from home as an officer and gentleman were as nothing. For three years, he had been as removed from his formative environment as if he were on another planet. He had seemed to thrive. He had left his mark across the country, but the country apparently had not left its mark on him—not if with one question out of his soggy "Fawvitz," his pop could devastate him. All that getting laid, all those wonderful exhilarating years—had it not meant anything? He had been sure he had made unmistakable penetration into the impenetrable mainstream of the U.S.A. He had screwed in the best and staidest hotels and in the seediest side-street Saturday-night joints in the heart of the U.S.A. He had laid all-American cunt in tourist cabins, in the first-built motels, in Ma Perkins-type rooms for tourists, in a barber chair of a small southern town in Alabama, in officers' clubs, in Army hospitals, in his '38 Plymouth on U.S. Route 40 and other seminal highways and byways, in a summer cottage in the winter, in apartments whose coffee tables contained pictures of smiling Jacks in uniform who were overseas and sending allotments to those apartments. He had screwed girls who were half-Choctaw, southern belles, all kinds of girls with delicious accents of the South, Southwest, Midwest, girls with mouth-watering names like Carol Sue Honeycutt, Yvonne Latimore, Joann Prentiss, Valerie Sargent, Gracia Truscott, Mary Czarkis. He had been happily astride Midwestern college students with sturdy Scandinavian vaginas; he had explored women whose ancestors had scouted with Kit Carson. He had had a West Virginia motor pool sergeant working and maintaining his little ol' '38 Plymouth so as to make it run and purr like a big-assed Cadillac, Lieutenant Goff, sir. He had had a Looziana mess sergeant making up hot steak sandwiches at midnight for him and his gal, Francine Devereaux, an Army nurse from Little Rock, Arkansas, who joined up because her brother was taken prisoner at Corregidor—no shit.

He had been invited to the home of a fellow lieutenant, whose family owned one of the largest potteries in Ohio, and whose father, around the dinner table, had said, "You couldn't find better people in the whole country than folks who work in these potteries—all mostly Scotch-Irish—finest stock in the world. What does your dad do, Lieutenant?"

My dad? I don't have a fuckin' dad. I've got a pop, and his stock stinks and he runs a shitty, break-your-balls grocery store with my brother-in-law, Murray, the *shmendrick*, and they sell matzo farfel and lots of pot cheese and unsalted tub butter and only Bumble Bee brand salmon. "He runs a food market, sir." Later his fellow officer's mother had said, "Bob, have you shown Lieutenant Goff his room yet?" Goff had never before been shown his fuckin' room in his life. The house was a twelve-room clapboard house with a glassed-in sun porch, set about a hundred feet off the road on tree-filled property that looked to him like the size of two football fields. He'd had the sixteen-year-old sister giggling and admiring him so much that it would have been a snap to have knocked her off, but he had refrained. He was an officer and a gentleman, and he had partaken of the popcorn made in their living-room fireplace. He had been admitted into the heart of Andy Hardy America. He would not betray their trust. He was an invited guest to the pottery magnate's home, and the crack about the finest stock had been the final inhibiting cruncher. It had tamed him good.

You'd think that all of this would have been more than enough to have immunized him from the scratchy kitchen remarks of his prickly under-weared old man. But when he said "Nu, Arneleh?" it was as if none of these things had ever happened. It was as if his balls had been merely puffed up with hot air. He would have to start out again like a scared kid. He would have to get away, but he was in panic, and his bouncy hot-aired balls of the past three years as a hot shot, shack-up lieutenant had collapsed at first pricklings of A.G.'s question.

With all his troubles getting the business off the ground, cutting the Brooklyn umbilical cord, he also had big problems with Gloria Goldstein, the girl he would eventually marry. It had been Murray, his brother-in-law, who still insisted on slipping Trojans to Goff, now a grown-up ex-lieutenant, who had nudged Gloria's phone number at him. She was the daughter of one of the customers at the grocery. "Arnie, trust me. She's built to the hilt. If I was a little younger . . ." He winked, still the schmuck. Hitler came and Hitler went, but Murray, his brother-in-law, kept on going, with a hernia or something around his balls that had kept him 4-F, but hadn't prevented him from unloading black-market cases of Bumble Bee salmon by the hundreds from Pop's handy Chevie and schlepping them into the cellar. War or no war, scarce, *shmarce*, give them only Bumble Bee and they pay. "She's gorgeous. You wouldn't take her for Jewish. I got a feeling you and her will hit it off. Call her. Whatya got to lose. I got the phone from her mother. Gloria herself wouldn't give it to me. I tell you she's something. She's got a good job with an advertising agency. Here, take it." He had wrapped the slip of paper around another of his inevitable packets of Trojans, and winked again as he pushed it on Goff. He had called her from the plant late on Saturday afternoon. He had been working like a dog, trying to get the bugs out of a solution that was damaging his main components. His fingers and hands were red-raw. Sheila, his sister-in-law's kid sister, was in Philadelphia for a cousin's wedding. He had been banging her steadily since his Army separation. He hadn't thought he would still have to resort to her after he came out of service. But there wasn't much else available. And she was a happy-go-lucky piece, and loved cock. He could do much worse. But it didn't do much for his self-esteem. He thought he'd be way beyond her by this time. She was such a dumb cunt, and occasionally would get sulky about his refusal to talk about marriage. But to her credit, the minute he drew out his cock, she'd forget about it and flounce happily onto it like a quoit plunking onto its peg. She was always scaring the shit out of him by telling him she was late with her period.

# Chapter 2

---

*How Goff met Gloria, his wife-to-be*

To make a comfortable phone call to a girl you don't know is an impossible arrangement. In the war, as a lieutenant, he had had all the elements working in his favor. Wartime conditions induced quick informality, and inhibitions were sanded down to smoothness by the rough times, either actual or conveniently and mutually fictionalized by all concerned. But now at his plant on a Saturday, with the gray of a raw November evening approaching, he was no longer a lieutenant. There was no war. He was in his dumpy deserted plant. He always insisted on thinking of it as "the plant." It had been a former fish market. He was deluged with uncertainties and fears about his venture and his future. The heat in the building had gone off and it had turned cold. The prospect of a cold Saturday without a date was very depressing. As the song said, Saturday nights were the loneliest nights in the week.

Maybe it was because he felt so low that it didn't much matter, the ordeal of going through one of those "you don't know me, but . . ." calls. The idea of hanging around home with the sure knowledge that Blanche and her putz husband Murray would be sure to drop over made him frantic. He shuddered at the suffocating dialogue: "If Arnie isn't going out on a Saturday night, he must really have combat fatigue, or should I say war." (With "war" pronounced with the old, inevitable clumsy lewdness of "whore.") "It must have been *hard* for you in the wars. Rest, bubie,

you earned it. The medals on a soldier's chest is called fruit salad. For Arnie, he got all cherries."

In desperation, he worked up his courage. He rationalized that if it
were putz Murray's recommendation, she couldn't be that great—so he
didn't have to get stage fright and choke up over a little shit of a spoiled
Brooklyn bitch whose mother fed her Bumble Bee salmon all through the
war. Murray said she didn't look Jewish; shit, Murray didn't know what
not looking Jewish looked like. Goff had been in places in the South and
west of the Mississippi, where they'd never seen a Jew before—and on
occasion when Goff didn't trouble to hide it, they'd always say, "You a
Jew? Well, I'll be damned. I guess you're the first one I seen." Murray
could very well be the Jewish counterpart. "You a goy? That means a
Gentile. I don't think I ever saw one before except for a policeman and a
garbage man." What a dog this broad must be. But maybe not—by some
miracle. He clenched his teeth and dialed the number Murray had given
him. He couldn't let this depression get the best of him.

"Hello, I'd like to speak to Gloria. . . . Well, I'm Arnie Goff. I think
you gave Gloria's telephone number to my brother-in-law, Murray Kritz-
er, of the G & K Dairy, to give to me . . . my father is Abraham Goff,
the big Bumble Bee magnate of Cortelyou Road. . . . That's right . . .
right . . . right . . . thank you . . . Gloria? Do you know anything about me . . . right, he's my brother-in-law. He insisted I call
you. . . . He says you don't look Jewish. . . . Is that a plus? No, it's
not. The more Jewish, the more I like it. When I was in the service, I was
stationed in places around the country where all we ever saw were natives. How I used to hanker . . . yes, hanker, for nice Jewish
girls. . . . My brother-in-law Murray—he's the younger one . . . the
older one is my father . . . for years and years Murray's been slipping
me packets of a commodity called Trojans. . . . Yes, that's what they
are, and he thinks I keep using them up. Actually, I have a drawer in my
room that contains 875 packets of Trojans—three in a package, and last
week he winked and gave me the 876th package, and with it your telephone number. . . . I assure you, strictly coincidence, and when I was
putting that package away with the other 875, there was your phone number, and . . . well . . . here I am—calling . . . absolutely no implica-
tion intended." It had come off smoothly. She had made some easy
cracks about admiring a prudent man who saves up for a rainy day, and
she hoped for his sake he would someday be properly rewarded for his
thrift and prudence. She hadn't put on any affectations or evasions about
being asked for a Saturday date on a Saturday yet. She had no date and

would be happy to see him—he sounded as if he had a good sense of humor.

They were exactly the same height, and she later learned to wear flat heels because of his height consciousness. They had spent an enjoyable evening on their first date, saw one of those new Italian films, later, a juicy pizza in a lively place in the Village that she recommended. There was a pleasant completeness about the date that had somehow eliminated the almost constant need of Goff's to push on to sex play. Not even a good-night kiss—it wasn't necessary. Was it because it was clearly understood between them that they would be seeing a lot more of each other? And that they would inevitably be digging into that reassuring supply of Trojans on hundreds of rainy days?

Those first weeks of Gloria had given Goff a momentary lift in his dark period. But before long she, too, became the cause of further complications, aggravations and uncertainties in his already beleaguered life. She, in fact, became his biggest aggravation and it stretched out for years until well after their divorce.

It wasn't long after their blind date that he started considering her for a wife. And it was quite unsettling to become burdened so soon with the knowledge of her "terrible habit." She, a girl well within the definition of a nice Jewish girl, how could she bring herself, with such ease and finesse yet, to get down on him? Could anyone blame him for being unsettled? It was a common enough turn of phrase in Brooklyn, when to allay parental concern about their sons, it would be said, "Sure, he's not settled yet. But, wait—he'll get married—he'll get settled." Goff laughed bitterly— yeah, he'll marry Gloria, he'll get settled. Soon! A cocksucker would settle him. The fickle finger of fate, as was said by the egg cream philosophers in the candy stores. Go know! Aunt Sadie, you didn't know I would get settled by a cocksucker. "It's not the most terrible thing, Arneleh." Aunt Sadie, do you really know what you're saying? Do you know what a cocksucker is? "I don't know exactly, but I got an idea. It's not the most terrible thing, Arneleh."

Goff, as sophisticated as he had become in those eye-opening, happy war years, was nonetheless downright shocked. He had known her for several months. He had never remotely expected it to happen in his sister Blanche's bedroom on the Fourth of July.

Blanche and Murray had gone away for a weekend. With winks and leers they had offered him the use of their apartment. "You can take *whorever* you like up there," Blanche said, making use of the old family joke again. The family joke exacted its traditional tribute of appreciative smiles from Murray and Goff. You couldn't discourage a family tradition. Actually, how many did they have? Murray made a dutiful attempt to give it a mature, respectful tone as befits grown-up guys who are beyond playing stink finger and are now ripe for major-league affairs.

Goff considered Murray the quintessence of ineffectual schmuckhood. He was a dark, curly-haired man who always managed to convey an expression of sincere and dutiful concern. A. G., a tattered buzzard with the eye of an eagle, had spotted Murray for Blanche and quickly held out a partnership in the grocery, and Blanche and old A.G. had proceeded gently, but completely, to peck the ass off him. Old A.G. contrived to work his balls off at the grocery, and at home Blanche broke what was left. No one seemed to mind this felicitous arrangement, including Murray, which was the main reason it was felicitous.

He was essentially a dutiful man and he did his duty. He blew his nuts dutifully, listened to dirty jokes dutifully, felt he had to tell them once in a while—did so ineptly, but dutifully. He considered he knew all about life, and if you didn't want to get fancy, he probably did. When his father-in-law, old A. G., cackled to their retarded delivery boy that a putz was more than just to piss with, Murray, in on the secret, would smile sagely. But it was an undeniable certainty that the poor schmuck never really knew that there was such a thing as a glorious, roof-raising piece of ass. He simply had not the remotest conception or imaginings of the pure wallowing pleasure; the dirtiness, the purity; the heights on heights on heights. The in-boring and the up-soaring. The slime sublime. The hearty zest, the yeasty nest. The perfect fit! It's you, darling! Whattya mean you not sure? Maybe if we let it out a little? Nah! Too loose. Something isn't right. It hangs by him. It'll never be a perfect fit. So for a shmendrick like him, it don't matter. So let it hang a little. Tell him it looks gorgeous, take his money, wrap it up and send him home—and don't forget—stamp his receipt, "Final sale—no refunds!"

Yes, alas, Murray would go meekly to his Maker, putz in hand.

When Goff had been a young man, sex, of course, and its pursuit had occupied a large portion of his life. It wasn't until now, in the full flower of his forties, that he realized sex was *everything*. Its pursuit was paramount. Somewhere out there was a perfect sex partner, a perfect snatch match. It was like the perfect wave. Like these surf riders roamed the world, schlepping their heavy surf boards behind them, to find that perfect wave—he was searching for the perfect ride. And fate could conceivably have it that his perfect ride might turn out to be the girlfriend of a surf rider, whom the surf rider had left behind for roaming the beaches of the world with his surf board schlepping behind him. Fate was funny. It was most unlikely that she would be Jewish, but he had become broad-minded enough and sufficiently free of prejudice to entertain that possibility. He would accept her. He realized he had striven all these years—amassed his million dollars, his prestige, his Park Avenue apartment, his self-acceptance—all, to prepare himself for the supreme fuck. And with that supreme fuck, you finally fulfill yourself. But you can't expect to bring off the supreme until you complete yourself. One must bring oneself to supreme readiness to obtain the supreme piece of ass. Or could he say, its not the fucking that makes the man; it's the man that makes the fucking?

"I don't know if I'm making it clear, Doc."

"You are making it quite clear."

"I've got to be in the driver's seat—all the way. I've got to feel I've achieved my ultimate development. Right?"

"It is extreme, but it is correct."

"Isn't that the core of creative selfishness, Doc?"

"Correct, Arnie. Selflessness through selfishness. The more thorough the one, the more thorough the other."

"I know what you mean, Doc. I know what you mean. I suppose I'm simplifying it, but it all seems as if everything I've done, my business, my investments, my art, my divorce, my therapy—everything—has been done to help me find the perfect piece of ass. Right? But is that a proper life goal for a man?"

"Why not?"

"Right. Why not." Another perfect answer, thought Goff.

Another perfect answer, thought Kummerlos.

When Gloria had gone down on him that Fourth of July in '48, he had been nowhere near the polished product he was now. He couldn't handle it with the nonchalance he would eventually acquire, but under the circumstances he had felt he hadn't done badly.

It was in the pursuance of a shaky courtship that Goff and Gloria found themselves in Blanche and Murray's bed that hot Fourth. It was as much the heat of the day as any heat of passion that made them take off their clothes. After eight months it still surprised him how far Gloria Goldstein had departed from her Brooklyn-influenced background in matters of sex. She wasn't so different from dopey Sheila, who was nothing but a natural-born cock-crazy cunt, a freak who could show up in the most sober socie-

ty. But while Sheila was dumb, Gloria was smart. She acted out of resolve
and conviction, and with a good measure of independence. A little too independent, Goff thought. She had a sharp tongue and mind. A source of
positive pride to him, however, was her un-Jewishness. What a sweet accomplishment—to simulate assimilation legal and kosher. To beat the
game and stay the same.

So, for Goff, Gloria Goldstein provided him with the best of all possible
worlds. Not yet ready to act on his lack of convictions, his Jewish conditioning still lay heavy on his stomach. Despite its repugnance, its outrageous demands, its irrelevance to his conception of life-style, its goddamn
nerve, he did not have the confidence yet to renounce its claims. In Gloria
he had a beautifully opportunistic out. She was Jewish, which was good,
but didn't look or sound Jewish, which was better.

And best of all was her un-Jewish behavior in bed. Goff, the lieutenant,
had had some fancy ride-'em-cowboy fuckin' in the South and Southwest, and Gloria, the Goldstein, wasn't taking second place to Carol Sue,
the Honeycutt. Well, maybe Carol Sue shaded Gloria a mite. Hell, no use
denyin' credit where it was due. And that might be just 'cause Carol Sue
set all her ass-twistin' in rhythm with that soft southern-style you-all cunt
talk. Goff's recollection was that of increased excitement and pleasure
caused by that soft southern drawl which was surely specifically evolved
to grace and mellow the basic violence necessary to a good screwin'. It
was a perfect accompaniment, like a violin section mellowing out the
thumping of the percussion section into a most felicitous blend. Goff
could be exquisitely sensitive to the refinements of fucking.

Having shaken off her Jewish fetters, Gloria sought reckless Christian
fulfillment, and Goff delighted at her un-Jewish abandon and wantonness—her delicate obscenities, "Fuck me harder, harder." Under the circumstances, absolutely in order, even obligatory for first-grade performances. It produced a hearty, arousing effect, although not as shivery,
slivery as a low, soft magnolia honeysuckle whisper, "Now jazz me
sweet 'n' hard, Lieutenant honey, y'hear."

Gloria Goldstein, the best of all possible matches for the Arnie Goff of
1948, who in spirit and looks could pass for Pat McSnatch, the girl of his
assimilationist wet dreams. He could now look forward to a quarter century of furtive, elbow-nudging questionings of envious Jewish friends—
"Arnie's wife, is she Jewish? I would've never guessed it. Did you ever
see anyone look more like a shiksa? She gives you the feeling she's wild in
bed."

*  *  *

Blanche's bed would finally be getting a proper workout. A Fourth of July fireworks display—a gala extravaganza—never before witnessed in these parts with startling sparklers, blazing Roman candles, soaring rockets, bursting cherry bombs. Goff would knock one off for Murray. "Let's make this one for the shmendrick," he whispered, breathing into Gloria's hot-tongued ear.

He burrowed into her, determined to show that bed finally what real fucking was like.

A pair of phonies, thought the mattress, whose name was Shapiro Bedding.

They lay on the bed. July the Fourth poured down its heat on their inert bodies. Gloria yearned to get up and get into a cold shower, but honored the sacred postcoital protocol by suppressing the clammy urge—lying in docile sacrifice with her hand resting on Goff's crotch—a tasteful gesture honoring their questionable sacred wild fires of a moment before. Gloria felt that even questionable manifestations should be honored.

In the unbearable heat, Gloria was now grateful that a few inches separated their main flesh masses, except for the isthmus of her arm and hand connecting with Goff's swampy crotch. Gloria could see Blanche and Murray's wholesale begot French provincial chest of drawers, crowned off by the display of a lucite-framed photograph of the couple in their wedding dress. She saw Murray's rented top hat and tails and his stalwart, vapid smile—the smile of the simple village lad in the fraudulent magnificence of his full-dress soldier uniform before the ravage takes over. Blanche in her wedding gown had removed the thick-lensed glasses she had constantly to wear—a myopic depiction of nearsighted fluttering maidenhood—all swindle.

Gloria had given it her best, but knew it had been a lackluster performance. He was an avaricious lover and had bored in with animal energy. She supposed he was moderately satisfied. He lay there sucking on a ci-

Goff thought it had been a pretty good fuck. He doubted that Gloria had come, but considered that she had been a good sport. She simulated; that spoke well for her. She hadn't lain back like a Hungarian heirloom goose-feather pillow—like his sister, Blanche, in the picture—like his mother—like his aunt Sadie—like it must be written in the Torah or Talmud or wherever it must certainly have been inscribed— "Daughters of Israel, lay quiet; let the man get done; it's not such a big deal, so don't make a *tsimmes* of it. It's enough the man will make a jackass of himself. You don't have to try to help him along."

Gloria, to her credit, despite falling short, had not felt shortchanged.

Goff puffed on his cigar and as a gesture of the warmth and appreciation he felt for Gloria, he patted her hand on his crotch. The pat clearly said that she was a bit of all right.

Gloria patted back. Her patting said, "I guess you're OK, Arnie. Your sex drive scares me. Chances are you're a prick at heart, but I'll gamble with you. I'll try to be a good wife if you ask me to marry you. I hope you just had a good lay—and if not, go fuck yourself. I tried my best."

Goff deciphered the tapped message and was pleased enough. Pleased enough for new stirrings in the sweaty heat. Gloria felt the unmistakable slinky little surges and tried stealthily to remove her hand. It was too late. Goff, quick as a cat, seized her wrist and forced back her hand to his resuscitated bird of prey—his phallic Phoenix.

Gloria resigned herself with practical realism. He's a very healthy boy, she thought, taking a positive view, but it was hot. The massive five-piece bedroom set seemed to be giving off its own choking heat in that airless room. The shades pulled down at the open windows hung motionless, exhausted. The odor of the heat was heavy and sour. Murray and Blanche had transferred their own smells to the room and furnishings, which had stored them up and now released them sourly to mingle with the heat of the room.

Fighting heat with heat, Goff pressed on doggedly. His hot passion progressed in geometric progression, and he quickly became totally committed to going another sweaty round with her. The environmental discomforts of the fucking locale were never a deterrent to his carnal appetites.

Gloria's grudging admiration for Goff gradually transformed itself into genuine arousal when she felt her hand now holding his full cock unfurled. He eased her over him and decided to try something new. Nothing to lose.

He started to nudge her head, which was kissing him up around his neck and ears—downward toward his chest. It complied with no resistance. He nudged a little more and the easygoing head drifted down further toward his belly. He nudged a little more. Ah, a little resistance; her head was now pressing back—of course. Goff pressed a little harder, fully expecting the return pressure to increase proportionately—but suddenly, the balking at his soft underbelly—gone—nothing! The resistance had collapsed. The head had raced to its objective. It swallowed up Goff's peninsula like a well-oiled blitzkrieg. He hadn't been at all prepared for such alacrity, audacity, voracity—for her aptitude, adeptness, veracity. She was indeed giving him a full-blown job. His sense of propriety was truly shocked. He had half a mind to disengage, but thought better of it.

Let her finish, he thought. Then I have some harsh talking to do. My God, he thought, she's better than that half-breed Indian gal in Oklahoma when I was a lieutenant. We're definitely going to have this out! But later.

So later, when Gloria tried to nestle up to him, she detected a sulky stiffness in his manner. She tried to kiss him. His lips turned petulantly tight. No lips that have ever touched cock will ever touch mine.

Gloria withdrew and lay silently beside him for several uncomfortable minutes. Goff was working himself into honest rage. She had betrayed him. To think he had been considering marrying her. There were few more broad-minded than he. He was no old-fashioned square. Christ, she didn't have to be a virgin. Why, he wouldn't even seriously consider a broad that wouldn't go to bed with him. No broad would ever have to fear that because she'd gone to bed with him, he would lose respect for her. Lose respect? It's in bed where respect begins. But for cryin' out loud, screwin' is one thing, but Gloria, the girl he was going to ask to marry him, had actually gone down on him. And she'd gone ahead and done a better job than that little half-breed Indian gal from Oklahoma when he was a lieutenant. He seethed.

"Arnie," Gloria said, "you're pissed off because I did what you wanted me to do."

His seething increased. He didn't care for her use of the expression "pissed off." "I wanted you to do that? I wanted you to go down on me? To blow me?" demanded Goff, working up the seething into genuine indignation. "Are you crazy?"

"Maybe I am crazy. Maybe I got crazy from all that nudging and pushing on my head you were doing—all in one direction—south—toward that upstanding member of that congregation of yours. Your hardon, to you."

There was some slight merit in her accusation. Goff reverted to seething. But he didn't like her use of the expression "hardon."

"I don't deny I was nudging your head. But I didn't want you to do it. I never expected you'd do it, and when you did do it, Jesus Christ, did you do it good. What form. What heart. That wasn't just lip service. Why, you blew rings around a little half-breed Indian gal that used to blow me in Tulsa when I was a lieutenant."

"Arnie, you're still a narrow Brooklyn Bar-Mitzvah boy, with all your Oklahoma blow jobs when you were a second lieutenant." He didn't at all care for the use of the word "second." She could have just left it at "lieutenant."

Gloria rose and started to put on her panties and bra. A glum Goff watched her tuck her attractive generous-sized tits efficiently into her bra.

Her good lines and her goyish-type angry face caused him to become even more glum. Never take her for Jewish, he thought sorrowfully. "Sit down," he commanded.

"Right, Lieutenant."

"I'm not the schmendrick you're looking at in that wedding picture. I'll never be in that picture. I've moved out of that picture for good, and I tell you I'm a little surprised that I got wrapped up as much as I have with Gloria Goldstein, made in Brooklyn."

"Tooshy for you, Arnie." Goff hated her wisecracky guts.

"And I promised myself," he continued painfully, "I'd never get trapped into a Gloria Goldstein setup. But yet, you're not as Gloria Goldstein as your name, and I didn't give a crap about your hot affair with your boss, the Madison Avenue executive. But a guy can only be broad-minded so much and no more. It's a little too much when I have to stack you against the little half-breed Indian gal in Oklahoma when I was a lieutenant, and you win."

Gloria stood up. "I'm sorry I couldn't live down to your expectations. I didn't realize I was that good. I thought you wanted it. I'm sorry."

"I told you I didn't want it."

"Okay, okay. So let's part friends—and do me a favor, will you, Arnie?"

Goff felt another wisecrack coming.

"Don't write my telephone number in public telephone booths."

Goff gave her a grim look; he got out of bed and put on his shorts while she completed dressing.

He was lacing his shoes when he looked up and asked tightly, "You did *that* with that Madison Avenue boss of yours?"

"Yes, Arnie. I'm afraid so, and I think he thought I was good, too. In high school I was voted most likely to suck seed."

Goff, enduring his pain manfully, asked, "Did you do it with anybody else?"

"No, I broke in with him and then you came into my life."

Goff gasped inwardly. Her timing was savage—professional Broadway. He had finished tying his shoes but continued to keep his head down for his last question. He almost choked on it before he managed to voice it. "Was he Jewish?"

"I can guarantee it," Gloria snapped with bitter flippancy.

Goff nodded, all stiff upper-lipped, as he rose straight and erect. A partial weight had been lifted. He knew he would have been completely shattered had Gloria's other blow job been a goy with foreskin. With silence and dignity, he escorted her from his sister's suffocating apartment.

\* \* \*

"I do and I don't, Doctor. She meets so many of my requirements, and yet after that incident I described, I can't bring myself to go through with it."

"Let me ask you, Mr. Goff, how do you think she would respond to your proposal of marriage?"

"I wouldn't have any trouble."

"What is the main obstacle of your reaching a decision?"

"I was all for it and ready to go, when she went ahead and did that unnatural act."

"The one with you?"

"Yes . . . but also with one other guy—that she admits to, anyway."

"Do you have reason to doubt her word? Is she generally trustworthy?"

"I'd say she's honest. Too damn honest."

"What if this unnatural act, as you call it, were confined exclusively to you. Would you then regard it in a more favorable light?"

"I think so. I don't know. It came as a shock, even before I knew she did it to somebody else."

"What do you regard as her favorable features?"

"Lots of things. She knows how to dress. She's attractive. She's smart. I would never be ashamed of her. And she is Jewish."

"How important is that?"

"It's very important. Why look for trouble. My family would never let me hear the end of it. And then if I have kids—who needs all the complications. Sure, Gentile girls are more attractive, usually. With Gloria, she makes it. She doesn't look particularly Jewish—and she doesn't act it, if you know what I mean. She answers a hell of a lot of requirements. She's not an embarrassment. You know what I mean?"

"Your parents approve of her?"

"More or less. They certainly wouldn't object. It would be satisfactory."

"They are not enthusiastic?"

"No, they think she's too distant, independent. But they know I was running around with Gentiles all over the country, and they'd be very satisfied to settle for Gloria. Anything is better than, God forbid, I should marry a shiksa."

"I'd like to get back to the unnatural act. Was there anything else besides blowing you?"

"No, I don't think so."

"What do you mean, you don't think so?"

"Well, sometimes we do it dog fashion. You wouldn't . . . ?"

"No, I don't think so. But blowing you—is it not possible after all to consider this as a sign of high regard and affection?"

"Well . . . if she doesn't particularly enjoy it for its own sake, maybe."

"Even with her previous affair, there are many ways to look at this. And most of them aren't especially unfavorable or without advantages. Think about it."

"Doctor, are you trying to tell me I should consider it in terms of my pleasures?"

"Why not? I don't see why it cannot be regarded as a positive contribution to the sum of your pleasures."

Goff then rounded the curve and saw the light at the end of the tunnel. Kummerlos had sanctioned Gloria going down on him, and as far as Goff was concerned the engagement was on. He felt relieved. Dr. Kummerlos had shown him the way. Of course. It was surely an addition to the sum of his pleasures. He would be an impractical fool to remain narrow-minded. There was nothing demeaning for your wife to blow you—done in the right spirit. A man would be lucky to have his wife display such devotion. He would not be a hypocrite. This was Gloria. If she gave, she gave with everything. Wasn't this actually what he was looking for? He would be a fool to be overcome with the very prudish limitations he so contemptuously attributed to his family and associates. And he would just have to stifle his old-fashioned repugnance about kissing a girl who had blown him. And, furthermore, in this instance, in order to have his cake, he might just have to eat it too. Well, he would see. Gee, it would be nice though—after a hard day at the plant. Just lay back and relax—no exertion. Not a dirty, shameful act, but clean and aboveboard, right at home, in your own clean bed, and then doze off nice with peace of mind for a sweet night of sleep. It could add ten years to a man's life.

So he resumed active contact with Gloria. He begged forgiveness for his momentary lapse into provincialism, and when his head nudges once again produced the results he desired, he no longer reproached her. It also occurred to him that maybe it would be the equitable thing to reciprocate, but he squirmed off the notion with distaste. How far can a man readjust on such short notice. And, anyway, didn't he deliberately put extra-added ardor into his kisses afterward to show his acceptance of what really wasn't (let's be honest) the cleanest practice in the world? But at least it was his uncleanliness. A man can always tolerate his own uncleanliness more readily than another's. Actually there were probably many more germs in his mouth than on his cock, clean cut and constantly exposed to the air that it was. But a pussy with its dank crevices and subterranean warm secretions was a natural breeding ground for corruption and abomination. Wasn't it well established that these were ideal conditions for bacteria to multiply in? She wouldn't seriously really expect it of him. *Feh!* And he lay back comfortably, content to have it remain at thirty-four and a half.

When she missed her period and thought she might be pregnant, he thought, fuck it already, it's all too nerve-wracking; and they got married. And as some women, after marriage, let themselves become slovenly and run to fat, Gloria became finicky and would no longer perform thirty-four and a half. No amount of clear head-nudging could set her off again. Goff felt cheated and trapped. Here he had gone ahead and made a most difficult adjustment, changed a very big value structure and given her absolution—so that he could marry her, and so that she could continue the practice, and there she had suddenly gone icy prim and proper. A complete shutout. What was his recourse? Could he very well remonstrate with his wife for refusing to be a cocksucker? It rankled deeply, and for years afterward he stewed. He was still working like a dog at the plant. But she would no longer budge to his nudge. Ten years of that extra life he was counting on—out the window! She had bamboozled him. She had sucked him in. He always felt afterward that that was the main reason for the eventual failure of his marriage—although this was not for publication.

"I don't want to sound like a crybaby, Doctor, but you remember my hesitations because of the unnatural practices I spoke to you about before marriage?"

"Of course," said Kummerlos, hoping he hadn't responded too quickly.

"Well, as soon as we got married, she shut up like a clam. I mean, she never once did it again, you know. And after I had torn myself apart to accept it, to learn to live with it and to get used to it. Frankly, I was beginning to count on it. You know, to add to the total sum of my pleasures. . . . I feel cheated in a basic way and I resent it."

"This is understandable."

Goff nodded, assured. He clearly felt he was receiving the doctor's full commiseration. And if he wanted a divorce, he was sure Kummerlos would grant it. Which he finally did.

"In the long run it will be best for you both, and infinitely better for the children. It is a fallacy that children are the worst victims in a divorce. It is much more damaging to them, living in a constant atmosphere of hostility, unrest and uncertainty."

Goff had to consider his children's welfare as paramount. "My children are my only religion. May I never have another hardon if I ever do anything to hurt my children," he vowed. So, of course, he must get the divorce, with Kummerlos' consent and blessing. What Kummerlos had brought together, so had he put asunder—on special request.

Having Kummerlos was almost as if he had captured a genie in a bottle. He would name his wish and the genie, Kummerlos, would grant it. What extraordinary good fortune to have found this magician. Kummerlos could grant him anything. He had the genie in the bottle by the balls and he would never return one night to find his Park Avenue apartment turned into a hovel. Arnie Goff would never screw up that magic.

# Chapter 3

*Goff finds it exhilarating to live on Park Avenue*

Goff had now arrived at the point where he felt completely at home in this high-strung, high-class, affluent enclave that was the fashionable upper East Side. Everything here had a neurotic, hyper-arty electricity. Goff took it all in and embraced it with affection and excitement. He dug the long-legged broads with their deceptively icy looks, who walked on the streets with their dogs, parading, clipped and groomed in defiantly grotesque contours. Dig me, dig my dog. He understood. He could handle them now.

Goff smiled at the overwhelming abundance of dog shit on these classy streets and pavements. These were the streets his ancestors had spoken of with religious awe, as paved with gold. The concrete of the sidewalks actually did contain glistening particles that produced the effect of diamond dust. And all over the elegant sidewalks shit these aristocratic, neurotic dogs. Their droppings reflected their high-strung creators. Not wholesome romping flop or honest, well-rounded country turds, their city shits were tortuously squeezed, twisted turds or brittle prissy pellets.

He walked with sure confidence now in avoiding stepping onto the turds on the shit-strewn sidewalks of Park and Fifth avenues, and their cross streets that were their rungs. It had taken time. Goff could remember when it had been impossible for him not to step into the sidewalk dog shit. But he had come to learn lightly and nimbly to trip through miles of it without over any more squishing into it. A middle-class or poorer neighborhood would never tolerate such shitness. He understood.

He admired the polished granite blocks of the buildings, the canopies, the elegant doormen. He felt virtuous tolerance toward the bustling black delivery boys, recklessly navigating their three-wheel bike carts with black dash and pepper through the mother-doublin' parked streets. The black Mercuries for gourmet groceries from the chi-chi markets and green grocers of Lex and Mad. They were to be commended for their industry and spirit. Goff always made it a point to tip them generously and never forgot to smile at them in a friendly, encouraging manner. Who knows? It was just this little display of goodwill and friendliness that was enough to tip a delicate balance. To be just the right amount of favorable experience to strengthen him at that critical point where he has to make his crucial decision as to whether to turn into a bitter "whitey" hater or a reasonable chap, who remembered at least one white man who was rather decent. It would be nice if he knew I was Jewish, too, thought Goff, but of course it would be most implausible for him to know *that*. Goff certainly didn't look it or act it. And for a *shvartzeh* how much didn't you have to look it anyhow? Could he, Goff, tell the difference between a Watusi and a Bantu? Goff daydreamed his just rewards further. A gang of them was about to mug him. Take his money and then beat the livin' shit out of him just for kicks, and one would suddenly yell, cool it! It was just a former delivery boy gone bad, but who recognized Goff and tells the gang to leave the mother alone, "Man, just leave the mother be. 'Cause I say so. Yeh, I know the cat and anyone that touches that cat's gotta tangle with my ass." Yes, all in all, it was a remote but reasonable investment in the future.

He didn't know why exactly, but in the fashionable upper East Side, the black delivery boys, their high spirits notwithstanding, still knew their place. It was the rare exception that was surly or didn't show at least reasonable appreciation of a generous tip. Was it because this was still one neighborhood where it was quite clear who was boss? And if the little bastard didn't accept it in the right spirit, he'd get his black ass kicked out quick enough—and he knew it—and acted sensibly.

Goff, walking on, took in the discreet, high-toned embassy and consular buildings with their porticoes, granite steps, iron grillwork and heavily draped windows. He recognized the stocky Middle-European or Middle-East characters with their stony expressions and their postures like tough, tight-stuffed acrobatic sausages.

He did not resent their DPL licenses and their conspicuous but neat and gleaming Police Department signs on lampposts giving notice of parking prohibited except for embassy cars. This was also all part of the exciting flavor of the scene. Wasn't this district, the Nineteenth Precinct, also called the Embassy Precinct by the cops?

Goff actually thought of it warmly as a neighborhood with its own cozy flavor, rather than an area or section of the city. He took possessive pride that the Whitney Museum was also now a part of the scene. The Cinemas I and II—perfect, just perfect. The foreign restaurants with their friendly easy-to-take ass-kissing, and the hearty, chummy saloons on Third Avenue where millionaire and show-biz and communications hotshots became hysterically regular guys and outdid each other with their down-to-earth enthusiastic appreciation of "the best fuckin' hamburgers in the world are made in this saloon." There were the antique shops on Third Avenue, with windows filled with Chippendale, cuspidors and old crank telephones. As an *arriviste* patron of the arts Goff also now knew the art galleries on Madison Avenue. The private schools, elegant English prams being wheeled by blue-caped nannies. He had laid one of them (from Glasgow she was). She had taught him she didn't have a brogue, but a burr. And he had nodded and burrowed into her burr. The kids of the area with their insufferable poise and their vexing (they should by all rights be inept sissies) agility at sports, not only in Central Park but even in skillful street games in the high-toned double-parked streets. And the careless air with which they ate hot dogs bought from the striped orange umbrella-covered carts of bent old Europeans, serving the young bloods of the fashionable upper East Side with scraping, gnarled-handed, broken English subservience. Goff himself could never bring himself to defy an old warning never to buy a hot dog from one of these guys. It made sense. Where did these guys wash their hands after they crapped? Where did they *crap?* There were the fags being pulled by their giant bloodhounds or whatever the fuck those ten-ton dogs were called.

He was acquainted with the food specialty shops. With the patisserie. The Viennese pastry shop. The cheese shop. Ah, the cheese shop. No yenta accents there. In this shop one heard only cultured tones with many an elegantly turned foreign accent, requesting Italian Fontegidia, or Camembert or Fontina or any hundreds of exotic names, all delivered with the correct pronunciation of the cheese's motherland. The shop, narrow like a shoebox, bulged with cheeses and their overwhelming ripeness of odor, and the cheeses were cluttered everywhere. Crammed on shelves, hanging gourdlike from ceilings, on counters, in iceboxes, in the show window. No other items whatsoever but cheese, cheese.

A customer's request was hopped to by clerks swaddled in oversized wraparound white aprons, like old-world gnomes, who might live in the holes of huge Swiss cheese. They served the clientele with intent, unsmiling briskness, skillfully carving and lopping generous wedges from robust, glistening, waxy wheels or loaves, or snapping large curved brass handles to open old-fashioned windowed doors on old brown wood iceboxes and trundling out their treasures of cheese with tender mother-hugging motions.

In the invariably crowded shop, the clientele never minded—obviously enjoyed—waiting in this cheesy atmosphere. They were enveloped in the wonderful fragrance of the near-fetid, almost sexual odors of the ripe cheeses. A living odor of sorts that only the near corruption of a ripened cheese can give off.

There was the silent camaraderie of the clientele in the cheese-crammed shop. Each secure in the elegant and comforting vanity that he was choosing that cheese which precisely and exquisitely matched his discriminating palate, *le fromage juste.* And each one graciously granted the other that same vanity, as if a felicitous unspoken bargain had been struck among them. I will grant you your exquisite taste, and you, of course, will acknowledge mine. Gnome, there, before you wrap it up, can you cut a sliver for the gentleman in back of me for to taste. Of course, I shall be delighted in turn to taste a sliver of yours. Ah yes, how like good brandy we must treat cheese. Room temperature—warm it in your hands if necessary—sniff the aroma—ah, the fecund bouquet—it's the sober cheese that puts the gorging banquet gently to rest. Cheese should smell like a peasant's asshole, *n' est-ce pas?* Fondue, my friend!

The residents of the fashionable upper East Side all knew that cheese, like a maturing mistress, had a unique value, intangible and wondrous—and deserved to be supported in a place of its own. Cheese was not to be shared with the other mundane groceries and comestibles. And the cosmopolitan customers, waiting to be served, were all brothers of the cheese in the fashionable upper East Side.

Goff enjoyed everyone's role, and he was comforted that everyone knew his role and was content in it in the fashionable upper East Side. Here roles and levels were clear and well defined. The call girl had her place and was content and was accepted and she accepted. The tradesmen, the endemic Yorkville delivery boys and the bused-in black delivery boys—all in harmony, living and flourishing off the great, fashionable upper East Side. Not like the jumpy East Village—or schizo Greenwich Village which didn't know what it was—or the decaying upper West Side. In the fashionable upper East Side knowing your place was the key to happiness.

It reminded Goff of a joyous medieval tapestry—a town fair with gay colors, pennants, lusty nobles and their lofty ladies in flamboyant finery; artisans, peasants and marketplace tradesmen, and impish, skittering boys. A latter-day carnival of high spirits was the fashionable upper East Side, and Goff, the jolly Jew, was in it.

# Chapter 4

*Goff sees Dr. Levine, the first item on his schedule for*
*his greatest day in his spring of '69*

Goff reached the building where the doctor had his office. Abraham Levine, M.D., it said. Such modest, unpretentious dignity—on the brass nameplate affixed to the polished granite block of the high-class, canopied, liveried, Fifth Avenue building. Abraham Levine, M.D. No pretense, no levity or brevity in the confidence-filling wholeness and wholesomeness of that honorable name. Quietly assuring, ancient priestly server, wisdom and humanity, Abraham Levine, M.D. That was good, but the whole area was also good—on every block on every building were seen these brass nameplates; the whole fashionable upper East Side was practically a medical center, mostly with impressive Mount Sinai practitioners. How reassuring to see all these names on their dignified brass plates, some old and weathered, signifing solid established practices, others spanking new, signifying erect, ninety-ninth percentile, shiny young men, the cream of Mount Sinai, who would soon roll in gilt. The names were good. Goff read the names as he strolled the area. Martyn Taub, M.D. (why the "y"?), Jason Kornfeld, M.D. (from Iowa?), Sanford Liebow, M.D. (no "itz" for him), Burton Pine, M.D. (Pinsky prick), Max Feinstein, M.D. (an honest man), Bruce Gordon, M.D. (Scotch? My ass!), Harvey Harris, M.D. (who you bullshittin', doc?), John English, M.D. (I wonder if he gets any Jewish patients?), Ernesto Sussman, M.D. (hah!), Abud Hakeem, M.D. (surrender, you bastard! You're surrounded), James Goldberg, M.D. (ah, poor mixed-up man). The area abounded with healers.

113

Plain Abraham Levine, M.D. How reassuring. A man whose competence and confidence in his chosen work were sufficient for him not to require false supports, pretenses and mannerisms.

At one side of the building a separate entranceway led to the doctor's office. Goff opened an outer door, took two steps down within a vestibule, pressed a buzzer. An answering buzz nervously signaled him to open the inner door and he stepped into a room tastefully furnished in decorum doctorum, with subdued, clean-limbed lamps and sensible clean-cut furniture. A few unobtrusive tables contained only the most current issues of *The New Yorker* and *Time*. No clutter of back-dated, rumpled magazines there. A little sign in quiet, discreet letters issued a modulated message that smoking was hazardous to health and would not be permitted here, thank you.

A "nurse" approached Goff. Her hair, blond, straight and short. Snub nose and big round Sunday-school black-rimmed eyeglasses. Goff immediately recognized the prairie heartland accent. He was amazed at the brevity of her nurse's skirt. She smiled an open country smile as she asked him his name. This native charm, a natural resource of Kansas and Iowa—a dime a dozen out there, but worth a lot of money when shipped into New York—and Goff was sure Dr. Levine wasn't paying the full value. The girl probably had no idea of her value, freely dispensing that easy, come-natural sunshine. She was the kind of girl that didn't have to take off her glasses to prove anything. She was the stuff of airplane stewardesses, of astronauts' wives. Of the young college instructor's bride. She was greater than that—she was the spunky monkey who slapped Tom Harper's face for his cheap, anti-Semitic remark and flew into the arms of dark, sensitive, brooding, curly-haired Bruce Ashkenazi, and sobbed in uncontrollable tremors, "Bruce Ashkenazi, I want to be your shiksa forever. I don't mind working till you get your doctorate."

Abe Levine is okay, Goff thought, as he gave the girl his name. And if he's screwin' her, she's giving him a good fuck behind those round black-rimmed eyeglasses of hers. He sat down and watched her corn-fed, contented, miniskirted ass wiggle back into another room.

He noted Dr. Levine's clientele. He sized up an elderly couple immediately. They had schlepped in from the Bronx or Brooklyn. His name was Sam and he was being smothered over by his wife, Sadie. Their speech was heavily inflected with Yiddish accents. They would be more comfortable speaking Yiddish, but here in this refined office it was not exactly fitting, so they painfully extruded a mottled English. Sam was nervous and frightened and Sadie, seeking to calm him by constantly reminding him it wasn't good for him he should get upset, naturally increased his uneasiness. When the nice nurse with a kind sweet smile told Mr. Shmulowitz he could now go to the examining room, Goff thought, how wonderful! Did Sam and Sadie appreciate that this Midwestern, blond American shiksa doll's total friendliness and warmth generously encompassed them too? Never. She was a remote fairy princess who regardless of her good heart, would never be able to change her father's royal wrath against Jews—and in the end would be dominated by him. Little did they dream that Arnie Goff could knock off these good hearts with his eyes shut and have them begging for more. Fuck her unbending, fearsome, red-eyed father. Bah, they had no conception. Ah, only in golden America.

Goff felt warm appreciation toward the nurse. More than that he felt tenderness. He would screw her, not just because "it's there," but with appreciation and gentleness. Sam and Sadie could never remotely conceive how much it would be on their account.

He watched her address another patient, a heavy, elderly black woman dressed in overdone tabernacle finery topped by a gravely ornate hat. Miss Peg o' the West showed the black lady her row of prize corn-kernel teeth in another wholesome smile and sweetly assured the lady that her turn with Doctor would come soon. The heavy black lady responded with a display of appreciation she couldn't handle comfortably, and overdid her protestation that everything was just fine, thank you, and I haven't been waiting long, and thumbing her unread magazine in a self-conscious attempt at casual absorption in its contents.

Good try, thought Goff. Sweet, sweet Peg o' the West. You didn't exactly do it, but it was a nice try. Actually, Peg, you don't have to go all out for the *shvartzeh* as you did for Sam and Sadie. Use a little selection. It sort of diminishes the value for Sam and Sadie if it's the same for the *shvartzeh*. To dispense friendliness universally on an equal basis? Did it not cheapen the value of the friendliness? Could Sam and Sadie Shmulowitz feel they had received full measure, if the same is accorded the *shvartzeh?* Goff felt that Peg had unwittingly tarnished her good act, but he couldn't work up a solid condemnation. He attributed her simpleness to a sweet *goyisheh kop*. She thinks she's doing right. It did not diminish his regard for her as a girl who would join him in a buddy fuck, but he didn't deceive himself that she would not equally fuck buddy-style with a spade. But today he couldn't sustain the narrow view. He felt so good, and Peg o' the West was really so sweet. What's fair is fair. What she gave to Sam and Sadie, he generously permitted the *shvartzeh*.

Goff next fastened his shrewd eyes on the heavy, elderly black lady. He

116 B. H. LITWACK

completely skipped over even a fleeting consideration of her sex life. He
didn't give a fuck about her sex life, but thought of her solely in terms of
the significance of a *shvartzeh* as a patient to *his* doctor. What did it signi-
fy with regard to his medical standing that he had a *shvartzeh* as a patient?
And a frumpy, worked-out houseworker type at that. No Lena Horne,
she. If he had one, he must have more. How many more? A doubt entered
Goff's mind. Was this doctor's a second-rate practice that he had to encourage *shvartzeh* customers?

Goff's slit-eyed appraisal concluded that she was a hard-to-replace
housemaid for one of Dr. Levine's colleagues who had asked him to treat
her on a reciprocal courtesy basis. The broken-down houseworker only
served to confirm the stature of Dr. Abraham Lincoln Levine. He was
chosen to treat the *shvartzeh* because he was deemed the best. For Goff,
she then constituted the good housekeeper seal of approval.

Goff saw Peg o' the West's sweet corn converted knees and luscious
corn-silk thighs approach him fetchingly in pure white nursey mini-wini
skirt. I could nibble her up, thought Goff. How clean and sweet she must
be. Goff knew the arousal power of purity, of innocence mixed cunningly
with a dash of wantonness. The slut angel. The "Lolita" thing. The
"Baby Doll." The childlike half nighty. The wide eyes. The thumb-suck-
ing. There was nothing more calculated to arouse the lechery of all good
men and true. This was sure fire. A saintly young nursey in a saucy-slutty
miniskirt was a supremely diabolical exponent of this trick.

As Peg o' the West told him to follow her into the next room, Goff hungered to ravish her, this wholesome corn-fed cock teaser. No more buddy
fuck. He would husk her down savagely and deprave her of everything.
He would scoop her out and nibble off her niblets without mercy. Goff
was fooled no longer.

The next room contained the stainless steel gadgetry and doctored furnishings of an examining room. The room seemed uncomfortably chilled
by the profusion of gleaming metal, the metal desk, a metal gooseneck
lamp whose light also gave off cold rays. The examining table's shiny imi-
tation leather also had a black metallic look. Its touch was sure to be icy.
On it a roll of paper was arranged to spread underneath each new patient
for reasons of sanitation. Goff felt uneasy about the effectiveness of this
thin barber-chair-type roller paper. Couldn't skin diseases, especially the
powerful, virulent ones like jungle rot and other African tropical kinds,
penetrate this flimsy tissue paper protection? For a hundred and twenty-
five dollars he might expect a surer antiseptic arrangement. Anyway, he
was glad the *shvartzeh* came after him instead of before.

Goff had not had too many girls like Peg o' the West. After his separation from the Army, he had hardly ever had a really hundred percent genuine, wholesome, open-cunted, four-H, Nellie Forbush hairwasher. Most had been blemished in their depravity. He thirsted for the wholesome depravity of Peg o' the West.

The closest he had come in recent years to wholesome, red-blooded depravity had been a brief episode with a former high school cheerleader from Trenton, New Jersey. It was, though, a short-lived locomotion. He had sensed her withdrawal soon after he had successfully urged her to go down on him.

What he wouldn't do for his wife he did for the girl. For her, he would nine to her six—an Arabic configuration he would never have contemplated in previous years. It had taken time and travail to acquire the exotic tastes for the perfumes and spices of Araby. To sin bad, assail her cunningly and wickedly, howsoever with pleasure for all, requires an ancient accommodation to corruption not easily adoptable to a common lad from rabbinical Brooklyn, but attainable, however, if worked on diligently.

Another consideration. For her to six for him and for him not to nine back for her was no longer cricket. And if a wholesome, clean-cut American kid is willing to accommodate you, it would be a slap in her face to lie aloof. It smacked of clannishness, superiority and cold exploitation. You don't have to supply them with *more* ammunition. Love America or leave it. It was tough, but fair.

But Goff no longer had to force himself. His tastes were now sufficiently catholic. Can a man rightly lay claim to the role of worldly gourmet if he has not yet sipped of bird's nest soup?

Perhaps it was due to overconfidence. He had not bothered to establish himself as a Basque with the Trenton ex-cheerleader. So he attributed it to anti-Semitism when she lost interest. It was at a highly charged Times Square kosher-style delicatessen that she remarked with apparent awkwardness and some gloom that she didn't much care for this highly spiced food. Goff took the remark as a much more general hint, and dismissed her with a "fuck 'er" when she didn't come to a party he was giving. But it convinced him he couldn't just disregard completely his valuable Basque identity, regardless of its occasional strident criticism in his group sessions. The group had swarmed on him and condemned it as a contemptible crutch.

"Mr. Goff," said Peg o' the West, "please have a seat. Mrs. Levine will be with you in a moment."

"*Mrs. Levine?*"

"Oh, yes. Miss Duncan, Doctor's nurse, is out ill. Mrs. Levine is pinch-hitting. She's a trained nurse. She'll take your medical history."

"By the way, honey, are you a nurse?"

"No, sir. I'm a medical technician and I double as a receptionist."

"Will you be the one giving me my cardiogram?"

"I think so, sir, if Doctor orders it."

"He'll order it. That's what I'm here for—to check out my heart." Goff then decided to move in a little. "This checkup is just a precaution. A good friend of mine, never sick a day in his life—heart attack. Keels over. Feenee—like that. Anyway, I'm a healthy man and I do healthy things." Goff grinned, edging closer. "And I'd like to ask you something from a layman's view, Miss . . ." Goff paused.

"Miss Seymour." She smiled.

How beautiful on her, he thought. How sure and proud she could always proclaim herself legitimately as Miss Seymour. She would never have to resort to snappy, sporty cover-ups and shortenings; She would never feel compelled to call herself Miss Sy or Miss Mel or Miss Marv or Miss Norm. Seymour for her was the norm.

How many of Goff's acquaintances would give their uneasy souls to awake one morning and find their name Seymour magically transposed from their flimsy first to solid surnames! If I marry you, Miss Seymour, can we use your name? We'll call ourselves Mr. and Mrs. Sy Seymour, and we'll live safely ever after.

"Miss Seymour, you're a very sweet and attractive young lady. Frankly," Goff twinkled heavily, "with you giving me the cardiogram, will it be me or you that shows up?" Goff suddenly switched to sincerity. "I mean, let's face it. You are an extremely pretty girl. I'm serious. Might a healthy sort of reaction or excitement show a misleading picture? Really!"

"Mr. Goff," Miss Seymour returned lightly, "Dr. Levine is a most experienced cardiologist, and I'm sure his diagnosis will take into account all your symptoms for a total picture."

Goff was pleased with the playful ease of her response. "I'll take your word for it," he said, "but if my excitement at taking my first cardiogram prevents an accurate picture, I only live a few minutes from here, and I can always come back for you to give me a quickie."

Mrs. Levine entered. Some Mrs. Levine, was Goff's immediate thought. Abraham yet. My proud, cool, fair beauty. What is your real name? Kathy what? Sullivan? Adams? Ipswich? Lobsterpot? You smile at me as if it strained every stringy muscle of your rockbound New England hide. Don't leave it out to me that you're going to divorce Abraham Levine. You look just like Gloria when she needed a new, stronger kind of tranquilizer. Is that what he gives you instead of what you really need, a good Arnie Goff-style fuck? You'd go wild, you poor, repressed darling. Let me make amends for my brother Levine. All us Jewish fellas feel mutual responsibility for one another's boo-boos. I would take you out to Montauk and, while the waves pounded the beach, we would fuck like crazy and I would encourage you to let everything out and I would understand, really I would, if you screamed out, Oh, you dirty fuckin' Jews. How I hate you dirty fuckin' Jews. And after, you would be refreshed and quietly grateful, and you would hold out your hand to shake mine and with a straight look in my eye, say sincerely, Thank you, Mr. Goff. I needed that. But you might still feel a little uncomfortable and want to apologize for the things you had screamed, and I would hold up my hand to show that it wasn't necessary. I understood, and then you would go back to Dr. Levine, your husband, and soon after he'd say, Is it my imagination, or have you stopped taking tranquilizers? And that night he'd say, My dear, things haven't gone like this for us in years, but he'll think, gee, that was a good fuck, and you won't mind it because even though you won't come, you'll still be serene. And he can continue his wonderful, rewarding work and your children will be spared the ugliness of a divorce. See. So come on along with me to Montauk. I could be a charming chap, worldly and witty. What do you say?

"Have there been any diseases in your family, Mr. Goff?" Mrs. Levine asked.

"Yes," said Goff softly. He now understood her distant, chilly manner.

Mrs. Levine completed her questions, rose briskly and asked Goff to follow her to another examining room. Goff followed, taking note of her purposeful stride. He also noted the flinty, New England ass. Rocky— hard-to-cultivate soil. People were known to have craggy jaws. She had a craggy ass.

She nodded him into a smaller room and told him his examination would begin shortly. He was to disrobe to his shorts. There was a white paper robe available to him. Goff said thank you in a sober, gentlemanly way. In the mood she's in, it wouldn't be smart to fuck around with this one. Let her know she's dealing with a gentleman of impeccable propriety. Have to lead up to Montauk with excruciating care, or blow the whole thing.

In the examining room Goff undressed, put on the paper robe and sat himself on a metal stool to await his next ministrant. He wondered whether he'd be seeing the doctor now. The door opened and a new girl inquired, "Mr. Goff?" He nodded. He saw that her nursey miniskirt was a bit higher than Miss Seymour's. Goff thought she was a good-looking piece. He judged her to be Puerto Rican. Her "Mr. Goff" contained a distinct "meester" and her dark hair, dark eyes and small features were almost replicas of the thousands of spics he had seen in the neighborhood of his plant. She sort of resembled Ramona.

"Miss, what is going to happen now?"

"Your blood test," she said as she glided in with deft little medical movements. She nimbly gathered up her materials as she told him in cool technical tones to have his right arm ready. "Roll up your sleeve, please."

Goff had noticed she had given him only the most perfunctory smile. He realized the little spic was trying to emulate her grand mistress, Lady Shiksa Levine. She wasn't going to get away with that. The tiptoe care he had felt was necessary with Lady Levine was certainly not the treatment he had to give this spicky span in white starched miniskirt. "Does a cardiogram hurt, miss?"

Disinterested, not giving a thing she didn't have to, she said, "No. Hold out your hand and make a tight feest."

"Miss Seymour tells me that it makes no difference how pretty the girl is who gives the cardiogram, it will record the same for a man. Is that right?"

She shrugged almost imperceptibly.

"I'm going to request that you not give it to me. Nothing personal, except you're a very pretty senorita."

"Miss Seymour will be with you for the cardiogram." Mrs. Levine's protégée was outdoing her mentor in cuntiness. Goff braced himself for the needle, but figured she would be adept as all Latins are with daggers, stilettos and needle-sharp instruments. He further imagined that screwing her would be accompanied by sharp, little happy, scrappy needle-like stings, bites and gashings. He would sure get her hackles up, whatever the fuck that meant, just as he would for Mrs. Levine—but he wouldn't have to waste Montauk on this one. A quick razzle-dazzle locally. Maybe his Park Avenue apartment—her color wasn't that dark.

"Open and close your feest," she said impassively as she brought the needle up to the vein in his arm. Goff smiled his confidence at her Latin deftness. In plunged the needle. Goff had had his share of needles in the Army and elsewhere. But never before had he felt such pain. It was as if a rusty, old-fashioned can opener had been driven into him. He bellowed out, "What the hell do they teach you in Puerto Rico?"

Unruffled, she held the needle in place and continued the business of withdrawing his blood. "I theenk you are meestaken, Meester Goff. I have learned my profession in Jerusalem in the Hadassah Hospital. I have not been in Puerto Rico, and I am not a senorita. I am Mrs. Chaya Antonovsky, an Israeli Sabra. You know what that ees?"

Goff felt his blood had been drawn out of him in quarts rather than the two cc's in Mrs. Antonovsky's syringe. She had now withdrawn the needle and Goff felt sure she had yanked it out zigzag rather than clean, straight pull. Having performed the preliminaries with sure deftness and then butchered the essential portion, she now resumed her small efficiencies in a lofty manner. The Sabra whipped out a cotton swab and planted it on Goff's gashy puncture. "Fold your arm, please," she said with aloof unconcern.

Goff folded his arm to pocket the swab. The blood that was left in him had turned cold at her revelation. Sabra, my ass, he thought. Although, come to think of it, she did bear a resemblance to the tubercular Moroccan street whore he had seen in Tel Aviv. But Sabras are blond and prickly on the outside, but soft and sweet on the inside. As far as I'm concerned she comes from a line of greasy East Side pushcart peddlers and I wouldn't screw her with my brother-in-law Murray's dick.

The contemptuous Sabra labeled her vial of Goff's blood and briskly started to leave the room, with not a word, but a final look of disdain. This Sabra also regarded him as a type likely to sell military information to Arabs. But Goff called to her, "When am I getting my cardiogram?"

Without as much as turning back, she told him with arrogant assurance that it would be next.

The Sabra was wrong. The chest X ray was next. It was a mournful-faced, slight girl who led Goff into the X-ray room. He thought she might be Oriental, but wasn't sure. Goff had seen better shapes on rag dolls. She must have been Dr. Levine's humanitarianism again. In barely audible, eye-lowered tones, she got a puzzled Goff to comprehend finally what was expected of him. Was he going to be fluoroscoped? He was beginning to worry. She might let too many Roentgen rays loose in the room. He had read that overexposure could produce cancer or stunted growth or, God forbid, impotence. Was that why this girl was so underdeveloped?

Where did Levine find her—in Hiroshima? The lights dimmed. "Say, Miss, am I in the right position now?" asked Goff with rapidly mounting concern.

"Yes," said the girl dolefully. "Keep standing, please, with your chest against the plate. Take a deep breath."

"I don't hear you."

*She* took a deep breath. "Take a deep breath," she said.

He took a deep breath.

"And hold it," she said sadly.

It was too late. He had let it go. "Wait. I'll take another one."

"Yes. Take a deep breath and hold it."

The room went completely black. There was a whine of machinery. Goff's chest pressed against the cold metal plate. His lungs were bursting with the effort of holding his breath. Was this some kind of radioactivated last mile? The lights went on. Blue in the face, he finally sputtered, "I can't hold it no more."

"Oh, that's all right," she said remotely. "You can let your breath out now. I have the picture."

Goff rarely had a pure, unpremeditated outburst of temper. He held that a tantrum should not be indulged in unless there was a reasonable likelihood of a fair return for the effort. With this hopeless girl it would be a complete waste. So with toneless resignation he merely asked her what was next on the schedule.

"You will go back to the other examining room. Doctor will examine you."

"Don't I get a cardiogram now?" asked Goff with slow-burn control.

"Oh, yes," she corrected herself listlessly. "Go down the hall to the right. Examination room B." She smiled at him sorrowfully as he put on his paper gown and headed for examination room B. He opened the door and the heavy, black houseworker, wearing only old-fashioned pink bloomers lumbered toward him like an aroused mud avalanche and slammed the door. "Ah'm awful sorry, Doctor, but ah didn't git mah gown on yet."

"That's quite all right, madame," said Goff with bitter elegance. "I'm not the doctor." He headed back to room C.

He sat down again on the metal stool. He began to have doubts about Dr. Levine. It was lucky he wasn't sick. He could relax. He had come to the doctor as a healthy man, and not out of immediate need. He was in the driver's seat. And if it weren't for that sweet-cunted Miss Seymour who now entered, he might just have a mind to get up, get dressed and take off. They better not send in any more foreign castoffs, and neither was he in the mood any longer for Mrs. Chanukah-Lights-with-Christmas-Trees Levine. And if he did decide to leave and Levine sent him a bill, he could go fuck himself. Goff, the proud Basque, would never pay. He could stand off armies of Levine's process servers in the fastness of his beloved Basque mountains. Hah, Levine in Berchtesgaden? What chance would he have? He'd shrivel him to nothingness.

But Miss Seymour was all reassurance, with her alert State U. comeliness and 4-H radiance. Goff swore her white mini was now higher than before, the perky-cunted delight.

"Mr. Goff, I'm going to give you your cardiogram," she grinned.

"Miss Seymour, I know you'll give me a very fine cardiogram. I trust you implicitly."

"Good," she said with her nursey cheerfulness. "Now, take off your robe. Were you weighed yet?"

Goff had gone into a cubicle off the room. "No, not yet. I want you to do it."

"I will. I'll get your weight later."

As Goff was untying his paper-string robe belt, he saw Miss Seymour daintily slip off her shoes and step onto the scale. She had decided to weigh herself while waiting for her patient. Miss Seymour's mild form of chaste disrobement somehow inflamed Goff. There was a strangely tantalizing intimacy about her act. Those silky white-stockinged toes. He felt a characteristic, general body limpness, as if all his body starch were draining out fast and rushing into his cock. He saw her now sliding the weight on the scale to get the reading. He hurried over to her, desperate to think up a snappy dazzler to crack. It came to him. "Let me hold your glasses. Every little bit counts."

Miss Seymour turned and gave Goff a smile right out of a golden Kansas morning haystack. It dawned up right from her golden cunt. She handed him her glasses, and the metal pointer clunked upward.

"See, you're lighter than you thought," said Goff, fondling her warm eyeglasses.

"Whatya know," she said with a kind of happy, open-legged forthrightness.

Goff became further inspired. "Don't move now. I'll show you a trick we used to do when I was a kid." He stepped up on the scale in back of her, taking hold of her waist. "We used to weigh ourselves, two for a penny. And we'd get a fortune card with the picture of a movie star. We'll get our combined weight, Miss Seymour, and then by the simple process of deduction, we'll get mine, my dear Miss Seymour. What's the weight?"

She adjusted the balance. "Two seventy-five."

"That makes it then one fifteen for you and one fifty-five for me. And I have the fortune card. It says, 'What a fortune, cooky. You two have achieved a perfect combined weight. It may never happen again. Don't wait. This is fate. For best results mix and shake well!' "

Miss Seymour adroitly but amiably squirmed herself out of Goff's increasingly tight hold and off the scale. "Mr. Goff, I have to give you your cardiogram. Please, my glasses."

Goff, friskily pleased with himself, handed her the glasses. "Fine, Miss Seymour. What do I do now?" He smiled at her. She grinned at him.

"Lie down on the table please."

He focused his total eyebrow on her. By incorporating his unibrow with a practiced smile tinged with a touch of leer, he felt he made a compelling communication to Miss Seymour. His instinct had guided his timing. That same smile at the wrong time could be disastrous. And by the way Miss Seymour met this look, a momentary, frank, head-on stare, and then a not-so-quick averting of the eyes, Goff knew he was in. Ah, pity he had this really big thing going tonight with Christine, the culminating piece of ass of his life. The pièce de résistance. Maybe though, he could work this kid in this afternoon (he *could* give up his nap), because after tonight—who knows? He expected never to want to look at another broad for years to come—and it would be a shame to pass up such a delicious one as this—not to squeeze in just one more before he shut the gates. Maybe Kummerlos' wife wouldn't be that great. Not a chance. It just had to be. He was finally ready, and Christine had to be perfect. But even if she was, even if she proved to be his queen of lays, why couldn't he still take a little excursion once in a while down from Mount Olympus and dabble with the rabble. The gods used to do that all the time.

Miss Seymour busied herself attaching straps and small metal plates on his legs and arms. "Raise your leg." Then, "Raise your arm. Oh, this is a dab of lubricant conductor which is needed under the plate. I'll wipe it off afterwards." And as she leaned over him on the table to strap on the electrodes, Goff, not missing a trick, pressed his elbow into her crotch. He was pleased to note that she hadn't tried much to avoid floating it right up to him.

Elbow snatching was new to Goff. It wasn't a breathtaking sensation, but it wasn't bad either. It felt rather nice. After all, when does an elbow get a chance for such rarefied contact? He prided himself on achieving just the right mixture of boldness and roguishness in the stare he designed and directed toward the unflustered Miss Seymour. How many virgin elbows had been wedged into her available crotch by cunningly opportunistic cardiacs who were getting cardiogrammed? Miss Seymour had undoubtedly long ago worked up a routine to meet these flattering attentions. She feigned unawareness and went on completing his strapping. Suddenly he lurched up. "Miss Seymour, I hope you don't mind my expressing myself, but I have grave doubts about the validity of this cardiogram, as I've already mentioned before. You're easily one of the most attractive girls in New York. We've been close together on a very small scale. You've been working very close to me these last few moments. And having very little elbow room, well . . ."

"Mr. Goff, please." She smiled evenly, completely ignoring the elbow issue.

"I want to remind you again," he said significantly, "I'm a healthy man, a very healthy man. And with the special excitement healthy men can work up under the circumstances, how, really, can this possibly give a true picture?"

"Oh, Mr. Goff, I assure you the recording will be fine. The basic pattern is not interfered with by any normal excitement or shortness of breath or anything like that. The main thing is that you lie quietly without moving or fussing." She widened her grin at him.

How Goff enjoyed her. He liked how she used the word "fussing"—so ingratiatingly heartland, mother-cunty. This was the language of a girl who knew how to care for man and beast. She would never say aggravation.

"I have complete confidence in you. I'm in your dainty hands," he said as he flopped back on the table with heavy aplomb.

"Good, it'll only take a few minutes. Lie still, including elbows, please." She flashed that grin at him again.

"I promise," he groaned. "Elbows and all, and I do mean all, I hope." He punched out the last crack brightly.

Having settled him into repose, all wired and strapped and lubricated, Miss Seymour began turning knobs on a somber brown mahogany box containing dials and black needle pointers on calibrated gauges. The whirring it produced lasted several seconds. A graphed tape two inches wide began to snake out of the box, piling in loops on the floor. It was full of sharply pointed peaks and valleys in black ink. This was Goff's heart pulsating out its state of health. He felt tense. He had to make that picture come out good. Stay calm. It was important not to let his heart wiggle wrong and show a questionable hill or valley. He must remain unexcited. What did that dumb cunt *know*—or was she trying to con him? Getting excited didn't matter! Who was she trying to bullshit? He had to be calm. He would try and concentrate on unexciting things. Thank God I'm healthy, he thought again. This was calming. I'll keep my weight down. I'll eat shitty cottage cheese more. I'll cut down on chocolate, all kinds—bars, chocolate cherry fills, egg creams. Fried stuff is out—never again. I'll walk more. I won't step in shit. Maybe I'll jog. I'll cut down on masturbating. I'll send my mother five dollars a month more. Make it ten. No more. Nothing between meals. Ah, the *shiksaleh* cunt is done with this part. She's stopped the machine. Is this all? I doubt it. Yep, she's putting that grease on my chest. A dab here, a dab there, all across my chest. Fuck 'er. I'm not even going to smile at her—cock teaser. This is serious. I'm going to make that cardiogram perfect. My heart waves'll be perfect. It's up to me to control it—to make it do what *I* want.

Miss Seymour applied a suction cup to the first position of the row of grease dabs on his chest, starting on the right side. She switched the machine on again. Again it whirred and issued the stream of graphed scroll scratching out the secrets of his inner heart. Goff reinforced his determination to think of unexciting things.

He thought about drugstore owners and their cousins, accountants. He went back to cottage cheese. He thought about operas, about synagogues, services and sermons. About taking his kids to Radio City Music Hall. The Rockettes. No, stay away from the Rockettes. Aw, why not Rockettes? You don't screw precision dancers. But when he was a schmuck kid though, he used to jerk off to them. What the hell had he known? When you're a kid, a flying fuck is a possibility, and you jerk off to trapeze artists. The Rockettes were the closest things to live naked girls he could get to—before he was old enough to go to a burlesque.

Miss Seymour smeared him up for another position on his chest. She attached the suction cup, closer to the center—going toward his left, closer to the matter of the heart. She smiled at him. Goff almost smiled back, but caught himself grimly. Can't fuck around, Arnie. Damn—it doesn't come too easy. What a complexion on that girl. What a belly and cunt area she must have. No acne there. With a massive mental tug he wrested his mind away. Cauliflower, boiled chicken, Bar Mitzvahs, visiting his mother, brother, his whole fuckin' family. Ooops, mustn't get excited.

Miss Seymour has clicked off the machine. All business now, as she shmeers him up for another chest position.

Goff shut his eyes. He could make her any time he wanted. Tea, tea
with milk. Open-school week. Listening to his kid play the clarinet. The
Olympics. Detailed weather reports. Poetry. My cardiogram should be
good and strong so I can fuck hard all night long.

Miss Seymour smiles now—the technician's smile. Another position
now. Aha, monsieur, but of course, one hundred and one! The electrode
sucks on to his chest again. It's sucking up good, strong pulsations from
his heart and recording them nicely on the ticker tape. Of course, the ticker tape! How's my ticker, Doc? Your ticker tape shows great, just great,
Mr. Goff. This broad smells so clean. I must get into her. We'll bathe
together. We'll scrub each other clean, assholes and all, then we'll fuck in
sterilized purity. No germ will pass between us. They can land us on the
moon. We can now take that flying fuck to the moon—without contamina-
tion.

"Are you almost done?"

"Almost." She was cupping the electrode onto his extreme left side.
She had traversed his entire chest with the couplings. "This is the last,"
she murmured.

Goff nodded. His cardiogram would be perfect. How just right her ass
had felt on a small scale. Not too hard. Not too soft. Just harft. The final
whirr of the staid mahogany box clicked off. She grinned, "Painless."
The spunky Nellie Forbush who has just washed the man right out of her
hair. Was the man Jewish? She started to roll up the graphed scroll that
was now a mile long—filled with the black-lined dragons' teeth of the secrets of Goff's heart. He lay there. The patient patient who has fallen in
love with his nurse and America.

Miss Seymour, having neatly rolled up the tape, unstrapped the electrodes on his arms and legs, wiping the grease spots off his skin. He sat
up. "How did it look? Healthy—right?"

"I'm not trained to read them. The lines were very firm. Dr. Levine will
interpret them."

"Miss Seymour, I'll never forget this cardiogram. This was my first
one. No matter how many I get in my lifetime, it is the first time that will
be the most precious and dear to me—and I just know you're the best little ol' cardiographer in the whole world. I really tried to stay unexcited,
but, frankly, I couldn't. But I trust you. I couldn't help thinking while it
was on, how it would be my pleasure to take you to dinner. I'm sure the
cardiogram will show that clearly."

She shook her head, smiling.

He pressed on. "Look what we could tell people. How we met on a doctor's scale. How you checked out my sincerity on my cardiogram. Maybe tomorrow night? I live close by. I can pick you up anytime."

"Mr. Goff," she almost giggled, her hand on the door, "you have to call tomorrow to get the report on your blood tests. Ask for me." She opened the door and flashed him her best smile yet, above and beyond the call of the doctor's office, and trimly pirouetted her ripe, miniskirted, corn-fed ass out of the room on hush-soled white shoes.

Goff glowed. And I did this all in my shitty-looking shorts, he thought.

Dr. Levine entered. Tall, stooped, he wore a long white lab coat with his stethoscope dangling from his neck. He also sported a beard. It was an unexpectedly bold beard, reddish and in fine trim, bushing gamely out of an unlikely pink and white face. This had not been a beard of impulse. Levine had considered it gravely before finally embarking on its cultivation. The bother of the actual growing of the beard had presented no problems. But sometimes, in the midst of his meticulous trimming and grooming, when he was called to the phone to answer a request for his medical services, he would shunt the caller to his associate. What else could he do?

"My most important commodity is time," he would explain with soft regret.

Before the beard, he had tried periodically to achieve a certain donnish air. Leather elbows. A mustache. Pipes. Cigars. Never cigarettes. Now it was his beard.

Levine had married Priscilla Plimpton soon after her glands had straightened out. She had always been a fat girl—from a small town in Maine. After her glands had unexpectedly straightened out, but before she could change her deprecating notion of herself as a congenital fat girl wallflower, Levine, first seeing her at her ebb and taking her for a genuine, congenitally lank, slender American beauty from old New England stock, dropped everything to court her and then hustle her into a quickie Jewish conversion and marriage. It wasn't long after that that Mrs. Levine realized she was no longer a permanent fat girl castoff, that her stock had permanently risen, but by then it was too late. Levine had snared himself a first-quality product at distressed merchandise rates. Resentfully, she tried to gorge herself with fat Jewish foods to bring back her flesh. The Yankee trader in her rebelled at having handed Levine such a bargain. But to no avail. Her basic, gaunt New England nature grimly stood off all her feverish Jewish attempts. Levine was so proud of her craggy, sunken-cheeked ass. So were his mom and pop.

When Dr. Levine entered Goff's examination room, he was jotting happily on a clipboard and annoyingly displaying his well-being by humming

and dumming "Tea for Two." He nodded a detached, smiling acknowledgment at Goff without pausing his jotting or humming and dumming.
The patient examined the doctor, his beard and his singing. I got him to a
T, thought Goff. I won't change a thing I've already figured out except the
poor prick doesn't know his wife is ready to screw off on him with the first
guy that fields her even fifty percent right. He doesn't have to rush his
throw with this one.

Dr. Levine made his final entry and looked up at Goff. "Mr. Goff," he
pronounced. He smiled, not a greeting, merely a reflex signifying lots of
money in the bank. "I'm Dr. Levine." He extended his hand, a pink, delicate hand, in a cordial manner. "Mr. Goff, the notes I have on you show
you feel fine and have no complaints. You're here for a checkup."

"That's right. My friend just died suddenly of a sudden heart attack.
He was never sick a day in his life. He went just like that." Goff snapped
the traditional finger accompaniment. "So here I am."

Dr. Levine smiled through his beard and resumed his humming of "Tea
for Two" waving his hand as he directed Goff to lie down. He then conducted a full examination.

> He listened to his chest.
> His balls he squeezed and pressed.
> He pried apart his toes,
> And then peered up his nose.
> He wrapped his arm to measure
> His current hemo pressure.
> He hammered his reflexes
> And crunched his solar plexus.
> He gave his throat a spy,
> And beamed light to his eye
> To look and see in vein
> His vascular terrain.
> And for the coup de grace,
> His finger up his ass.

While Levine wiggled his exploratory, rubber-covered, greased finger
in Goff's ass, the "Tea for Two" still kept pouring out. Son of a bitch,
thought Goff, who found the wiggling finger extremely annoying, especially since it seemed to be keeping time to the humming. His baton was
the finger up Goff's ass.

Levine withdrew his finger. The humming stopped. The examination
was over. It had taken two minutes.

As Dr. Levine bent over the bowl to wash his hands, he told Goff to

dress and wait in the reception room. He would see him later in his office
to discuss his findings. Gliding out with sterile pink hands, Dr. Levine resumed his humming and dumming of "Tea for Two." It sounded to Goff
as if the tea for two were in a glass.

When Goff had been in the reception room several minutes, the Sabra
entered and lobbed him a sour look. Sabra Antonovsky's look suddenly
turned to a smile. Goff was momentarily puzzled until he saw it was directed not at him, but the *shvartzeh.* "Please, Mrs. Hareeson, come. The
doctor weel see you een hees offees now."

The heavy *shvartzeh* arose in a queenly manner. She smiled graciously
at the Sabra, as she walked regally through the door held for her in defer-
ential dignity by the Sabra.

Goff was furious. They had deliberately and humiliatingly taken away
his next. The WASP, spic and the *shvartzeh* had teamed up to give him a
shafting. This was typical of the trend all over the city, and they had as
their dupe and ally the mushy-minded liberal-thinking of the two-teaing
Dr. Cuckold Levine. Well, he wasn't going to have that medical putz win
the annual Brotherhood Award at *his* expense. He wasn't Sam and Sadie
Shiteatin' Shmulowitz.

Christ, he had a busy day ahead. He still had to go to the plant. He had
that damn lunch date with Leon Finger. He had his regular Kummerlos
appointment at three. This was a real big one—he had all the intentions
and expectations of screwing the man's wife tonight and he had to get
some final sightings and clearances on the thing.

And what was the big rush for the *shvartzeh?* What did *she* have to do
so important? Cash her relief check? He wasn't going to let this Levine
crew here give him this two-bit penny-ante shuffle. Shit, he was going to
barge the fuck right in, right now and raise a bloody stink. Fuck them.
Shit, he, a millionaire Park Avenue college graduate, World War II officer, veteran, industrialist, cash customer. Taking his next like that! What
fuckin' gall!

Fired by this healthy indignation, Goff burst into the adjoining examining room and into the presence of Mrs. Doctor Levine. He was glad it was
her that would get the full blast of his hot indignation. She was certainly
the one who had maneuvered this calculating slap in his face. He had been
nice to her enough. But no more Mr. Nice Goff. And to think he really
would have extended himself sincerely out at Montauk for their brief
affair. But fuck that now. She'd lost him and that therapeutic lay she so
desperately needed. Of course! Look, the proof. The remains of a glass of

water at her desk. Probably just taken her Librium or some other soother-smoother.

At one time he would have frozen before a type like her, steely bitch-schoolmarm Mother America, part-time floozie, part-time Indian fighter, part-time widow of men that go down to the sea in ships, silent kneeler at wintry graves.

No longer did he quail before broads like these, and this one—who had married Levine—her escutcheon had really taken a blotting. This one could claim nothing—she had forfeited her claim to her ancient airs and privileges. As Mrs. Doctor Levine she could never again pass herself off to Goff as unattainable. The holy grail could never be hers—and she was now fair game for a congregational gang-fuck.

Goff thought he had done a magnificent job in weaning himself off all Jewish reliances and alliances. At the occasional family or social function, be it a *bris*, Bar Mitzvah, wedding or funeral—or any of these things where a heavy Jewish flavor predominated, he kept a cool spiritual distance and eased away from the beckoning bejeweled pudgy arms temporarily opened for either festivities or fatalities, as the case might be. At these functions, let the Jew be unconfined didn't apply to him. But that didn't mean he wanted to sit at the goy table, the one table where the business acquaintances of one of the principals are bunched, secluded and liquored up for the duration, except perhaps to introduce eighty-year-old Aunt Sadie from New Haven, who never yet has missed a family *simcha*. Aunt Sadie is always marched out with false hearty pride, and Aunt Sadie always tries to explain what is a *simcha*. She knows when she's been trotted out to the goy table. "A simcha is an occasion for joy and happiness. The liquor is always good and I never miss it." The chief goy delegate always responds to that with hearty good fellowship and agreement about good whiskey. The lesser goys smile uncomfortably as Aunt Sadie is led back again. The Jews hope they've taken her for a salt-of-the-earth kind of Sophie Tucker type. She is then conducted back to her table, where the occupants have been sensitively selected for their compatability. Aunt Sadie is always seated with the ancient family collection of silent widowed or bereaved septuagenarians and octogenarians who still hang on. To that table, there is always one other addition—the faithful long-term *shvartzeh* cleaning girl, who, despite her theoretical eligibility, is never placed at the goy table. Their adjudged compatibility is based on their total and mutual noncommunicativeness. They nibble and nod away for two

expressionless hours and are then led away by heavy short-winded, eve-
ning-dressed *machers* who cannot conceive of themselves as soon to be
noncommunicables also.

Goff would allow his presence to grace the affair. But to join the feverish, hysterical circle of dancers for the hora, as dished up by a four-piece
band featuring a wailing clarinet in heat—thanks, no. "I've got to save my
strength for a horizontal hora." In this atmosphere it didn't matter his using of the hoary family joke again. And Blanche, breaking up, would gleefully shout that Arnie never changes. "He's waiting for a horizontal hora.
Come on, Murray." And Murray, puffing a fat, caterer-supplied cigar,
and a little high, would give his admired brother-in-law an overripe, man-
to-man wink, as he was dragged off by Blanche for his enforced hora
duty.

Goff would quietly turn down the fat single cigar that was offered to all
the men as part of the package deal the caterer provided. He preferred to
smoke his own thin, elegant, non-Jewish cigar. Before his sophistication
had set in, he also had favored the paunchy, dark cigars that looked like
stubby garment manufacturers. Now, only the long sleek tan cigars that
looked like the sun-tanned blond surfers he saw at Montauk.

And when the time came for him to say *Mazel Tov,* he managed to express it like the character of his cigar, smooth, clean-cut, streamlined and
modern. The lean enunciation he gave it anglicized the pronunciation.
The bite end was clean, firm and dry—in contrast to the garment manu-
facturer cigar: heavy, schmaltzy tonal productions, the bite end a shred-
ded, sopping mash.

And he would never lapse into a Yiddish inflection anymore. In the early years he might have been guilty of it and used dialect jokes. His repertoire of jokes no longer included the blatant ones. No more "Becky,
make like this."

He had covered this ground with Dr. Kummerlos. "I feel uncomfortable at these things. Sure, when I take a drink with someone, I'll say
*L'chayim.* I'm no snob, but, hell, if I'll go much further."

"Let's stop. First, you are a snob. A snob by common definition is one,
who by various degrees of subtlety, demonstrates to those he meets that
he considers himself superior to them. It is only a truly saintly man with
genuine humility who can avoid it; or else someone completely lacking in
self-confidence. Be glad you have something to be a snob about and don't
fight it. But also don't flaunt it. Let yourself be comfortable with it. Don't
display it when it works to your disadvantage. When it serves to raise

your ego, use it. When it causes resentment in somebody whose antagonism you don't need, bury it. If it makes you uncomfortable to adopt modes and mannerisms that you feel are too Jewish, don't do it. As with all other behavior, the course which seems socially unacceptable may be just right for your particular needs. We will not be rigid.'' The doctor concluded his counsel with the serene conviction of a nonsectarian holy man who has never been handicapped by an excess of either Jewishness or humility. His expression clearly conveyed to Goff that Kummerlos could also be relied on to supply calm reason—and if it necessitated unorthodox and bold new approaches, so be it. Kummerlos would supply them.

"I knew you'd feel that way," Goff said.

Priscilla Plimpton Levine looked up at Goff icily. She waited for him to speak.

Goff felt unnerved. Here in this first-class, Fifth Avenue physician's office, a hundred twenty-five dollars for a checkup, the look he was getting from the doctor's wife was deadly. Its intensity was unaccountable—weird. She should be rolling out the red carpet. What the hell's the matter with her? He'd had enough. He started to speak. When he had decided to burst in, he had no doubts that his remarks would be fast-flicking rapier thrusts. But to his consternation he began to stammer. "I . . . I had . . .a . . . originally, I had a nine-thirty appointment, and . . .''

She cut him short and spat out venomously, "Look, heebie-jeebie, if you're here to complain about the black woman being taken before you, and I can see that's what it is—I can tell by that heebie-jeebie look of righteous hurt that's coming over your face—just stow it and go back to the waiting room and be a good little heebie-jeebie.''

Goff was staggered by this unexpected right cross. Instinctively he defended himself. "But I'm Basque, Mrs. . . . .,'' he said, blinking and dazed. He couldn't remember her name. Groping, he finally stammered, "Mrs. Nurse.''

She continued lashing out. "Don't give me that Basque tripe. I've known enough of your kind now to know one when I see one." Her eyes narrowed to slits. "You may have momentarily forgotten my name, but you know I'm married to and share my bed with a heebie-jeebie. You couldn't hide that arrogant smirk—thinking what a pushover she is. She's already been laid out on the mat by a *landsman*. Softened up for any wondering Jew that passes by with a Yiddle yen.''

Goff tried to shake off the blows. "I only wanted to find out about my next." As dazed as he was, he realized he had lapsed into give-away phraseology and he tried to blur it out. "I mean, I thought my turn had been skipped."

She was relentless. She disregarded his amended version and mimicked scathingly, "About your next, he who sullied me, your Doctor Levine, decided I needed a houseworker today, so he hustled her in to finish her up to the loss of your contemptible next. The good *schvartzeh* is now on her way to our apartment where she will have full access to our bedroom. But not you, you drooling jewling. Wretched descendant of King Solomon with your lewd Jude shrewdness enabling you to fathom that I had just taken my black and green Librium capsule. You guessed right, of course, Jewpig. The good Doctor Levine is not the right meat for this Christian maiden. But with your gall, sure of yourself and domineering, you think you can charge up with your black pushcart and spirit me away into your black orgasm world. And with your elite genitals set me aright. Take the girl out for a bit of exorcise in the pushcart and with your ancient and cunning mastery of prickery, flail the living dybbuk out of her."

"No, no," gasped Goff. "There is some truth, but it is distorted." To his horror, he now found himself on his knees.

Sensing the kill, Mrs. Levine became as one possessed. "You dare," she spit, eyes blazing hot blue flame, "to say I distorted! You admit to my accusations and then grovel in excuses and exceptions. You slimy mendicant people! You parasites, pimps, pornographers—philanthropists!"

Goff pleaded upward, "I had no special lust for you. No offense intended. I could see you were troubled. I wanted to be of service. I would not have pushed. I would have invited you to Montauk. It is beautiful in April. The beaches and dunes are deserted. We could have gone on long walks, you wearing your tweed skirts and soft cashmere sweaters. In my scarlet imported cardigan, I would have walked beside you, silently, not touching, but somehow more closely brought together than any physical contact could possibly have accomplished." Goff's eye began to water.

"You're a liar, presumptuous pimp, *paskudnyak*," she hissed.

"No, no," Goff beseeched, "I would not have asked more. That is not to say more would not have come. That mighty surf—its rhythms—in turn wild and gentle would have affected us. But it would not have been my intention. No offense, again, Mrs. Levine, but I don't need you. I have so much. Why, even tonight I expect to culminate a dream of a lifetime. So—see?" Goff smiled up at Mrs. Levine sickly.

Mrs. Levine would not let up on him. Her savagery gave him no quarter, and cowed, he remained on his knees. "You are a transparent liar and devourer of flesh. You are an insatiable Hebrew swine. Even on your wedding night you were not above sniffing and rooting for other mucky rutting.''

How did she know? He had discussed it with Kummerlos, of course:

"By the way, that's one thing I sort of feel guilty about. I mean a quickie with a broad I picked up in the hotel lobby on my honeymoon night. I'd like that to go in the record. I mean, that I felt sort of guilty. But the main thing I want to bring out is I want to cooperate because I think what you're doing is really worthwhile. It's clear you need to know about the things that make me tick. I now realize a lot of things that didn't seem important were of the utmost importance. You remember *Citizen Kane*. Well, where Orson Welles had his Rosebud, I had my dog Queenie. It was in the country. A Gentile farmer up there gave her to me, and it was me that named her Queenie. I was nine when I got her. I remember because it was in the country—where at the same time I got the dog, I got my first real sex with my cousin, Florie, who I mentioned before. Anyway, we hit it off together right away—I mean Queenie and me—and it was in the country, and for two weeks except for having relations with Florie, I was like a Jewish barefoot Tom Sawyer and his dog. And I wasn't botherin' with Florie anymore. I didn't want to be annoyed, because I had my pal Queenie. You know how a dopey kid is. And then my father came out on the weekend and I ran up to him and Queenie right behind me, both of us all excited—and I said, 'Poppa, Poppa, look at my dog. Her name is Queenie,' and my pop wants to look at the dog and she sort of playfully runs away, and I tell him to call her, she'll come; her name is Queenie. And Pop laughs and calls her—the old bastard—may he rest in peace—but he doesn't holler out 'Queenie,' he hollers out 'Schmunzu,' and somehow, I swear, I knew immediately what it meant—it was Russian or Hungarian for 'cunt.' And Queenie, sure enough, answers to the name and comes running right up to Pop wagging her tail. After that I never felt exactly the same about Queenie. Queenie remained her official name; I tried to keep calling her that, but my father's name caught on much stronger, and around the house, it was really more 'Schmunzu' than ever Queenie again. Before our second week was up in the vacation, I was having relations with my cousin, Florie, again. The barefoot boy really blew it.

"Remember when I said the best sex I ever got wasn't a shiksa—but that she was Jewish—It was my brother Armand's sister-in-law, Sheila, which you might have guessed. Well, anyway, I'm making it official for the record. Who would think—right in my Jewish family—what a sex-crazy girl she was—the older I get the more I look back in appreciation. For day in, day out, sustained sex; you know, it was like she'd squeal with delight. A girl squeals with delight when you buy them a gold wristwatch or something—for an actual person's organ I never heard it yet—they got other sounds for that. But Sheila, when she saw it, smelled it, touched it—anything—it was a pure squeal of delight—I can't describe it any better. She was best—and she was Jewish. Can you beat that?"

Mrs. Levine's vilification of him was unfair.

There were certainly mitigating circumstances beyond his feelings of guilt. First of all, it wasn't as if Gloria were pure. Ha, Gloria—some virgin! The look the blonde with the book had given him in the lobby of the Miami Beach hotel was absolutely 200 proof. After all he was only flesh and blood. He had told Gloria to freshen up—call up her mother if she wanted. He would step down to the lobby for cigarettes, cigars and arrange for some liquor. The blonde with the book was still there. Goff could practically hear her beckoning lava bubbling and gurgling in her box. He knew it was wrong, but the pull was impossible for him to resist. A man sometimes becomes inflamed with an irresistible urge to plunge from the edge of the crater into the volcano. What he told her—without any further preliminaries—was: "I just checked in on my honeymoon. I know it's crazy." She nodded with a smile. She understood. A quiet mystic understanding suffused her face. "Are you Jewish?" she asked softly. The question somehow was no surprise. He quickly began to computerize her at the normal 186,000 miles a second—her clothes, her nose, her book, her look, the place, her grace, her speech, her feet—and came up with the correct answer. "Yes," he said.

"I am too," she said with muted sadness. "I'm divorced."

Goff repeated with urgency, "I'm on my honeymoon."

She nodded and arose immediately and led him without more ado to her room. With the solemnity of ritual they disrobed in measured movements, and then as if by signal, they both released strangled cries and immediately engulfed each other.

It had ranked with the finest fucking he had ever had, and it had been attained without any of the mandatory prerequisites. It was guilty, transient, Jewish, furtive, casual, vital—with no endearments, no liking, no longing—with no foreplay, buildup, anticipation. Nothing. And yet one of the greatest. It was fuck at first sight, a flaming celestial collision most rare. Absolutely incomprehensible. He learned a lesson: many a good fuck is born of a mysterious alchemy, and has a life of its own unrelated to and unencumbered by the before and after life of the fuckers.

When he rolled off her, she sighed that he was very, very good, and said wistfully that his bride was lucky and she wished them "a *mazel tov.*" He examined her sharply for traces of irony, but he saw she was in earnest. He rushed back to Gloria.

His guilt worked beautifully for Gloria. Another alchemy took place. The droplets of guilt that dripped into his spheres of feeling converted his renewed lust to tenderness and tempered his blustery hardon to a gracious jewel-tipped scepter. He behaved like a Rudolph Valentino to his bride, and Gloria, who had always had basic misgivings, found new hope that honeymoon night—thanks to Goff's strange quickie with the strange Jewish divorcee.

"It was beyond my control. And I was remorseful." Goff, from his kneeling position, continued abjectly to plead his case with the implacable Mrs. Levine.

But she continued with Christian Crusader steadfastness. "Your words condemn you. Covering your treachery with a show of remorse. You vulpine scavenger who would offer solace to the grieving widow, who would hoist her weeds and slither into her with your evil-beaked blackness. You swamp creature who would bring a sewage to her grief."

Goff pondered. What on earth could she have in mind? He finally figured it had to be one of two incidents or possibly both. And in neither case was it the way Mrs. Levine colored it at all. He sincerely wished she'd check her fact sources more thoroughly.

When he was a lieutenant he was assigned to tell a girl her husband had been killed—not even in action; it was an accident on the rifle range. It was in a small Alabama town near his base post. She was the town barber's daughter. It was after closing hours. She lived in back of the shop with her daddy and old granddaddy. When he knocked she opened the screen door and let him in to the living quarters. Her daddy was out, but her granddaddy was in the rocker. Lieutenant Goff delicately suggested that she might want to receive his news privately. She opened a door and led him into the barbershop. All the green shades had been fully drawn for the close of business.

He told her she had better sit down. She sat down in the barber's chair, leaned back, spread her legs, heaved up her chest to brace herself for the news. Goff told her. She began to weep and moan, and told Goff through her tears to lower the lever to flatten the chair some. "Lieutenant," she sniffled, "bear with me for just a little while." She was true to her word, and when she had sucked in a final sniff she tore off one of the tissues on which the barber slaps down the used lather, and wiped her eyes and blew her nose. Goff, all the while, stood at respectful attention.

She rose and told him she was truly grateful to him, and then softly insisted on giving him a shave. "It'll calm me, and allow me to show in a small way my appreciation for your gentility, Leiutenant." Goff automatically felt his chin and acquiesced, and lay down on the barber chair.

And while the hot towel covered his face, he felt her unzipping his pants—and putting her razor aside, she blew him. When she finished she utilized once again the little square tissues for used lather.

Of course he stopped using the post barber after that, and became a steady customer there instead. What the hell kind of advantage taking was that? You don't have to be Jewish to take that kind of advantage.

And just the other day, when C.P.A., his accountant, died of that sudden heart attack, the major reason for his being here now—didn't he show proper restraint, when that Cookie cunt, a fresh widow, had pressed it into him in her uncontrollable grief—and her uncontrollable churning it right into his tired balls? That fat cunt, disgracefully allowing herself to put on all that weight. The nerve of her, manipulating her grief so clumsily and transparently to get him aroused so he would screw her. He knew her game. How she would gush tears afterward, wailing that she didn't know what came over her, but that the emotional strain must have done something, and that the reason she felt so terrible was that Chaim would have been *sure* to forgive her. He was so good and clean. A *malach*. He would have understood and even urged it. Oh, how she hadn't deserved him!

Crap, it would have been so easy, but he had respect for Chuck. He would just simply not allow himself to get aroused. Christ, he'd already had her—and slightly more than once. But that was before she had married C.P.A. and before she had gone to fat.

She had always been such a pain in the ass in that Jewish way. Whenever he had banged her, he had to submit to a torrent of Yiddish *bubelehs* and *zeeskeits* and *shtup mir, mehr,* harder, *mehr! Oi* it's *azoi git.* It was plain disgusting. And all right—there *was* one more time—but a real quickie—once during C.P.A.'s heavy tax season. But after that, never! She had already started to pile on the flesh, and she had got to the point where hardly an English word passed her lips anymore.

Who was he to stop them if they always threw it in his face? But with Cookie Addelson, he was clean, absolutely clean. Where did Mrs. Doctor Levine come off accusing him of that hoisting her weeds stuff?

And Mrs. Levine, the twisted darling bitch, would do the same. Her ranting was her guilt showing. Goff pictured her on the lonely Montauk dunes. Who was he to stop her if she suddenly turned to him and pressed her soft cashmere-covered tits into him.

Mrs. Levine would never resort to that cheap, greasy, pussy-grinding into him. Just a clean-cut, hard, refined press of snatch, nicely tweed-covered, and maybe one sensibly loafer-footed leg bent back gracefully as they kiss on the deserted dunes silhouetted amid the high, wild beach grass against an early spring sky, and the white-capped ocean and the wind in her hairs—and the spray too.

And he'd say to her, as they stood there in clean, honest embrace, "You may call me John or Jim or Tom if you want. I know how you must long to say these words. I don't mind, although I am Basque." And she would snuggle against him and nod softly in trustful appreciation. And she would murmur in response that he could call her Pat or Kathy, and he'd say that Priscilla was perfectly fine.

And since he was only five foot six, with his foot he would carefully and unobtrusively work out a hole in the sand and nudge her into it, so that in embrace, he could be taller than she for a more heroic tableau out there on the long, lone dunes of Montauk.

But Priscilla Plimpton Levine would have none of it. She opened the desk drawer and reached for a pill container and tapped out a green and black Librium capsule and held it displayed between two fingers. She looked at him with now weary scathe. "You would stoop to anything to debauch me," she said woodenly. Her ass lines melting, unable any longer to contain the fine sharp crags.

Goff lowered his eyes. She had some justice. The poor thing—already in need of another tranquilizer. Lookie, for her he would paint his dong from the roots up to midpoint, green, from midpoint to tip, black. He would offer her then the king of tranquilizers. Lookie, I have the mightiest Librium of them all. Take it. It will cure you. One massive dose. I give it to you in true friendship. I wish to be a true, good friend, and I wish you to be my good, true friend. It's sure to bring back your wonderful crags.

She swallowed the pill in her hand and rose at her desk. In a friendly tone she requested him to get up from his knees. Dr. Levine was waiting. He might now want to take a shower to prepare himself for his final examination.

When Goff looked up from the magazine, he heard the smiling Miss Seymour calling his name. "Mr. Goff. Doctor will see you now." He scowled as he rose and followed her to Doctor's consultation room. "It's not your fault," he grumbled, "but frankly, I'm amazed that the colored woman was taken before me."

"Oh, I'm sorry, Mr. Goff. I hope it didn't inconvenience you, but Doctor asked that she be sent in first. Seems that she had to get to her job. Didn't the other girl tell you?"

"She did not. But I sort of figured it out. I'm not mad at you, Miss Seymour." He decided to smile at her as she opened the door of the Doctor's consultation room. As she stood aside to let him enter, he made sure to bunk his arm against her chest. As she closed the door to return to the corridor, he managed to tell her that he would be calling her tomorrow to get the results of his blood test.

The consultation room labored to achieve good taste. It contained an overlarge glass-topped desk. Oak-paneled walls honeycombed by lots of bookshelves laden with the appropriately heavy medical tomes. Subdued lighting and a few deep leather chairs facing Doctor's desk. Dark carpeting on the floor matching the dark draperies on the windows. A shrewdly high-class touch was the omission of the usual diplomas, certificates, pedigrees and citations that less secure medical men hung conspicuously on their walls to bolster the confidence of nervous patients. Rather than the brittle, pragmatic atmosphere of a doctor's office, the room strove to attain the well-rubbed depth of a gentleman's study.

Goff noticed some half-dozen hand-carved wooden figurines on one of the bookshelves. About three and a half inches tall, they were German carvings of German doctors, cleverly detailed. At the base of each of the wooden statuettes was carved out in German the title of the doctor's specialty. There was the skin *arzt*, the tooth *arzt*, the woman *arzt*, the nerve *arzt* and others. Each one was a unique individual, with painstaking detail having gone into the facial expressions, the instruments, the big bellies, the various postures of comic pompousness. Ach, what droll, exacting care went into these handmade creations! Ach—zo cute! Ach, but Goff's ass they burned. Goff knew why they were there. The precious, droll wooden German doctors were there to demonstrate that Dr. Levine didn't take himself all that seriously. Oh, but that pissed him off. Who the hell was Levine not to take himself seriously? The conceit of the smug bastard! Telling everyone with those German statues, "Seriously, all that seriously I don't take myself. You see? I am though in earnest. Clever, aren't they?" When had that prick earned the right not to take himself seriously? Not at my expense is he going to not take himself seriously! Goff wasn't going to fall for Levine's double whammy.

In the Schwarzwald the jolly woodcutter, quietly yodeling while he worked, with loving care carved out the happy little wooden doctors and then sold them to flesh doctors in New York, and it vas a good feeling because the woodcutter knew his liddle statjews were given a goot home and they vuz really loved dere.

Shit, a Volkswagen is different. Goff, a one-time owner, defensively forced the thought. It's made out of heavy steel machines, not intimate, ass-wiping hands.

Goff's eyes then lit on a good-sized photograph on the doctor's desk, and his mopey disgruntlement sniffed off into a tidy sneer. It was a family grouping. In it Dr. Levine was beardless, but droopily mustachioed and smiling. Mrs. Levine stood alongside. Before them stood their three Levantine-featured children, one of which was a boy in his Bar Mitzvah regalia—shawl, suit and Bible. The smiles told the story. Levine in mustachioed bliss seemed to be saying: Behold me and mine. Pray, let all men flourish like me. I have been righteous in the eyes of the Lord and the Lord's blessings are upon me. I do not covet the miraculous blondness of my swarthy cousin Sheldon's children. The Lord has granted me this fair beauty from a distant land and has shown her the pathways unto Him together with Abraham Levine, M.D., in sanctified union. And now in New Canaan we have a beautiful home smiled down upon by Him, in addition to an apartment in the East Seventies, that He doesn't frown on either, thank God.

And Mrs. Levine. The patrician smile plays on her face. She has her hands on the Bar Mitzvah boy's shoulders. Her eyes say: he is a good earnest lad, her Seth James. His brooding has to do with her. She will smile publicly and even privately sometimes. No one will be permitted a glimpse of her private torment. No one, but Goff, the shrewd, lewd Jude. He sees all the Librium capsules that have fortified the smile. He sees the stubborn streak that shall never permit her to admit it was a mistake. He sees her parents who have never fully reconciled themselves to Abraham Levine. Never fully reconciled themselves, my ass. They hate Levine's guts—and he just shrugs.

Goff had reached the conclusion that Levine had sold out. Where had Levine first seen her? Most probably as a young nurse at Mount Sinai. And where the majority of hot-nutted, Jewish interns and residents chased robust shiksa nurses for honest screwin', adultery and general fuckin' around, Levine would function with unction. He acted within the cowardly, protected precincts of legitimacy. For Levine would never serenade with the savory lines of false exhortation of lyrical truth inspired by the hot pursuit of seduction, but rather intone the ponderous, slovenly

falseness of the truth of bloodless courtship. None of the poetic truth—
the sweet forgivable cunning of a red-blooded line of roses and wine—of
everything's fine. Nay, Levine felt compelled to his furtive truth, which
in truth was a boring lie.

This was Levine's lie: to keep his faith, he rejected the faithful. In Levine's scheme he would lose nothing, gain all. He would never have to
leave the comforting hearth and ark, and if in the bargain he could also
share it with someone desirable, instead of those he had come to disdain,
albeit gently, even affectionately—ah, wouldn't it be a cause for celebra-
tion and jubilation? If Levine could arrange for a fair, blue-eyed benedic-
tress, haloed in soft Sabbath light and lace to light his candelabra,
wouldn't that be heavenly? Baby, light my candelabra. Hot dog! To win
the game and stay the same—a one-in-a-million accomplishment.

Retain the comforting, traditional Sabbath table—always snowy white
linen, never soiled by spillings of red horseradish or greasy drippings.
"Try this stuffed fish, Roger. I think you'll enjoy it. This is the *gefilte* fish
you've heard about. It's ground or chopped, a mixture usually of whitefish and pike. Priscilla cooked it. My mother marvels at her and admits it's
more tasty than hers. Oh, you must try it with this red horseradish. It's
the red beets ground in that does it. We call it *chrain*. Priss can never
quite learn to pronounce it. Well, pretty damn good, huh, Roger? And
now the matzoh balls. . . ."

"Damn good is right, Abe. Priss, you're great. It's actually fantastic.
Y'know, actually, some of my best foods are Jewish."

Levine was such a good wholesome boy—and bright! Listen: Class
valedictorian; editor of the *Silver Trumpet;* assistant to the rabbi; leader
of the junior congregation—conducted services by himself; got a hundred
percent in five Regents exams; Dean's list all four years at Cornell; a major in the Army—could have been a colonel but turned down the promo-
tion so he could start his civilian practice; arranged for a small kosher
kitchen at the base hospital. Everybody loved him—he was so good—if
the *shvartzeh* ate tuna fish, he just wouldn't touch his lamb chops, he
also had to have tuna fish, and he had to eat it with her—and he would
make her share his chocolate milk that he made himself.

Levine thought: It is no use denying that I may be amused and sometimes intrigued by the Jewish girls whom I have known in Brooklyn,
Bronx, West End Avenue, Boston, Philadelphia, Chicago and even Dal-
las, Savannah and Phoenix. But the truth is they lack a certain quality.
They are often too gross, too materialistic. Often too coarse, too aggressive, too demanding, assertive. They are often too pretentious, too de-

signing, conspicuous, downright exhibitionistic. They are often too ugly, ungainly, insensitive. Their laughter too raucous. They are too often spoiled, artificial. They are either not their mothers or else too much their mothers. And they *do* say they are not ideally responsive in bed. Alas, Jewish girls there are aplenty, but there are no longer to be found any Jewesses. The rare Jewess nowadays marries an elite goy and merges into upper-class indistinguishability.

What to do? What to do? I will *not* end up with Sandra, Beverly, Sheila, Florence, Helen, Norma, Mitzi, Pauline, Evelyn, Laura, Muriel, Dorothy. Let Mel, Artie, Murray, Sherman, Sy, Hy, Leon, Howie, Sid, Jerry, Milt, Harold end up with them.

If I cannot find me a Jewess, then with God's help, I shall fashion one. And she will be tall, lithe and, God willing, blond, the tresses down to her milk-white bottom, and she will carry herself with grace, and her speech will be well modulated. And her benedictions will be soft and reverent, with lingering and lace. At the lighting of the Sabbath candles how soft and fair and spiritual will be her effulgence. A Princess Grace or a Jacqueline Bouvier of a Jewess. Hot dog!

Levine's mother says: Oh, my daughter-in-law, the Jewess? What a doll! What a treasure! God has blessed us in fullest measure. And she knows! Everything about the religion she knows. Her matzoh balls are unsurpassed. We are constantly amazed. A shiksa? All our sons should have such shiksas. All mothers should have such shiksas for daughters-in-law. And you should see the children. Like . . . like . . . regular Vikings, she lied (unconsciously). You know what I mean? Gorgeous, simply gorgeous! God bless them. *Kine-ahora.*

So, Levine beat the game. He pleased his mother, his father, God and himself. But to Goff it was a sellout. No honest, clean-cut mess like an honest fool gets into by marrying a shiksa, unconverted, and drifting off unsure, a little guilty and furtive and defensive. Not Levine. Organize it and legitimize it in fact and spirit. Proudly hold her out—look, the shiksa goddess converted to my Sabbath queen. Oh, Sylvia, what a nice surprise seeing you at services. And these must be your children. How's Milt. Milt—right? He's a converter—textile? Right? Of course, I remember. I'd like you to meet Priscilla. She'll be along shortly. She's chatting with the rabbi about the plans for setting up the Succoth in back of the temple. Yes, the blonde, that's her. She used to be much blonder.

LEVINE! UP AGAINST THE WAILING WALL, SHIKSA FUCKER! YOU'RE UP ON CHARGES!

# Chapter 5

*Goff puts Dr. Levine on trial*

In one of the basement Hebrew classrooms of Goff's synagogue-plant is assembled the *minyan* that will hear the charges against Levine. The room, even in its best days never much above steerage-class level, still maintains itself in its original peeling decrepitude. Cracked walls match cracked blackboard, match scattered splintered desks and chairs, match limp, frayed prayer books, match sagging cartons overflowing with stuffed, crumpled, stained prayer shawls and yarmulkes, match the present seedy occupants, the members of the minyan. This room is the essence of the Hebrew school, whence tumbled forth in resentful, methodical bewilderment thousands—millions—of slap-dashed, half-assed Hebrafied Bar Mitzvah buchers, but who at least had learned to mouth their prayers with the "s" sound of sweat and sorrow intact, unlike the current candidates, who have been airlifted to suburban, half-glassed Hebrew school classrooms full of sunlight and lollipop colors, and been turned away from that earthy Ashkenazi "s" to its displacement by the titless sephardic "t" of tut-tut and tone poem. But once exposed, even to the most bumbling, most frayed, most indigestion-wracked teachers and *melameds*, not even the most scornful scoffer can ever completely shed himself of its tacky traces. Amen.

The minyan consists of Goff, the leader, seated at the teacher's desk, and twelve Jews previously mentioned sprawled in indolent and haphazard fashion at the scattered students' desks. The twelve are Mel, Artie,

145

Murray, Sherman, Sy, Hy, Leon, Sid, Howie, Marv, Milt and Harold. Levine, in bewilderment, stands at Goff's desk.

Goff: "I have been designated as grand inquisitor of this duly constituted minyan. The charge against you is 'selling out.'"

Levine: "Selling out? Selling out what? What kind of a vague and ambiguous charge is that? Come, gentlemen. This is ridiculous. A charge has to be specific. There's no such charge as 'selling out.' There's treason, conspiracy, adultery, sodomy and dozens of other mis- and malfeasances—there's malpractice. But no 'selling out.' There are moral and ethical charges. There are ecclesiastical charges. Pray tell, gentlemen, selling what out?"

Goff: "You sold all of us out. You better sit down, Levine."

Levine sits down.

Leon: "'Selling out' is the right charge. You went against your kind—that's selling out."

Levine: "What kind? What going against?"

Harold: "You went against us Jewish guys in a sneaky way. You tried to beat the rap by trickery and sharp practice."

Hy: "It was a slap in our faces."

Levine: "What are you fellows talking about?"

Goff: "Look, Levine. A Jew is either a Jew or he's not a Jew. In either case he suffers."

Levine: "You're talking in riddles."

Howie: "No, he's not. I know what he means. He means a Jew either holds himself out as a Jew or to varying degrees he doesn't. To the degree that he removes himself may warrant labeling him un-Jew. Non-Jew would be inappropriate, and 'not a Jew' may be ambiguous. Arnie, would you say 'un-Jew' captures the meaning?"

Goff: "Yeah. I accept that. Are you suffering, Levine?"

Levine: "Present occasion excepted, no, I'm not, Goff."

Goff: "Do you at least brood?"

Levine: "No. Why should I?"

Goff: "Well, that's what it looked like. What kind of Jew, including un-Jews and all the rest, doesn't suffer unless he's really made a pact with the devil? Leon and Harold, faithful observers, married good Jewish girls, keep strict kosher homes—they suffer. Artie and Sherman, not such wonderful observers, they suffer. Milt and Mel married shiksas, never go near a synagogue—they suffer. And you know Howie and about his marriage? You don't ask 'How's Howie?'"

Levine: "Of course I do. Hi ya, Howie. How's everything?"

Howie acknowledges with impassive nod.

Goff: "Well, Howie, whether he's got guts or he's plain nuts, married interracial, and he'll never admit it, but he suffers."

Levine: "It's really the children that suffer."

Goff: "Even me. I've achieved everything, and I'm a *cockamamy* Basque-type un-Jew, and I suffer. I want to ask you a question, Milt and Mel. You married shiksas, you're suffering and you don't really give a crap about Jews, right?"

Milt and Mel, both indifferent sufferers, nod.

Goff: "Milt and Mel, tell me do you feel contempt or condescension for Leon and Harold for their strict observance?"

Milt and Mel: "We don't give a crap."

Goff: "Leon and Harold, does it rankle or disturb you that Milt and Mel have drifted off and married shiksas and have become un-Jews, or don't you give a crap either?"

Leon and Harold: "We don't give a crap either."

Levine: "I object. Gentlemen, I object, not so much to this highly irregular interrogation, but we are in the House of the Lord, formed in a duly constituted minyan and I vigorously protest the use of uncalled-for vulgarity."

Goff: "You are right, in form."

Sid: "What are we beating around the bush for? I gotta get to work. The charges. The charges. I vote guilty. He was too proud to marry a good *haimisheh* girl. He built himself an idol to worship, the bastard, and said, that's no idol, that's my wife. Guilty, guilty."

Artie: "I'm with Sid. Guilty. That son of a bitch. You don't mix milk with meat. Guilty."

Howie: "I wish you'd explain that, Artie."

Artie: "I'll try. You remember the picture *The Graduate*. That schmuck, the hero, was screwin' the mother, Mrs. Robinson, when all of a sudden, he's just gotta have the daughter too. I maintain, once you got the mother, the daughter is strictly off limits; it's too fuckin' bad if the daughter turns out to be a tasty dish—you've had it, and you don't go cryin' after the daughter and making out it's a far, far nobler thing you do, fighting the establishment and all that shit. It's like incest. You don't mix milk with meat. Okay? And that schmuck was Jewish too! Did I explain it, Howie?"

Howie: "After a fashion. I incline toward guilty. What Levine was doing in effect, was passing."

Levine (incredulous, near-shriek): "Passing! Passing!' You mean assimilating?"

Howie: "You dig, man."

Levine: "Are you crazy? Why, except maybe for Leon and Harold, I have no earthly doubts that I exceed anyone here in my devotion to strict practices and observances of Judaism. I have never hidden it or under-played it, but have followed these practices with open pride and joy. I am no mere high holy day observer. Day in, day out, I lay *t'fillin*. I wear *tzitzi-ot*. My family and I are strict observers of the Sabbath. I observe all the tenets. In my community, among my colleagues, everywhere, this is well known. There is no hiding. There is proud proclaiming. And this is pass-ing?"

Sid: "You're way off on that one, Howie. Levine is like a regular rabbi in that respect."

Howie: "No, fellas, no, I'm not. Levine is passing, but with diabolical cleverness. He's passing with all the trappings of not passing. A beautiful camouflage. You see, it's much too tough—too many inner hangups and outer obstacles to buck when you try to portray the false or less than com-pletely revealed identity necessary for traditional passing. That's for suckers only. So Levine, who is Phi Beta Kappa material, thinks: what are the purposes and goals of passing? And he concludes, it's to establish yourself harmoniously and homogenously in your greater society, fully accepted, with liberty and harmony for all, including Levine. So Levine says to white, Gentile America: 'Look, I'm Jewish—plain and proud—nothing up my sleeves. I'm with you chaps. It's not just talk. Look, I'm God-fearing and an excellent citizen. And except for my Hebraic commit-ment, of which I am proud and don't deny, I am just like you fellows. I like what you like and I dislike what you dislike. I hold no brief for the atheistic, spuriously liberal, libertine Jew and faker, believe me. I do not take my God lightly. Yes, every Sabbath, you will know where to find me. I shall be found in my House of Worship. By the way, have you noticed my wife? How well modulated are her tones? How fair? And other fea-tures and refinements? And they'd respect me for all that.'

"And the white Gentile community answers, 'Levine, we're mighty proud to know you. You can consider yourself fully accepted, dammit. What we ask of you, we ask of everyone—just be a good American, dam-mit. This fellow makes no bones about being a Jew. You know for sure when he goes to his church and you know for sure when it's Fourth of July. He gets the flag out, dammit. I'm proud to know him. Good citizen. If only they were all like Levine, dammit! Ever notice his missus? She's a beautiful gal. His children are kinda funny-lookin' though. But Levine is A-OK in my book.'

"Well, brothers, do I begin to make sense about Levine's passing? His master detail was his marriage—and that sweet conversion. That extra point won him the game."

Sherman: "You've sold me, Howie. He didn't have to marry the shiksa. He rejected his own kind."

Levine: "I loved my wife."

Artie: "A man can psyche himself to love anyone he chooses. It's an insult to all us guys that chose to love Jewish girls."

Levine: "But she *is* Jewish."

Marv: "Jewish, my ass. Kosher, I'll grant you—but not Jewish. Kosher and fit for consumption, but I don't swallow it, Levine."

Sid: "He's what you'd call a house Jew, huh, Howie? He signed away his basic right—to be obnoxious when he feels like."

Goff: "OK, fellas. The sentiment is pretty clear. The charges hold up."

Levine: "What are you going to do?"

Goff: "Nothing. The charges hold up. That's all. The minyan is dismissed."

Leon: "Wait a minute, Arnie. Don't everybody start rushing out. I want to say a *Kiddush* for my father."

Harold: "Schmuck, it's not *Kiddush*, it's *Kaddish*. Kiddush is for drinking wine. I'll stay."

Goff: "Hold it, everybody. We have to respect Leon's request for his pop who passed away. We only need ten men for the minyan. We've got fourteen. Four of you can leave, if you have to." Goff looks at Howie, the interracialer, Melt and Mel, the shiksa marriers and Levine. No one goes.

Goff: "OK, good. I don't know how to conduct this thing. Does anybody here know how to do it right?"

There's a lot of shrugging. Nobody knows. Finally Levine sighs and stands up.

Levine: "I am familiar with this service. I'll do it."

Levine walks up to the teacher's desk as Goff moves off to join the others.

Artie: "No disrespect, Levine, but just one question before you begin, a hypothetical one: if two guys were drowning, one a God-fearing goy and the other an atheistic Jew, and you could save only one, who would you save?"

Levine (with martyred resignation): "I would save the Jew. The other one is already saved."

Harold: "Wrong reason—right guy."

Levine: "Gentlemen, please let us begin the services. Those who have no yarmulkes, please get one from the carton here. No *talaysim* will be necessary." About half the men go to get the skull caps. "Now you will find *Siddurs*." Levine expertly riffles to the page he wants. "Open to page one oh two. Rise, and starting at the top of the page, read with me."

The men all rise and Levine starts to read the Hebrew in full resonance. All the men start to read following Levine—some expertly, some haltingly, some barely moving their lips, emulating the sounds a fraction of a second after hearing, but all respond and read.

Artie (whispering to Goff): "Arnie, doesn't this make you *kvell* with pride? It's like something out of live television with tasteful commercials."

Goff nods, glowing. The door bursts open and Malcolm Feiler, Goff's bustling, hyperefficient shipping clerk, enters, followed by a crew of Puerto Rican workers carrying cartons.

Feiler (loud): "Arnie, we just got a shipment of five hundred cartons. This is the only room with enough space to pile them. It's the copper oxide for the final solution."

Goff (testily): "Okay, okay, but work around us."

# Chapter 6

*Dr. Levine completes Goff's examination*

Dr. Levine glided into his office wafted on his own air of "Tea for Two," his constant self-accompaniment. As he slid behind his desk into his seat, he favored Goff with a fast shuttered flick of a smile. He had set focus at infinity. And so, having completely assured his insulation within the self-created, floating bubble of his hum and dum, he was completely oblivious to the rays of distaste which emanated from a sour, disgruntled Goff.

Dr. Levine examined several documents, ran the yards of Goff's cardiograph scroll through his fingers and nodded and hummed and jotted. He finished, placed his pen down, placed his hands together to form a prayer tent, looked out at Goff through his bubble and continued to hum for several more seconds. He then clapped his hands, opened up a small porthole in the bubble, leaned back in his chair and said, "Mmm." This finally signaled the end of his "Tea for Two" and his readiness for interplanetary communication. The distant bearded star twinkled out a dim smile at earthling Goff. He was ready to communicate his findings.

"Mr. Goff ," said Dr. Levine, "I'm not unhappy to say that I find nothing to indicate poor health. Your cardiogram shows no weak areas; your blood pressure is not abnormal, your X ray is devoid of anything that should concern us, your urine fails to show up any positives." (Goff couldn't remember having donated a urine specimen.) "Everything is fa-

151

vorably negative. Your weight, though, is a little high. I'm surprised to
see it at 170. I would have taken you for about fifteen pounds less." Goff
realized that the sweet Miss Seymour with her goyisheh kop had goofed
in her subtraction. But he would accept that failing any day in preference
to the inevitably correct arithmetic of Mildred, the bookkeeper type. "So,
I'd not hesitate to say, it would not be unwise to lose ten pounds or so."

"I don't think I'll have any trouble in losing *those* ten pounds very
quickly," said Goff. "I have some questions, Doctor."

"By all means," said Levine, and leaned farther back to demonstrate
his accessibility. He would keep his small porthole opened as long as his
patient wished, unlike other practitioners who might open them briefly
with impatience and then curtly slam them shut, or others who would never even open their bubbles at all.

Goff asked, "Do you consider me in good health?"

"As I said, Mr. Goff, I find nothing to indicate anything but good
health." Levine smiled, inviting further questions.

Goff finally realized he would never get a straight answer from Levine.
He decided on a different approach. "I have a special question. I believe
it was your Miss Seymour who gave me my cardiogram. She's a very
pretty girl and I think I was excited too much. Might this distort the true
picture on the cardiogram?"

Levine smiled broadly. "Mr. Goff, I cannot disagree with you about
Miss Seymour. She is a far from plain girl. The reaction you had, I have
no doubt, is not an uncommon one, or abnormal, and I'm not unhappy to
say that neither was your cardiogram abnormal. It would not be unlike a
temperature that is not abnormal. In a man devoid of infection, his temperature will not be far off the norm of 98.6, regardless of outside environment and influences."

My God, thought Goff, can't that noncunt talk in anything but nega-
tives. Goff dimly perceived that the whole doctor business was built on
the inverted foundation and protection of the negative. In medical par-
lance negative is good, positive is bad; or—negative is not so bad, positive
is not so good. It occurred to Goff how Levine got that Plymouth Rock
wife of his. He could never have swept her off her feet. He had had to
sweep her under the rug. And when the rabbi said, ". . . so let them now
speak or forever hold their peace," when no one spoke, they were married. Two became an odd one.

Desperate now to get out, Goff said, "Thank you, Dr. Levine."

"You are not unwelcome," smiled Levine, his hand already on his

small porthole. As Goff started moving to the door, Levine smiled for the
last time, firmly shut the small porthole and resumed his "Tea for Two."

Goff nodded. Thank God, he was healthy. Thank God, he had his Dr.
Kummerlos to fall back on. Yes, even though he could see through him
now, he was still the real doctor, the real mender.

# Chapter 7

*Goff recalls the Battle of Yorkville, his triumph and
Leon Finger's defeat*

When Goff left·Levine's office, he sprang up the three steps of the
sunken vestibule, not only to quit the place as quickly as possible, but
also to forcefully confirm his well-being. He stepped into the street, just
around the corner from Fifth Avenue, a stone's throw from Central Park.
With relief and then exhilaration, he took in several deep breaths of the
stiff breeze that always seemed to rush up the East Seventies from the
Park. His examination, although performed by a well-trained schmuck,
was the extra percentage edge to confirm what he already knew. He was
in top shape. It would have been foolish not to check out the checkable.
Goff was fast but not impulsive. And it had paid off. He had applied this
principle to all phases of his life, except for that one fatal time he had
allowed himself to marry Gloria without checking out her overdue period.
But even that gaffe was now like a lump in the smooth rich mixture of batter—steadily dissolving in the constant churning, as newer and richer ingredients poured in. Everything was converging so beautifully and right.
Batter up! Goff was now at the crest of his finest hour.

When he looked back at his accomplishments, his amazement invariably turned to giddy, guilty satisfaction, which he hoarded in deepest inner secrecy, like a monk on a rainy day with pornography stashed in his
cell.

From his schlep-father's accident to cool millionaire. To savoir faire
and up-to-date awareness. To new wisdom and sensibly selected sen-

155

sitivities. To art. To with-it. And tonight—above all—undoubtedly the ultimate. To hold out his hand and liltingly minuet into his bed the bluest,
blondest, most gorgeous creature he had ever seen and fuck there her ass
off to exaltation. The magic flying fuck to the moon was within his grasp.

What a delectable and daring move, cuckolding Kummerlos! What a
crowning triumph! But could Kummerlos appreciate that he didn't really
wish to hurt him with this hurt? That as he sneered, he also revered. And
wasn't that a normal filial feeling? Kummerlos ought to know *that*!

Daddy Doctor, grant me this wish. I shall positively ask for no more if
you just grant me this last, oh great wish Doctor! This will at last fulfill
me. Allow me this ultimate in Creative Selfishness.

How would Kummerlos take it? Goff had to admit he was handing the
doctor a big conundrum. On the horns of a cuckold's dilemma, what
might he do? Christ, this might turn out to be a bigger test for Kummerlos
than for him.

Goff felt that in the end the doctor's professionalism would prevail over
his provincialism. He would subordinate his personal defeat to his smash-
ing professional triumph. How perfectly obvious, the shattering enormity
of the psychological break-through! Goff, a certified accident of lifelong
standing, a questionman of small stature, bearing crushing psychological
burdens, is miraculously brought by the Great Physician to the point
where with one last mighty tremor, as he consummates violent possession
of his father confessor's wife, he heaves off the last vestiges of his crip-
pling burdens. This was of energy-of-the-sun proportions. This was
Prometheus, psychologically unbound. And that she was a breathtakingly
beautiful shiksa? Hardly incidental or without deep significance. An Au-
gean stable of psycho-muck cleansed clear in one epic gush of *shpritz*.

Dr. Kummerlos, like any father, would be sure to be understanding in
the end. He would even be more than that. He would be demonstrative.
He would finally rush up from behind his desk, clap him on the back, and
enthusiastically acknowledge Goff's boldest of trespasses as the culminating phase of his greatest medical triumph. This was his likeliest response. He was, after all, first and foremost a healer. Would he then,
however, consider the case closed and finally discharge him? Goff wasn't
sure he liked this idea. Invulnerability wasn't built the way it used to be in
the old days. There was a shoddy fragility about it nowadays. There was
always something coming up to scratch, dent or penetrate, and he would
surely continue to need his handy physician.

But if by some remote chance Kummerlos decided to be small about it,
if he decided to be offended, to stand on ceremony and take it too person-

ally—then fuck 'm! Thanks to Kummerlos, Goff could now fend for himself—he could thrive and survive without his mender physician. But he
would still give credit where credit was due. Kummerlos had earned it.
Whichever way it went, Goff couldn't lose.

Nineteen years ago when he had first started his therapy, he had been a
shaken man—anxiety-filled, hypertensioned, a nervous vessel filled with
that whole range of ever-sapping mental secretions that collect in a man
and seep through to debilitate and wear him away. He had offered himself
to Charles Atlas Kummerlos as the puny, sunken-chested, ball-less vege-
table in ill-fitting sagging trunks, with forlorn eyes desperately imploring:
change me from a Before to an After! Make me into an After-*mench*, with
well-hung bulges bursting from tight hugging trucks, and all the rest of me
brimming with the psychological muscle necessary to carry and support
that ultimate weapon in its rolling, ball-bearing caisson. So in this logical
way the treatment had begun.

"In the Army, I guess I had inflated false balls. Balls falsies. When I
was discharged, they collapsed, and I realized it was all done with hot air
and mirrors. I guess the Army charges a man's balls up with hot air."

Kummerlos had him working out with Freudian exercises three times a
week. He became good at balancing the ambivalences, softly pedaling the
Oedipal. He got to know and understand the use of all the equipment. It
had cleared up a lot of things. He could understand the acrobatics of his
hardon for his doctor's wife. He was father-fucker motherfucker. Am-
bivalance times four—balance it behind your back—and then juggle it.
Now take a deep breath and sublimate—now exhalate—now sublimate.
Down, up. Down, up. In, out, in, out.

So after all these years of soul-rending preparation, after surmounting
so many incredible obstacles, after so many agonizing false starts, he was
now purified, purged and tempered. Galahad Goff was ready to possess
his Christina grail, but all that sexy stuff would have to wait for tonight.
Oh, what an elemental basic-rock, hardon of hardons he had for Christine. But none of that for now. He had to get to the plant.

The plant, once a pulsing synagogue of piercing rams' horn cries; of
uninhibited worshipers crowded together, swaying in unison, and also not
in unison, in ecstatic oblivion to one another's overpowering, bad breath.
Now it was Goff's "plant," no longer in the teeming Jewish ghetto, but in
the cha-cha-cha jangle-jungle of bongo drums and streety babble.

For Goff, going through the streets on a warm early evening was like passing through a never-ending ghetto carnival of chattering monkeys all equipped with bongo drums. Everything moved in high-strung bongo beat animation whether singing, darting or quarreling. Tired old shops with dingy looks and impoverished, near-bare sagging shelves lined the street. Each one seemed to be a grocery store, called *Bodega;* only *Bodegas*—no other type of store appeared on the block. Was there no need for anything but food? And what food! It looked as if all they ever carried for sale were bunches of what looked like green overgrown bananas and six-packs of beer, and nothing else.

Informal groups in their undershirts gather around a record player joining the already loud music with louder bongos, guitars and impassioned vocal accompaniment. Frequently, one will impulsively step away from the group and uninhibitedly break into a scorching dramatic aria as an undershirted street soloist. Goff is constantly struck by their undershirts. They are invariably sharply white and clean. Maybe even cleaner than his. Nah, it's an optical illusion. It's the contrast.

All the men hold cans of beer which are immediately tossed clinking into the street on consumption. Kids are skittering all over the street propelled by zigzag waves of high-pitched jabber. Many of them are throwing baseballs. Grown-up men, many fat and thick, intermittently jump up from the stoops or milk crates and join in the ball tossing for short sprint dashes. With uncanny vigor and elasticity, they toss the ball around with fast, scissors-clicking sharpness. Completing their quick turn, they flash broad grins as signs of satisfaction with themselves and hustle back to melt into their stoops and groups.

Goff was amazed at how they could get up all that energy on just beer and bananas.

This was where Goff had shrewdly chosen to locate his plant. His original plant was an oversized former Jewish fish market. He had chosen the lower East Side because of the cheap rent and the availability of cheap spic labor, and the former fish market because he needed the old abandoned zinc fish tanks for the manufacture of his electronic components. It involved a plating process that required tanks.

In the early days before he had got rid of his partner, he had been visited by his boyhood friend, Leon Finger, who had become (Goff maintained he wasn't surprised) a forest ranger, a genuine, permanent employee of the United States National Park Service. When he had been drafted, he was assigned to one of the last real horse cavalry units in the Army, in Colorado. He had taken to horses and the outdoors, and after discharge and a few months of trying to work with his Trotskyite father, a small-potatoes capitalist proprietor of a constantly near-bankrupt luncheonette in the garment district, Leon threw in his hand and got back on his horse and moseyed out of Seventh Avenue back to the West as a U.S. forest ranger. One thing Goff had to give him was that he didn't burden you much by overplaying his Wild West role. On his periodic visits to New York, a former member (as was Goff) of the Church Avenue Shamuses Social and Athletic Club, he tried to be one of the boys. He would get various assignments which actually could take him to any part of the country even including Manhattan. He always sought Goff out when in New York. Goff found it more nuisance than pleasure. Actually, what did he have in common with a forest ranger?

At his visit in those early days, Goff had resented Leon's heavy-handed derision of the term "plant." "So this is the plant. I guess 'plant' is the right description. It's certainly not the Botannical Gardens." He laughed that stiff dumb horselaugh he always had ready—had even before he joined the last horse calvalry troop in the U.S. Army. "Say, Arne," he continued, not letting a good thing go, "from the smell of it, maybe a better thing to call it is the aquarium. Maybe in the tanks is still swimming a nice fat live carp, I could bring home to Mama, hah, hah." Goff could have sworn Leon deliberately avoided making his mocky accent perfect. Leon continued, "I gotta hand it to you, Arne, you must have got your plant dirt cheap. And it sure looks like you got your money's worth—with all that dirt, I mean, hah, hah, hah. Hey," he said, picking up some old fish scales, "is this what you pay your spic help, scale wages?" He was convulsing himself with his laughter.

Goff could usually handle most situations with a sharp, controlled, sarcastic thrust, especially with his clod pal Leon Fickle Finger, but in that instance, he couldn't bring it off and he flew into a rage, almost stammering with fury, "If you don't like it here, get the hell out. I didn't ask you to come here. You barged in unwanted" (and Goff finally thought of the crack—still in time to get it in) "like you've been doing since the second time I ever saw you."

Leon laughed, a hearty appreciation of Goff's cleverness. There was only the slightest trace of quizzical searching in his broad grin that followed. Goff always had to remind himself that you just couldn't dump this guy. He was thoroughly uninsultable—stupid, thick-skinned bastard. How could this dumb hardon understand the anxieties, doubts and dangers—the back-breaking work that was involved in this business venture? Did this hyena-schmuck notice his hands, the rawness and stain from the acid he was constantly working with? Did he realize how important it was for him to succeed? Did he notice the lines of strain in his face from being at the plant fourteen to sixteen hours a day—and on top of that the constant aggravation he got from his fancy partner with his time-consuming life of more important things? Nah! What the hell did he know? With that stupid goyishe job he had. Low-grade security. His ass growing fat on a horse. No worries. A watchman for forest fires. Eat like a horse and live to be a hundred.

Leon stemmed from a father, a soft-on-capitalism Trotskyite who tried to straddle both worlds by running an honest-value luncheonette, serving good quality, keeping the prices low, paying living wages and treating the help like humans—an impossible arrangement—which finally killed Leon's constantly bewildered mother, who, with her unquestioned poodle devotion, always waddled along after Leon's pop at 5 A.M. to open the luncheonette, and came home fifteen hours later in bewildered exhaustion. So was Leon's pop enabled to maintain his socialistic ideals at the expense of the exploitation of his wife's labor. As both of them were always out breaking their hump, Leon was left almost entirely on his own. Goff strongly felt the resultant parental neglect of Leon must have somehow contributed to his total schmuckhood. The father weathered best and lived to turn from a defensive, sore-pressed Trotskyite to a fiery adamant, battling octogenarian Zionist. Leon resolutely maintained a state of contempt for his parents. Goff grudgingly conceded it was more healthy than the sulky, deep-seated contempt he, Goff, had for *his* parents. Leon displayed it so openly and, Goff suspected, with affection. When Goff had occasionally heard Leon tell off his pop to go take a good shit for himself, he suspected a portion of it was genuinely for his pop's constipational benefit. Goff didn't know how, but he was sure all these factors had played an important role in shaping Leon's incredible choice of nomadic lifework—a U.S. forest ranger. In this line of work, Goff wondered what kind of nookie he was apt to be getting. Did he screw indigenous timberland maidens on beds of pine needles or did he prey on macomberlike tourists or hunting party nymphos, sneaking into their tents when their husbands were on trail or stream. Did they know he was Jewish? Or maybe he was fucking sheep. The big bastard—he was six foot one, the dumb bastard. Goff always had resented his bragging that he hadn't been Bar-Mitzvahed thanks to Trotsky. Damn it. That was rubbing it in. Goff figured it gave him a slight edge with the blond campers in the West. Not being Bar-Mitzvahed also gave him an edge with the sheep. Goff figured he'd give his kids Bar Mitzvahs, but he wouldn't hold them to it. And then they could root for themselves. Leon, who had always fancied himself irresistible to blondes and Aryan types (to a man, it seemed, every former member of the Shamuses had preferred shiksas), had said of himself with his loud horselaugh that he was a "wandering dude" and was well equipped for his chosen work because he could sure take care of all the "wild life servicing out yonder."

One other thing about Leon; he was one of the few kids in the neighborhood that had taken German in high school, and he took it seriously. He actually enjoyed strutting the language and allowed it to shape his posture and facial expressions. He began to fancy himself as an aristocratic Junker officer type, and he would adopt stern, ramrod poses where he forced his mouth into a grim line and compressed his chin into tight-ranked military folds of flesh, and spoke deadpan gutteral, chopped-meat German, and only half kidding. He used to enjoy barking the expression *"Raus mit den Juden."* He blatantly bragged he would never end up with a fat Jewish mama type, which to Goff was understandable and okay, but he was too obnoxiously boastful about it with his superior six-foot-one assurance.

Any time he was in town, Goff could accurately predict he'd be running up to Yorkville to those beer-barrel polka joints on 86th Street trying to pick up a German housemaid or some Irish cunt. With his half-ass German and tucked-in chin, the Prussian aristocrat would order of the scum behind the bar to fetch *"Zwei Bier, Herr Ober, bitte."* He had urged Goff to go along with him one night in those early trying years.

Goff felt downright uncomfortable and even menaced on that street and in those dance halls with their heavy-assed roll-out-the-barrel *gemütlichkeit.* He felt completely alien to the men at the crowded bar making the rounds of tables trying to start a thing with the girls. For Goff there was an ominous assurance in their manner, as if they weren't pressing too hard, because it was certain that for them they would have their Ilse Kochs before the night was over, not like the little Jew bastard who would get his balls smashed if he overstepped. Most of them looked like guys who had been captured German prisoners of war in good, bending-backward-to-Geneva-Convention American camps in Arizona or Texas, and who regarded Americans contemptuously as fools because their treatment was altogether uncalled for; it was much too good and foolish. They looked as if they had made fast friends with the sympathetic guards and officers and had enjoyed together their common bund: detestation of Jews. Their arrogance to Goff was plain; and the girls looked like the kind who would have had themselves smuggled into these camps to have the privilege of giving themselves to these *Herrnvolk* losers. Many of the girls reminded him a lot of his Brünnhilde girlfriend in Columbus, Ohio, during the war, except she had way more class. This kind of thing at a public dance and especially in this goosey kraut atmosphere was not for him. If he were still in uniform as a lieutenant, he could better take it in stride. But it didn't faze his schmuck pal Leon, the baron.

Goff, very uneasy, had remained at the crowded bar while the baron made forays to tables to select braided-tressed maidens who would dance with him now and warm his bed later than night. He took his rejections with Teutonic dignity. He'd pick himself up with stiff and monocled expression and pompously clump away to another table. He looked cumbersome but untroubled in the turgid beer-hall atmosphere and never sensed what Goff sensed. Goff felt sure that if that oompah, pah, pah band ever struck up the Nazi Horst Wessel song, it would electrify the place and everyone would rise and sing it with fierce, murderous reverence. And with all probability his pal Leon would be right along with them with his half-ass German—the schmuck. Although he never denied he was Jewish, he proudly felt his looks and outlooks sufficiently transcended the general mucky Jewish type to permit him complete freedom of movement in all possible worlds. He strove for the role of nonsectarian citizen of the world, with always a slight leaning toward a German baron being. He would choose to be Jewish when he felt like being Jewish. And usually when he wanted to be, he assumed a broad mocking pose and speech to clearly establish that he was only temporarily putting it on. Goff couldn't understand his ability to be so insensitive to Jewishness and concluded it was mainly due to a general, low intelligence.

Goff was angry at himself because for one, he had allowed his schmuck pal, against his better judgment, to talk him into coming and further for allowing him to persuade him to remain. His instict was all against remaining in the beer hall. He felt as if the Allies, in overrunning and conquering Germany, had completely forgot about this place, which was still sovereign, hostile and deadly. But shrewdly, Leon had appealed to his cock. "Arnie, look, we're here already, and this place is loaded with ass. It's just a matter of time. I'll take care of making the connections, you just relax at the bar—what've you got to lose?"

The dumb prick didn't realize what he had to lose. To lose was the precious, fading remains of his torturously built-up confidence. He had already drawn on most of the reserve he had accumulated as a hotshot officer in the Army, and all the broads he had shacked up—all the wonderful types and varieties, all over the land. America was a vast wonderful country of pussy in all glorious regional varieties. And now here in this soggy untaken enemy pocket what if one of these Nazi-loving bitches, after scrutinizing him, and guessing right, made some crack? Who needed that! Who needed even a routine rejection from some nothing-bitch *mädchen* who, waiting for some Hans or Fritz or even Jimmy O'Neil, intuits that he isn't quite the genuine article. He didn't have his lieutenant uniform anymore to create the self-assured roles and illusions. At any sort of these public dances, he just couldn't fortify himself against the kind of rejection a guy can get. He had long ago learned he didn't perform well in this kind of situation, where he was vulnerable to a snotty turndown. He couldn't shrug it off and move imperviously on to the next cunt like dumb schmuck Leon. Arnie Goff could perform best in a controlled situation. He just needed a little structure to get a foothold and then dazzle them with his footwork. Dammit, he had it, if he wasn't flattened out before the gong even rang. Even blind dates had a certain ordered structure to work within. By the convention of it, he had a captive audience for a certain prescribed amount of time. And if she were a good-looking piece, he had the time and drive to make his points.

This whole setup, a Nazi lonely hearts club, was not for him. He conceded that his incredible horse's ass pal, Leon, with his nervy approach might fool a few of them who, for any particular reason, weren't too sharp in sizing up only genuine Jew-exterminating types. He saw two of those blond, beefy Klaus and Helmut types go up to a table with a kind of swaggering bumpkin courtliness. The two blond twats at the table who immediately identified the ex-Afrika Korp troops as willing Jew stompers turned up on them smiling, animated faces. In two minutes the four were as congenial and congealing as if it were ach, such a happy reunion of staff of good old Camp Dachau. Goff could guess the arch German dialogue when one of the bitches stood up. She would be saying with German toilet-trained coyness that she was going to the little girls' room. Ach, ja, they would all grin broadly. She would be momentarily peeing out a gallon of beer piss. She could probably do this three or four times a night and never entirely shed a deep-rooted lumpy sobriety. Her eyes would only begin to flicker with real excitement when she began to sense the promise of his Jew-killing zeal and dedication. And she would get shmoosey on beer and bloodlust. And she would work up a voracious appetite for her beer and bloodlust sausage. So the fires kindled, would they then proceed to fuckel and furgle one another to the beat of the oompah-pah band.

Goff observed them hooking arms with beer steins aloft to entwine in a coupled, drinking swastika. The swastika turned to Goff and smirked. It offered a toast: tonight the smite, tomorrow the welt. Tomorrow, however, the blond twatsies would be back at their jobs at the bank, punctiliously groomed and shined with faultless devotion to their columns and figures and calculating machines.

Goff saw the swastikas disentwine and the two storm troopers get up to move on. The girls bade them *auf Wiedersehen* with glistening eyes. Goff, with left-out bitterness, admitted to himself he wouldn't at all mind banging them, but he knew he couldn't qualify. They'd know him for a ringer. That Basque stuff wouldn't work either. And then he saw his putzy pal marching over to the table. Yes, he was actually marching. Leon halted, nodded his head with a snap to the two girls. He was absolutely all erect and *korrekt—alles in ordnung*—in beer-hall pickup style. But the shrewd, intuitive Fräuleins smelled a rat. In complete contrast to their simmering response to the storm troopers, their eyes clouded into quick blue ice in Teutonic precision. And quickly, as if to punctuate their attitude beyond any further doubts, the maidens, without a word, both popped up like two icicled exclamation points, paired up and stiffly polkaed off, to the middle of the crowded dense floor.

The band musicians, all with knockwurst bodies, were dressed in jolly Bavarian getups. The short *lederhosen,* the knee-high socks, shirts with frills and broad, bright-colored suspenders and the alpine hats mit the cute feder in it. And everybody clomped and stomped to the belly beat of the oompah, pah.

Leon took his rejection with stiff Junker stoicism. He clicked his heels at the deserted table, pivoted and marched away to engage another table.

Goff despondently observed this from the crowded, hostile-feeling bar. He thought about his Nazi darling in Columbus. Unforgettable. She could have held court here in the crowded, beer-sodden *Deutschland uber alles* stomp and romp beer hall. He was beginning to savor his reverie, when he became aware that Leon was waving him over to a table. He saw that Leon had finally got himself seated with two blondes. Goff picked up his beer and, cursing Leon, went for the table. He was pissed off. He shouldn't have been here. He could already see from the distance that by their posture the girl krauts weren't exactly welcoming Leon with open arms or open anything. Even their pores. Everything was shut tight and waterproofed. As Goff approached them he finally felt a good healthy nastiness surging up to challenge and diminish his menaced feeling about the place. Shit, he thought, I'm a grown lieutenant and these are the beaten enemy. It emboldened him even more when he got up to the table and he, a man who could recognize his enemies, suddenly concluded that the krauts weren't German; they were Polacks. He wondered whether they were trying to pass themselves off as Germans. Were they trying to achieve status as Germans as he tried to do as Basque-American? Do Poles strive to be Germans? Was that why they strive to be better Jew haters? Goff was convinced they do try harder. Why had they ended up second best? Because they were dumb Polacks? No. It was because they were romantics. They were the Baltic Irishmen. Very emotional. This prevented them achieving the dispassionate efficiency of the Germans.

The two girls did not have the preferred, lush golden tresses, but rather limp and lemony hanks. Leon was trying his stiff-lipped German on one of the girls. She had a long goosey neck upon which perched a corresponding goosey profile, bound to become more so with age. She had a wooden air of self-satisfaction about her—a dumb, cared-for look, as if she were being bred for her liver. You had to grant her, however, a certain prettiness. But it was the dated prettiness of styles long out of fashion, found in back-issue magazines. It was the trussed prettiness of an old Jeanette MacDonald with cupid bow lips. It occurred to Goff, that for a dummy like Leon, who now spent his life mounted on horses, it might just be his type. Goff figured her for a spiteful deadass, but who still might be brought to life by a dumb muscle-bound meat and potatoes bruiser who looked like his name was Mike. His pal Leon could have been that type if he didn't take himself so seriously and wasn't so stupid. Leon sat there talking to her, trying with effort to spark the fire with his damp German.

The other girl had watery, red eyes and a sniffly sourness of expression that bespoke a hapless pugnaciousness. An embittered loser who kept on punching. Goff was seized with the replusive notion that her twat matched her eyes, likewise red and watery. If her girlfriend was a goose, she was not quite a duck, but half-duck and half-Pomeranian pup, nasty and distempered. He figured if you could pet her, you could have her.

"Arnie, meet Tessie and Della." Della, Goff supposed, was to be "his." She was the short ducky one.

"Hiya," said Goff with ironic, nothing-to-lose expansiveness, as he pulled up a chair; he felt fed up and tired and simply wasn't going to be menaced by these two Polish Kunsczs.

Leon insisted on pressing his German onto the goose girl, who remained aloof, barely acknowledging his presence. What gave her the right to be aloof? She looked to Goff as if she had a trick where she could activate a nerve mechanism and cause a circle of sharp little teeth to snap shut in her snatch and claw and nibble away at unwary Jewish cocks foolhardy enough to venture in. Her followed response then, Goff further envisioned, would be an ugly guffaw. How else did Polacks react to the discomfiture of Jews?

"His" girl, the punch-drunk duck—eighty-five bouts, no victories—perked up, sniffing expectantly for yet another go at it. She tried to put her two pfennigs in. Goff changed it to zlotys. He didn't know German, but he knew all three of them spoke it lousy. They said they were Sudeten Germans. My ass. Polacks through and through. Oh, what the hell's the difference. It was getting so late.

"I'm a forest ranger from profession—in Oregon. Do you know where is Oregon?"

Tessie, the haughty goose, shrugged no indifferently. Della Duck quacked bitterly that she knew all about Oregon because her good-for-nothing brother-in-law had borrowed money from her to open up an ice-cream parlor in Portland, but it had gone kaput. Did Leon maybe know an Otto Skorzeni there? Better he didn't, the liar and swindler. He was now a milkman in California. When she and Tessie were working in Merkel's in Jamaica, she had met Otto and they were going out for a while and then he had deceived her and chased after her sister and married her. Della considered herself lucky that she hadn't ended up with that liar. Della turned to Goff. "You heard of Merkel's, ja? You didn't? Where you been?" she demanded, beginning to bristle. "You never heard of Merkel's frankfurter or bacon? Must be something wrong somewhere. It takes me two hours to go there, but I wouldn't work no place else. Everybody is German or Polack and I got seniority and they can't fire me. You must've heard of Merkel's. You must've forgot. We get $1.37 a hour. Just let that Otto swindler ever ask me for money again. I got no sympathy for my sister. What's your name?"

"My name is Anton Lochinvar."

"Lochinvar? What kind of a name is that?"

Fuck'r. He wouldn't even bother to use his Basque identity. "Lochinvar is Turkish."

Della looked at Goff with ruffled hurt, preparing to tangle herself up in yet another defeat. But, as always, she intended to go down battling. "Nah," she snapped, her lips starting to curl. "You not Turkish."

"Scimitar my poopick and hope to die if I'm not," said Goff, describing an elaborate motion of crescent around the vicinity of his navel.

"Do you believe in God?" she demanded aggressively.

"Ja, ja, of course."

"Oh, you do speak German."

"Nah, I speak English, Turkish and a few words of Polish."

"Ja?" Her red eyes happily glowed ruby.

He knew it! A Polack!

"What can you say in Polnish?"

Goff knew how to say good morning; kiss my ass. He said it.

Della laughed with girlish glee and eagerly nudged over to her pal, Tessie, the contents of Goff's startling linguistic display of Polski. Goff saw Tessie's decades-old cupid-bow lips thin out to a refrigerated meat-packer's smile. Goff's "good morning; kiss my ass" had broken the Polish ice. Della fetchingly rammed her bony meat-packer's elbow into Goff's ribs. Goff woofed his acknowledgment of his Jew-boy acceptance by Della the Polack. In her cranky eagerness to ensnatch a boyfriend she had completely overlooked his detestable origins. Goff thought this was a good illustration of why Polacks were second best.

So Goff saved the day. As they drank beer, he drew on the bittersweet ironies, the gently biting fun-poking in the classic Jewish tradition of the self-effacing humor of the Diaspora, of the *shtetl*—the vital humor of survival. So was Goff, like the gentle *shtetl* tailer, able to weave the foursome into a mellower cohesiveness. He poked gentle fun at Leon's job— about Leon earning money on the side by renting out sheep to lonely woodsmen; about the girls' job at the sausage works. After handling baloney all day, could they still bring themselves to regard it with any affection when they came home? Sure, he was Turkish. Chinese girls have it sideways, and Turkish girls have it crescent shaped. Again with the sure fire: scimitar my poopick and hope to die, if it's not true. Leon, don't let everything out; save some for the trip home in case we run out of gas. Sausages again: Aren't some sausages already ready-made? Isn't that called sweetmeats? Take this straw with you, honey; keep the hair dry. She was so ugly, every time she brought the sausage up to take a bite, it would shrivel away.

Goff was a big hit. He could easily see Della would be his reward if he wanted her. He had her quacking deliriously. But he didn't want her. Even Leon, he thought, now had a chance with the new loose goose, Tessie. Leon, the schmuck, was smitten by her. Goff wanted to go home. Leon gave him an imploring look. Goff relented. He would be a good scimitarian. So he continued to play the jolly Turk. He said Allah be praised. He couldn't do the polka, but could do the Turkey Twat; scimitar my poopick. . . .

Goff finally maneuvered their departure by suddenly clutching his poo-pick area. "I must have halvah. It is almost twenty-four hours since I had my last halvah."

The girls tittered, "What is halvah?"

Leon grasped the halvah strategy and explained it was a Turkish delica-cy. Turks are weaned on it. The girls would love it. They must find some. They would not be deterred by the lateness of the hour. Goff understood the roles they must now play. They were the madcap aristocrats who must pursue their madcap whim regardless of cost and availability. Inn-keeper, innkeeper, rouse yourself. Rouse your musicians and your good wife. Prepare us the rabbit ragout for which you are famous. Hang the ex-pense, my good man.

So Leon was the Junker baron and the two damsels were of the oldest Polish nobility with some excellent strains of German blood, and Goff was their guest from Turkey, an irrepressible, fabulously wealthy emir who was here in Yorkville to study Prussian military science. The game wasn't bad, thought Goff, except he didn't want to screw this Della pig under any circumstances. How had he gotten himself into it? And did these two Polish cabbages know they had been transformed into the land-ed nobility? Tessie, the goose, never knew it, but surprisingly, Della Duck allowed the enchantment to take hold, and she flapped eagerly for mad-capping for halvah.

So the four left the German beer hall—to find halvah for Anton Lochin-var and make zany—all so Goff's friend Leon, the soft-on-capitalism Trotskyite's son, the U.S. forest ranger, could get himself a piece of cold Polish nookiewurst for a midnight snatch, that Goff wouldn't screw with his brother-in-law's (always poor Murray, his brother-in-law's) dick. Why should he fuck any of those two Polacks? Had they ever done even one good deed for a Jew? Name one good thing you ever did for a Jew, you miserable Polack, Katszka, just one—and I'll let you screw me.

Out on 86th Street Goff was inspired. Purely for the sport. "It has come to me where to get holy halvah! Allah has revealed. Into my car. *Allons.* To Zabar, the grand appetizer. The cunning Zabar is sure to supply us. On to Broadway across the park." The three followed Goff into his car, and with a counterfeit screech and zoom he U-turned his east to west and went shooting across the park to Broadway, and on to the establishment of the cunning Zabar, grand appetizer and palatier for the exacting gas-tronomies of hawk-nosed pickers and choosers of the upper West Side.

The Zabar establishment: storehouse of savory and smoky delights from Mediterrania and trekking north along the random flowings and inlets of the wandering Jews through the Balkans and Slavia and Mitteleurope and the Baltic and finally Scandia. In each place, a delicacy of the area was noted and adopted and Zabar had collected them all. His main counter, a thirty-foot showcase and nestling place for the delicacies of the soft underbelly through the white scaled topside of Europe. Perhaps it was Zabar himself behind the counter. With black walrus mustachio and enormous snowy apron bellying out in tight crease and fold lines, he stood with jolly ferocity brandishing his two-foot-long flat carving knife for belly-lox slicing. Before him on the counter were laid out the delicacies of the house—and mainly fish it was. And what fish! The product of man's final mastery, emerging after a thousand years of man's worthiest applications, his attempts to contrive a tastier morsel for himself. From within ancient smokehouses, tenderly hung to capture and take on the smoky flavor of hickory, cedar, balsam and juniper, and throw in a sprig of spruce.

And Loki stole an earthen jar of the secret smoke from the underground dwarfs and then he stole the sacred salmon from Odin and hid the salmon in the jar. And Odin in his wrath was about to slay Loki, but on tasting the salmon, his heart melted, for never had he tasted anything so delicious. And soon after, a wandering Jew who had just rowed over from the Skagerrak heard of this wondrous food. It was originally called Loki's, finally corrupted to lox, as we now know it.

There was the lox in huge teardrop slabs, deep rose-hued and glistening in velvety texture. The lox that was severed off the finest salmon caught by disgruntled fishermen who begrudged that the best of their catches was earmarked for express delivery for fat Jews in New York.

Other fishes at Zabar's. Fish in savory picklings, covered in spiced and garlicked garnishing. Jews would flock to Zabar on Saturday to provision themselves for their Saturday-night fish bacchanalia.

With hands diamond bedecked, the ladies would point resolutely to the fishes of their choice—to the herrings they favored, to the whitefish most moist. With frenzied anxieties they would direct the the resigned appetizing man of Zabar's to their precise, severely considered choices within the glass-enclosed counters. All appetizing men had expressive eyebrows, their most important tool in soothing and serving the hyperanxious ladies.

"Murray, Murray, I'm having a big bacchanalia tonight. I've got to have perfect stuff. It's gotta be all fresh stuff."

Murray's eyelids lowered reassuringly.

"I want today's delivery. I know you get a delivery Saturday morning.

A nice whitefish. No. Not that one. Further up—no—to the right—no, no, my right—your left—yes, that one—yes—hold it up—I wonder if it's not a little too dry looking—you sure? Maybe you better give me this one here in front instead. Murray, this is no joke. I'm depending on you—pull off a little wing—let me taste—good—slice it nice—no—it's too big pieces—keep the tail—my husband likes to suck on it—don't be fresh. Now pick me out a dozen nice chubs—fat ones and not dry—no—I don't want that one—that one's nice—better make it a dozen and a half—those *fressers!* And I'll want some nice herrings—schmaltz, matjes, pickled, filleted, chopped, mopped, kippered—and some nice sturgeon—and lox—half nova half belly—better, more heavy on the nova. And some nice carp—k'nubbel carp, winter carp, sable carp, sliced and chunks—and I want some nice kippered salmon—make sure it's not dry pieces—and smoked sprats—oh, yes and some nice butterfish—fat ones—not dried out. Gimme a taste of that lox. Why don't you start a fresh lox—I don't want the end slices— and don't give me the first slices—put in the skin—my husband likes to suck on it—the comedian again—slice it nice and thin, *tateleh*—I want it should look nice—wise guy—it's not because it should go further. After you weigh the carp, before you wrap it up, give me a slice, to taste. I don't want Zabar to lose money on me. Yes, it's good. I wouldn't say I haven't tasted better—but it's good—it better be for the prices he charges. Also let me taste the sturgeon—this is definitely too dry. Murray, I've been eating sturgeon all my life—it's dry—*I* don't know what's dry? But I have to have some—but make it only half a pound. I can't help it if you already sliced more—it's dry. That's your problem, *bu-bee*—don't worry so much. You're talking like it's coming out of your pocket—you call that loads of onions? For the prices he's getting, Zabar could afford to give me an extra container of onions—charge me if you have to; don't think I wouldn't resent it, but I must have more onions—and don't be so stingy with the juice—it shouldn't get dry. Murray, you get me so tzettittered, you almost made me forget—I want some pickled lox, too. You say, no, Murray? Okay, I get the message, *meshuggeneh*. So let me have another whitefish instead. I trust you. Slice it in nice pieces. The main thing it shouldn't get dry. How many people am I having? Four."

Murray ticked off four reasonable twitches of eyelid and continued slicing.

So that night in hundreds of West Side apartments and elsewhere, tables would be loaded in Jewish Saturday-night smorgasboard style with

Zabar-supplied appetizings. A herring and lox, smoked fish saturnalia. Platters of sliced snowy sable carp. And chunks of rusty paprikaed carp, garlicked and herbed, rows of bursting full-fleshed, juicy, golden-skinned whitefish. Their flat cousins, the butterfish, in skins of glistening bronzed parchment. Plump herrings in bowls of pickled sauce, in beds of creamy onions. Oval platters of lox in salmon-colored slices of cream-soft salty piquancy. Urns of crisp green scallion shoots rising out of tender milky-white roots—and extra bowls of creamed onions—their raw angry sharpness subdued, relaxed and mellowed in the thick pickled cream sauce.

The white mounds of cream cheese. The black glistening meaty olives. Baskets piled with freshly baked, rich earth-scented thick-cut slices of coarse-grained black bread. Piles of gold-crusted, still warm plump rolls with full cheeks generously seeded. The sunken-centered *bialys* with their arid, gone-dry wells spread with a tantalizing onion mash. The flattened onion rolls crisp crusted, with large onion flakes baked boldly into their top crust. The darling bagels, plump and pampered favorite of New York. With all his finagle, 'twas only his bagel that gained the acceptance he sought for himself. The burly trailer truck drivers carried the Jewish bagel from New York over the cross-continental highways into backwater bayous and main-street cafes and jazzy, chrome diners. The bagel rolled out over America, and scrawny shiksa country counter girls cried out for "toasted bagel" with unearned familiarity.

Goff realized the power of these magical foods. Maybe not him, but others would surely be sensuously overwhelmed by these (admittedly) miraculous food creations which could conceivably generate so much pleasure as to suffocate the sex urge. Goff admittedly derived enormous pleasure from shmeering a healthy glob of rich cream cheese onto a crisp fresh onion roll or bagel or bialy or fat slice of black bread—and then slapping on generous slices (the thicker the better) of smooth glistening belly lox and then crunching into it with a follow-up garnish of firm new, cool milk-and-green scallion that snaps off clean to the bite. For a man who wasn't quite that dedicated to the primacy of pussy he could well concede the overpowering near-sensual pleasures this kind of Norse-gods fressing could produce. Yes, he would concede the close competition of a Saturday night of assorted smoked fish and herring fressorgy.

Goff spotted a huge conical mass of sand-colored halvah. With a huzzah of triumph, he ordered the clerk to cut off a kilo's worth, and to make sure to use his halvah cutter so as not to risk crumbling the delectable mass of crushed sesame seeds and honey. Goff went into mock fumery when the appetizing man told him he didn't have a halvah cutter, but he could use a nice milchikeh messer to cut off a piece. He was basically a churl. Appetizing men are rarely appetizing.

The girls were uncertain joiners in the appetizer fun. Their smiles were a little forced and bewildered. Leon and Goff also bought some salami and cheese—to continue the party. Didn't the girls share an apartment on East 85th Street? Salami and cheese on Russian health bread and then get high on halvah. Goff now knew his purpose clearly. He was going to be the instrument to get his pal laid. He selflessly sought only his friend Fickle Finger's pleasure. He wanted no part of the prickly Polack meat-packer girl. "I'm tired as hell, but I'm doing this for you. I hope you appreciate it," he whispered to Leon. Goff was satisfied with big Leon's look of response. It was filled with appropriate gratitude. Goff figured that it was the kind of limpid look Leon's horse gave him when he sponged him down around his balls.

The girls shared a walk-up apartment next door to a firehouse. A couple of firemen were smoking outside, and one of them, a husky brute who manned the back wheels on the hook 'n' ladder, called Tessie over. Goff noticed for the first time that night Tessie, the goose girl, lost her aloof goosiness and went into a genuine smile. She walked up to him saucily.

"That's Mike, right?" said Goff to his duck.

Her bill flapped open in amazement, "How you know?"

"I am Turk. I know," said Goff, screwing up his unibrow into occult undulations. The duck flapped a shrug.

"Ja, sometimes he her boyfriend. But he too crazy and he married."

"Won't he be angry, us coming up?"

"Maybe, but is not his business. We do nothing wrong anyway."

"Don't forget what you just said," said Goff who was glad to volunteer himself as her conscience.

"Cross my poopick—hah—how you say it in Turkish?" She jabbed her elbow into him again with ducky glee.

To Goff it looked like the burly fireman, in the shadow of the firehouse, had his hand casually on goose girl's ass, and poor Leon felt himself no other course but to assume the stolid Prussian look of defeat—the grim, wait-till-next-war expression on his face.

Leon was saved by the firebell. Inside the firehouse the bells clanged like muscular brass bulls' balls and Mike stiffened happily—released. He pulled his hand off goose girl's ass, gave a happy whoop and joyfully clumped into the firehouse. The anticipation of humping over that great big back wheel to steer around treacherous corners the wild, swinging back end of that long, siren red, gleaming thousand-wheeler gave him his supreme excitement.

The doughty Yorkville firemen electrified themselves out of the firehouse with red flash and dash, and with a screech, clang and clash they were off—with big Mike humped and helmeted majestically over the great back wheel.

The four frayed fuckers watched fascinatedly, despite themselves, as the hook 'n' ladder snazzily navigated the corner and disappeared clanging uptown.

Goff, the first to snap out of the hypnosis, energetically reminded them of the salami and halvah feast that awaited them.

"Ja," said Della, who sensed a romance with the delightful little Turk—or whatever he was.

They climbed five flights of stairs bathed in old reekings of long-ago cooked cabbage and pork.

The two girls shared a three-room apartment. More neat than clean, it was festooned with the novelties and gimcrackery of counters and sidewalk schlep-cartons outside of cut-rate houseware schlock stores on Second Avenue. The slum baubles that had been tendered to buy Manhattan were still being traded to maintain it. A shiny-faceted framed photograph of Jimmy Cagney, the grinning scamp, was prominent. He was Della Duck's favorite guy.

Goff took charge. "Bring out some plates, a knife, a fork, some glasses, some ice and turn on station WNEW for all-night music. Darn, we just missed the Turkish hour on WEVD. The Turkish hour is five minutes. It goes on from 1:20 A.M. to 1:25 every night. Every nationality gets its hour on WEVD."

"Ja, that's true. From nine to eleven is the Polish hour," chimed in Della.

"Now everybody take off their shoes. A Turk never goes into a house with his shoes on—and certainly never eats halvah with them." Goff winked at Leon. Leon smiled wisely in answer.

Masterfully, Goff the wily Turk blended the four frayed ones into a harmonious group. He got them to drink, to dance in their stockinged feet to the radio music of WNEW. He made a big production of the halvah—grabbing up a bathroom rug and using it for his prayer rug, getting on his praying knees, and pointing toward Mecca. ("Which way is Mecca? Which way would you say is Orchard and Delancey, Leon?") More scimitaring his poopick, and the ecstatic first taste of the holy halvah. "What did I tell you? Ever taste such a paradise taste? There is a dance called the

Halvah. It is danced when the first batch of halvah of the season was produced—all the Turkish people in the village gather around and dance the
Halvah." And of course to the tune of "Havan'gehlah," Goff danced and
sang the Halvah; Della was delighted. Tessie was transformed. Della
hooked arms with Goff and urgently pushed herself into the spirit, impro-
vising Polish wedding dancing to the Halvah. "I think I heard that song
somewheres already," she told Goff suspiciously.

Goff, the Turkish dervish, suddenly gyrated to a collapse, and on his
knees faced Delancy and Orchard and went into a strangulated muezzin
prayer of Yiddish gibberish, telling Leon he was cholishing from fatigue;
that he wanted to go home; take the broad into the bedroom and *zetz* or
get off the pot; please. Allah have mercy—he was so tired. He would wait
in the living room with his dog; did Leon ever have a better friend than
Arnagoffa, Arnagoffa, Arnagoffa?

Leon danced the goose girl into the bedroom and Della was finally alone
with Goff. An immediate strained air filled the room.

Goff thought: I'll give Leon twenty minutes—half hour tops. This sad
sack'll be climbing over me in a minute. I'm so tired. She's so repulsive.
Allah, this may come as a shock to you, but I don't want to get laid.
Please, keep her away from me. Let Leon blow his nuts quickly so we can
go home.

"Della, eat more halvah. Is good, no?"

"Anton, halvah is prima. I like it. I like you."

Della thought: I will sit next to him on the couch and we'll eat this wonderful halvah together. I do like him. Maybe this is my lucky day. He
would be a first-class boyfriend. He could put his baloney in me anytime.
I would never get mad at him. He's so cute. Would Tessie be surprised
and jealous.

"Anton, you not a Turk."

"What you mean, I not Turk?"

"You some kind of Greek, I think."

"A Turk is some kind of Greek, ducky."

"I don't care. Whatever you are, you cute. You like me?"

"I'm not allowed."

"Because your religion?"

Goff nodded wretchedly. Della moved closer to him and took his hand.
"I respect you more for that. But what is the harm if we just like each other?"

"Is bad," said Goff staunchly.

Della nestled up closer, and put her head on his shoulder in respectful
admiration for his principles.

Goff patted her hand. "Go get me more halvah, ducky." Della smiled at him in sweet martyrdom and arose to fetch him more halvah.

"Open your mouth," she instructed, and she fed him chunks of the crumbly confection. The halvah was becoming a little sickening to Goff now. When was putz Leon coming out? He better have got himself laid. He'd give him ten more minutes. But what the hell was he going to do with this nudnick of his? She was rubbing his stomach. He was so tired—and it would take another hour for the drive home. How had he fallen so low? That halvah had made him nauseous. What the hell was she droning on about—she still respects me for sticking to my religion—oh, shit—what a pain in the ass. I might as well screw her, and Leon better be finished when I'm done. You will never know my little ducky—I'm fucking you 90 percent out of sheer boredom—and 10 percent out of the charity I always show to my enemies. There would be no war if everyone was like me.

And Goff threw the happily docile Della flat on the couch—groaned a dramatic "Allah forgive me," and without much more ado pulled off Della's panties from a completely cooperating strained, lifted-up ass and put his baloney into her. As he expected, she had a funny liquified snatch. Also, he was amazed how, for a small girl like her, what a tremendous hole she had. Under these circumstances, he surprised himself a little at how quick he had shot off. But as soon as he had, without further ceremony he pulled out, smiled at her courteously, adjusted his clothes, looked at his watch and resumed his company-mannered position on the couch. Della looked at him a little anxiously, forcing back a wave of her customary hostility. She slipped on her panties.

"Your mother and your father was both Turkish?" she probed, hoping for a loophole in his religious commitments.

"Yes, both."

"Oh. But, anyway it was good, Anton?"

Goff nodded, pained at the abstentions his religion enforced on him. "I'm Catholic, but I'm not so strict. I believe in different religions."

Hah! You believe in Jewish, you Polack cunt drip? Goff thought bitterly of her reaction if he told her: I'm a Jew boy, Polack.

*"No. No, you fooling me."*

*"No, I no fooling."*

*"Oh, Holy Mother. You put your baloney in me."*

*"Yes, Big Hole, and my baloney is 100 percent kosher."*

*"Oh, I'm ruined," she would wail—the fighting duck finally defeated.*

Nah! Even with this nothing cunt, Goff felt uncomfortable at the idea of revealing himself. Sure, her cuntooze would freeze right up if he told her—and with the expansion taking place at four degrees Fahrenheit, it would finally bust her big box wide open.

Tell her anything else and it would be fine. Jehovah's Witness: fine. Hindu: okay. A cannibal, a thuggee: terrible, but tolerable. But a Jew boy! *Oi gewalt,* my delicate Polack meat-packing cunt is undone!

No. Fuck her. It would of course serve her right, but it wasn't worth it for him. It was really so unfair. Even an inconsequential, ludicrous twat like her could use this knowledge to cover him with embarrassment. He had played, God knows why, a Turk. It was schmucky, but was it really so innocently haphazard and prankish? Of course not. Yes, even for this big-holed little Polack, he would rather avoid having her know he was a Jew boy.

Goff again looked at his watch. He had given Leon enough time. He smiled at Della. "I must go now. I will call my friend." Della looked at him with eyes starting to get red at the rims. The duck was holding back the fighting cock in her. Goff knocked gently at the bedroom door. Amid the sound of tussle and rustle, he heard the goose girl breathily inquire as to who and what.

"Leon, it's late. We gotta go home," said Goff with conscious, whining, perverse pleasure.

"In a few minutes, will ya," returned Leon through the door in a protesting, snarling whine.

Goff returned to the couch, again smiling courteously at Della. Della's eyes, more red-rimmed than ever, fixed Goff with a piercing sulk and sneered, "What kind of name is Leon?"

"Leon is a boy's name," said Goff, on the alert.

"What nationality?" she persisted duckedly.

"French, I think. Leon is Noel spelled backwards."

Della considered this with brooding concentration. The angry suspicion in her face started to drain, and she nodded her head grudgingly. "I was beginning to think it was Jewish. I didn't like that."

"Leon? A Jew? Ha, ha. Don't let him hear you say that. He get very mad."

Della looked at Goff searchingly and asked, "You like Barbara Stanwyck?"

"Sure."

"You like Ducky Medwick?"

"Sure."

"You like the movie *Fantasia?*"

"No."

"I don't like it either. What about Leopold Stokowski?"

"Okay. Why?"

"They all Polacks." Della seemed mollified by all his answers. Her red rims paled. "Barbara Stanwyck married Robert Taylor. Stokowski married Gloria Vanderbilt. They not Polish, either of them."

Goff shrugged.

"Rita Hayworth's boyfriend is Ali Khan. You and Ali Khan's get the same religion?"

"Yeh, but he's not religious."

Della moved in close again. "I like you, Anton. You gonna call me up?"

"Of course." Goff had his hand taken by the broad-minded Della.

Leon was still smothered in the bedroom. Della was moving in on him again. He was so tired, but he would continue to be a gentleman. He remembered the words on an old cereal bowl he had had when he was a kid: "Higgledy, Piggledy, my black hen; she lays eggs for gentlemen." As a gentleman, he would lay the Polack girl—and Leon better be out by then—positively. He thereupon nudged her and she immediately flopped flat again on the couch—with, again, her ass lifted for Goff's convenience in removing her pants. To reassure him that this was not her customary mode of behavior with every guy that took her out, she whispered, "I don't want you to get the idea I let every fella that takes me out put his baloney in me. I go for you a lot, Anton."

Goff nodded as he packed his baloney into her again. Boy, will I sleep tonight, was his predominant thought; also, he would never eat baloney again; also, as a former commissioned officer, recent World War II veteran, this was a disgrace. He hadn't been mistaken on his last round; she *was* tremendous—and awfully swampy. Goff had to work harder this time to finish off his higgledy piggledy, but he managed it, again with surprising dispatch, and it was none too soon that he had again resumed his gentleman-caller deportment on the couch, because the bedroom door opened and out came Leon blinking blankly, a signal mechanism out of whack for general communications, but fit enough to tick off messages of disaster. Goff got the disaster signal: putzy Leon Fickle Finger had not got himself laid. Goff had fucked the duck twice for naught.

In Goff's car driving home, after making sure Leon understood the sacrifice he had made, he asked Leon what had gone awry. Leon, a little punch drunk, kept repeating with awe and amazement, "And you got laid twice—just to kill time?"

Goff dismissed the accomplishment with modesty. He pressed Leon.

What had happened in there? Shit, he'd been in there long enough. "Wasn't that long," said Leon peevishly—and he shook his head again in admiration at Goff's getting laid twice.

Leon knew he couldn't hold off endlessly on the details of his fiasco. It was the oldest code of the street that made it mandatory for guys to reveal all postmortem details after going out with broads together. "She just wouldn't let me get in, the cunt," he blurted out finally. Goff waited, delicately, without interrupting. "She's some kind of nut. All she wanted was me to play with her. I had practically my whole hand in her hole, and she wouldn't let me take it away." Goff nodded. There would be no stopping Leon now. "Every time I tried to take my hand away, she'd grab it like a maniac and put it back."

Goff finally had to ask, "Did you have your cock out at least?"

Leon answered with manly indignation. "Of course I had it out, but, like I said, every time I tried to take my hand away so I could put it in, she became a maniac."

Goff nodded clinically and asked, "How undressed was she?"

"I had her skirt up," said Leon defensively.

"What about her pants? Did you get her pants off?"

Leon was honest. "No."

Goff couldn't help injecting some sarcasm. "So, you were working through the side of her pants?"

"Well, they were loose. There was plenty of room," said Leon, no longer a Prussian baron.

"You should have taken her pants off and plowed into her. That's what she wanted."

"I couldn't, Arnie, and every time I tried to put my dick in, she'd say, 'Not now,' so I thought, with the way she was going crazy with my fingers in her, it was just a matter of time," he tried to justify.

Goff shook his head in honest criticism. "What about her tits?"

"I had my hands on them."

"Bare tits?"

"Sure," said Leon curtly.

"Did she have her brassiere off?" asked the ace shrewdly.

"No."

"That was loose too?"

"Well, it was. I got my hand under it without any trouble."

Goff shook his head again. "You fucked up, Leon," said the two-time fucker straightforwardly. "You gave her a good time. Did she give you a crummy hand job at least?"

"No," said the forest ranger, shaking his head miserably.

"You know, Leon, maybe she knew you were Jewish, and that's why," needled the wily Goff.

"She had no such idea," said the proud forest ranger firmly. "She was just plain wacky. Just plain loco," he concluded, changing his assessment into cowboy lingo.

Goff shrugged charitably; he was too tired to rub it in anymore. Wacky indeed. That dumb putz friend of his would have to go home and wacky it for himself. Right into his American Standard. Goff didn't feel so satisfied himself. He might consider it for himself also so that he could go to sleep with peace of mind. He had shot off a double load, but it had stunk in that big, damp cavern of hers. There had been no real satisfaction with that Polack bitch. And it wasn't because she was a Jew hater. He had had some of his finest nookie with a real blue-blood Nazi in Columbus during the war. Maybe he would conjure her up again when he came home. Get off a pleasurable load this time, sleep late Sunday, and get in shape for Monday at the plant. He had to be in good shape for his plant; he had to do the work of two. His partner wasn't worth a fuck. With all that aggravation sure to be encountered during the week, he owed himself a soothing treat. Yes, he would go home and pay homage to his Nazkeleh. That's what he should have done in the first place, instead of going through this whole ball-crusher night.

# Chapter 8

*Goff remembers his great Wagnerian fuck; a hero's
joust at Ebbets Field*

He had been temporarily assigned to a base outside of Columbus, Ohio, in '43. While playing basketball at the base gym, he had sprained his ankle. He had already been commissioned a second lieutenant several months before. Taped up, and with the help of crutches, he had gone into downtown Columbus one afternoon. He noticed that old ladies, girls and children looked at him with sympathy and encouraging smiles. Gallant young Lieutenant, where did you get it? Kasserine Pass? Some atoll in the Pacific? No, lady, I slipped while making a lay-up. He was enjoying the misleading picture he was creating.

He had decided to go into a restaurant, and preceding him was a haughty, blond beauty. Her hair was fixed in long braids wound tightly around her head in classic Nordic style. It was obvious that she knew he was directly behind her, and he, a "war casualty," fully expected she would patriotically hold the door for him. But quite the contrary, she strode in, head and ass high, and not only did she *not* hold the door for him, but seemed even to fling it back at him.

Goff knew an opportunity when he saw one. He considered the aggressive act an overt invitation for him to advance, hobbled as he was. In his uniform, and with the assurance that it gave him, he felt his pulse rise, as he saw his first vision of those braided blond tresses unfurled, long and rich, framing her pink body in gold, down at least to her rich proud ass— to fringe his horny pleasures in gilt.

She had seated herself in a booth, and he followed her, sliding in to face her and making an elaborate show of standing his crutches in the corner of the booth. She appraised him icily. Goff fixed his features in the most un-Jewish cast he could arrange, and put on a slight sardonic grin. He thought of Clark Gable, raised half an eyebrow and hoped he had thought himself into that kind of look. His instinct told him he'd better get himself looking as un-Jewish as possible. His face should show debonair nonchalance. Keep away from intellectuality. Show more insensitivity and nonchalance. Wipe off concern and guilt and conscience. He sensed he had to put all that into his face or risk failure, or even worse, humiliation. He remembered Bernie Bender, one of the guys in the Church Avenue Shamuses SAC, who had tried to get a commission in the Navy as an ensign and had gotten a notification turning him down because of "negative physiognomy." How they had to run to the dictionary to look it up. Goff believed you could mime your face ethnically to a degree by thinking "goyish," and he wasn't going to physiognomy up this chance, if he could help it. He felt in his bones a terrific piece of ass in this cold blonde.

Her face had cold blue eyes, a sensual mouth and a complete air of disdain. Goff made his smile and slouch more careless. He had to get across to her that he didn't give a shit.

She slowly opened her purse without looking at it or changing the direction of her hard gaze. She took out a pack of cigarettes, slid one out and placed it between her lips. Goff didn't move. It would be Jewish now to rush out a book of matches and light one for her, regardless of how blasé it was done. The mere act of attendance on her might tinge his color as fawn Jewish. He must give no hint of scraping or ingratiation. No breath of the humanitarian, the conciliator. She had flung the door at him. No turner of other cheeks. No matchbook. No books! He would not light her cigarette. She waited the imperceptible second for Goff to light it. But he didn't fall for it. He didn't move a muscle, except make his smile a mite more sardonic, and tilt his one eyebrow a little higher and bunch it up a little more to make it bushier and more swashbuckling.

Goff sensed he had scored a point. Her cold hostility had reached its peak. She had been sharply taking measure of him, but when she reached for her own matches and lit her own cigarette, he sensed the crisis was over. And out of this icy blond creature of the North, smoke from within poured through nose and mouth. What a wild fuck she'd be, felt Goff, straining to the utmost to look casual, languorous, long-legged and Gentile to this implacable Valkyrie. She finally spoke. He had been right!

"For a minute I thought you might be a Jew," she said with cool matter-of-factness. She was still watching him with intense scrutiny. His response had to be flawless. Pure inspiration suddenly seized him. Her first probings had been a crude jab. He would respond audaciously with crudity in kind. He would counter with a deliberately clumsy, overdone Yiddish accent. He had to clothe the accent with the heavy-handedness and grossness of a guy who might be a casual dabbler in Jew hate. He had to avoid the overcommitment of a fanatic, not only could he not bring it off convincingly, but it would also be out of character for the nonchalant hotshot he had already started to portray. It had to be somewhat inept and offhand. "Vell, vell," he said. "Iss dot a reason vy you trying for to kill a crippled solja?" Goff stoked his smirk up a bit. It had come out right. The inflection was overdone just right and the phrasing and accent were clumsy and exaggerated. He had brilliantly sold his people down the river Rhine.

She appraised him a moment more and then favored him with a kind of smile of tentative acceptance. "Actually," she said, "I didn't notice you in any particular detail outside. I'll be blunt. I'm irrevocably opposed to our involvement in this war. The Jews have manipulated us into it and I'm not particularly inclined to show any special courtesy to anyone in uniform. And as far as I'm concerned, a door slam into a soldier on crutches illustrates my feelings without any room for doubt. And as long as you're not a Jew, nothing personal, Lieutenant." The smile she now showed him was warmer, the creases of suspicion ironed out. The firing squad was dismissed for the moment because the stranger had known the proper passwords.

Was it worth this degrading deception to screw this bitch mädchen. Shouldn't he now dangle his dog tags in front of her, show her his "H" for Hebrew, make a mocky face at her and tell her in high Brooklyn sing-song to go fuck herself. He looked at her blue-diamond blondness, the blue-hot passion that was certainly the reagent that transformed it to hot hate for Jews—signaled by her contained cruel mouth and eyes; and the alchemy he could bring to bear to retransform it to supersex. With luck he could be a bronco buster and fuck her tame. He weighed his loyalty to the guys who hung around all the candy stores in Brooklyn. Goff concluded they would, to a man, cheer him on. Go boy, get one for the Kipper! Zetz her good! Once and for all—for all the times the blond Irish cunts from Gerritson Beach scorned us and made us feel like dirt; for all the times those blond kraut whores from Ridgewood would just as soon cut our balls off as look at us; for all those Bay Ridge blond Swedes who made us feel like small greasy monkeys; for all those blond Polack *pyrges* from Greenpoint who considered *us* inferior.

He thought about his pop's wheezy encouragements—*geh, Arneleh, geh, ess ist ahyn mitzvah.* You shouldn't let politics mix in. How good and proud Pop would feel.

He thought about the guys at the Church Avenue Shamuses SAC and his later frat brothers at Brooklyn College. How Mel Goldbert, Murray Nadel, Bernie Schuster, Harvey Spieler, Lennie Slutsky, Kenny Hirschkorn, Manny Seltzer, Sy Fiegelman, Bob Cohen, Leon Finger, Ben Lemlich, Jack Grabelsky, Seymour Schlusselberg, Norman Weissman, Louie Schoen, Donald Furst, Harry Siff, Al Schindler, Sol Serota, Milt Feiffer, Irv Mayrowitz, Burton Davis, Arnie Slifky, Lionel Rosen, Anthony Gargarella, Nat Wasserstrom, Lester Leshevsky, all would cheer and shout in fraternal unison, "That's Arnie, our frat brother! Hurrah!" A slight improvement, what, over that retarded, god-awful smelling zombie they had all, every one of them, gang-fucked (or so every one had jauntily said they did) as they smirkingly came out of the room at the "frat" house on Bedford Avenue.

And he thought about his sister, Blanche, who would screech with glee, and her husband, Murray, who would start winking with compulsive camaraderie. He thought about his mom, who would shrug and go bake a *challa.* He cut her out, and let his imagination drift on beyond, and he saw the circle of cheerers widen and widen. All of Brooklyn was cheering for him. It would be an exhibition at Ebbets Field—a special event.

Traffic on Bedford Avenue would be clogged. The Brighton line would be discharging them by the thousands at the Prospect Park station. Ebbets Field, normal capacity 34,000, would buckle to bursting that day—cramming in 42,621—and outside, unable to get in, thousands more of hyperexcited Jewish guys milling around the entrance gates and parking fields and gas stations. Nobody was going home. The roaring electric excitement from the ball park overflowed the fortresslike walls and held the crowds on the outside in a magnetic grip. All the guys on the street were compulsively eating out of nervous excitement. Either they were digging into stained brown paper bags coming up with thick, kitchen-knife-sliced salami sandwiches on oversized seeded rolls, or the more audacious ones, daringly eating prohibited Stahl-Meyer frankfurters from the many shacklike stands in the vicinity. Mounted red-faced Irish cops, cousins of Cossacks, always impatiently raring to get hot and ride their beautiful brown horses to control the mobs of excitable Jewish guys. The beautiful brown horses themselves obeying with impassive detachment. Always aloofly neutral, always above the battle, they never became inflamed like their riders—not like intemperate emotional dogs would. But today, somehow, those cops weren't the usual sadistic pricks they habitually were. They would be cheerfully puzzled, head-scratching and good-natured. And so too were the cops' pint-sized, wizened shrewd-eyed uncles, who, unable to make the cops, were given jobs as ticket takers at Ebbets Field. Tending with skinny-knotted arms their turnstiles at the gates, they would be shaking their heads in amazement at the enormous outpouring, and despite their normal inclinations, they too found themselves rooting for Goff.

The Jewish guys poured out tumultuously from all the burrows of Brooklyn—all to see Arnie Goff and this big Teutonic amazon, pitted one against the other—like David and Goliath. The Aryan Nazi bitch would be on the mound. Would Goff even have the balls to walk up to the plate to take a turn at bat? Even more, would he then be able to hit her? This was destined to be the event of the century.

The Jewish guys had streamed out from all the candy stores in Brooklyn. All the splintery, weather-beaten wooden newsstands outside the candy stores would be for once emptied of these loutish newsstand loungers, who gave such aggravation to all the Hymies and Sols, the nervous wrecks of candy-store owners. This one time they wouldn't be sprawled indolently drinking, nay, nursing their Pepsi Colas—(Grepsi Colas, more familiarly). These were the grepsi generation—their loyalty easily won over by a simple twelve full ounces, that's a lot—and twice as much for a nickel too—so, of course, why not? This then was the chosen drink by the chosen—by far. The candy-store penny-ante hustlers, pool hustlers, handball and punch-ball hustlers.

Pinball-machine virtuosos who could make these machines perform tricks with tap and tickle as an expert gentleman horseman in his habit could get his thoroughbred steed to go through his intricate blue-ribbon leaps and paces by the merest flicks and nudges. These candy-store-spawned guys devoting themselves to these machines as if these were the delicate instruments for which they had been trained a lifetime to master. Tensing those spring plungers to the infinitesimally correct degree of pressure to launch those steel balls to wonders of peregrinations upward and then magically down the inclined flashy, gaggle-lighted course of its run. Through the maze of bumpers and traps and cunning entryways to the grand 100,000 slot—to cause the ball to bump and nuzzle again and again against the mounds that released multicolored flashes and scores that mounted and mounted on bright-hued tote boards. To control the ball with a just right tap, a propitious pat, a teasing tickle, a squeeze and wiggle or twist of ass, a body's English to keep the ball bumping along—bumping along—to stay as long as possible its inevitable descent to the final gully trap. Or even worse, to topple into TILT. The awful tilt of totality—of all wasted labors and nullity.

But on occasion a knight of the Order of the Pinball, in his heady tilt with TILT, would emerge victorious, "Hola, Hymie, I hit 890,000. That's a fifteen-cent payoff." And Hymie would pull his hair out and wail, "No cash, no cash—only merchandise." And Sadie, his moustache-brewing wife, would butt in and holler. "He's not supposed to shake the machine. Don't give nothing, Hymie." But today Hymie would sustain no aggravation. Even *he* would be at Ebbets Field. "Sadie, mind the store. I must go. I won't hear no. I'll be back by five for sure."

From fancy Flatbush the rich kids from Ocean Parkway and Ocean Avenue and Albemarle Road would forgo the library—put aside either their research or tennis rackets—riding on horses on Ocean Parkway.

The handball players at Avenue P, Brighton Beach and Beach Fifth Street, all the schoolyards in Williamsburgh, Boro Park, Bensonhurst—all would give up four precious hours of handball to get to Ebbets Field.

The poolrooms in Brownsville and East New York would be empty—balls neatly racked, untouched.

No ringo-levio; no Johnnie-on-the-pony; no hanging around Dubrow's Cafeteria on Kings Highway today.

Williamsburgh cheders and yeshivas would be near empty. All Hebrew schools would be out.

East Flatbush Jewish sharpies would forgo their cellar clubs and gang fucks. Sperm production for Brooklyn for this afternoon would be off by sixty gallons. Jerk-off artists by the thousands would lay down their palettes and would forgo jerking off to the hot drawings in *Breezy Detective*.

Bar Mitzvah lessons—piano, violin, clarinet, sax and accordion—forget it for today.

Young Communist League meetings—canceled.

Lone, poor, scared, pimply Jewish kids whose stoop-shouldered fathers ran drab musty candy stores, marooned in distant goyishe sections like Red Hook or Bay Ridge or Park Slope or Marine Park or Ridgewood, would slink timidly away through the hostile streets and only begin to straighten up with joy and exaltation as they approached Yiddishe Eastern Parkway or crooning Crown Heights and its crowning castle, glorious Ebbets Field.

Candy-store card games would go unplayed. Pennies remain unpitched. Buchhalter would decree a holiday in Brownsville, and Murder, Inc., would close down business for the day.

The excitement would reach an unbearable pitch. Would Goff even come out of the dugout? And—yes! It's him! Goff is coming out of the dugout on the first base line. And forty-four thousand Jews from forty-four thousand shuls of Brooklyn rose as a congregational one, and a mighty roar rent the air. (Why rent? The air is free—no?) It was after all, thank God, not for nothing that they had all made their pilgrimage to their hallowed Field of Ebetz.

Ebetz Field was the true gateway to America for all those Brooklyn Jews. Ellis Island—baloney! Ebetz Field, I tell you. Ellis Island was the back stoop for the I-cash-clothes peddler who would barely be tolerated one foot in the house. Ebetz Field was the front portico where the doctors, insurance agents and relief investigators were ushered in with—if not full honors—at least respect.

Ebetz Yisroel—we kiss your bleachers, your pitcher's mound, your infield, your outfield, your whaling right-field wall. You holy Field of Ebetz—you allowed us to worship you—through you we first saw America; through you we showed how we loved America and wanted so much with all our hearts to love America and for America to love us in return. Look America, we love the Field of Ebetz! All our love and emotions go out to her. So have we therefore not earned your love, America? For we love the same thing. It is as genuine as mother love. Our reputations for our devotions to the Field of Ebetz are well known among you all. Our loyalty is legendary. Are we too extravagant in our love? Maybe, but that's our way. It only signifies our deepest wishes and hopes to join and establish ourselves among you. This is our first contact with America—do you see?

Ah, the players of Ebetz Field, the esteem in which we hold you all! We love you, Johnny Cooney, Billy Cox, Frenchie Bordegeray and your comical cutups. Hot Potato Luke Hamlin. Hot potato! Hot dog! Lonnie Frey. Hot Potato. Who has it? Buddy Hassett. We had such fine hopes for you Long Tom Winsett, Hal Jeffcoat. Van Lingle Mungo! Van Lingle Mungo—bingo bango bungo—Van Lingle Mungo! Oh, my. Babe Phelps held up his mitt for a target and Van Lingle Mungo smoked in his fireball. A swing and a miss. We hope you're not bitter that you could have been a thirty-game winner with another team. What grace and form. You were our first real contact with the heart of America. You guys with your rangy loping grace. Your fine long graceful necks. Your beautifully shaped heads—close-cropped, blond, bristled—arching out in perfect curves underneath the backs of high worn baseball caps—visors tilted, deep forward in nonchalant gum-chewing assurance. As a chin has distinct shape and character, so has the back of a guy's head. There is the noble open rotundity of some. You guys had it. And the way you all spoke. The same, no matter from where you came—it was always a kind of southern drawl of cowboys and country people.

We got to know you—to worry and be concerned about you. You got to know us—to know our interest and concern were genuine. We wanted to know all about you, your wives and children, your parents, what you did during the winter. You knew that. You learned about us too. Most of you had never seen a Jew before. You finally saw we were OK guys. Our speech was a little funny, but so what? You could see we were colorful, generous, argumentative—and loyal—above all that we weren't mere rooters—we were always called "faithful rooters"—as if it were one word. Admit it—how false and misleading were the descriptions you heard about us in your small, far-away towns and whistle stops—your little cowboy shtetlehs. And you would go back to your towns and ranches and farms around the hot stoves. And tell the people in your drawls, "Those Jewboys in Brooklyn, ah reckon, they're OK. Have to admit ah was surprised—but they fine people—when you get to know them. Yep, this little shiny ol' convertible—they give it to me. No special reason. Ain't nothin' wrong with them that, mebbe, a little less talkin' wouldn't fix. They like to talk you to death if you let 'em. You cain't understand everythin' they sayin' at first, but you come to after a while. That's true. They do use their hands a lot—but other'n that, ah cain't say ah got complaints."

We suffered with Pete Reiser, that gallant, hard-luck guy. We shook our heads sadly with embarrassment over our Dixie Walker. Come on, Dixie, straighten up and fly right, a good guy like you. Don't be a stubborn mule about Jackie Robinson. "You wanna be stubborn, be stubborn." A parent's distress about a beloved son who insists on being unreasonable.

"Come on, Jackie. Look, he's driving the pitcher crazy, dancing up and down off third base. Oi, my God, he's going!" He streaks for home! He slides! Safe! He stole it! Pandemonium. But give a look at that stubborn mule, Dixie, in the dugout, *angeshpart*. He's looking the other way. For cryin' out loud, give a little credit. Dixie, Dixie, why can't you be like Pee Wee Reese. Pee Wee is so sensible. He's shaking Robinson's hand. Pee

Wee, so reliable, so steady—brings you so much *naches*. And Pee Wee is no Northerner either. He's from Kentucky. "Hey, Moish, you know why they call him Pee Wee?"

"Because, he's small, he's a small scrappy shortstop—that's why."

"No. He ain't as small as he looks. He's five foot ten. Don't you know anything? They call him Pee Wee, schmuck, because he was a marble-shooting champ in Louisville when he was a kid."

"Hey, Schloim, gimme a bite o' your hot dog."

"Fuck you, Moish. It's not kosher. I thought you were so religious, hypocrite, prick."

"I'm allowed when it's not at home."

"Well as far as I'm concerned, Ebetz Field is home, so fuck you where you eat." And he gobbled up the last half of that limp characterless goyishe hot dog in one gluttonous, pagan bite.

And so it was when Goff was sitting in that restaurant booth in downtown Columbus in '43, across from that blond murderous Nazi bitch, he knew for sure the forty-four thousand Jews at Ebbets Field would be screaming for her blood, and he decided, for them, for pop, for the family, for his self-respect—and above all for the marvelous lay she promised to be—to give it an all-out try. He would go up to the batter's box.

First, he thought, he would have to allay her fears that she might be giving too much aid and comfort to the enemy. He said easily, "By the way, I didn't come by these crutches in combat. The embarrassing truth is, I was working out on the high bar at the base gym and my grip slipped and when I came down, I had me a sprained ankle." Goff had quickly decided to avoid telling her that actually it had happened playing basketball. He figured it was too Jewish. What with CCNY, Brooklyn College, NYU and St. John's in Brooklyn fielding those tremendously hot basketball teams loaded with skinny high-strung, glandular-long Jewish talent. She would respond better to gymnastics, which was more a muscle-bound kraut kind of preference. It did the trick.

She smiled away the last traces of her mean cruel eyes and mouth—and replaced them with a show of large, open healthy teeth. "If I'd known that your injury came from that, I might possibly have held the door open for you. Held for the hero." She laughed gaily and explained that *Held* was German for "hero."

Goff, the debonair goy, who would tolerate girls' exhibitions of useless erudition—*he* certainly wouldn't bother with 'em—put on a reckless, devil-may-care semiconspiratorial grin. His Jewish bones told him he had a sure thing. The mating rites between Nazi lass and Jewish lad had been set in inexorable motion—the curtain was going up for *Abie's Iron Cross*.

When the waitress came, Goff ordered bourbon on the rocks because it was more ruggedly Gentile than scotch or rye. She ordered a Jewish whiskey sour—it was after they had both had their second round, that he mentioned casually that he was of Basque descent and didn't much concern himself with the ideologies of the war. "I guess I just like a good scrap," he lied dexterously in accordance with his role.

Yes, she knew, she nodded. She was a student at Ohio State University. She was passionately interested in anthropology, and racial studies were her specialty, and she knew the Basques were fiercely independent mountain people—who would never submit to a master. They were a pure Aryan strain, who had in the mountain fastnesses steadfastly resisted mongrelization by numerous inferior strains who throughout history had attempted to overwhelm them. They had never allowed the Moors and Jews to penetrate and debase their noble line. She thrust out her hand with salutelike precision because she wanted to shake his. She was glad to know him. A pure people were a joy to the earth, and to the life spirit that was really the sole deity in this threatened world. She was working herself up. Her eyes started to flame the hotter blue. "A mongrel people defiles the holy life spirit. They are quite literally an abomination, offal to the earth. These mongrel people have to be expunged, eliminated without mercy."

Goff, a typical exponent of the mongrel class that his Nazi acquaintance would without mercy disembowel, sat peculiarly undisturbed. He nestled cozily into his corner of the booth, declining to take her increasing ravings as a mortal threat, but on the contrary as a positive confirmation of the passionate, hot piece she would be for him. He saw them as the blind ravings of hot-twatted ecstasy and not to be stupidly and self-defeatedly taken for cumbersome genocidal intentions. Goff figured he knew his customers. He would ignore the irrelevant.

And so he was beginning to feel an actual warmth for her even as she expanded her murderous talk, and he decided it would now be proper and even expected to move himself closer to her. So, as she paused for a moment to nod assent for yet another whiskey sour, he eased himself over to her side of the booth and hove to, pressing against her. After all, wasn't her self mesmerization her way of inviting him? Of course it was.

The positioning completed, their thighs pressing, she resumed her raving. "The life spirit will, of course, eventually and inevitably triumph."

Goff put his hand on hers, a sympathizer signifying his sympathy. "And, of course, you know who is the herald and prophet?" Goff correctly interpreted this question as rhetorical and responded only with a tighter hand squeeze. "It is Adolf Hitler, a supreme visionary, who has been miraculously—there is no other word for it—imbued with the zeal, the iron will to act as a holy missionary to lead the pure peoples in a holy crusade against the mongrels. The most insidious and virulent—the Jews, of course." Of course, thought Goff. She paused, smiled at him, well satisfied with him as worthy of her efforts. In a new relaxed tone of the pastor who, having discharged his fire and brimstone sermon that morning, is now mingling with the congregants at the buffet supper in the church basement, she smiled. "Don't you see—or begin to see . . . ? What is your name, Lieutenant?"

"Goff, Armand Goff. And yours?" He had long before considered the name he would use for her. It was best to avoid "Arnold"—"Goff" was all right, a tough little guttural bark of a name that could be anything. But Arnold was suspect somehow—too many soft consonants. . . . He knew too many Jewish guys in Brooklyn who were Arnolds. Maybe this prevailed in Columbus too. Why take foolish chances—give away percentages? And as for the name "Armand," his Nazi anthropologist would be sure to remember that the Basques bordered France. He also congratulated himself on the finesse with which he had said "Armand"— looking at her with that peculiar tone and twinkle that strong men use when they thrust on you their soft and sissy names, just daring you to make a crack, because with even one wrong flicker they were ready to kick the living shit out of you. In the end, then, their sissy names enhanced their ruggedness.

"I like the name Armand," she said forthrightly. "My name is Frigga. Yes, actually. Frigga Schmidt." She awaited his reaction.

Goff knew he had to reassure her. A beautiful broad—and she was stunning—can get away with any name, but "Frigga Schmidt" was a handful. It so happened that in Goff's rather meagre reading, he had come across a book of the Norse myths, and he knew Frigga was one of the goddesses.

"Ah, Frigga, a goddess in the Norse myths. . . ."

"Right," beamed Frigga as she squeezed his hand and pressed closer, obeying the wonderful fateful bond that was enveloping them. "Frigga was the wife of Odin." She began to ooze and again the zealot's haze overcame her. She started to talk about Norse mythology. How the subconscious *geist* of a people would shape their myths and folklore. How

the Jews, like diseased rats and vermin, were gnawing away at the roots
of *Yggdrasil,* the sacred Tree of Life. How the promised rich blossoming
could never be fulfilled until the sinister despoiler and corrupter was ex-
terminated once and for all.

Frigga kept waxing hotter and more passionate and Goff felt he could
(nay, must) take a liberty. He placed his hand on her luscious Teutonic
thigh and began a temperate pawing. This seemed to be her signal to further mesmerize herself, which in turn was Goff's further signal to
advance. Her ranting became more feverish, but Goff paid no mind to its
contents—a lot of Nordic-Aryan crap. It all translated to: "Feel me up—
more, more, more. I am not responsible—more. More—I have transported myself beyond these earthly, carnal cravings. I am spiritually beyond
the reach of dirty pawings and filthy feeling."

And so with the aid of raptures transcended and unsullied, she had no
need to block Goff's earthbound pokings, his crass caresses. Goff understood and rushed his hot fingers up from her formidable thighs to her
pussy unhinged. He noticed that from the moment he attained fluttering
possession, her mention of Adolf Hitler increased, both in frequency and
passion. When she suddenly uttered his name in a sliding, whimpering
catch, Goff guessed she was now coming with Adolf Hitler. She finally
trembled off a mighty, epic tremble as befitted a lusty, dewy-eyed Valkyrie, and then concluded her fervent paean. "And with all his steel and sacred determination, he is still known as *der schöne Adolf.*" She smiled at
Goff and he was not at all surprised that she now grasped his wrist and
firmly forced his hand out of her and away. However, she gave him a
peck on his cheek to demonstrate she was not angry with him. Goff wiped
his fingers with unobtrusive tact on a napkin, and he thought about the
opinion of his frat brothers at his escapade. Would they appreciate that he
was instrumental in having a *Deutsche bundes Mädchen* come in her pants
over Adolf Hitler? He could imagine their comment: "Jesus Christ, Arnie, we're all for you, but being a proxy for Hitler! Even for a piece of
ass, a guy's gotta draw the line somewhere."

Frigga leaned contentedly into the corner of the booth and smiled approval at Goff. He lifted a friendly eyebrow back at her. She said finally
with a considered, crooked smile, "Armand, I don't think I would at all
mind having an adventure with you."

Goff quickly selected an answer, "Frigga, you're a very exciting woman, and I'm sure it would truly be an adventure. I look forward to it. I consider that it's already started."

The response was just right. Her smile broadened. She was pleased and squeezed his wiped hand. This Basque chap was very interesting. As crippled as he was, he gave sufficient evidence that he was a real man. She lifted her drink. "Let us drink German style as comrades. Take your drink." She hooked her upraised arm with his and they drank with their faces close together. She smiled with the undisguised sensuous promise of complete, bovine availability—a complete reversal of her icy hostility of less than an hour ago. *"Zu unserem Abenteuer,"* she said breathily.

Goff leaned back companionably. "That means, 'To our adventure,' right?"

She nodded deeply and they both drank, enhooked, taking on a dramatic solemnity—she with natural devoutness; he with the ecstasy of expedience. When they had drunk and unhooked, she said, "I see you have an understanding of German."

"Well, I think I have a feeling for it," he said with a bright smirk. Frigga smiled at the irreverent scamp. Goff thought about the origin of his understanding of German. Every word he knew stemmed from the Brooklyn-yammering Yiddish he had heard so often at home. So near and yet so far. The contrast between the clang and harangue, the blood and iron, the leather-strap snappings of the German tongue against the soft boiled chicken soup, the limp-noodled bendings of its unlikely sighing offspring, *Yiddish mama-loshen.* Oi, thought Goff, if she knew how I happened to understand her, that crazy Nazi bitch'd cut my heart out.

Frigga then went on to tell him that her full name was Frigga Unity Schmidt. Her father was Horace Greeley Schmidt, professor of German at Ohio State University. Her mother was British and an amateur anthropologist. It was the English mother who had instilled the currently modish racial ideas in her daughter, rather than the German father. Mrs. Eunice Schmidt had studied with Houston Stewart Chamberlain, who had also had such a profound influence on Hitler and Rosenberg. The notion of Aryan superiority rested on solidly based scientific evidence.

Would her new friend Armand like to join her that evening at a gathering at the German Turnverein beer hall, where he would have the opportunity to witness a display of traditional German *Gemütlichkeit;* where good Germans join in rousing good fellowship. Where eating, drinking and singing become elevated to the kinship of folk spirit, a mystique really impossible to describe—which really must be witnessed? Frigga didn't suppose Armand had ever actually participated in this.

Goff shuddered. Thank God, he had been spared the pleasure. He didn't want any part of it. He didn't relish close scrutiny from her crowd or her father at any German beer nest. Someone might see through him. It could be a mortal piercing. He hesitated.

"I must go there tonight, Armand. Frankly, I'm not all convinced tonight's get-together will be all that genuinely German. My father is a complete simpleton, but I have promised him. Such a naive soul. He is on the faculty of the German department at the university. They have undertaken to train a group of about one-hundred common enlisted men for the occupation of Germany. Idiots. Hitler, of course, will never, never allow it to come to pass. Nevertheless, my father and the German department are committed to a crash program for production of little tin American Gauleiters. They will not only speak German, but be thoroughly indoctrinated in total German culture. They expect to put teeth in the lore, ha ha. The better to eat the Germans with, my dear. Father feels it is his duty to do a thorough job. Mother is furious at him. If you think I'm an ardent disciple, you should see my mother, a fantastic fanatic. She will not speak with him because he allowed himself to be drawn into this despicable program behind whose evil spirit lurks the insidious Jew, Morgenthau, the evil genius behind Roosevelt, who would turn Germany into dung and scorched earth—the new ordure, ha, ha. But I am not that severe with my father, mainly because his efforts are totally childish. Germany will triumph. No question. But naturally he and his colleagues in the German department are going about it with typical German thoroughness, and are not only holding twenty hours a week of actual classroom language study, but have also persuaded the authorities to grant an additional two hours a week for German folk singing. They feel that one cannot grasp the full German flavor without joining in singing the traditional German songs, the *Lieder*. In their *Lieder*, it is felt, reposes the soul of the German. This is true. So, twice a week, all six professors join with these sorry soldiers and have themselves a German singing society in an assembly hall, and believe me, if I know them at all, they put their whole heart and soul into it. In addition, to show you the thoroughness and dedication of these foolish men, they encourage those scum to gather every Saturday night at the Turnverein so that these—ech—soldiers can further drink in their feeling for the German *Geist*—spirit—in a more natural atmosphere. They are really crazy. They are meeting tonight at the Turnverein. The other professors usually bring their wives. My mother has absolutely and correctly refused to accompany him. So he has asked me to show up, because he says it is becoming very awkward for him, always there alone. I told him I would do it this once and that he should not expect me again. I admit that it is awkward for him, but I feel no guilt. My best girlfriend once dated a Jew. I have to thank Mother for spotting him. She said she could tell by his walk. Imagine?''

(Goff was grateful his need for crutches had probably brought on enough distortion.)

"And when I asked Pam directly about her date, and she said yes, I cut her dead at once and forever. It shows you how serious my feelings are. Anyway, tonight I have promised, so tonight I go, for first and last. I strongly suspect these scum soldiers are mostly Jews, and I've told my father so. He doesn't answer me on that. Oh, well, so hopefully we'll go together, Armand. To be escorted by a disabled soldier. Father will be delighted.'' She laughed raucously.

Goff tried to talk her out of it. But she was quick to point out her promise to Armand that they would have a glorious adventure together. Would he want her to be one who could not be relied upon to keep a promise? Again she laughed loud and lewd and kissed him hard on the mouth. Goff had no choice.

When she asked him to pick her up that evening at her home, Goff had panicked inwardly in dread of the scrutiny of that eagle-eyed Jew spotter, Frigga's mom, who could spy a Jew seven leagues away. Maybe the crutches wouldn't fool her. But if his crutched walk was undetectable, maybe she could tell by the way in which he held them—maybe he had a Jewish grip. God knows how diabolically subtle were her black arts. He had stretched his portrayal of a tough, carefree Basque to the utmost of his creativity. Frigga had been tough enough, but to go on to fool her mom, the master detector, could be fatal.

He pictured Frigga's fierce mom on a lookout platform atop a soaring tower rising out of the highest peak at Berchtesgaden. On constant watch, provided with the finest German binoculars, she peered relentlessly at hundreds of square miles of Bavaria for any trace of a Jew. On sighting one (she could tell him by his peddler's stoop), she sings out the battle cry of the Valkyrie, wafting it downward to *der schöne Adolf* who usually stands in trancelike meditation leaning over the railing of his terrace, enjoying the pressure of the balustrade on his questionable balls. Jolted from his gauzy ruminations, he springs erect to perform his quick stiff French jig of delight, smiles up and waves gaily at his loyal lady eagle, as he shrieks out an exultant order to a detail of handy SS men to outflush the Jew.

Goff felt he must avoid Frigga's mother at all cost. So resorting to his Basque air of fierce mountain independence, he laconically told her he

couldn't get around too much on his bad ankle. There was Clark Gable
moxie in his cocky, eyebrow lifted, crooked grin. The message was clear.
He didn't especially need Frigga or any other dame, if it meant giving him
a hard time. All dames were pushovers for him. If she couldn't make it
convenient for him, it was just tough tootsie.

Frigga recognized the manifestation of fierce mountain independence,
reminding her oddly of the dark brooding expression of that Jew actor,
Paul Muni. She quickly conceded that not only would he not have to pick
her up at home, but moreover she would call for *him* at the base. Forgive
her for being so thoughtless. She would have a car which she could get
from a swain, a 4-F, madly in love with her. He was very rich, his father
ran a brewery in Cincinnati, and he was able to get all the gas ration
stamps he wanted.

That afternoon, back at the base, Goff was feverishly excited. With this
Frigga, he knew he could look forward to such screwing as might only be
found with high-soaring eagles in high craggy eyries. Her screeching hatred against Jews surely hid the presence of a wild eroticism. A substitute
passion transmuted by a demented society, which hysterically condemned someone who offhandedly fucked a Jew, but easily shrugged off
the casual killing of same.

It was only by the most stringent exercise of will power that Goff held
himself from dashing to the officers' toilet and wacking off. He had to re-
pel the terrible pressure that screamed within him "Release! Release!"

"No. No," said the harried jail keeper, who was notorious for his leni-
ency, who hated to say no.

If he could only take a nice nap. He lay down. God, he thought, how his
balls were churning. He could feel—never before had they whipped up so
rich, so frothy a brew. He figured if he fell asleep it would be impossible
for him not to have a Niagara Falls of a wet dream.

But snooze off he did, and oddly he didn't have the wet dream, but a
rather singularly dry one. He dreamt Frigga's fierce mom came down the
ladder from the high observation tower. When she reached the terrace,
she sighed heavily and wearily removed her horned Viking hat and white
silk robe. And out came his mother in her shapeless housedress. She
shlumped into Hitler's house and she was in her old kitchen. Hitler sat at
the kitchen table. Hitler was his pop with moustache, stubbled face and
scratchy long underwear. He was taking his usual pleasure, flailing a *shul*
crony with his raspy sarcasm, as he slurped a glass of tea. The discomfort
of his victim brightened the glint in his sharp eyes as he rasped triumphantly, "Look at my Arneleh. He was an accident." His mom looked at

his pop with her flat condemning look and silently proceeded to prepare the ingredients for baking yet another *challa*.

Awake, Goff dwelled on his dream for a moment, shrugged and forgot it forever.

At eight o'clock, pulse racing, Goff, perched on crutches, waited at the camp's main entrance gate. The two sentries were only mildly curious as to whom the looie awaited, but naturally they hoped she'd be a dog.

The sentries sucked in their breath and turned camouflage green when they saw Frigga driving up in a flashy convertible, looking like a Viking goddess at the prow of a raiding ship. They barely noticed Goff hobbling into the car, waggling his crutches behind him. The blond goddess smilingly leaned over in a generously revealing bend and held wide the door for her wounded warrior. Goff was sure he heard one sentry whisper awesomely, "This sure's one looie that don't have to beat his meat on the company street."

Goff felt elation. The mighty struggle in holding off the devil's hand had been worth it, and the whispered admiration he had heard was its sweet reward. His true worth had been recognized. A good ol' American looie shavetail. Clean-cut, and take no shit from no one. No beat meat on company street. No Meyer Muck Masturbator, but Tom Straight Topfucker, all-American. Goff pushed his gilt-trimmed overseas cap rakishly forward and leaned back feeling the sweet peace of a totally accepted hero being whisked off to Valhalla.

Meanwhile, back at the sentry box, one of the soldiers, slowly coming out of his gawk, scratched his head incredulously and asked his mate, "Did I hear him right? Did he call her Frigga?"

The room that was the banquet and beer hall of the Turnverein was done up mainly in old delicatessen brown. The wooden chairs were brown, and even darker brown were the scarred wooden round tables. The walls were dark mustard brown. Antlers hanging on them were grease-filmy brown. Scattered all around hung country style sawtooth wooden plaques inscribed with home-brewed German folk sayings in Gothic printing—all done up in customary cow-dung rustic brown. An American flag, going brown with grime, hung limply on a brown combination window and flagpole in a corner. Everything was sour beer suds, brown and down.

Goff saw no pictures of Hitler, saw no swastikas, but saw the faded rectangular areas on the wall where he was sure they had once hung. He felt the whole place's drooping apologetic air to its Führer for the omission. "Oh, beloved Führer, we know you understand. We cannot hang you on our walls, but you know in our hearts is where you hang."

Eight tables at one side of the hall were occupied by the student-soldiers and their professors of German. Soon after Frigga and Goff arrived, the soldiers began singing a German marching song. Although they had started slow and ragged, the pitch and fervor quickly built up steam, till they were in full, rousing step. It was astonishing. Goff had never seen or heard such loud, fervored, ringing, thumping, enthusiastic singing. At other tables many stout burghers of Columbus looked on with approving double-chinned smiles, and soon joined in the singing. A few even carried their beer steins to the soldiers' tables, joining them and bellowing together in close, true, stein-waving, beer-sloshing sentimental comradeship. Steins aloft, they all tried to outdo one another in beery brotherhood—the louder, the more brotherly. When not engaged in song, they would punctuate every few minutes with a sudden burst of exaggerated bellow of the traditional sing-song snatch, *"Ein Prosit, Ein Prosit, und Gemütlichkeit!"*

The entrance to the hall was not directly in view of the singing soldiers, so enabling Goff and Frigga to make their way in unobserved. Frigga started to lead Goff to a table well away from the group. A fat waiter built like a beer keg with stumpy legs who spotted the impaired Goff slipped up to them, oozing thick guttural greetings and solicitude. *"Guten Abend, gnädiges Fräulein Schmidt.* Your *vater ist schon mit den* soldiers." Then turning to crutch-borne Goff, he shook his head, and oozing with soupy round-eyed sympathy and sorrow, said, "Ach, shame, Herr Lieutenant, please sit. *Kriegsverwundet?"* he asked Frigga respectfully.

"Nein," she laughed. "He fell out of bed."

The waiter's bleary sorrow transformed itself into incredulous hilarity. Holding a chair for Goff, he laughed and shook as if it was surely the most comical thing he had ever heard. Frigga ordered two steins of beer and a plate of roll mops. The waiter clapped Goff on the back and waddled away still shaking with laughter and repeating delightedly "From da bett he fell." Goff tried, but couldn't manage to stave off the wave of pleasure he felt at having been accepted even by this laughing fat prickwurst of a Hitler-loving kraut. He tried harder to suppress it, to replace his gratitude by dredging up contempt and hate for the fawning Jewhater waiter, but he couldn't bring it off. It was awful, but all he could retain was pleasure. Like a stray hound, whoever patted him received his instant love and a grateful wag of tail. But Goff quickly shrugged that one off too. Fuck 'em all, he rationalized. He was soon going to plunder their princess.

The song ended and immediately a new one bellowed out. Spontaneously Frigga grasped Goff's hand and began to thump the table with it in time to the heavy cadence. "Sing," she urged, pushing her flushed face close to his. "It's easy. Follow my lead. It's just a song asking for more beer." And she lustily sang along with the soldiers, the professors, and now, the whole beer hall. "Sing, sing—*Bier her, Bier her, oder Ich fall' um—Juch hei!*"

> *Bier her, Bier her, oder Ich fall' um—*
> *Soll das Bier im Keller liegen—*
> *Und Ich hier mein Ohnmacht kriegen.*
> *Bier her, Bier her* [now loud as hell] *ODER ICH FALL 'UM!*

The hall had been churned up into a boiling froth of beer and booming brotherhood.

Goff grinned and Frigga kissed him a smack with the same heartiness she might put into a backslap.

Another chorus started, louder than ever. Frigga thumped with increasing vigor, pulling and pressing Goff to join, join. Goff grinned and told her to carry on without him—he himself was deriving tremendous enjoyment just watching. She shrugged convivially and soared up in a solo flight.

Goff looked at the soldiers and professors. One of the professors, with a long gentle horse face and deep-set eyes and the frizzled electrified hair of an Einstein, waved merrily toward them. Frigga, amid her transported singing, waved back. Goff assumed he was her father. He had no worry with a guy that looked like him, and he went on to examine the student-soldiers, all enlisted men.

They all clutched oversized steins of beer aloft and were all fiercely immersed in a group effort to portray a roistering bunch of devil-may-care young blades from Old Heidelberg. To a man, they tried to bring off a look of sabre-scarred arrogance and dash. Goff granted they might have pulled it off, if only they didn't all have such Jewish noses. He smirked as he recognized—their army getups didn't conceal it—types he had seen all his life in the candy stores, libraries, schoolyards and social-athletic cellar clubs all over Brooklyn. Frigga was absolutely right. All Jews. All yelling their heads off with their beer steins, trying to make like German aces at the officers' club. *Trink, trink, Brüderlein trink,* tonight ve make merry, for tomorrow ve die in our Fokkerspads!

And those professors! They were really going along with this incredible pageant. A clowns' opera. They were waving their arms, leading, bellowing, encouraging. With pathetic, but indomitable, stubborn good will they were really trying to turn these schmucks into Germans, and in some crazy way they were doing it. Ja, truly, if there is a spark of willingness in the pupil, a dedicated teacher can bring about miracles. Goff marveled. Tonight they were Germans—with blutwurst and beer. Tomorrow, a package from home—a salami, strictly kosher, Hebrew National, and wash it down with a glass of celery tonic. The purge was in. The *putsch* was over.

Goff settled down to smug enjoyment of the scene. The jolly round waiters, like puffy medicine balls, were rolling and waddling in and out of the tables, deftly balancing heavy trays filled with foaming steins of beer. Their flushed, perspired faces beamed with pleasure at their labor of love. The singing grew louder, more uninhibited, more carousing.

One singer seemed to be outshouting all the rest in a frantic high-pitched rendition of a swaggering German marching song. His stein waved more violently, his foot stomped harder, the veins in his neck strained bluer, and his pop eyes glazed deeper in their Prussian reverence. His face! He wasn't wearing his thick-lensed glasses, but Goff knew him! There could be no doubt this crazy bastard wasn't just another one of those Jew boys from Brooklyn, temporarily bewitched and transformed into a raving maniac, beer-hall German. Goff felt his stomach collapse and mush up. That sallow, pop-eyed Prussian was no other than Ira Mittelman. There could be no mistake. Despite his overseas cap, a shaken Goff could see that awful kinky hair springing up under the sides of the cap. There is kinky hair and there is kinky hair. But Ira Mittelman was cursed with the kind that for most men is mercifully reserved and secreted tactfully around their balls. But for poor Mittelman, this ugliest of hair had been destined to crop up where it had no business, not on his balls, but open, on his head! It was cruel and indecent.

Goff began to feel panic. He could feel his virile confidence crumpling and slinking back into his scrotum. Because—if Ira Mittelman, that sallow-skinned, prick-nosed, four-eyed, shriek-laughing, compulsive talking, spit-shpritzing, hand-waving, snot-picking, balls-haired Hebrew school toilet jerk-off artist, prize of pets of all Hebrew schoolteachers, rabbis, rebbitzens and shul hangers-on—if that putz of all pets somehow came over to him and claimed their acquaintanceship—he was DEAD! As dead as Kelsey's balls. Frigga would know the truth and blitz him to smithereens with one mighty thunderbolt of Thor's hammer, which Goff knew she could borrow any time she wanted.

Goff continued staring at him despite the danger. Like a creature hypnotized into immobility by a snake, Goff couldn't tear his unblinking eyes

away. The showpiece of the Ocean Parkway Jewish Center who could in-
cant three hours' worth of Saturday services in Hebrew without a single
mistake. There he was: instead of chanting the reverent, the eternal
*sh'ma Yisroel,* he was shrieking the German rathskeller swilling song,
*"Bier her, Bier her . . ."* with the crazy zeal and feeling of a beer-bloat-
ed storm trooper at a party rally at Nuremberg.

There was no mistaking him, even without those thick glasses he always wore. It was the same Mittelman who used to raise his hand in Hebrew school to ask Mr. Wolofsky for permission to leave the room. Mr.
Wolofsky would nod gravely to his prize scholar. He was certain Ira was
not leaving for frivolous reasons or worse. So sincere and serious was
Ira's devotion to the sacred teachings. In retrospect, Goff felt that, ironically, Mr. Wolofsky's faith was peculiarly justified, if you looked at it in a
cockeyed way, because when Ira left the classroom, he wasn't going to
the Talmud Torah bathroom to jerk off like so many of his adolescent
coreligionists. With him it was different. Because, whereas the other artists, after maneuvering themselves to the toilet, would quickly pull out
their schlongs and with no wasted motion jerk off to pictures they'd cut
out from *Breezy Detective* or movie magazines, or of whore divorcees and
breach-of-promise cuties in the *Daily News,* Ira Mittelman, in peculiar
loyalty to his religious teachings, piously jerked off to pictures of Queen
Esther in his Bible stories book. Goff had seen it with his own eyes. There
propped up on the urinal altar was Ira's Bible stories, opened to a picture
of Queen Esther on her knees, begging King Ahasuerus to save her people from wicked Haman. And Ira was whacking away, inspired by good
Queen Esther. It was interesting to speculate then whether Mr. Wolofsky
would be apt to look less wrathfully on Ira's sin than on those of the other
Hebrew school jerk-off artists, the assimilated ones.

Goff himself had been outraged. He couldn't exactly explain it, but he
knew you just don't fuck your religion. It was disgusting and perverted. It
was like jerking off to your old aunt Sadie. Maybe that was the way these
hypocrite rabbis justified *their* jerking off. Ira was sure to become one
when he grew up. That was clearly his calling.

It had been there in the Ocean Parkway Jewish Center where this miracle had been revealed to him. It had been Shep Grossman, whom Goff had
envied because he was good-looking in a non-Jewish way, and because he
lived in a private house on Beverly Road and whose parents spoke without accents. Grossman had signaled to him to follow after he'd received
permission from Mr. Wolofsky to leave the room. When Goff saw him a
few minutes later in the bathroom, Shep had already propped up on the

urinal a drawing torn from *Breezy Detective*. He had told Goff to watch him, and had then gone ahead without further ado to jerk off with quick practiced strokes into the urinal. The picture was a crudely drawn illustration of one of the stories showing a sexy-looking shiksa with big tits sticking out, in a shiny black dress. The art work was beautiful, with the highlights and tit lines drawn by a truly master illustrator. The drawing was indelibly etched in Goff's mind forever. How she reclined on a couch, with a lot of thigh showing, because of the Chinese slit in her tight black dress, and she was holding a gun pointed at a suave guy in a tuxedo. This had been a normal enough kind of picture for jerking off. But then there were really all kinds of pictures a guy could choose, depending on what was his type. There was Carole Lombard, if your type was someone who was quick on the uptake. Jean Harlow was great if you were in the mood for a wild, crazy, go-for-broke fuck. God, those nipple bumps in the cloth of her dress could drive you wild. You'd want to suck on them right through the cloth. If you were tired of blondes, Paulette Goddard—or maybe Claudette Colbert. She was American-French. But for the real French, for real connoisseurs—Danielle Darrieux. Madeleine Carroll if you wanted a high-brow sincere piece with an English accent. For the college coed type, Toby Wing, Betty Grable, who really went on to hit the jackpot. You could have floated an aircraft carrier with all the juice pumped out on her account in WW II. There was Eleanor Holm when you felt like it in a warm bathtub. For wholesomeness, or the girl you wouldn't do it with until you were married, who was better than Priscilla Lane? Deanna Durbin for the starry-eyed juvenile schmucks. For guys who liked their hot-blooded Latins, Dolores Del Rio, Lupe Velez. If you're in a mood for a zany one-night stand, try crazy Betty Hutton. I guarantee it. Try. You'll see. And millions more, unknowns, from bathing-suit ads; unknowns till you saw them, recognized their talents, and made them stars in your production. Murdered models whose pictures were plastered all over the *Daily News* and *Mirror*. You brought them back to life with a twist of your fist. Gangsters' broads, like Gae Orlova, girlfriend of Lucky Luciano. There had never been a time in history when a guy had so much choice and variety. And if you felt like changing your luck, there was Lena Horne. She could just about pass anyway, if you felt funny about it. For every taste, for every twist, a guy could find the jerk-off princess of his dreams.

Considering all that choice available, Ira's selection of Queen Esther was even more reprehensible. The other guys around Ditmas Avenue and Ocean Parkway were equally incensed, and they had lain in wait for Ira one night when he was coming home from Hebrew, dragged him onto an empty lot and painted his balls and cock with bright red Red Devil paint. And they warned him never to pull off to anyone in the religion again.

And now, here was Ira, singing these German songs with frenzied eyeballs and his crazy high-pitched hollering. Goff's eyes caught Ira's and Ira in turn pushed his eyeballs out further in strained nearsighted peering in Goff's direction. But his wobbly focus fell short of a direct hit on target. But Goff knew that Ira had perceived a hazy glimmer of the familiar through his watery eyes.

Frigga rose to go to the john, and Goff seized the opportunity. He quickly hopped over toward Ira's table and waved him aside. "Ira, quick, meet me in the john."

Ira grinned craftily as the recognition set in. "Arnie!" he screeched with exaggerated joviality. "I was lookin' at you, I thought . . ." Goff interrupted, "Please, Ira, in the john."

"Sure, Arnie, we'll go to the toilet—what kind of john?" Ira laced his speech with a strong overdone mocky inflection. Goff realized he was being reproached. The word "john" was unacceptable to Ira because it signaled an adoption of high-class goyische airs. "John" was not a Jewish expression of the old neighborhood. Ira would not grant him the privileges of his new membership as a commissioned officer in the U.S. Army. Ira, very high and brassy on his beer and indoctrination of old Munich, told Goff with a self-satisfied smirk, "To the toilet I'll go, but not to no john. In a john I'd feel like a *shvartzeh* in a gent's room, for whites only."

"OK, OK," conceded the jumpy Goff, "to the toilet, Ira." Ira nodded gravely, and they proceeded to the beer hall toilet.

Inside, Ira said comfortably, "Excuse me, Lieutenant, sir, but I gotta go pishin. I gotta lot of beer in me." He turned to the urinal. Goff, leaning against a washstand, told Ira, "I gotta talk to you fast, Ira."

"I never talk business while I pish. Wait. I'll finish. Then we can have a nice chat, a short chat, a long chat, whatever you want. Yes, sir." Ira snapped his head for finality and continued his pishin, granting it now his undivided attention. Time passed and Ira pished. Still in full, undiminished flow, Ira started singing his German beer song, waving his cock and stream gently to its infectious rhythm.

Goff waited. How much could that guy hold? Goff was sure that Ira had clocked off easily five minutes before he finally dribbled off the last drops.

Now, with the serenity of one whose burden has been lifted, Ira turned to face him. Letting loose an elongated guttural sigh of relief, he smiled and asked chummily, "Nu, Lieutenant, howze by you—aside from the blondie?"

"Aside from the blonde, nothin' to rave about. But it's the blonde I'm worried about now. Ira, do me the biggest favor, please?" Goff studied Ira's crafty look, heightened and emboldened by the beer still in him. How could he persuade Ira not to acknowledge him in front of Frigga?

Ira smirked. "What flavor favor you want, Lieutenant, strawberry, raspberry, cherry, orange, lemon or lime? I bet you it's closer to cherry than all the rest," hee-hawed Ira, pitching high, fracturing himself.

Goff knew he had a tough job ahead. He figured Ira for one of those whose slyness and perception registered sharpest when they were semi-loaded. Goff ruled out lying; it wouldn't work. A few auxiliary minor lies maybe, but only to bolster the main core of truth. But the truth he would present to Ira had to be a carefully selected truth, one that would best harmonize with his loaded condition. He would appeal to Ira's honor. That always went good with a drunk, any kind, Jew, goy or *shvartzeh*. The last refuge of a drunk is his honor.

"Ira," said Goff with throwing-himself-at-the-mercy-of-the-court candor, "I got a very good chance of *shtupping* that blonde I'm with. . . ."

"And you need my help, Lieutenant?" giggled Ira.

"Listen, Ira, seriously, she happens to be such an anti-Semite Nazi that she even criticizes Hitler for being too soft on Jews. She doesn't know I'm Jewish. I'll be dead in a minute if she even so much as smells it. Ira, the big favor is that if this Jew boy is going to get his Nazi nookie tonight, I gotta have you promise me something."

"What?" Ira looked at Goff crookedly.

"You've got to promise to make like you don't know me. She spotted all you guys, and she picked you out especially. If it was up to her, she'd have all your balls cut off."

Ira cried with sudden pain, "Even without my glasses, I look Jewish?"

"Ira, promise, please. My nookie is in your hands."

Ira turned dignified. "I don't owe you a thing, Goff, and don't think you can go ordering me around because you're a ninety-day *vunder*."

"What kind of ordering you, Ira? I'm making an appeal."

"Yeh, a United Jewish Appeal," said a suddenly sullen Ira. (Goff had deliberately used the word "appeal" to elicit just such a wisecrack, figuring if he gave Ira an easy hanger, he'd be in a better frame of mind.) Ira continued, but Goff was sure he detected a tone of relenting. "Look, Goff, all of a sudden you're a real *haimisher landsman*, talking to me like one real mockie to another. I can see right through you. The way you're talking to me now is not the way you talk at your officers' club with your Johns and your pootang or whatever the hell they call it out here. You can go fuck yourself. I'm not making any promises. If I feel like coming up to you and that cunt and saying 'Arnie, *boychik, vuss macht a Yid?*' that's what I'll do."

Ironically, Goff thought Ira was still flattering himself. He didn't have to come over and say all that to screw up the works. All he had to do was come over, period. He would have to lay his cards on the table. "Ira, you were never anybody's fool. Sure, I'm putting it on a little thick, which you recognized" (he'd flatter him a little). "Sure, I'm talkin' *mama loshen* to you."

"Na," mumbled Ira truculently. "That's not *mama loshen*. *Mama loshen* is straight, clean Yiddish, not that singsong shit you're pullin' on me."

"All right, Ira. So do you blame me? I'm trying to get through to you." Someone was coming in, and Goff cautioned, "Let's hold it, Ira."

The fat waiter trundled in. Seeing Goff roused him to a fit of laughter again. "Ho, ho, out of bett, ho, ho."

Ira glowered at the waiter, and Goff dared not display any friendliness. It all went past the waiter, who proceeded to the urinal, shaking and gurgling. He opened his fly and groped around before successfully pulling out his pecker and getting his grip on it for aim and steadiness. Goff noticed he held it with a full-handed clutch rather than with the common three-fingered light support. Like with cigarettes, he figured the European holds it differently. This guy was also one of those long pishers, and as they waited, he and Ira simultaneously looked at the printed sign over the basins directing all employees to wash their hands before leaving the lavatory. The same question occurred to both of them. Would the kraut wash his hands or not? They went on to figure it was a foregone conclusion. Coming from such a clean race in which obedience to rule and law were so deeply ingrained, he would certainly follow the directive to the letter. They watched the German zip up, still laughing as he started to make his way out. He would be passing the washstand. Goff and Ira turned from the Health Department sign to look at each other. Would the Kraut stop at the washstand or not?

The waiter didn't give the washstand a glimmer of a look. Laughing and shaking, he passed it right by, threw the door open and waddled back to the hall to resume his duties.

The two Jewish-American spectators were nonplussed. Ira blinked unbelievingly. "The Kraut didn't wash his hands, the filthy, sneaky, phony

bastards, the fuckin' frauds—they're full of shit! That's why they're going to lose the war!'' he shrieked in his hysterical high-pitched voice. Goff
had already recovered and was anxious to return to his original business.
But Ira had been shaken to an extraordinary degree. "They are misrepre-
senters," he said. "Do you know, the whole war depended on what that
Kraut was going to do. The fate of his whole country was in his hands!
*These* are the dirty bastards that are killing the Jews. They have no right,"
he said, shaking his head in stunned bewilderment. For the first time the
unfairness of it had actually hit home.

"I think I know what you mean, Ira, but getting back to the
blonde . . ."

"Your Nazi girlfriend! She's sure to have the clap," said Ira woodenly.

"I'll risk it."

Ira shrugged.

"So, it's a deal, Ira?"

"I didn't make any deal." Ira was beginning to bristle again.

Goff had to resort to the loyalty of the street code of the old neighborhood. "Ira, a piece of ass is at stake. Christ, we've got to come through
for one another—like it was back in the neighborhood." Goff recited all
the codes and rules of the Church Avenue Shamuses Social Athletic Club.
Never crash a brother's gash; and, you never tresp ass.

Ira burst in to point out bitterly that he was never even a Shamus; how
he had always hungered to be one; how they had always rejected him. He
well knew all the club slogans regarding the sanctity of the almighty getting laid. He knew: *"The only thing better than cash is gash"* and *"You
never duck a fuck."* Ira increased his crescendo of long pent-up agony,
humiliation and hurt. He remembered—oh, too well—Goff spreading the
word about him in the Talmud Torah toilet with Queen Esther and how
they ganged up on him and painted his schlong red. The hypocrites with
their righteousness. "You don't fuck your own religion," they had ordained wrathfully in unison. How they were responsible for keeping him
from getting his share of nookie, his rightful heritage. He held them all responsible for keeping him cherry until he was almost twenty-one, when it
was only right here in Columbus that he *finally* got his first piece, some old
bag who had a son his age in Guadalcanal.

"You fuckin' Shamuses kept me from my rightful heritage. With all
your slogans for the sacred rites of getting laid, you blackballed me—red-
balled me—out of the running, and turned me into a fuckin' baseball accountant. While you guys went to your gang fucks and cellar parties, I
hung around Hymie's candy store to learn every batting and earned run

average of every player in the National League—so that when you were finished and came around, I would be ready to give you all the runs, hits, and errors from the pink edition of the *News*. Is that a way to grow up? And now I know why all you guys always gave me the shit end of the stick. Plain and simple, though you'd never admit it, it was because I was the most Jewish of you all, and you bastards punished me for it."

Goff said soothingly, "Aw, Ira, don't hold a grudge. We were dopey kids. Let me tell you something. Nobody was getting it as much as talking about it. Even me, the only reason I was in fair shape was because I had it in the family. If it wasn't mostly for my cock-crazy cousin in the Bronx, I would have been just as bad off as you. And those gangfucks, believe me, you were better off. Maybe it's hard for you to believe, but it wasn't pleasant. If they weren't retarded—I mean really mental—they were the doggiest of dogs. And most of them stank. I mean odor. Phew! And this'll knock you out: You remember Shep Grossman?"

Ira looked at Goff with mopey suspicion. "Sure. Don't tell me he wasn't getting into Rhoda Sacks."

"He wasn't. I swear it to you. Look, Ira, my point is getting laid never came easy to anybody. That's why I'm begging you, don't screw me up. Please, please, don't know me out there. It's a very delicate thing."

"Goff, they tell us you salute the uniform, not the man. I got respect for getting laid, and I wouldn't hurt any man's chances. You don't have to be afraid. I won't know you. As far as I'm concerned, you can tell her you're Goebbels, who—I hope you're not insulted—you resemble. But I want you to know, you hardly deserve it. You guys in the Shamuses could have given me a permanent complex."

Goff grasped Ira's hand. "Thanks, Ira, that's damn white of you." With that, he quickly hopped out, like a rabbit. Ira followed, shambling at first, but suddenly snapped himself erect and *korrekt,* tried to pat down his springy hair, and joined his group of fine Heidelberger fellows in their *singen und saufen.* He studiously avoided looking at Goff's table and his blond Nazi.

When Goff returned, Frigga showed annoyance at his drawn-out absence. Goff laughed it off, telling her he had got into a little argument with some private in the john. "I bet," she said, quickly switching her peeve, "it was with one of those Jew bastards. Oh, how it galls me that they should be singing these wonderful German melodies, and the airs they put on—unbelievable!" Goff patted her milk-white knee.

Frigga's papa, Professor Schmidt, left his crowded table and came to sit with his daughter and Goff. Flushed by the beer, excited by the singing and his daughter's appearance, the professor greeted them with the excessive cordiality of one generally unaccustomed to easy gregariousness. He immediately subjected them to an effusive lecture. "The German is credited or discredited for many characteristics, but it has never been acknowledged that the German, more than any other group, has perfected the art of creating the perfect feeling of harmony derived from an evening of communal singing and beer drinking. It cannot be achieved by any other combination. The quaffing must be of beer, and the songs must be the German songs. There is between them a unique affinity. It produces that rare, special *Gemütlichkeit*. No other elements can quite produce this blend, this magic."

Goff nodded aggreeably: he wasn't about to reveal that he could remember when his pop and his devout cronies did pretty damn good on a glass of tea with a piece of sponge cake—that was pretty good magic too.

Frigga attempted a cold surgical incision. "And, Poppa, this magic seems to work on everybody without discrimination, *nicht wahr?*"

"Yes, yes," agreed the good, innocent Herr Professor Schmidt, never feeling his daughter's razor. He invited Frigga and Goff to join him, the other faculty members and the students, but Frigga pointed out the lieutenant's incapacity. He must be excused. In any case, in a few moments they would have to leave. Adding that the lieutenant was on duty that night, she directed at Goff a gross leer.

"Even with your incapacity, you are obliged to be on duty?" asked the eternally naive academician.

"Yes, sir," responded Goff, the officer and gentleman. "My bad ankle won't interfere." He returned Frigga's message with his own quick, deft smirk. But he felt uncomfortable despite these easy intimate exchanges. He couldn't eradicate the old discomfort he always felt in front of the father of the girl he was taking out to lay. He wished he wasn't burdened with these old-fashioned scruples. Even in this instance, where the daughter was a Nazi.

Frigga rose. "Sorry, Dad, we have to go."

"Glad to have met you, sir," sirred Goff, who felt very squirmy. Not only was he going to screw the sir's daughter, but in addition, "sirring" a girl's father was so alien to him. He felt as if he were sneaking in a knish at a New England church supper.

At this moment Ira staggered up to their table. Goff cursed under his breath, and shot him a hard, warning look. The professor attempted to introduce him. Goff and Frigga were icily rigid in their avoidance, as the professor innocently described Ira as possessing the most remarkable aptitude for the German language.

Ira maintained a rubbery grin at Frigga as he acknowledged the praise, which he volunteered was really undeserved, because his parents spoke a German dialect at home which had gone so far as to give him a basic grounding in German. He reported this information gleefully, especially searching out Goff's eyes to make sure he got it. Goff became ossified with hatred, which only egged Ira on even more. "Professor, the gang sent me to bring you back to the table, and also to invite your beautiful daughter and her handsome escort to accompany us." Ira was at his gallant best.

Utterly ignoring Ira, Frigga told her father they had to go now. Goff nodded grimly and raised himself laboriously from his seat. While he was adjusting his crutches under his arms, Ira staggered up to him and, grinning maliciously, said, "Lieutenant, don't we know each other from somewhere maybe?"

Goff hissed, "Step aside, Private," and started to move forward, but Ira grabbed his arm. Leaning on one crutch, Goff took the other and drove it up viciously, in uppercut style, so that the underarm section smashed wickedly into Ira's jaw. The blow produced a tremendous thwack, and Ira spiraled into collapse.

The professor went into immediate slack-jawed shock. Frigga went into instant shining-eyed delight. She grabbed Goff's arm tightly, and started to lead him away. Goff tried to suppress the sick feeling billowing up from his stomach. From the floor, Ira torturedly stretched out an arm toward Goff, and through a bloody mouth blubbered in dazed bewilderment, "Fuckin' Arnie, I wasn't gonna tell, I wasn't gonna tell," and he lapsed into unintelligible sobbing. And as Frigga and Goff reached the doorway, Ira pulled himself into a sitting position, and with great effort sobbed, "An officer isn't allowed to hit an enlisted man. He's not allowed to hit-t-t-t . . ." He trailed off in a whimpering spasm. It took a few moments before he could catch his breath again. "It's against regulations," he managed finally, a strangled, legalistic denunciation.

Ira then looked up pleadingly at the bewildered Professor Schmidt; he felt a vital need to obtain the professor's full understanding and sympathy, his respect, even his love. And so with supreme effort, despite his shock and bleeding, lacerated mouth, Ira repeated the regulation again. However, this time, to please the professor, in perfect idiomatic German, perfectly enunciated, as his professor had taught him. *"Es ist gesetzlich*

*unerlaubt für einen Offizier, einen Soldaten zu schlagen.* " With this astonishing display of scholarship under stress, Ira crumpled again.

As he now gazed down at Ira, the professor's bewilderment dissolved
into a look radiant with inner delight. How exalting! Enunciated in perfect
*Hoch Deutsch,* in perfect grammar, in perfect idiom. A humble teacher's
supreme reward. The quintessential manifestation of a teacher's *raison
d'être.* A perfect student who had mastered the teachings impeccably,
there lay, miraculously before him. The good, wild-haired professor quiv-
ered gently from his core.

Frigga was filled with exhilaration as she and Goff entered the convertible. As soon as they were seated, she turned to him, opened her arms so
they could envelop each other in an ardent kiss, a kiss of victory, a kiss
for her Siegfried. "You were magnificent, Armand," she panted huskily,
as she plunged her tongue ferociously into Goff's mouth. Officer and gentleman Goff responded in perfect taste. He tongued her right back, placed
his hand on her palpitating breast and gently drew her fluttering hand onto
his genital area—all in the chastest manner, under the circumstances, for
he strove for no bare skin in either of these reciprocal courtesies. The
truth of the matter was that Goff found himself surprisingly devoid of the
vigorous responses that sex play invariably induced. He simply couldn't
abandon himself. It was the memory of Ira that debilitated. That crunch
of crutch against poor schmuck Ira's jaw still resounded in his ears. And
as his tongue flapped listlessly in Frigga's mouth, he realized he was not
completely without sensitivity. The terrible curse of being Jewish.

Frigga suddenly withdrew her tongue, and in a spontaneous outburst of
joy pushed Goff away. "Armand, *liebchen,* we must spare ourselves for
later." Goff made a halfhearted attempt—out of good form—to continue.
But he was more than content to abandon it when Frigga showed
firmness. "It is better to stop now," she said with protective Nazi mater-
nalism. Goff leaned back relieved, glad for the opportunity to fish out a
cigar and light it. Frigga concentrated on the driving, while joyously humming intense, German-sounding musical passages. After driving for some
time, she humming, he puffing, Frigga turned to him. "Armand, your cigar smells so good. Let me have a few puffs."

Goff passed it over to her readily, but he resented it. He smoked a cigar
cleanly and didn't relish it returned to him soggy and munched up—or
even if it wasn't mangled, just the thought that it would soak up even a
minute bit of her slobber was repugnant to him. He didn't mind French
kissing or even French anything, but he had always smoked a cigar clean,

and he couldn't help being pissed off at this invasion of his cigar. This sharing shit had to stop somewhere. But he wasn't going to make an issue of that now.

Frigga puffed the cigar for a minute and then handed it back to him. Goff immediately planted it in his mouth, but tenderly, with the air of a cavalier who has just been tossed a rose from the bosom of his beloved. Frigga smiled at him benignly. She had fucked up the cigar, sure enough, Goff detected. Its spring had turned to sog.

Frigga drove on, her humming surging with enthusiasm and good feeling. Goff, unable to extract his accustomed satisfaction from the now-tainted cigar, finally threw it out the window, and trying to keep annoyance out of his tone, asked her what she was humming.

"Wagner, Armand. Do you know his music at all?"

"Can't say that I do."

"After tonight, maybe, you will become good friends with Wagner," she said, flashing him a lewd, companionable smile. She nodded several large nods to usher in her next statement. "It is certainly proper and fitting, after your victory over that slimy Jew. Oh, incapacitated as you were, you were able to overcome him with that lightning stroke of your crutch."

Goff sank a little deeper into his corner. Goff, the crippled Jewish Thor, lashing out thunderously with crutch instead of hammer. He definitely felt bad about that shmuck Ira; and this overpropagandized cunt was ready to give him the Iron Cross for it. He decided to be grim about it for half a minute and then ask her where the fuck they were going.

Frigga took Goff's grim silence as he had expected. She concluded that this was the typical reluctance of a good soldier to talk about the bloody battlefield. She was pleased, extremely pleased, with this wonderful Basque.

Goff's prearranged timing now called for him to ask carelessly, "Where are we heading for, baby?"

"Armand, I said we would have an adventure. My family has a summer cottage. It's about twenty-five miles from town. We will be there soon. Are you pleased?"

Yes, yes, he assured her. He was very pleased. But it would have been better without Ira. But maybe the bastard, in some obscure way, had even contributed to the success of the mission after all.

They pulled up into a thickly wooded pine area. The headlights picked out a cottage in log-cabin veneer and latticed windows. Keeping the headlights fixed on the door Frigga stepped out of the car, proceeded in grand processional to frame herself in the spotlighted doorway and raised her arms to welcome her hero to Valhalla. The hobbled hero started to stumble forward toward the exciting apparition that was the gloriously illuminated Frigga. The powerful effect of this tableau had easily driven out all further thoughts of Ira. Goff was reaching unbearable excitement as he feverishly clattered closer—but already a gnawing thought began to mar the purity of his pleasure. Ira was gone, but only to be replaced by a new concern. He began to worry about the car's battery running down—and in these secluded woods . . . .

Goff cursed his Jewish anxieties. What the hell made him start worrying about the battery running down? Out! Out! He commanded. And as that worry was extinguished, a new one was already waiting in the wings. This spectacularly seductive enticement, set in this dark, heavy pine forest, was menacing. There was this glowing blond-braided North woman luring him into a Hansel and Gretel kind of cottage. Would this beauteous blondie turn into a hag-witch and lock him in a cage to take him out only when she wanted him to screw her? Would she shuffle up to the cage every day and command in a cackle to hold out his cockel. "All right, dearie, hold out your peter through the bars so that I can feel it." And her fingers, turned into sharp talons, would pinch his wee, timorous Jewish prick and she'd curse, "Drat it, still too skinny and scrawny. We'll have to fatten it up some more, drat it, drat it, drat it." Shuffling off, muttering, she'd return a few minutes later with platters heaped with potato *latkes* and *blintzes* and *knishes* and place them inside his cage, squawking, "EAT, EAT, EAT! You've got to get your *schmekeleh* fattened up, drat it!"

And he *would* eat, eat, eat. And he would get pudgy and fat all over, except for his *schmekeleh,* which stubbornly continued to remain skinny and puny. But isn't that what he wanted—to thwart that witch? Maybe not. He was mixed up. Maybe he did want his *schmekeleh* to get big and fat; but if it did, then maybe he'd resort to the old Jewish chicken-bone trick. But maybe he wouldn't. The witch wasn't *that* old. What about: never duck a fuck. What a conundrum.

Suddenly Goff was in Frigga's arms. She hadn't turned into a hag after all. She kissed him ardently, and he returned her ardor in full measure, clinging to her with tremors that surprised him. He had been scared, and he would not let her slip into a hag. He wanted to be protected. He clung on and they kissed and pawed and slobbered over each other touchingly. Nazis were, after all, also people, thought an inflamed and infatuated Goff. They were both panting furiously, when again as before, Frigga broke away. "We must wait a little more, darling," she said breathlessly.

"Yes," back-panted the wobbly Goff who could barely hold himself up. "You'd better turn off your headlights, baby. The battery is running down." Goff was leaving hangers all over that night. He knew what he was doing, and he was racking up. So having handed her the cue stick, he was not surprised at how promptly she sank the shot.

"I don't think so at all," she gasped, as she nipped Goff's ear and tapped his straining crotch playfully.

Goff asked whether there were lights in the cabin. Frigga thought there were some candles, but couldn't find them. Using a flashlight, she found, however, a Coleman lantern and asked Goff to light it while she brought some things in from the car. He had seen a Coleman lantern only once before, at night field exercise, but he had paid absolutely no attention to its method of operation, because he had been teamed up with a guy named Murphy from Montana who knew all about lanterns, half hitches, slack, lashing, lean-tos, and all that great outdoor goyishe stuff. A Brooklyn boy would hardly have the occasion to become adept with these things.

Having this guy Murphy, Goff never again gave the Coleman lantern another thought. But now, Frigga expected him, a Basque Buckeroo, from a long line of fierce, independent mountain lantern lighters, to light it with firm, ridgy-veined, outdoor hands. She probably expected him to be able to do it blindfolded.

Goff fucked with the lantern for a few minutes, straining to recall what Murphy had done, and then slammed it on the table. Dammit, he'd come right out with it and tell Frigga he just didn't know a fuckin' thing about lighting it. It was *her* responsibility to provide some civilized means of lighting. Anyway, he figured shrewdly, he didn't have to be so meticulous in his role anymore. She had accepted him and committed herself to him, and he could now ease off some. He didn't have to strain to be so goddam un-Jewish anymore. She would never notice now. She wouldn't dare to notice. It was all in the psychology.

Frigga came in and asked whether Armand was having trouble lighting the lantern. Goff blurted out that he didn't know the first goddam thing about it. She quickly shushed him with a kiss and told him sweetly not to fret. She would do it. Handing the pouting Goff the flashlight, she instructed him to keep it trained on the lantern. She bent to it and began expertly turning some knobs, pumped another knob, lit a match, and—poof! The thing exploded softly into light. She made a further adjustment and produced a bright, even glow. Just as Goff had expected, she then turned to him, shaking her head in gentle, mock annoyance at his lovable clumsiness. So typical—his masculine ineptness with small delicate parts. Goff well knew that the notion that he might be plain Jewish unmechanical was the most remote idea in her accepting, silly, blond, Nazi *keppeleh*.

In the surprisingly far-reaching light, Goff saw a room containing the traditional features of rustic coziness. Dominating the room was an imposing stone fireplace. On the floor before it was a thick oval shaggy rug. Arranged comfortably were a couch, two deep red leather chairs, a rocker and alpine bench which doubled as the lid of a storage box for firewood. One wall contained built-in book cases, and the remaining walls were paneled in dark pine. Frigga told him the cabin consisted of four rooms. What a place, marveled Goff, to settle down with a pipe and write a book, if you could combine it with, let's say, two good pieces a day—one to put you to sleep, one to wake you up—and if the broad kept out of your way the rest of the time, you had it made. He could go for that. Maybe he could be a writer some day.

Frigga invited him to sit in the deep red leather chair. She fetched a bottle of brandy, poured two generous half glasses and sat on the arm of his chair.

Accepting the brandy, he reminded her she had not yet turned off the car headlights. "You are such a worrier," she said, tousling his hair affectionately.

Goff continued heedlessly, "And you'd better run the motor hard for a few minutes or we might have trouble starting it up." She shook her head in playful despair, and stood up to do as her grouchy beloved had bidden. Goff sat back in a triumphant sulk. He had to get back at reveille. He no longer feared his anxieties would be regarded as Jewish. Frigga would now consider them sound and level-headed, the proper concerns of a solid man.

Frigga returned after a few minutes flashing an affectionate smile. Goff thought that she no longer looked like such a hard, murderous bitch. She knelt on the hearth and got a fire going. While it blazed and crackled, she wound up the phonograph. Taking her glass of brandy, she sat herself on the rug at Goff's feet, intent on the music.

It seemed to Goff he had heard it before as maybe the theme of some boring, high-brow radio program. It was slow and draggy, ponderous stuff that never made money on its own, always in need of sponsorship or subsidization. How he wished he could tell her to knock it off—didn't she maybe have a copy of Benny Goodman's "Sing, Sing, Sing," a solid sending, self-supporting work. But that was a liberty he was not yet ready to take. He would try to go along with Wagner—and either get into the mood or simulate it. He stroked her hair and she reached up and held his hand, and he slipped out of the chair onto the rug with her and began to peck her cheek, ear and neck with the sobriety that befitted the mood. Gently he eased her head onto his lap, and careful not to jar the rapture of his misguided Nazi girl, he placed his hand with infinite delicacy on her breast (clothed)—and it was a movement, a touch of sheer poetry. It promised to be a generous breast, once bared.

Here he was now with this exciting homicidal Nazi. She was in a moony trance listening to this Honus Wagner crap. Her head was blissfully in his lap, and his hand on her tit.

At intervals Frigga rose to change the music, confining all her selections to Wagner. It became a brooding surge within the cabin. Imperiously it commanded them to go on and on and on deep into the hot fire center core of the universe. This was clearly Frigga's music, Frigga, who had been conceived with a heaving primal roar over towering spruces and pines, deep in the forest.

And Frigga and Goff obeyed the stern Wagnerian command.But first Frigga threw another log on the fire, wound the victrola up again, and with breathless haste set thereon the record containing her climactic music, *The Prelude to the Third Act of Lohengrin.* All in readiness, Frigga then threw herself down on the shaggy rug and clamped onto Goff, panting hoarsely that the moment was now upon them. Prepare.

"Sure, sure," Goff agreed quickly. "Let's get into the bedroom."

"No, no, Armand. Here we must remain. Trust me."

"Sure, sure."

"I promise you an adventure, *Liebchen,*" she panted into his ear, already saturated with ardent salivations. Her hand was inside his shirt, petting him soothingly. "In a little while I will turn on the phonograph. It is all set to play Wagner's *Prelude to the Third Act of Lohengrin,* and I promise you, Armand, there is absolutely nothing in the world as thrilling as making love to Wagner in front of a roaring fire." As she murmured, she kept licking into his ear. "Don't you sense the truth of it?"

"Sure. Sure," said a frenzied Goff, who was bursting with Teutonic lust. But as insanely inflamed as he was, he still couldn't stave off a characteristic intrusion into his moment of approaching ecstasy. It would continue to plague him all his life; he couldn't completely abandon himself. Who needed Honus Wagner? He could do just as well with Horace Heidt and his Musical Knights, or better yet—nothing. Who needed a roaring fire? And on a hard floor, when there were three beds available? Roughing it was for jerk-off Boy Scouts. He didn't need that kind of nonsense thrill. And how about how drafty it was on the floor? With the way she had soaked up his ear, he was a prime candidate for a draft getting in there and bringing on a bad inflammation. He had always had inflamed ears as a kid and mastoids and that awful pain, and his father pouring hot camphor oil into it. That's what brought it on: drafts into damp ears. And he had to be in that jeopardy, because his crazy Nazi wouldn't settle for sensible civilized fucking. Goff had to blend the expression of his preference about fucking in bed with his undiminished ardor. So, his pettings and pawing became half-disguised tuggings; and his choked ardent murmerings, if translated accurately, would emerge something like, "Come on, Frigga. Enough. This is Armand, your wild mountain lover. We don't need all that crap. Let's just fuck, Frigga baby. You're lovely and beautiful and have the sweetest Nazi pussy this side of heaven and, besides, I really like you a lot; and I don't give a shit about how you hate Jews. Aw, come on, sweet Frigga. You know, I'll bet I could make you see things differently. I'll marry you, Frigga, I really will. I'll tell you the truth about myself. You won't have to convert, but you have to promise to bring up the children as Jewish—not strict, but at least so that they should know they're Jewish. But I'm reasonable. We'll make a deal. They should go a little to Hebrew in the school season, and summers they can go to the Bund camp in Jersey. Oh, you stubborn Dutch squarehead. Will it make you happy if I'm finished before I start? What good would it be for you? Please, let me put it in now, and stop playin' around, baby doll. Fuck Wagner. Now! *Meine zeeskeit, meine schaeneh maideleh. Oi veh, ess tut mir veh!* Please! I'll heil Hitler for you—howzat?"

And Frigga finally felt the time was ripe. She bolted up, threw off her clothes, and hissed at Goff to take his off. She then ran to the fireplace to throw another log on the fire, snapped on the victrola, and rushed back, clambering breathlessly onto a nude, shivering, crazed Goff.

And Frigga took charge. She conducted him through the whole of Wagner's *Prelude to the Third Act of Lohengrin*. It takes exactly eleven minutes and twenty seconds. Considering he was a novice, unacquainted with the music, she conducted him masterfully. She brought him into the lyrical passages, the somber swayings, the sudden stayings, the crashing crescendos and subtle innuendoes.

In grim control, hanging on like onto a wild roller coaster for most of the piece, Goff finally succumbed to the intensity of performance—got himself carried away, but regrettably reached his finale before Frigga's baton called for it. Frigga synchronized herself perfectly with the recording, and surprisingly, when the music reached its final cymbal bang, the adroit Goff was there together with his inspired conductor; he having faked the last two minutes manfully.

Frigga sprawled blissfully on the rug. Goff felt clammy after his sweaty Wagnerian fuck; he was beginning to feel the tricky little floor drafts swirling and licking around his moist unprotected balls. His predominant impulse was to jump up, get as close to the fire as possible and get dressed, but Frigga in sweet spenthood wiggled next to him to convey to him silently that she was cleanly sated. She hoped she had brought him equal fulfillment.

Goff wondered how clean the rug was beneath him. How many guys had she given a Wagnerian screwin' there? What moldy corruption lay imbedded in that rug to cause him skin infections? He resigned himself to remain for a few minutes. He owed it to her, he guessed. She wasn't such a bad broady. Maybe he had misread that cold, sadistic joy in her face when he had clumped poor Ira cold with his crutch. Such blond angelic repose in her clear-skinned, blissful face, as it rested on his shoulder.

"Was it good for you, Armand?" she finally whispered.

He assured her it had been glorious. She smiled and nodded, eyes closed. "There is nothing like Wagner to bring out the highest response of lovemaking."

"I swear I won't ever be able to do it again without Wagner."

"You are teasing, Armand. But I'm sure there is some truth in it."

"A hell of a lot of truth. I will never be the same again."

Again she smiled and purred contentedly.

Goff felt expansive and had an impulse to test out the truth—to tell her about that Basque crap. Would she still react that bad if he told her he was a Jew? Wasn't it possible she might nestle closer to him and lower her eyes and whisper half-ashamedly, "Yes, Arnie, I began to suspect sometime ago. There was a certain characteristic humanity, so beautifully blended with soft, gentle wit, and then I knew for sure when you made love to me with a compassion combined so excitingly with that vital, vigorous pushiness that is so typical of you Jewish people. I was a fool, Arnie, with my barbarous ignorance. To think I was such a scatterbrained, silly little Nazi. Please, can you ever completely forgive me, Arnie? I'm really an entirely different person now. And you made me that, Arnie. Can't you see, bubie?

Or would she rise up in a consuming wrath, whirl herself around seven times and turn into a pile of salt, like in Ira's Bible stories. But then where would he ever find such a piece of ass again if he happened to be in Columbus, Ohio? So he decided to take no foolish chances.

So seven hours later his wisdom was to be borne out in the cold, gray dawn. While he huddled in the car fretting over whether the engine would turn over due to Frigga's Nazi-goyische, lightheaded irresponsibility,

Frigga, still with cheerful unconcern, told Goff, as she worked the ignition, that it had been a memorable night for her not only because of their lovemaking, but also because of the thrilling way he had laid low that insect Jew. To Goff, her continued relish over the Jew laid low was truly astonishing, considering what a good screwin' he had given her. He accepted it philosophically.

When the motor caught, Goff relaxed and considered that he had also had a memorable night. He had notched up some very fancy fucking. She hadn't steered him wrong. They had gone at it a second time with Wagner, and a third time without—in a bed, civilized, for the last. He had to admit, good old Honus definitely made a big difference. The music grew on you. He was converted and he had learned fast. He had succeeded in pacing himself with her to a grand synchronized finale—to come with his conductor.

As the car started to move, he patted her on the knee appreciatively, as much for her fine fucking as for her success in starting up the car. He went on to philosophize further that that's what life was all about, and if you could combine good fucking with true love, man, then you've made it, assuming you had a little financial security.

That had been Goff's first formulation of the true key to happiness. He then shut his eyes and thought about how good a steaming hot, soap-sudded-scrubbed-balls needle shower would feel. He would cleanse himself completely of all that come, sweat and cheese that had crusted into his skin and his pores.

He shipped out and never saw Frigga again, and he never forgot the Wagner. In the course of years after the war, he learned the name was Richard, and he would rarely miss the chance to point out his familiarity and appreciation of Eudora Welty and Richard Wagner. If challenged about his competence or intimacy, he might back down on Welty, but never on Wagner.

# Chapter 9

---

*The return of Ira Mittelman; his revenge for the crunch
with the crutch*

One Tuesday morning, Goff arose and decided to approach the day lei-
surely. He phoned his plant and told Ramona not to expect him before
noon. He spent the morning luxuriating. In his acoustical bathroom he
turned on Wagner's *Prelude to the Third Act of Lohengrin* and went on to
salute and relive that night with Frigga Schmidt. The aftermath was never
depressing. Dr. Kummerlos had assured him it was not only OK, but use-
ful and beneficial. Guilt and self-recrimination were only products of narrow thinking.

So it was with perfect tranquility that he then went on to shave and
bathe. Now, afloat with well-being, he busied himself happily, preparing a
modest, health-giving breakfast. Some nice orange juice, freshly
squeezed; one jumbo double-yolk egg, soft-boiled; a thin slice of whole-
grained pumpernickel with a schmeer of cream cheese topped by a velvety pink-rose slice of Nova Scotia lox.

He was about to top it with the brewing of a fresh cup of coffee, when
he suddenly had the urge for some chocolate milk instead. He always had
a jar of chocolate syrup on hand and poured a sizable amount of the thick
chocolate into a tall glass. He filled the balance of the glass with milk and
stirred until the chocolate was evenly distributed. He had, from early
childhood, always favored chocolate drinks, and his father, a grocery
man, always saw to it that his Arneleh could have chocolate milk whenever he wanted. To Goff, there was nothing like a good chocolate drink. It

could take diverse forms, either chocolate milk, an egg cream, a plain
chocolate, an all black ice cream soda, or a malted. Milk shakes and thick
shakes were bullshit, although you had to settle for them out of New York
or in PXs. He had long ago learned that outside of New York, if you
asked for a chocolate malted, the flat-chested shiksa countergirl just
stood there and looked at you as if you spoke Hebrew or something to
her.

By far the most popular exponent of the chocolate drink class was the
chocolate soda, with its inspired refinement, the egg cream. Maybe the
Jews didn't discover it, but they perfected it and took it to their hearts
with love and affection. In New York anyway.

Goff acquired the learning regarding the currently fashionable drinks,
the drinks considered suitable for assimilated chaps like him, and at a bar
or party or even soiree, seemed quite at ease in ordering from the wine
list. He knew he had to swish brandy in the belly of the glass; never drink
anything less than twelve-year-old Scotch, and martinis were fashionably
vodka now. He almost even knew the correct name of the showy key-
bearing wine waiter. It was something like "Lavalier"—not quite—but
he'd have it nailed down in a week or so, tops. His polish was getting shi-
nier every day.

But as Brer Goff is tom-cattin' around, the plump old egg cream pa-
tiently waits for that sure-to-come time when her scalawag man will tire
and stagger home from the supercharged high-yaller dazzle-drinking to
the quiet sweet brown softness of a good virtuous chocolate lady egg
cream. Oh, Goff would readily agree, the egg cream was a prime item in a
Jew's soul-food cuisine. You certainly couldn't deny, on a sweltering day
when you are shvitzing like a hairy, undershirted, flour-caked bagel bak-
er, there is nothing, *absolutely* nothing that poured down a dry, flour-dust-
ed throat so cool and soothing like a egg cream. A beer, a Coke, a Pepsi, a
plain seltzer—they never came close. Strike that. A plain cold seltzer
came close.

When Goff finished his chocolate milk, he smacked his lips with the
gusto he would never show in public. It tasted delicious. He went on to
get himself attired in conservative mod. Quiet, buckled shoes, just falling
short of being boots. A brown polyester suit, the pants with just a touch
of flare. A fourteen-dollar knitted shirt, no tie. He combed his still-thick
hair stylishly forward, something like Hitler used to favor. Patted down
his moderate sideburns, whisk-combed the hairs of his unibrow, and
sauntered comfortably out of his bachelor's pad, $950 a month mainte-
nance charges.

Even before he had stepped one foot out of the lobby, Ira Mittelman stepped out of a thirty-year past and blithely strolled by. Instantly, Goff was thrown into stunned disorientation. Where the hell was he? There was schmuck Ira, the very same of thirty years ago. Or had thirty years actually gone by? Was this Park Avenue or was it Ocean Parkway with Ira on his way to Hebrew? It was scary. Ira looked exactly as he had thirty years ago when he was a boy rabbi. Again, as in Columbus, he wasn't wearing his usual thick black-rimmed glasses. But there was one unusual difference. His hair had straightened out. The passing years had somehow mellowed the tense coiled springiness of it, and it now reposed, relaxed and calm, no longer bristling hysterically to claw and attack. Goff snapped himself into verified reality. It was now. It was Park Avenue. And this was Ira, phenomenally unchanged.

"Ira," shouted Goff, not only excited, but quite delighted at seeing him well and prosperous-looking. Goff had never totally rid himself of an occasional haunting of the specter of Ira with outstretched arms on the floor at Columbus, bloodied and blubbering in impeccable German. At best, it had been an irksome memory. Also, corraling Ira now gave him the always pleasant opportunity of displaying himself a little in his resplendent setting.

Ira's recognition of Goff was likewise immediate. But as to any pleasure it contained for Ira, Goff wasn't at all sure. Ira's smile wasn't all that ecstatic. But the guilt-tainted Goff wasn't going to miss his chance for a little expiation and a dash of showing off. He managed, by deft, rapid references to his plant, his six-room Park Avenue cooperative and "its crazy maintenance charges," his recent trip to Europe, his costly divorce, to establish himself clearly as a man of estimable wealth. "And what about you, Ira? I swear, you never looked better. You shook me up for a second when I saw you through the lobby door. It was like thirty years never went by. I was beginning to curse the goddam dream I thought I was having—making me think I'm going down to my plant, when I'm really going to Cortelyou Road to work in my pop's grocery store, because the retarded delivery boy was out with a fit or something. Maxie Cockteppel—you remember?"

Ira, who was nowhere nearly as excited as Goff, nodded politely. And Goff became determined to infect Ira with enthusiasm. He wanted to embrace him, render him good. He wanted forgiveness. Maybe, if he could persuade Ira to come up to his apartment for a while to permit him to dispense largesse, even graciousness. He could adopt the regular-guy-millionaire pose any time he put his mind to it, and thereby put a less fortunate chap at ease as quick as you could say, "Sit over there, Ira. This chair was custom-made orthopedically to tenderly fit the contours of a man's ass regardless of size or shape. You'll feel like your ass is floating on air." For the hour or so they would spend together, they would both derive a world of good. Guaranteed.

"Look, Ira, I'll call up my plant and tell 'em I'll be detained. Come on up. We'll relax. I'll fix a drink, a *nosh*. We'll shoot the shit and catch up on old times." Goff tugged at his arm.

"No, really, Arnie, I'd love to, but I've got to get going. I have to leave tomorrow morning and I've got a million things to do." Goff noticed he spoke with a slight cowboy accent. Without his eyeglasses, Ira still looked unnatural. Ira was basically a four-eyed jerk type, and with bare eyes he would always look unfinished. He could never establish for Goff an un-eyeglasses identity. His thin, hooked, waferlike, sallow nose looked indecently exposed arching out of his eye sockets without the chaste enclosure of eyeglasses at its source. Like a shaky leg coming out of loose-fitting shorts on a pallid clerk on his two-week vacation (before the Charles Atlas course).

"Well, if you can't, you can't," said Goff, feigning finality. He was determined to have Ira up. "So what are you doing here? Are you married? I heard you're teaching or something."

Ira smiled, reserved and quiet. It irked Goff that Ira was so self-possessed, but he was still determined to tender him only generosity and good feeling. There must be no skimping. But Ira stood there with that unmerited air of assurance that bordered on arrogance—insufferable little prick that he always was.

Ira told him he was teaching German at the University of Nevada. His army training and experience had produced a good command of the language. During the war, he had gone on to become an interpreter in military government, and had seen duty in helping put an occupied German town on its feet. Right now he was just coming from Hunter College, where he had met with the chairman of the German department about their collaboration on a forthcoming German textbook.

Goff noted that he had lost almost all his nasality, and the prick hadn't once laughed that high-pitched shrill *kvitch* that had been his trademark. It must be the dry desert air that had dried up his drippy adenoids. But where did he get the nerve to keep on talking like a cowboy from Marlboro country? He was making it difficult to continue being sweet to this *momzer* with his airs—who used to whack off to Queen Esther's picture in his Bible stories book in Hebrew. Goff stubbornly persisted anyhow. Was he married?

"Yes," said Ira evenly.

Probably to a fat little Jewish social worker who now perspires like hell as she runs around the desert with a big fat ass bursting out of her jeans, finding meaningful employment for clapped-up Indians. And they must have two pudgy, clumsy kids who are the best readers in all Nevada.

"I have eight young 'uns," said Ira cowboyishly.

Of course, thought Goff, that orthodox animal under that civilized exterior. His poor *schleppy* wife has to take the brunt of all the years that hardon starved for a piece of ass. Now it's kosher and he's merciless in his observances. Drags them all to *shul*, too. "Bet they have to travel two hundred miles to a temple," he snickered.

"No, we don't." Goff thought Ira was beginning to answer a little nasal now. "As a matter of fact, we're Unitarian." There was just a trace of high titter.

Unitarian? Wasn't his wife Jewish?

"Well, she was, but we talked it over, and agreed that under the circumstances, Unitarianism was a better deal." Goff thought he detected a sly flicker in his ugly face. Traitor prick. Should have guessed. Once you fuck your religion, you always fuck it. It was in the cards all the time. A better deal! And this schmuck had been practically a rabbi. God! Fuckin' squaw man. "We're quite happy."

And what was her name?

"Sylvia," said Ira. Another titter skittered out, slightly shriller than the last.

Despite his growing disgust, Goff was now obsessed with bringing Ira up to his apartment. He wondered whether Ira remembered the incident in Columbus. He had been very high, but Goff guessed he remembered. He had an inspiration. "Ira, Ira, you gotta come up. You'll never guess what I'm gonna make you."

"Really, Arnie, I can't."

"But I'm gonna concoct you something that is irrefuckensistable." Goff tried to be as tantalizing as possible. "Ira, how would you like a big cold glass of delicious . . . " He halted dramatically, working up a taut excitement.

Held by Goff's glittering eye, Ira couldn't hold off a fishy grin, coming on unwanted like a developing sneeze.

"*Borscht?*" offered Goff teasingly. "No. *Schav?* No. Dr. Brown's Celery Tonic, maybe? Nah. Ira, listen, old friend, I'm gonna make you a scrumptious, delicious, cool-cold, rich, yummy, cummy, creamy, chocolate, Fox's U-Bet, eggy, egg cream," he finished triumphantly.

That broke Ira. His old, full shrieky laugh, engirdled no longer, suddenly burst out.

Goff pressed on. "A deelicious chocolate egg cream, double sweet, right here on Park Avenue yet, where a man, even if it meant life or death, couldn't find a place within three miles of here to fix him an egg cream." Goff had again clutched onto Ira's arm and now was beginning to feel the inertia break of movement out of Ira. Ira was giggling with uncontrollable nasality. Goff tugged him toward the building entrance. He slowly started movement. Ira had succumbed.

"But just one, Arnie, I'm really in a hurry. You really hit my weak spot," tittered Ira, his cowboy accent now completely dissolved.

"Ira, we'll make sure I don't tie you up too long." He turned to Fitzsimmons. "Fitz, would you please buzz me in forty-five minutes."

"Yes, sir, Mr. Goff," affirmed the perfect doorman's doorman.

"You'll get the same time it takes for a good session with a shrink or a gentleman's piece of ass. I read once that a gentleman properly should get his screw loose in about forty-five minutes—because if it takes less time, you risk being vulgar for undue haste, and if it takes more, you risk being boorish for ineptness or overstaying your welcome. I think that's as good a rule of hump to guide yourself by as any. I always do, naturally. That's how I first suspected I was a natural-born gentleman. How about you, Ira?" Goff nudged him. Ira hee-hawed, and Goff began to feel a little better disposed to him. But he still had too many airs for the basic schmuck he was. A schmuck with earlaps had been transformed into a schmuck with attaché case, Unitarian style. "Yeah," opined Goff, still cottonin' up to Ira. "I reckon a good *shtup* is often more therapeutic than any psychiatrist. Out West, I hear tell they're great believers in home remedies." Ira, the Nevada mountain burro, hee-hawed again.

When they were in the apartment, Goff told Ira he would like to show him around, but first to the kitchen; the egg cream got first priority. Ira followed gingerly. Arnie told him to leave his schoolbag on a chair, sit down and feast his eyes on the way Arnie Goff would fix up a deelicious chocolate egg cream. "Notice, first, a heavy glass gallon jar of Fox's U-Bet syrup—just like what gets delivered to Hymie's candy store—not the *pishachtz* you buy by the can or jar at your better grocers and food markets. I'm very, very *futzy* about the chocolate in my egg cream." Goff continued to mug and ham up his production. He had Ira in a state of uncontrollable sniggering, and his performance was spurred on and inspired by Ira's total captivation. Goff succedded in presenting the complete, down-to-earth millionaire art collector—a swell-guy aristocrat who puts his guest at an uneasy ease by picking his nose.

"We pour the syrup into the glass one-fifth up. You never *jalliveh* on the syrup, and risk a flat egg cream. It's always better more than less, because oversweet might hurt it but can't kill it, but under is fatal—*toyt, du herst*?" For some reason he couldn't account for, he was incorporating more Yiddish, speaking with Ira, than all of the past five years added together. Curious. He would make it a point to tell Kummerlos. And the way it came out. No struggling—just falling from his lips naturally. Some of the words he hadn't recalled ever uttering before.

"Now, a dash of milk. Strike that. Make it a *shpritz* of milk. Now for the critical part." With a flourish, he opened the refrigerator door and extracted an old-fashioned siphon seltzer bottle. "Seltzer! You need seltzer. Not vichy, not *pishy*, not carbonated water, but seltzer. Seltzer, made from heavy water, with unrefined, lumpy, sluggish bubbles that lay in your stomach like cherry bombs and then explode into a mighty *greps* of relief. Seltzer! Not pinpoint carbonation club soda. Seltzer, that could never get into the club.

Ira was mesmerized. Goff, the inspired impresario, caught up in a momentum of wild creation, perspired on. "You squirt the first shot in hard to agitate the chocolate molecules good. But then after, *pamelach*, you gotta flow the rest in easy, because the agitation can get out of hand. You can drive them molecules *meshugge* with excitement and they blow up and run out over the glass. So you gently trickle the rest on a spoon to cut its force even more. You fill it now to a little below the top. Stir firmly until you get a uniform color and a quiet head of brown foam. There. *Nehm*, my good friend. Take it. Look at the color. By the color you can tell the quality. Ira, I ask you honestly, did you ever see a more perfect egg cream?"

Ira grabbed the glass of egg cream eagerly, but then hesitated, waiting for Arnie to make one for himself. But Goff, the perfect host, insisted, "Drink it now. This second. An egg cream is best while it still has *zetz* in it—to be drunk down immediately. Drink, drink, Ira, *tzim gezind*."

Ira giggled with near-hysterical anticipation and, acknowledging Goff's gracious permission with a little nervous salute with his glass, drank it down in one mammoth, primitive gulp.

"A *mechaieh*, hah, Ira?"

The Unitarian nodded avidly. "A-OK," he said breathlessly, trying to sidestep Goff's Yiddish lingual assault.

Goff then deftly mixed another one. Drank it down quickly, smacking his lips voluptuously. "*Azoi geschmack*! Another round, Ira! *Vuss zugst du*?" Goff was still trying to break Ira down; to elicit a Yiddish word from him.

"If you don't mind," Ira giggled. This time Goff, the slick soda jerk, rustled them up in twos. They drank these down with more leisure, with the lingering, studied drawing-room appreciation of brandy savorers. They chatted about mutual acquaintances of the old days. And Goff went on to make some more of the chocolate drinks. The cool chocolate creaminess continued to feel good and a kind of peculiar mellow inebriation began to set in. Ira's giggling and laughing lost all restraints. The high-pitched braying went all the way back in time when he had nothing to offer in the way of street skills like ball playing, brashness or being a wise guy with girls, and the only way he could bring attention to himself was with this crazy, goony laugh.

Goff was now in full command. Ira was high on egg creams and Goff's flattering attentions, and he had reverted against his will to the stooge role to which he had been accustomed when he was a *schlemiel* punk.

With glasses of egg cream in their hands, Goff conducted Ira around his apartment, showing him his paintings, his marble statuary and his African primitives. He pointed out that the furnishings were mostly of Danish design. "I like the clean lines," he said, waving his glass airily toward a grouping of stark naked blond-wood chairs.

"These paintings and sculptures must have set you back a pretty penny," said Ira, likewise waving his glass of egg cream toward some paintings on the wall.

"Yes indeedy, but they're good investments. You acquire beautiful things, and they increase in value in very short order. A sound investment, yes indeedy."

Ira nodded his nose in understanding. Goff insisted Ira have one more for the road. No use rushing out on such a sweltering day unfortified. He was now feeling warm toward him. He figured Ira did remember. "Ira, I want to tell you I've never forgotten that night in Columbus, and I've felt terrible about it for twenty-five years. I hope I've been forgiven." The egg creams were producing a bloated feeling and making him maudlin.

"I understand, Arnie," said Ira forgivingly. "I think I better go now."

Goff, mellowed with brotherhood, said impulsively, "Look, Ira, your wife, Sylvia, is she in town with you?"

Ira tittered affirmatively.

"Why don't we arrange, the three of us, to have dinner and maybe a show tonight. No—no show. It's too hot. The air-conditioning of these Broadway theatres stinks. And, mainly, I'd like to spend it with you and your wife. I could get a date, but I don't really want to—I want to give you my full attention. I'd consider it a pleasure and a privilege. Dinner at any place you like. Whattya say, old buddy?"

Ira shook his head.

"Why, do you have something special you're doing?"

"No, not really," said Ira uncomfortably.

"Then come on—don't be a *yold*."

"No!" Ira almost screeched.

That schmuck can't go five minutes straight without pissing me off, thought Goff. "What's the problem, Ira? I'd like to meet your wife, for cryin' out loud. I'm sure she's a charming bright girl, and we'd all have an enjoyable evening."

Ira lowered his eyes and giggled nervously. "You wouldn't want to meet her, Arnie."

Again Goff thought of Ira as a schmuck, but this time, a little compassionately. The poor schmuck is embarrassed about his wife. Or maybe the jerk was even afraid he'd make a pass at her! Christ! Really—a schmuck is a schmuck is a schmuck. "Hey, Ira, you have anxieties? I'm gonna goose her or something? It's unfounded, completely unfounded."

"Look, Arnie, I assure you I have no anxieties," snapped Ira in a worm-turning tone. "The egg creams were delicious. I'm glad you're doing well, and I'd better be going, right now."

"OK, OK, Ira, don't get sore. I wanted to do right by you, that's all." Goff turned from Ira, and began fixing another egg cream. He wasn't offering any more to Ira. Fuck'm, he thought. The egg creams were starting to turn sour in his stomach.

Suddenly Ira sprang up, positioned himself directly in front of Goff, and with fire in his eyes and his hair starting to frizz up, said bitterly, "You're no fucking good, Goff, and you'll never see Sylvia. I never forgot anything, and you can go fuck yourself with your art and your Danish egg creams."

This bitter vehemence caught Goff completely by surprise. He had thought he had put Ira completely back in his place.

Ira shifted into high whine and a secret in his eye. "I'll tell you what, Lieutenant Goff. I have a family picture in my wallet. Would you like to see it? There's my mother, my father-in-law, my mother-in-law, my kids and my wife, Sylvia. You want to see Sylvia? That's the only way you're going to see her."

Ira's whine had turned wheezy with emotion.

Goff steadied himself with another sip of his egg cream, and said, "Look, Ira, you better calm down. As far as I'm concerned, you can keep your family and your Sylvia packed away in your back pocket next to your ass forever."

"I insist," hissed Ira.

"As you wish," said the debonair art collector.

Ira fished into the jacket of his summer seersucker suit and brought out a leather billfold designed in burnished lariat cowboy theme. Flapping it open, he drew out a photo, and handing it to Goff, fixed him with an intense look.

Goff glanced wearily at the picture. He saw some elderly people, some children. He made out Ira, and standing next to him, presumably his wife, Sylvia. Goff raised his eyebrow a shade. Sylvia wasn't a bad-looking broad, blondish and rather pretty. Goff studied her casually. And suddenly he felt a whomp in his stomach. It was as if all that egg cream had fermented and brought on a violent agitation down there. He turned pale and weak. That was no fuckin' Sylvia. That was Frigga! But it couldn't be. Those fuckin' egg creams must have had some dope in them and given him hallucinations. Maybe the syrup had been too old and turned into LSD or something. He examined the old man with crazy electrified gray hair sizzling out of his head. He dimly remembered Professor Schmidt. That must be him. The elderly blondish old bag must be his wife, Frigga's Nazi mom. The other old lady was, sure enough, Mrs. Mittelman. Sylvia was a blond, maturer, serener Frigga. His Wagnerian, whack-off queen all these years—Ira's wife, Sylvia? What the hell was going on?

"What the hell is this, some jerk-off joke of yours or something? Is this your wife, Sylvia?"

Ira nodded, trying to keep solemn, trying to suppress the bursting triumphant, revenge-is-sweet look.

"But, this is that broad Frigga! That crazy Nazi cunt from Columbus."

"I guess you're entitled to that description, which I'll grant she once was," said Ira primly.

"What are you talking about, Ira? Please, for cryin' out loud, what are you talking about? Is this some crazy revenge you're taking? Is it some trick photography? What do you mean calling her Sylvia? What do you mean, she was Jewish and now she's Unitarian? What in the hell are you talking about? You crazy jerk-off artist. What did you put in my egg cream? Have you been scheming all these years to get revenge on me? That was no accident, your walking by my building. You're a warped jerk-off, that's what you are." Goff had to sit down. He was on the verge of spasms.

Ira remained erect, composed. He was prepared to speak, as soon as the mob quieted down. "I'll tell you the whole story," he began. "I didn't want to, but I guess it was inevitable once we ran into each other—and it was simply that. I had no idea you lived here—or anywhere," he needled.

How he burned Goff with his calm, snotty control! He violently lit a cigar. He would try to control himself and listen fairly and objectively to what that crazy prick was going to say.

Ira related how a few days after the beer-hall punch, he had run into Frigga at her father's house. He had needed some help with a difficult translation, and Professor Schmidt, who had been so impressed with his phenomenal ability as a German student, had extended an open invitation for Ira to visit him at home any time. When Frigga had seen him there, she recognized him and laughed in his face and called him the Jew who my father is trying to turn into a German. He, in turn, had answered heatedly that Goff, her boy friend, was one too. She turned to ice, slapped his face and with compressed fury hissed that he was a Jew liar.

When he had visited Professor Schmidt's house a week later, Frigga seemed to have been waiting for him, but she was no longer composed. She appeared quite distraught and accosted him. She insisted frantically that he had lied and demanded a retraction. He would do no such thing. If she wanted proof, he would get it. He wrote to his mother to mail him his junior high school yearbook, and went on to show Frigga a class picture with him and Goff in it; it also contained their names and predictions. Even now, he remembered Goff's. Although it had scandalized the school, it seemed to Ira that it had been aptly prophetic.

"You remember it, Arnie?"

In spite of himself, Goff grinned. He remembered it perfectly. He and his sister Blanche and old A.G. had always been proud of it. It had been the brainchild of ugly, but enormous-titted, sarcastic Laura Sadowsky, the school genius, who had been editor of the yearbook, and whom he had once tried to feel up among the book stacks of the neighborhood library, the Kensington branch on McDonald Avenue. For years to come, that little jingle had been worth its weight in gold to him.

Ira recited it:

> Blue as a violet, red as a beet,
> If not always in love, always in heat.

Goff couldn't help softening a bit toward Ira. He did have a most admirable memory, and of course it was flattering. Goff, adopting a kindlier tone, asked Ira to please continue about Frigga.

When Frigga had seen the incontrovertible evidence, she was stunned. To make a long story short, she had quickly sunk into a deep depression and proceeded to have a breakdown. She was privately institutionalized, and Ira, obtaining the consent of her Jewish psychiatrist, visited her faithfully each visiting day. Her mother turned violently passive and offered no objection. Professor Schmidt was delighted. Frigga remained completely withdrawn, although she had not actually recoiled from his presence. Ira also wrote to her daily. When Ira passed her psychiatrist in the corridors, the psychiatrist had invariably nodded his head and winked an eye at him.

On the day he told her he had received orders to ship out to an embarkation point, she had silently reached out her hand to him.

He had gone on to England, through Europe, and with the invading forces into a defeated Germany, where he, with the rank of T/5 practically single-handedly undertook the governing of a small rural town in Bavaria. He had been part of an eight-man military government detachment. Two were captains, whose chief occupation in the occupation was charging around the countryside in their bouncy vehicles, scrounging furnishings to crate and ship home. The other five, enlisted men, immersed themselves in the single greatest activity of the war, "shacking up." But not Ira. He had plunged himself completely into the officially stated mission—to reeducate and rehabilitate, to root out all Nazi influence and replace it with democracy. His method was benevolence, constant indefatigable benevolence. He scurried around and made the public utilities function again; he reopened the schools, got the newspapers going, the police department revived, the library, a museum, the hospital—and his finest accomplishment—which earned him the everlasting love of the simple townspeople—he reestablished the town band. They dedicated their first concert to their beloved Amerikanisher Korporal T/fünf Mittelman and played—so earnestly in his honor—a grotesque oompah-pah rendition of Gershwin's *Rhapsody in Blue*.

Ira continued to write Frigga daily. He told her of his accomplishments; how rewarding it was; how people were, after all, people. His letters were laden with detail. He gave her to understand that in this devastated land of the Hershey bar pushover, he remained completely celibate. He hoped she would understand, would fathom the reason why.

Goff was too much of a gentleman to interrupt; and as nauseous as he was, it still didn't choke off his thinking. Sure, he believed, a jerk like Ira would act that way. With more ass than you could shake a putz at, Ira solemnly decides suddenly to become celibate. That, for a putz like him, figured. But what he wasn't telling—Goff was sure—was how many times a day he was helping himself abstain by resorting to his tricky toilet training. Goff gave up on his cigar and mashed it grimly to shreds.

When Ira had come home, he had shot out immediately to Columbus. There, he had learned that Frigga had been discharged from the santiarium. Her depression had not completely lifted, but she was functioning, although in a limited way. She had turned to religion. Also, she was about to marry the Cincinnati beer heir.

Ira at last became irate. He stormed up to Professor Schmidt's house and roared that he would allow no beer heir. *He* wanted Frigga. Frigga had walked over to him in a stately, remote manner, held out her hand to him, clasping it resolutely, and stationed herself alongside him. Her acceptance of him was clear. Professor Schmidt nodded his acceptance, and the Nazi mom shrugged her acceptance.

Frigga then told him evenly she wished to convert to Judaism. Ira, in turn, told her he appreciated the gesture, but it wasn't necessary on his account. She insisted. The reactions of the professor and the Nazi mom were the same as before: he nodding and she shrugging.

Frigga further insisted that she shed the name Frigga. Ira was agreeable and suggested that since his Aunt Sylvia had just died of a severe malpractice, the name was now available. Would Frigga care to have it? She said that would be fine. And so had she become his Jewish wife, Sylvia.

He had then gone on to get his degree under the GI Bill, and had become an instructor in German in Nevada. He had sensed the strain and effort Sylvia had been making to be a perfect Jewess. And since it was becoming a strain on him too, because he wasn't that crazy about being Jewish anymore—it had all been much too wearing—he suggested they turn Unitarian. If that was what Ira wanted, she would be happy to go along.

And so it had been, and it had all produced an idyllic happiness for them, Ira said.

Ira's tale was finished.

Goff was momentarily shattered. Slimy Ira had beat the game. That warped bastard had rewarped himself straight back into crazy health and stability.

Goff's dream girl, unfettered Frigga, pure American Nazi nymph, had turned into Ira's docile Sylvia. She had ceased to exist long years ago. Fantasizing with a phantom; deluding himself with a delusion. When you draw double delusion, you're automatically out.

Ira announced he would have to leave now. It had become much later than he thought. He would have to phone Sylvia. Might he? Goff gestured listlessly to the phone. Those egg creams had definitely turned sour in his mouth and stomach.

The prospect of Ira any moment talking to Frigga was shattering. His Dr. Kummerlos had not prepared him for this, and he couldn't suppress a bitterness worming in among all his other feelings. He told Kummerlos all about Frigga and his long-term utilization of her with Wagner and the whole push-button production whenever he needed it to tide him over between gigs. Kummerlos, if not actively encouraging it, had certainly at least sanctioned it. In fact, he had congratulated him on his healthy form of outlet. What was wrong with reliving a lusty night with a lusty Viking maiden, Kummerlos had offered clinically. He had no objection to an occasional tryst with the wrist. But the sting of it was that all these years, the Viking maiden was Sylvia, that putz Ira's wife! Goff felt besullied, besmirched and beswindled. Because all these long, lack-love years, he had been jerking off to a lie. Kummerlos had been remiss. He had not had quite enough vision to foresee the jeopardy for Goff. He simply had not properly prepared him, had not adopted sufficient preventive precautions. And his negligence was now hurting—bad. A severe confidence crisis was engulfing Goff.

Ira spoke into the phone. "Hello, Hun. I'm sorry. I've been delayed. I ran into an old friend. Hah, hah, no, it's a man."

Goff leaped up. He was suddenly seized with the notion that he must speak to this Sylvia/Frigga. He gestured to Ira strenuously, urgently, that he be permitted to say hello. Ira, as he continued talking, shook his head and waved him off. But Goff persisted, adopting smiles, toning down his frantic gestures; an old friend just wanting to say a friendly hello. Ira maintained his headshaking—firm, pendularic, unyielding.

Goff pretended resignation, but only to put Ira off guard, because he suddenly lunged to wrest the phone from him, but Ira neatly dodged him. Goff snatched again. Ira pivoted and blocked him off with a well-thrust elbow. Throughout, Ira had succeeded in maintaining an even conversational tone. Completing his conversation without any jarring, Ira slipped the phone softly into the cradle just as Goff, shedding the last semblance of dignity, in mad desperation, finally hollered out, "FRIGGA, HELLO FROM ARMAND!"

Ira the Unitarian gave his former coreligionist a look of thorough disdain as he collected his attaché case.

"She heard me," wheezed Goff with feverish malevolence.

"It really doesn't matter at all," said a supremely confident Ira, his cowboy accent fully restored, as he sashayed out the door.

For a moment Goff was numb. Then he dashed to the phone and dialed furiously. "I would like to speak to Dr. Kummerlos." There was a pause. Goff was drumming his fingers like pistons. He finally yelled, "Well, tell that son of a bitch to call me *immediately.* Arnold GOFF!" Another pause. "I'm sorry, Answering Service, I'm a little upset. You know that Dr. Kummerlos is a psychiatrist?" Another pause. "Thank you, Answering Service. I appreciate that." Chastened, he softly placed the phone down.

# Book III

Book III

# Chapter 1

*Goff begins to see Kummerlos in a new light*

The sequence of events had been exceptionally critical. As it happened, he had first laid eyes on Christine only one day before experiencing the shock of Ira. And although the first sight of Christine had produced a sensational wallop, Goff hadn't lost his basic sense of proportion or natural order. Christine, as the wife of his most esteemed doctor, was really unobtainable—and properly so. His doctor was still an enthroned personage, a regular father figure, and as such had a natural superior claim on the Queen. To seriously challenge this? Not really. The authority whammy to which he was subject was total.

But then Ira's appearance, his incredible accomplishment—transformation—from frizzy-haired jerk-off ghetto *shmegegge* to calm-haired drawling assimilationist prairie cowpoke had shaken Goff's guts from their moorings. The ignominiousness of it. To think that what Goff was still jerking off to, Ira was enjoying in the living, fair-skinned flesh. Utterly unbearable.

And Kummerlos! Kummerlos had for once not measured up. He had failed to recognize a basic upheaval, a crisis; failed to realize that this time Goff needed more. Kummerlos' standard *shtiks* would no longer suffice.

A man comes into his own only when he finally hurls off his father possessor—and replaces him. Grant the poor father his dizzying ambivalence. To bee or not to bee. The sting needle once imbedded presages

237

doom. It is a wise father who adopts a rigid ambivalence. Often wise is a
farther father. Tug, tug, my son. Pull me off, if you can, my precious lout.

When Kummerlos had finally responded to his distraught message to
Answering Service, Goff's shock had subsided enough to permit the doctor's velvety telephonic calm to persuade him that the matter might safely
await discussion for their regularly scheduled appointment.

"Frankly, you sound like perhaps an hour ago, this was a matter of critical urgency, but now, it sounds to me like all is under control. But if you
feel it should not wait until tomorrow, tell me. I will fit you in."

"No, Doctor, you don't have to bother. You're right. Tomorrow'll be
fine. I was just shook up for a while."

For nineteen years straight Goff had flourished under the absolute guidance of his venerated physician and healer, but now he just couldn't dis-
miss the awful thought that Kummerlos had been a sucker all these years.
Goff reverted to the simplistic characterization of exploitive doctors nor-
mally used by his immigrant parents and their contemporaries. He had always felt irritated at their greenhorn misuse. The simple literate was
adopted by the illiterate. According to modern usage, the milked patient
was correctly the sucker (not he who sucked, but he who got sucked; the
suckee was the sucker). But in his distress he lost touch and fell back to
the artless literal. Kummerlos sucked patients and was thereby the sucker, plain and greenhorn simple. The psychosucker! Kummerlos was not
only a sucker, he was also a patronizer, a common condescender.

Goff, high in his condominium, heavy with brooding, stared down at
Park Avenue. If absolute power corrupts absolutely, then God perforce
should be the Supreme Offender. But this perhaps applied to all bosses. It
certainly applied to Kummerlos. A man must be on constant guard. A
man must remain unawed.

Goff would not allow Kummerlos to sink him to second-class citizenship. He would no longer toady to him. He had reached the point where
he was no longer content not being his own man. He had gotten as far as
he could go in that capacity.

"Doctor, I wasn't prepared for this. I believe I've had a big setback."
Kummerlos pursed his lips into a fat noncommittal funnel to receive
Goff's outpourings. "It's very complicated. It has to do with everything, I
think. He made a jerk out of me. It was no small thing. This *shmegegge*

did something nobody I knew ever did. A perfect assimilation. Just what *I've* been trying to do all my life. Isn't it, Doc?''

"In a manner of speaking."

Goff was encouraged. "The schmuck tamed the consuming fires of hell and converted them to a domesticated four-burner range."

Kummerlos was astonished at Goff's kitchen poesy. He hadn't thought his patient had it in him. His Goff had been sufficiently agitated to produce a rough, primitive artistry.

"I'm all shook up, Doc." He paused, awaiting the supportive response to which he had been conditioned. It came.

"I'd classify it a little tremor. It's no earthquake, Arnold."

"I don't know, Doc," said Goff, who now knew. "I was on the launching pad, ready to rocket into the great belonging. You see, what Ira did was go into orbit when he turned that blond Nazi shiksa to a devoted Jewish wife—and then—both into Unitarians—it was genius. Don't you see, like that old joke—when they ask Frigga—but what were you before you were Unitarian, she can say, 'Jewish.' It makes my blood boil, but it's the most beautiful thing I ever heard. It's like he superkoshered her. I don't know if I make myself clear."

"Absolutely clear, Arnold. But this friend of yours made an unnatural accommodation, and as such, his seeming tranquility is in constant jeopardy. Let me ask you. Honestly, would you say this Ira has a joyous bed? Honestly, now?"

Goff had to admit he couldn't picture Ira and a defused Unitarian Frigga as capable of producing a joyous bed.

"So there you are," said Kummerlos, unpursing a little. "So what's the big accomplishment? What you are now on the verge of, my good Goff, is so much more solid, so much more real."

"What do you mean, Doc?" Good old Doc was ready to spring another vitalizing insight.

"I mean, you are ready to assimilate beyond assimilation—to belong beyond belonging—to identify beyond identity." Goff listened intently. "What I mean is, you don't need the shiksa any more; you're ready for assimilation via nonassimilation. You are ready to be complete—all alone—without props—without crutches—or crotches." He smiled.

"You mean I won't have this thing for turned-up nose, blond, blue-eyed shiksas anymore? I can have my supreme sex without them?"

"Exactly. Your ability to achieve your maximum fulfillment, your supreme sex, comes from within. So it may happen that you will find your perfect partner as a shiksa, but not *because* she's a shiksa. That's the big point. She could just as well be Jewish or Chinese for that matter.''

Goff felt he wouldn't mind a cute little China doll. Maybe Kummerlos was right. Maybe he had been too quick to condemn.

"What about a colored girl or a Puerto Rican?''

"That too, why not?''

Now, he was full of shit. Big democrat! Willing to pawn off any kind of a greasy twat on Arnie Goff, the patient-peasant, while he, the high priest, gurgled and cooed into that odorless blond Scandinavian pussy of shimmering northern lights, Christine from Lapland. Well, that's what he wanted, too! Christine! No one else. His good doctor wasn't going to palm off any lesser merchandise on him! And if that was the sign of a man who still hasn't made it, so be it. He'd take his assimilation straight. Straight with his doctor's wife, Christine. What was good enough for his doctor was good enough for him: Kummerlos' Christine, in the flesh! No use living in a jerk-off dreamland any more—encouraged, yet, by his doctor—to undermine him and keep him in eternal subservience. Unconsciously, he got her for me anyway, divined Goff, who was thrilled by this daring insight, the first independent insight he had ever had.

For the first time, Kummerlos was a bum.

What means motherfucker? Once the vilest obscenity, to shock the most calloused, now a tired commonplace—a herd word—uttered often, but rarely heard. Why did the black matriarchal society adopt "motherfucker'' as its catchword? Its most comforting, nourishing epithet? Massa Froid in the cold, cold ground, oh Jew king of motherfuckers—how you, ol' rascal, knew us darkies. You'll notice that not one of the Ten Commandments says, Thou shalt not be a motherfucker. Wise old Yiddishe kopf Ten Commandments. Why legislate the unenforceable?

Goff would lay his trap artfully. It had to be a masterpiece. Anyone intent on motherfucking can't be too careful.

# Chapter 2

*Goff has it out with Phoebe Shissel*

The following night, Thursday, at their regularly scheduled group session, Goff forced himself to greet a frazzle-nerved Meltzer enthusiastically, to Meltzer's grateful surprise. "I have to congratulate you, Sher," he flattered.

"What do you mean, Arn?" Meltzer was ready to tremble out of gratitude but held back because of the many times Goff had zapped him.

"Really, the way you described Kummerlos' new wife, 'shimmering northern lights'—letter perfect. She's quite a knockout. What is she, Danish?"

"No, she's Dutch. Some Dutch treat, ja ja. So you finally saw her?"

"Yeah. She peeked in his office to tell him the final score of Monday's game."

"It's a shame you missed her at that session about a year ago. You were in Europe then, right?"

"No, Venezuela. Was that the only one she ever came to?"

"Yep, just one. And then Kummerlos must have stopped her for obvious reasons. He went crazy over her and pulled her out before she went public in the group."

"Did she say anything revealing that night?"

"Not really. That was Phoebe's famous night, when she played that crazy tape she recorded of her rabbi banging her so the group could get a better idea of the reality of her situation. Anyway, aside from the novelty

241

of that tape, the session finally turned into her old song and dance, how she basically doesn't respect herself because she screws for everybody. And how the rabbi represented her final desecration of herself, and all that crap. You know how she tries to monopolize all the group time for herself. Anyway, Kummerlos' *tateleh* did ask her if she actually got sexual satisfaction from all her affairs. And Phoebe says, of course, that's the damn trouble, her salvation would come if she didn't have satisfaction from all of them. Then she could start to weed out. And then she brought the house down when she complained, yet. . . . 'But they all give me orgasms.' I happened to notice that this Christine didn't join in with the big yoks like everyone else; she sat there nodding seriously like she was learning something about another tribe or something. Maybe it all had to do with her problem."

"Her problem? Which way, her problem?"

"That she too has hot nuts, naturally. Don't you think so?"

Goff shrugged. His own guess would be just the reverse. His guess was that the plucky dear, like so many of her sister pilgrims nowadays, had stumbled across Kummerlos and his group of Jewish-flavored neurotics because she too was groping around for her big "O" (make that double OO—in America the wheels of fortune spin with the double OO, the better to screw you with), the Organizational Orgasm. If you can't get the preferred old-fashioned hand-crafted one, American genius can always supply the mass-produced, production-line version. Better than nothing.

Goff asked Meltzer, "How long was he married to his first wife— Miriam, wasn't it?"

"No, Muriel. Over twenty years. I used to know her. We went to the same public school and high school. She really got a raw deal. She put him through medical school while she was teaching. He had a damn good practice as a G.P. on the lower East Side, but it was too hard for him, or he wanted something with more prestige, or where he wouldn't have to move his fat ass or something—so he went back to medical school and Muriel went back to teaching, and he became a psychiatrist. I can't deny he has the touch, though; that is definitely his field. And Muriel is back at teaching again. Ech, what chance did she have against a gorgeous shiksa like that?"

"Yeah, a stunning girl. If only she weren't so flat-chested," said Goff. He figured he had milked all the information he could get about Christine Kummerlos.

As usual, Goff was the host, and he had set out coffee, soft drinks, peanuts, cookies and pastries, some quite expensive. But no liquor.

Although Kummerlos hadn't arrived yet, the group got underway at 8 P.M. with Meltzer reminding them that the previous session had ended with their agreement to give him first crack at getting a few things off his chest. Goff, who ordinarily gave the group's words his complete attention, tuned completely out. He couldn't be bothered listening to any of them, especially Meltzer.

Goff wondered whether he was finally beyond them, beyond Kummerlos. Dare he toss them aside? In the main, he had always treated the group, their problems, their suggestions, with the utmost seriousness— even Meltzer. Group was really great. His residual street-corner cynicism and disdain arose only outside formal sessions. It was pretty much the same with all of them. In session, they really took it seriously, and Goff felt they all curbed their meaner instincts and genuinely tried to be helpful. And they had been to him. And he had been, in turn, to them. As far as he could remember, he had never been sarcastic to Meltzer. And Meltzer was such a putz really.

Goff dwelt briefly on Phoebe sipping on Tab and munching on a Japanese rice cracker. Slightly taller than himself, slender appearance (it was her clothes, not her flesh), long legs, always fashionably turned out and smartly *betchotchked*, she liked to point out that her extremely arched nose was not exactly Jewish. "Don't you think it's more Persian or Turkish, Arnie?" She was usually animated. Men always sniffed around her. She permitted *tohpping*. He liked her for her penetrating views, but not for penetrating. Maybe they knew each other too well, like close cousins. Anyway, she didn't get him hot; he'd had to push himself the two or three times he'd screwed her.

In his final lay analysis, she was an uninspiring piece. Yes, she carried on like a wild woman with her thrashings and mighty earth-mother moanings. But somehow there was a false ring to it. Man does not live by bread alone. As soon as she had squeezed out her last tremor, she reverted immediately to Phoebe. Even before the last sweet spasm, to say nothing of the proper grace period—Phoebe, already 186,000 miles away asked him blandly, as if he were her steady garageman who had just filled up her tank with gas, "Arnie, would I do better taking the Queens Midtown Tunnel or do you think the Triboro?" He himself almost always preferred quick quits, but there's eat and run and there's eat and run. The least you do is allow time for a smoke—if not a cigar, at least a cigarette's worth. But Phoebe meant well; any chance she'd get she'd really try to say something to boost a groupie's ego. She even told Meltzer, in a group session, that she'd love to have an affair with him; she found him very attractive;

there was something old-fashioned about him, a solid reliability which was one of women's basic needs (regardless of women's lib); a big brother quality, a Jewishness, if you will, with its sensible, responsible instinct for survival. Meltzer was more Jewish even than her rabbi lover, to his credit; but alas, being in the group, it was like incest—a veritable taboo. How Meltzer had glowed, with a sweet and sour shrug of Jewish resignation, of *Takeh, es ist schwer tzu zion a Yid*. But what can you do? You go and jerk off, Meltzer, that's what you do! But of course, before you do, you go up to Arnie Goff's gorgeous spread, laid out on the grand piano, and you take one of his scrumptious gooey chocolate strudels or matzopans or whatever the fuck they called them at the classy Viennese pastry shop on Lex and 85th Street. Meltzer, while talking, would keep getting up from his chair, and with apologetic twitches, keep stuffing the gooey chocolate into his fat orthodontist face; he had to *fress* it up before his big competition arrived: Kummerlos, who also was no slouch when it came to *fressing* down those Viennese delicacies.

Phoebe was a canny one. She wasn't exactly overwhelmed by any group incest taboo when she didn't want to be. After one recent session, when everyone else had gone, Phoebe'd stayed. She took Goff into the bedroom and sat down on the bed. Besides wanting to go to bed with him, she told him candidly that she also wanted to discuss further his motives about his Basque identity *shtik*. It was the oldest standing joke the group had. She thought it was a little sick, but she had congratulated him anyway on the brilliance of the concept—how people's vagueness about Basques played right into his hands. What did she know about Basques? They lived in the Pyrenees, played jai alai, were fiercely independent, and spoke their own peculiar language.

"What else, Arnie?"

"Nothing much, except they're good with sheep."

"How long've you been using it?"

"High school. I was taking Spanish, where I first heard about them, and this little shiksa—she was taking French—she was French. I wanted to make points with her, so I said I was Basque."

"Did it work?"

"Yep. I'm not going to say I made it all the way, but it was the most beautiful stink-finger and dry-hump combo—you'll excuse the French—a young lad ever got—which, I swear to you, wouldn't have been possible if she knew I was Jewish. And the fact that she was French—Phoebe, it just added something—an excitement, a glamour, that's hard to describe. Do you want to get into the sack now?"

"No, not yet. What was her name?"

"Lorraine Metzdorf."

"Metzdorf?"

"Yeah, Metzdorf. I know the name doesn't sound it, but she was French, believe me. She even called me *'cheri.'* Without a Jewish accent like Meltzer's interior decorator's wife. And she had the softest pussy I ever felt. Excuse the French. Like creamy French ice cream. She *was* French. What did you want to know her name for?"

"Curiosity. Y'know, it's very curious, Arnie, to what extent so many of you *narrishe* Jewish men continue to play down your Jewish backgrounds. Oh, I know about the alleged glories of the shiksa pussy; feh, what a horrible word, but it goes way beyond that, and it applies to so many of my Jewish sisters, too. They'll put live lobsters into boiling pots of water in their own kitchens. They'll learn how to make clambakes, they'll become bourbon and branch-water drinkers, to avoid any semblance—don't get me wrong, the girls don't usually put out for a goy, but they die if they think they're giving off identifiable signs of Jewishness. Oh, they won't lie about it if they're asked, but they'll do everything in their power to avoid raising the gruesome question. They'll follow all sorts of goyishe pursuits, become outlandish things like boating enthusiasts and encourage their offspring to become surf riders, even stifle sensible aptitudes for traditionally Jewish trades and professions and force themselves to adeptnesses at completely unsuitable jobs. My cousin, a perfect pharmacist type, became a reptile keeper in the Bronx Zoo. I'm sure you know what I mean."

"Sure. I understand you and you understand me. Phoebe, I wanna move further into the good life, and if comes the time it helps to be a Jew, I'll slap on my yarmulke and be first on line, but if that's not the ticket, I'm always ready with my black beret. Arnold Goff, Basque American, heavy interests in sheep, at your service. And present company excepted I'm sure, but it's an absolute established fact, a shiksa is better in bed than Jewish."

"Bullshit."

"Can I fix you a drink?"

"OK. A little scotch, a lot of soda. You don't have to get me high. Jewish girls either come across or they don't; you don't have to ply them with liquor, which works so well with a shiksa. Did I say a true thing, *tateleh*?"

"By George, I believe you did, Phoebe, ol' girl! But true doesn't mean good!"

"Also, I'm gonna conduct a little poll now with you, and if you're honest, I'll bet you'll learn something startling."

"Yeh, what?"

"I want to shake that insufferable opinionated conviction of yours and so many like you that a shiksa is a better lay than a Jewish girl. That's sheer prejudice. Now honestly, who did you start with?"

"My cousin, Florie. She was ten, I was nine."

"My God, honest?"

"Scimitar my poopick and hope to die."

"Come again."

"Oh, my God, Phoebe. I just reminded myself of the worst lay I ever had. She wasn't Jewish; she was *takeh*, a Polack."

"Aha!"

"But wait, the best and next best, and next best, and next best, in that order, were all sweet shiksas. I had me a beautiful blonde in Columbus—I never had it so good—she was a *verbissene* Nazi, but what a lay. Then I had Kit Carson's great-grandniece or something in Oklahoma. What class, bedrock American, and more and more too numerous to mention."

"And other than the *Polnisher* they all came up to your high standards?"

"Well, come to think of it, I had me a little Irish twat recently; by all outward appearances she should have rated very high. She was frankly from hunger. But the score is so overwhelming—it's no contest, Phoebe. Unless you can turn the tide. Come, I'm in the mood."

"Not yet. What about your ex-wife, Gloria? Don't be colored by your later difficulties. But at the beginning . . . "

"No, no, at the beginning, at the end, in the middle—no. She had a certain talent which I won't go into, but you can't call it good humping."

"That's interesting, Arnie. Can you elucidate?"

"No! Oi, wait, Phoebe, I just remembered. On our honeymoon, the most beautiful piece I ever had—we were like ships that pass in the night. I have to admit, she was Jewish—and she wished me the most sincere *mazel tov* on my marriage that I ever got from anybody, bar none. Wait, for cryin' out loud, the second-best piece, on a long range, day-in, day-out basis, was right in my family—my dopey sister-in-law, who shall be nameless."

"I assume she was Jewish, yes?"

"I also assume so. Actually, it never came up. All she ever had on her mind or ever talked about was my putz."

"So, Arnie, the *shtarkeh shiksavist* is crumbling a little bit."

"Not at all. You don't understand. They were good, but—"

"Not good, Arnie, best."

"All right, best. They were best in the flesh, but not in the spirit. And in the end, you can't hold onto the flesh; what you have left is the spirit, right?"

"Quite a philosopher you're turning into."

"Look, the exact same steak you eat at home doesn't taste half so good, isn't half as enjoyable as eating it served up nice in a nice restaurant."

"Arnie, you know, I wouldn't call you exactly a self-hating Jew. You're too practical. I'd say you were an all-out goy lover. Haven't you any ethnic pride?"

"Why should I have ethnic pride? Let someone who needs it have it. Let the *shvartzehs*, the Polacks, the Italians have it. Let the Armenians have ethnic pride. I don't need it. I can't be bothered with it. What good did being Jewish ever do me? It never promoted me a piece of ass yet."

"It's gonna get *me*, Arnie."

"Hah!"

"Don't laugh, Arnie, because I swear to you if you weren't Jewish, I wouldn't flop off to bed with you. Don't laugh. I know I have an unfortunate reputation for promiscuity. But think back—of every attachment I've ever spoken about, there was never anyone but Jewish. The truth, Arnie, right?"

"Hmm, I think so."

"I know so, Arnie, and the reason is simple. I don't like *goyem*, I'm not comfortable with goyem, I can't relate with goyem. Furthermore, I think—unspeakable snob that I may be—that I'm vastly superior to goyem. I simply can't understand Jews kissing their ass, ingratiating themselves with them, adopting their ways. Oh, I'll *shmeichel* at them, I'll be charming and disarming. At school I'll flirt with goyishe department heads and district superintendents, I'll be helpless and cunty to Italian gas-station owners so my darling little Volvo can get the benefit of better servicing, but actually I can't stand them. I love being with my own kind. I'm only truly at ease with my own kind. I recognize it and proclaim it. Fuck all closet Jews—of all shades. It is no accident that my most exciting lover is my *meshuggeneh* rabbi, God bless his awesome and wrathful virility. Goyem stink. Sleeping with one, feh! With his unclean foreskin, feh!"

"Phoebe, Phoebe, you surprise me. You are actually a bigot. Do you mean to say there are no good goyem and no bad Jews?"

"Don't be simple, Arnie. I'll say it slowly. All goyem are initially unworthy until they prove themselves otherwise, and all Jews are worthy from inception until circumstances and the unimaginable pressures they endure transform the poor dears into bastards. *Du fershtest*? Tell me, Arnie, what turned you into such a goy lover? What trauma did you have that turned you against your people? Did the *shkutzim* chase you home from Hebrew school and call you kike, dirty Jew, Christ killer? Did they beat you, pull your pants off? Did your perfume-smelling Irish schoolteacher in 4A turn up her nose when you brought in the absence excuse note that your mother wrote with chicken fat stains on it? What turned you against your people? Explain."

"Look, Phoebe, I'm not against my people. For one thing, they're not my people. I can like everybody. But I like a nice shiksa a little more. I'm not interested in being a Jew, and nothing traumatic ever happened to me growing up in Brooklyn, except that I learned soon enough that Brooklyn wasn't the whole world. I knew that from my first reader, *Dicky Dare*. It said 'Dicky Dare went to school. On the way he met a pig. Oink, oink, said the pig.' It didn't say, 'Shloime Rabinowitz went to *cheder*; on the way he met a nice fat pullet. Oi, oi, said the pullet.' Correct? I had Irish teachers with fascinating wrinkles on their necks I never saw on Jewish women and rouge on their cheeks. They did smell of perfume or goyishe soaps and toilet water—no smell you ever found in a Jewish apartment in Brooklyn. And they made themselves completely *unvissidig* come Christmastime and went full steam ahead with Christmas carols and that shitty striped colored sugar spice candy in those animal cracker boxes, as if there were an unspoken understanding. They would go ahead full blast with their Christmas shit, regarding us as a church's children's choir, and the Jewish class accepting the role because it would be in the worst form to remind the teacher: 'But, Teacher, haven't you noticed? We're Jewish!' And I don't care what anyone says, the little blond shiksa girls were always the prettiest. So I didn't have to be called kike or anything like that; I didn't suffer. I wasn't victimized. But I got the message anyway, loud and clear."

"You're a perfect example of what I was talking about. You've been turned, *nebech*, into a bastard by those impossible pressures you've been subjected to. Let me finish! With your unusual sensitivity, you quickly sensed the constant threat of anti-Semitism in the air. You didn't have to be hit on the head. And there is your misfortune."

"Ha, ha, Phoebe," said Goff, sweeping his arm around the apartment. "You call this a misfortune?"

"Arnie, sweet, you're being simple again. What good is your whole *fercokteh* Park Avenue if it's a beleaguered fortress defended by an intermittent Basque? Poor Arnie, you never had that warm, supportive, close-knit family to sustain you against these awful assaults, like I did. I can honestly tell them all to *kush mir in tuchis*. You know what I am. I'm not really what you see, Phoebe Schissel, smart fashionable matron of Forest Hills, educator, mother, mistress, wife, career woman, committee woman, analysand, somebody definitely to be reckoned with. My real inner core self is little *Faygeleh Seeskite*, six years old, all spiffed up in Dr. Posner's arch-supported white-strapped shoes with white anklets, a big pink bow on my *keppeleh*, with hair pulled back and a mass of Shirley Temple curls, and my doting parents and grandparents are leading me to the stage in the casino of Kochansky's Pine View, with my big shining brown eyes and my freckled eager face, and I get on the stage on guest entertainment night, and I've got the audience in the palms of my *kleine hendelach* when I sing my Yiddishe number, *The Greeneh Kozineh*. It always brought down the casino. "Well, Arnie, is that touching?"

"Not in the way I think you mean. You see, describing the little Jewish *madeleh* in a funny way turned me on something awful. Come, Phoebe, *shayndeleh Faygeleh*, I'll take you behind the casino by the lake with the two rowboats."

"Arnie, if a little innocent Jewish *mamaleh* in Dr. Posner shoes singing an old Yiddish melody can provoke these strange stirrings in you, maybe there's hope for the prodigal son yet. I'm ready. Let's hurry, *tateleh*. Take me in back of the casino. I've got to get back to Forest Hills by midnight."

# Chapter 3

---

*Goff yearns for a Jewish St. Patrick's Day*

They were all trying to mold him and fold him into a neat package. Now the new line he kept reading and hearing: Jewish was "in." Like, in a pig's eye, in. Fool's gold.

He had read that Rabbi Putzenluch was concerned about the high rate of intermarriage; the Jewish race would be lost; the race would be lost by a nose. Yes, siree, ladies and gentlemen, coming down the home stretch. Galloping Galut lost by that shade of nose so recently bred out of him. His sire, Galloping Galoot, would surely have finished first by the strength of his protruding proboscis, hah, hah. Well, if all Jews became indistinguishable and disappeared, well, good riddance! Let's have a diaspora that's a real diaspora! It would be good for a Jew to be to Israel like an Irishman is to Ireland. Jesus, comes St. Patrick's Day, everyone becomes an Irishman and it's all good-natured horsing around and getting loaded, wearing of the green. There's got to be a holiday—a fun holiday—none of the existing ones is suitable. Maybe Tisha Be-av? No! Shit, the Irish didn't pick out Potato Famine Day, like the Jews would be apt to do. They're all too tied up to religion and tradition, all inappropriate.

How about Auschwitz Day? Is *that* your idea of comedy? It has to be a new thing, a fun holiday.

Of course. Golda Meir Day. Brilliant. Jewish Mother of Her Country, or Founding Mother of Jewish Women's Lib. The color'll be blue. On Golda Meir Day everyone will wear something blue. It's a fun concept. . . . What did she chase out of Israel? Nothing, except maybe Ben-Gurion and the Arabs. Chaim Weizman Day? Theodore Herzl Day? No, no, too serious. Sounds like you're collecting for the Jewish National Fund.

No, it's gotta be something that's gonna make you smile. Golda Meir!

Have to think of another angle. Golda Meir—she took a Jewish mother and turned her into a Prime Minister. It'll signal a national orgy of ethnic eating. On St. Patrick's Day the country drinks itself into a stupor; on Golda Meir Day the country eats itself into a stupor—the whole shmeer of Jewish food, and if bagels and lox are the prime symbol, so be it. Like turkey for Thanksgiving, lox and bagels for the whole country on Golda Meir Day. By this phony attachment to Jewishness, like the phony attachment to Irishness, we can advance tremendously to visible invisibility.

A holiday shouldn't be for collecting, for beating breasts; no atonements for repenting, for lamenting; no six million Jews; no building tabernacles; no Torah stuff; no Chanukah, which isn't first, but it's trying harder.

And one day in the year, on Golda Meir Day, everyone in America is a Jew and you hoist a glass of tea to Israel, *l'chayim*, and you have a parade, and all the politicians, including the Jewish ones, become Jews on the reviewing stand every Golda Meir Day. And the next day, everyone's back to normal, and you resume not being Jews again—until one year later, on Golda Meir Day—when you binge again. 'Tis a grand, grand day—on Golda Meir Day.

Goff'd be a Jew like that. If everyone was a Jew, shit, he'd be glad to be one too, on that grand, grand Golda Meir Day. The phony Irish have monopolized that thing long enough. They're not even drunks anymore! Actually, they've all but disappeared, but they still hold their old membership cards. And six-year-old blond blue-eyed kids (all right, woolly-headed black-eyed kids too) tugging at their mommies' miniskirts (if they can reach that high)—Mommie, Mommie, today is Goldamire Day. I want my lox and bagel—and I gotta wear something blue, 'cause today is Goldamire Day. Teacher says. This same blue-eyed twat twenty years hence will say, "Gee, when I was a kid, you know, I thought it was really one word, 'Goldamire' Day. How I love that day, love that yummy orgy of food you have to eat on good old Goldamire Day. I can't get out of the habit. Who the hell, exactly, was Golda Meir anyway? Was she the one who drove the snakes out of Israel? St. Patrick's Day is a drag, but Goldamire Day, I love it. I think my great-grandfather was Jewish, so I can really wear the blue, and it's so much better for my complexion than ghastly green. But what the hell, Orlando, don't get uptight, put on something blue, we're all Jewish on Goldamire Day. Israel go bragh. Oh, silly, you've heard that a thousand times, Orlando. It's Hebrew, Orlando, it means God bless Israel." Jewish being *in*.

In today, out tomorrow. Goff didn't trust it. In his bones he didn't trust it. He'd hold on to that Basque gag for another decade or so. And then either renew his option or not. Christ, he really ought to make a study of the Basques.

# Chapter 4

*Goff steps up his machinations to possess Christine*

The holiday season was coming. For many months now Goff had been having a special kind of open house on the fourth Sunday of every month, which had become known as the Arnie Goff Fourth Sunday Brunches. He had thrown himself into the project feverishly, trying to make them an *in* thing. A happening. He spared no delicacy carried by Zabar the Appetizer. These brunches had actually achieved a fair social success for him, especially after they were mentioned in Lennie Lyons' column.

He had succeeded in enticing several congressmen to his brunches, a hungry Jewish senator and his jet-set Jewish wife, the divorced wife of a famous novelist, one famous novelist, several minor novelists, TV people, a renowned Israeli general, some black militants (who had grown fond of Jew soul food as children because of leftovers brought home by their mothers from their day-work jobs) and others. Once Elizabeth Taylor, whom Jews worshiped like a Queen Esther, almost came.

Goff decided he would invite Kummerlos and his new wife. It was the holiday season. He would insist. They lived only two blocks away. Hadn't he just gotten him that Saturata color TV wholesale for his mother? Hadn't he been his best customer, steady, nineteen years, and besides, hadn't Kummerlos made a bundle on that stock tip he had given him a few years ago? Kummerlos couldn't turn him down.

Everything you've ever dreamed of eating on a Sunday morning: whitefish, sturgeon, carp, lox, novie and belly, lox in lox omelets, lox in every

255

form imaginable, caviar, and bagels, bialys, onion rolls, and Russian pumpernickel, tiny tender scallions, twenty different cheeses, glistening Danishes and Martinson's coffee only. Or, if you like, chocolate milk; mix your own. Or egg creams, even. He had siphon bottle seltzer, the real McCoy.

How could an East Side boy resist?

The fourth Sunday in December fell on the day after Christmas. Goff figured his brunch would be welcomed as a godsend by his guests—get that sugar plum fairies shit taste out of their mouths with some food and atmosphere that had some tang and *zetz* to it, some *Yiddishe tahm*.

On December 1, a Wednesday, at his regularly scheduled session, Goff threw out his firmest invitation yet. He had already mentioned these brunches before, the satisfaction they were giving him, the success they had turned out to be. Kummerlos had been fairly attentive, nothing spectacular, and Goff several times had issued an offhand invitation for him to drop up some time. It was open house. No formality. He was only five minutes away. Bring his wife, have Sunday brunch. He was welcome any time from eleven on.

"Doctor, I insist. I want you to see with your own eyes how I've adapted myself to Park Avenue and the whole shmeer, thanks to you. It's my Christmas brunch. It's going to be the best one yet. You have got to come." He then listed the menu. Sure enough, he caught a watering glimmer of appetizing gluttony in the doctor's eye. "You've got to promise me you'll be there . . . with the wife." He made "with the wife" come out like a polite afterthought.

"We shall see, we shall see, Arnie."

"Good." He had called him Arnie instead of the usual Goff or Mr. Goff or the occasional Arnold. He was now Arnie Appetizing. He was going to make it.

At their next session, December 3: "Say, Doctor, how's the TV set working, OK?"

"Fine, fine."

"I'm counting on you now . . . and the missus, Sunday the twenty-sixth." The missus. Oh, Arnie, you're so shrewd. How disarming. Who ever tampers with a guy's missus? For a missus you don't get tamper tantrums. Hee, hee. Goff figured he had the doctor faked out as to his true motives.

He brought up his shipping clerk, Malcolm Feiler. He had rehired him. His shipping department had fallen into an impossible tangle. But it was still mainly out of the milk and honey of human kindness that he was taking him back, because even with an impossible tangle you could manage to keep going. But on allowing him to come back, he had made that free-with-his-hands Zionist prick crawl. Had he done right?

Yes, he had done right, affirmed Kummerlos.

Goff had thought so all along. "I'm really glad you see it that way, Doctor. What about my brunch?"

"Most probably, most probably."

One week, three sessions later, on the tenth, Kummerlos relented to the persistent patient who was so anxious to have his doctor see the wonders he had wrought. Yes, yes, he would be happy to come to his brunch. "Yes, yes, ha, ha, I will bring the missus."

Whenever Goff had his brunches scheduled he would call in Wandalee Williams on Saturday to get the apartment into shape, and he would also have her on Sunday from ten till about five to help set up, serve and clean up the mess afterward. She had been a houseworker for him and Gloria before their divorce. Also she allowed him to bang her whenever the notion seized him. She had been allowing it for ten or twelve years, having started in their apartment in Flatbush, mostly on the wall-to-wall carpeting near the closed door outside the bedroom while Gloria slept late mornings. He had derived a perverse pleasure doing it in that particular spot, and had told Kummerlos—not that Goff required any explanation—it was so obviously a rebuke to his wife. But besides the perverse pleasure, it was also very nice. He didn't have to put on any airs. No mask, no Basque. No roles to play, just relax and be a massa. And she gave you a damn good fuck. Leave the drivin' to her. Sensational twisting and bucking in a certain slithery way she had; a beautiful ride, and silent, silent like a sleek black Cadillac. It had to be quiet, right there outside Gloria's door. He had never quite had anything like it, so much motion without commotion.

Wandalee was a handsome statuesque black girl with an attractive sexy kind of impassiveness just bordering on surliness. She would accommodate a man because it ain't gonna do her no harm, more likely good in one form or another. Mr. Goff for instance was generous—in money. He paid her time and a half for Saturdays and double time for Sundays, but the extra twenty he slipped her for each time he fucked her was the same regardless of the day.

Because of the frenetic *fressing* and because the preceding night, Saturday, with its hangovers and bangovers and the enervating results thereof, these brunches usually found Goff completely exhausted when his last guest had departed, and almost invariably he would summon Wandalee to service him. Unsmiling, always managing to maintain a dispassionate dignity, she'd work her way underneath him on the couch and ride him to glory. Goff by this time would be ready for the well-earned sweet repose of an afternoon nap. This was his favorite sleep. Always had been. And just before he conked out into serenity, he would mumble, "Just work around me, honey, and take the money out of the wallet in my pants, plus a twenty for you, and when you slip out, leave the latch down."

As his last words yawned out, Goff was already lambie-pie adoze. It was understood that she could take home any leftovers she wanted.

On Friday the twenty-fourth, Christmas Eve, at his last session scheduled before the big brunch, Goff spoke about his still deep yearnings to make a permanent attachment. So many things had been resolved, but yet—it was ironic, but now he had to worry about whether a girl was attracted to him or to his money.

"Now I guess I really want perfection. I guess I can afford to hold out for it now." Kummerlos lapsed into the role of golden listener. "My pop calling me his accident—I know now all the grief it brought me. I guess I've always wanted to be born again—not as an accident, not as a joke—because to Pop it wasn't even a bad accident, it was more a joke. Between the two, I think I'd rather be a bad accident than a joke accident." He paused. It felt appropriate. Like the parts in shul when the *Siddur* directed, "Continue in silent meditation." Kummerlos went along, honoring the propriety with him.

Goff resumed, "But in the end I suppose it was for the best. You've explained transference. I guess I'm sort of an accident to you too, eh, Doctor?"

Kummerlos waggled his head slightly, signifying a slim possibility; not more than a one-out-of-ten shot.

"Well, I haven't given up hope. I mean, having my rebirth, sort of, by finding the right girl. You know, I've always said I'll know the right girl by the sex I get. But it's very very tricky. Maybe it's by the sex you *don't* get. Maybe I'm looking for someone who will excite me *not* to want intercourse with her. Who'll turn me off in such an exciting way that it's turning me on. Something spiritual. Crazy talk, isn't it?" Goff thought his question was rhetorical, and was a little surprised to hear his doctor reassuring him with considerable animation, "No, no, not crazy at all."

Goff mentally overruled him. It *was* crazy. "I'm gonna stop having relations with my maid, Wandalee," he announced.

"Why?"

"Because I think keeping up these relations may relieve me of a pressure that I really need to push me to finding the perfect girl—whatever she turns out to be."

"Perhaps."

"But then what about masturbation, Doctor?"

"Well, Arnie, we have to close now. We will take up next time from this point."

"OK, Doctor. Don't forget now, I'm going to see you and the missus Sunday, right? Eleven-twelvish?"

"Right, right; twelvish, twelvish—ha, ha."

Yes, he just might do that, stop screwing Wandalee. The fewer pieces of ass available, the better it would be for him. He felt a strange need for something like purification to fortify him in what could otherwise be considered a sleazy goal: to steal Kummerlos' doll, a missus to the good doctor, but a hotly desired momma to the transferee son. So Wandalee would have to go. Common enough. In times of retrenchment, blacks are most apt to be let go first.

As for stopping his jerking off, that was ridiculous. No use making that resolution again. At least he felt virtuous insofar as he had given Kummerlos a fair hint of his intentions. If he didn't get the message, tough shit. It should be as clear as day to any competent psychiatrist that his patient was saying, "Stop me, stop me, before I kill again!"

Oh, tantalizing forbidden fruit! What hope that I shall pluck thee! And if King Kummerlos in patriarchal wrath banishes me as a blind wanderer to roam the earth, I shall still have tasted of his delicious fruit. Oh, happy Greek tragedy! Because in truth, King Kummerlos would never banish me.

Greek olives by the quart arrived, carried by the bearers of Zabar, Grand Appetizer, at ten o'clock sharp on Sunday morning, the day after Christmas. Dozens of bags and cartons marked with the living stains (growing right before your eyes) of the oozing fat of rich smoked fish which even countless layers of heavy wax paper couldn't contain. Huge bags of hot bialys, bagels and onion rolls. Black breads, rich and hearty enough to substitute for meat and potatoes, cartons of still warm Danish pastry and cheesecake in special chilled wrappings.

Everything had to be perfect.

Goff had been up at seven, at Zabar's at eight, personally selecting every item for his order. His painstaking scrutiny, his fussiness, surpassed by far any of the old lady hawks he had always derided.

Everything had to be perfect. Friday morning he had been in a dither, rushing into Georg Jensen's on Madison Avenue and loading up on Delft dishes. His look of wild urgency was tolerantly accepted by the purring clerks as the plight of a harried Christmas shopper getting caught in the last-minute rush. Goff gladly accepted their misidentification and echoed their parting "Merry Christmases" as he hurried in and out helping pile four heavy cartons into a waiting taxi. "Merry Christmas!" he rang out.

Everything had to be perfect. From Jensen's he hurried to the cheese shop and bought from the solemn cheese dwarfs a dozen varieties of cheese from Holland.

Everything had to be perfect. He called up the Netherlands consulate to identify Dutch delicacies. Schmaltz herring? Matjes herring with sliced onions? Well, whattya know? The Jews had left their stamp on Holland, all right. "Well, thank you. Merry Christmas."

Everything had to be perfect. Goff importuned Wandalee, "Please, honey, I know Saturday is Christmas. I'll make it worth your while. This brunch coming up is a very, very important one. I *gotta* have you Saturday, honey, to set things up." Wandalee had been adamant. This was *her* holiday.

Goff was up against a religious fanatic. He really couldn't see what the hell was so much her holiday about it. What happened? Because Macy's put in a *shvartzeh* Santa Claus all of a sudden? He conceded. "OK. But can you come early Sunday? Let's say eight instead of ten?" She agreed to nine.

Everything had to be perfect. Goff remained in his apartment all that Christmas Saturday, dusting, vacuuming, polishing and cursing Christmas. Now he knew how the other side felt on Yom Kippur when they couldn't get a newspaper, cigars, nothing, because everything was closed.

When Zabar's massive order arrived, Wandalee received it and set it out in sumptuous smorgasbord style on Delft platters. She made sure that the blue-hued bottles of siphoned seltzer were well chilled and that the chocolate syrup was room temperature.

Egg creams were very big at his brunches. All the egg cream cognoscenti preened with pride as they introduced the special mix for goy noncognoscenti. "I promise you you never had nothing like this in Nebraska. Don't ask me why it's called an egg cream, but watch: you take a Coca Cola glass—always a Coca Cola glass . . . "

It was the great leveler, the great ice breaker. It bonded the bonhomie and shmeered them all up with the same brush of nostalgic candy store blues. The egg creams brought out the chauvinistic soda jerk in all the boys from old New York.

"Hey Mel, get a load of this: you can make your own egg cream! No, schmuck, it's six parts syrup to one part milk and you shpritz the seltzer on the spoon. What's better to wash down a good salty fat piece of white-fish than a geschmaka drink of egg cream? Arnie, you're a fuckin' genius. Nebraska, honey, this is the sacramental drink of New York Jews and to tell you the truth, it's been so long I almost forgot. Oh, egg cream, if I for-get thee, may my taste buds rot so that everything tastes like peanut but-ter and jelly on white bread. Ha, what did I tell you, Nebraska baby? Ever taste anything so . . . so . . . scrumptious? *That* word you know, right? My Nebraska shiksa doll. So go tell him, Nebraska, tell Arnie he's a fuckin' genius. I'm getting high on these egg creams. I better eat some-thing. Nebraska, shmeer a dab of cream cheese on a bialy and put on a thin piece of novi and bring it to me like a good girl. Mel, Mort, will you show Nebraska what's a bialy and explain to her the difference between novi and belly lox?"

And Mel and Mort, two curly-haired ad executives, flank Nebraska, each eager to fill her in.

"A bialy," says Mort, "is a roll with a fantastic belly button."

"A bialy," says Mel, "is the arid moon with an onion-flavored crater."

Mort quickly realizes Mel has just moved ahead in the plowing of Ne-braska.

Kummerlos wasn't twelvish. He was twelve. On the button. And he looked starved. "Come on in, Doc. I'm so happy you could make it."

"Ha, ha, Arnie. I said I'd be here. I'm here."

Goff searched the hall back of him. No Christine!

"Where's the missus?"

But the corpulent Kummerlos had already slid by him, had already wormed his way through two dozen people to the table laden with Goff's extra-specially selected appetizer *fresserei*. Roughly clanking a twenty-five-dollar Delft serving plate off a stacked pile, he started filling it up. Disregarding all civilized buffet table amenities, aiming at the choicest smoked whitefish chubs, the richest sturgeon slices, the fattest herring pieces, he ruthlessly slashed through all arms and utensils, spearing sen-sationally beneath the prongs of all the other *fressers* to take in his haul. He was an Eskimo d'Artagnan gone berserk. After topping it all off with a healthy scoop of black beluga caviar, he backed off from the fish and dug through a basket of bagels, handling a dozen before he found two to his liking. He then emerged like a slippery halfback wriggling through a line of scrimmage, his high-piled plate protected and intact. Nobody was going to grab his brunch ball out of his hands. Kummerlos' eyes shone with gluttonous greed as he darted around looking for an isolated ice floe on which to devour his catch undisturbed.

When Goff walked up to him, his jowls were already crammed with multimashings of half a dozen varieties of Zabar's finest deluxe. Goff cornered him, forced a casual smile, and again asked, "Where's the missus?"

Kummerlos held up a pudgy finger. "Wait," said the finger, "let me clear my gullet and I'll answer." His Adam's apple signaled all clear; he looked at Goff, as he tore a bagel in two.

"Where's the missus?" he laughed, still getting a big charge out of the word. "The missus went to stay with my mother; she got sick—an emergency. She sends her regrets," he said unregretfully. "I was prepared to go, but the missus knew I had promised to be here, and she understands how I feel about keeping my commitments. So she volunteered."

He had shmeered a rich glob of cream cheese on his ripped-off chunk of bagel and was trying to spear a slippery slice of matjes herring filet. "I like a piece of herring on my bagel and cream cheese. Better than lox. I recommend it," he endorsed stoutly as he finally impaled the herring.

That prick, thought Goff. From observation at group sessions, he had suspected that Kummerlos was a gluttonous slob, but he had never guessed to what extent! It must have been more than the "emergency" that had persuaded his doctor to ship his wife this morning to the Lower East Side, crawling with all those P.R.'s and *shvartzehs*. They didn't wait for dark anymore to jump you. It was now 'round the clock that you could get yourself jumped, humped, lumped, dumped—Saturdays, Sundays, holidays. Continuous performances. The only thing, Goff figured, that would most likely save her was her extraordinary, startling beauty, those shimmering northern lights. Those clapped-up bastards would probably freeze into slack-jawed paralysis at the sight of a dazzling cunt like her.

Kummerlos was afraid to expose her to Goff and his fast-flying crowd. The old East Side caution, suspicion, takes no chances. Slippery prick, gorging, gorging. Goff felt like slapping an uppercut to his plate and sending all that expensive smoked fish shit flying right into his fat *fresser*.

"Well, Doc, I host these things the fourth Sunday every month. I hope you and the missus can make it next time. I'm going to keep reminding you about it."

Kummerlos grinned. "Well, I'll tell you, Arnold. I don't think I ever ate such good quality smoked fish and everything else like this before. And this is from an old East Side boy who knows. Simply fabulous. And the missus, I tell you, she loves this stuff, so I'm sorry she couldn't make it, but . . . " He shrugged up a continental c'est la vie.

Just then Phil Epstein, the president of Saturata Electronics, walked by, in one hand holding a bialy whose onion well was stuffed to overflowing with cream cheese and topped by a dainty slice of moist pink lox. His other hand held a large glass of foamy egg cream. His pink face, framed by snow-white hair, matched the color scheme of his lox fringed by cream cheese. He smiled broadly at Goff and holding up the bialy said, "Arnie, this is *geschmak*. And washed down with an egg cream—it's inspired. Nectar and ambrosia."

Goff, a dim idea beginning to form, put his arm around the *haimisher* gourmet and said, "Phil, I'd like you to meet the man I've so often spoken to you about. Dr. Kummerlos, I'd like you to meet Phil Epstein, who runs Saturata Electronics."

"Of course, Dr. Kummerlos. Arnie has indeed spoken so much about you. And if I recall, he arranged for you to get our top color TV model. I hope you're enjoying it."

"Oh, yes, yes, "said Kummerlos, "me and the missus—ha ha—enjoy it immensely. It is giving us superb service."

"You and the missus? I had the impression it was for your mother," said Goff, on the alert.

"Correct. Correct. But then I discussed it with an ophthalmologist who recommended that for someone of advanced age, for certain technical reasons, it would be better for her eyesight for her to watch black and white. I didn't want to take any chances."

Lying prick, thought the newly awakened Goff.

Epstein felt a gentlemanly defense was in order. "Oh, not at all, Doctor. Oh yes, when color TV first came out, there were some bugs about microwaves, which were never dangerous, totally distorted reports. In any case, our sets—and frankly all the competition's too—are perfectly safe."

So I was wrong; so do me something, was the expression on Kummerlos' chomping mouth.

Goff had to advance his fledgling idea. "Gentlemen, I'm so happy you two have met, because in a certain sense I owe so much to both of you. You, Phil, for trusting me and extending all that credit I needed when I first got started, and your continuing help and business advice. And you, Doctor, for that great support, without which I shudder to think where I'd be today." He paused. Both were tut-tutting between bites. Could he get away with his next piece of bullshit? He thought he could. "You've both, in a way, been like fathers to me."

Their tut-tutting continued, accepting his appreciation agreeably.

When Kummerlos was preparing to leave, Goff had Wandalee pack up a huge bundle of assorted goodies. He had to watch her because her inclination was to go light. Otherwise there'd be less for her black ass to take home.

"More, more," he ordered. And for further inspiration, he grabbed a blue Delft plate and set it flat in the bag, and had Wandalee place the package on top of it.

And when Kummerlos was ready to leave, he pressed the package on him. He didn't need much urging. "Please, I feel so bad. And when you told me that the missus loves this stuff, I really feel she shouldn't miss out on it because of the emergency you had. And anyway, there's always so much left over that I have to throw out. It's a shame. Please, Doctor, for the missus. And I put a plate on the bottom. This stuff is so rich. No matter how well it's wrapped, the richness comes through."

Kummerlos eased back now to his professional role. So broad professional acceptance covered up narrow greedy acceptance, and he took the succulent package and left.

Son of a bitch, thought Goff. She'll be lucky if she ever gets two bites of it. The fuckin' pig.

It worked! It worked!

The next day in his shul plant, Ramona told him a little sniffily there was a phone call for him.

"Who is it?" he barked through his cigar smoke.

"Your psychiatrist's wife, or maybe hees mother," she said, increasing her Puerto Rican accent out of pure bitchiness.

Goff had kept it no secret from her that he had been seeing a shrink named Kummerlos for nineteen years. He felt it a shrewd strategy to hint to Ramona that he might be a little unstable. See, that's why sometimes he couldn't help what he did.

He grabbed the phone. "All right, I got it. Hang it up, please."

"Si, si, señor," and she slammed it down.

A quick thought flashed. Jesus, her Spanish was starting to have a mocky accent. "Arnie Goff here. Mrs. Kummerlos?"

"Yes, Mr. Goff. I'm calling to tell you and thank you for your thoughtfulness yesterday."

Tell him and thank him. That same classy English-Scandinavian-type accent. That was shimmering northern lights, too.

"Oh, not at all. It was nothing. I'm so sorry you couldn't make it. And when Dr. Kummerlos told me how you like . . ."—he couldn't bring himself to say "herring, lox, whitefish" for so ethereal a creature—"er, the kind of stuff I usually have at these spreads, I insisted he take some home with him. I always have loads of leftovers anyway after my brunches."

"Well, I'm grateful. And I'm so sorry I couldn't come. But when I came home last night, I was a little hungry, and that piece of delicious lox and that herring were delicious. It was a perfect little snack. I finished every drop."

Why that son of a bitch Kummerlos, thought Goff. A little snack! Finished every drop! I gave him a ton of stuff. That fat bastard must have been stuffing himself on Zabar's best all day. He must have eaten up ninety-five percent of it, the load I gave him. Just as he suspected! She was lucky to end up with even a couple of slivers for her snack.

"Well, I'm glad you enjoyed it. Your husband practically promised me I could expect both of you when I have my next brunch."

"Oh?"

"Yes, I get a really big kick out of it, and everyone enjoys it. I have these brunches the fourth Sunday every month. I hope you can make it next time. Is there anything you especially like? It would be my pleasure."

"Oh, really, I wouldn't want you to go to any trouble; I'm easy to satisfy."

No you're not, he thought. You need very, very special attention. "Mrs. Kummerlos, you really didn't have to call, but I'm happy you did. By the way, how did you get my number at the plant?"

She was very matter of fact. "I asked my husband. I told him I must thank you. He gave it to me."

"Oh. Good, good."

"Mr. Goff, it was most thoughtful of you to include the Delft serving dish, and I thank you very much. I will have it wrapped with Dr. Kummerlos for your next visit, so he can return it to you."

"Oh, no. I don't want it back. I included it because the richness would have come through the bag. But I also meant for you to have it. I thought you might like it. I understand you're Dutch.''

"No, I'm Danish.''

"I'm Basque, myself. Of Basque descent, that is.''

That fuckin' Meltzer.

"Thank you, but I know how expensive is Delft, and I wouldn't think of it. I will have it with Dr. Kummerlos, wrapped for you. But again, I thank you.''

What class! What richness!

"As you say, Mrs. Kummerlos. I'll be looking forward to seeing you at my next brunch.''

"Yes, perhaps. Dr. Kummerlos seemed very pleased. I shall hopefully look forward to it. Good-bye and thank you again.''

"Good-bye,'' said Goff, strangely stirred. Sitting in his shul plant, he wondered if there were *broches* for brunches. If there were, he would recite them. One thing irked him; Kummerlos had apparently been very casual about giving Christine his phone number. The overconfident schmuck! He'd show him!

During Goff's subsequent sessions with Kummerlos, he introduced a new anxiety element. He wanted to start futzing around, experimenting, feeling his way with his new idea.

"Doc, I feel like a shit. I *am* a shit.''

Kummerlos studied the self-proclaimed turd, but as usual spoke not. Let the patient unload first, before he examined the specimen.

"You see, I've been trying to suppress it. You remember at my brunch I introduced you to Phil Epstein?''

Kummerlos gave it the old puckered lip with the old well-oiled barely perceptible nod combo. God, did Goff understand that bullshit nod now.

"Well, to make a short story long, heh, heh'' (he got a pained twitch of polite smile for his effort) "Epstein is like a father to me, a dad, a real dad.'' He'd be fair and sporting with Kummerlos. He'd give him clues every now and then to put him wise to what a crock his story was. But Kummerlos would have to be sharp enough to catch the clues, and Goff didn't think he was. Because if he were that sharp, he'd catch the phoniness of Goff calling a father a "dad.'' "I was with him in the hospital when the doctor came out to tell him his wife passed away. The shock to him was terrific. He was so crazy about her. Six months later he married this Greek girl, which to me proves how crazy he was about his first wife. Because I believe the theory that if you have a great marriage, you marry again soon. The proof is in the pudding, heh, heh. And my case is further proof. My marriage was for the birds, right? And it's been six years, and I'm still in no rush. Except this new thing that's making me feel like a shit. I think that I'm crazy, starting to have a thing about Phil's Greek wife. Phil Epstein's, who's been like a dad to me. She was at the brunch, maybe you noticed her." (Shit, he didn't notice nothing, blinded and crazed by all that food he was *fressing*.) "She was that short, dark, lively one, a little on the *zaftig* side, pitching in helping everybody, serving, and very lively. And the damndest thing is, you know how that kind is completely the opposite from my type, or so I thought. I always told you how I go for the blond, slender type. Well, now, complete reverse, this Greek girl, her name is Alexandra, short, dark, very Jewish-looking, but she's not, and I can't stop thinking about her in a way that I don't want to."

"How far has this advanced?" Kummerlos had perked up a bit, as Goff noticed he always did when he sniffed the hot parts coming up.

"Well, I sort of held her a little bit, put my arms around her after the brunch. Everyone was gone. Phil Epstein must have overeaten a little, he had some chest pains. He always gets them, and he took a nitro, and then he dozed off on the couch. His new Greek wife became very alarmed, and I put my arms around her, you know, just to comfort her."

"After Epstein fell asleep, she became alarmed?"

"No, before, but she had to keep up a brave front for him. You know how the Greeks are. But when he was dozing she felt she could show it. Well, I swear I meant to reassure her like a brother, but—well, to my astonishment, really—I started to get a feeling. It hit me like a ton of bricks, beyond just sex, even. I don't know if she got it too. It could be. Anyway we both pulled away. But it took some effort, believe me."

It was all bullshit. He and Phil had both taken a snooze after the brunch, and his new Greek wife, the fat little dark kind he could never stand, was really pissed off.

"In your ordinary course of affairs, would you have occasion to be seeing her? I mean, in business, do you have much contact with Epstein?"

"Yes, Doc."

"Well, I'll tell you, Arnold. Regardless of the seeming intensity, these are just preliminary feelings. Not yet rooted. It would seem sensible, and for practical as well as possibly psychological reasons, for you to try and curb them while they are not yet firmly embedded. I say try—and if it doesn't work, well . . . " He shrugged his up-to-date tolerances and permissions. "We'll cross that bridge if we come to it. We must close now."

"Thanks a lot, Doc," said Goff, rising. "Oh, don't forget, my invitation still stands, my next brunch, next month—you and the missus."

Kummerlos smiled broadly. "Perhaps, perhaps. Oh yes, I have your plate to give you. The missus told me I shouldn't forget to give it to you. She thanks you."

"Oh, yes, thanks, perfectly OK. She called me, y'know."

"Yes, I know."

"Well, so long, Doc."

"She enjoyed the tidbit very much."

As Goff walked out he scowled at the ungainly Hunter College receptionist, who scowled right back. She knew him for what he was.

"Tidbit, tidbit," he muttered, "the fat prick."

As the sessions continued, Goff kept feeding his doctor more details about his anguish over Epstein's Greek wife. How he was trying to curb this powerful fascination she had for him. He hadn't done anything overt, thank God. All other women seemed to have lost his attention. But he was masturbating, using her as his fantasy figure. That was the only thing that kept him from exploding.

Kummerlos nodded his approval.

Sure, thought Goff; it keeps the natives from getting restless.

Oh, yes Epstein and his Greek wife were expected at his January brunch. Could he expect the doctor and his missus?

Yes, yes, he could. Kummerlos would be delighted. And Goff could perhaps point out this Greek woman to him. It might be helpful seeing the actual instrumentality of his patient's anguish. His missus? Yes, yes his missus too, ha ha. "It's a date," he said jovially.

# Chapter 5

---

*Goff's brunch pays off*

Before his January brunch, Goff got rid of most of his Delft.

"Of course I'll take it!" cried Phoebe Shissel on group night. "I love Delft!"

Meltzer, who thought it would be beautiful in his dining room, looked on enviously after the group meeting broke up as he watched Fitzsimmons, the doorman, schlep down four cartons of the stuff to pack in Phoebe's Volvo. As the doorman struggled out with the last carton, Phoebe flashed him her special ingratiating smile reserved for goyishe service people, and turned to Goff. "Arnie, I hope he doesn't get a *killah*. How much shall I give him? Is a dollar all right?"

As Goff shook his head in genial amazement, it finally dawned on Meltzer that Goff had been screwing Phoebe Schissel, the Forest Hills Hadassah nympho.

And again Goff prepared meticulously for his monthly brunch. Again he called the consulate, this time the Danish. Schmaltz herring, matjes herring. Here too! Again he hurried to Georg Jensen, this time purchasing a large order of Royal Copenhagen. His apartment was already furnished in Danish modern. How electrifyingly provident! His usual guests, mostly slobs of various kinds, would never notice what they ate off. Like Kummerlos, although he was the extreme. Only interested in what was piled in the dishes. You could pile up a *cocktepel*. It wouldn't slow him up a whit.

269

But Christine would notice! It would create an affinity between them. Have to start somewhere. . . .

"Ah, Mr. Goff. Your Danish decor. It is delightful. Ah, Royal Copenhagen. Ah, Mr. Goff. The matjes herring is superb, and even more so on the Copenhagen. Ah, Mr. Goff. What do you call this, an egg cream? Ah, delightful. Ah, the lox, ah, the bagel, ah, the sable, ah, the table, ah, ah, ah, ah, ah."

Kummerlos was so confuckinplacent sure of himself!

When they arrived, Goff was again struck by Christine's beauty. But alas, his eyes made the final confirmation: no tits. He would no longer continue to hold on to his wishful fantasy. He was struck with a thought: with that flowing clean-limbed beauty of hers, tits on her would actually be gross. She was the only girl he had ever seen where tits would be surplus. She was like Danish furniture—clean, uncluttered lines. Isn't that what he actually selected for his apartment? How well her titless form would fit into his decor. Unconsciously, wasn't this what he always wanted?

Sparkling blue eyes, long blond hair. A smile to melt the North Pole, from which she had sprung. How could Kummerlos fuck her? How *actually* could he fuck her? Didn't he have any shame? Sitting there, in his same corner, shoveling it in. How could such a slob have the chutzpa to fuck this beautiful creature? The most beautiful shiksa he had ever seen. The prototype, the mother stamp, the acme of shiksas.

And then it struck him. *NO!* The answer must be—Kummerlos *doesn't* fuck her. Was that possible? But it must be. It must be! He had some kinky relationship with her. That the poor dear probably didn't even know about. He growled.

Goff told Kummerlos the Epsteins couldn't make it. Alexandra had called to tell him Epstein was having angina. The truth was, they were in Greece; the cold weather didn't agree with Phil. But no need to announce that. And he tried to put on a distressed demeanor whenever he felt Kummerlos might come up for air and look at him.

His sweetness to Christine was subdued, a careful, brooding melancholia. She likes that, he thought. The Danes love brooding. He was showing her a Hamlet quality. I definitely intrigue her. Hot shit!

When they left, he offered them a bundle of fish. Christine thought not. Goff didn't pursue—withdrew. A gentleman does not get all worked up over minor material things. Goff felt Christine liked that, too. Kummerlos looked irked and puffy, but didn't dare speak up.

In the succeeding sessions he brought in photographs of Alexandra the Greek to show Kummerlos, who couldn't hide his surprise. Her schlumpiness pleased him, thought Goff. Yes, he still saw her, only with Epstein present. . . . Their eyes would meet occasionally. He was sure she felt something for him too. Epstein was still subject to angina. Goff darkly suspected he was hoping him to die. He must suppress that, mustn't he? Kummerlos agreed he might try.

Although Epstein had always come to his brunches, Goff couldn't any longer guarantee he would be able to make his February brunch. Would Kummerlos come?

Goff saw Kummerlos wasn't fucking around anymore. He agreed greedily and noted it on his calendar. "That makes it official, Arnold."

Goff looked on with satisfaction. Kummerlos had become a trained seal, lured by promises of belly lox and other fishy morsels. As he closed the door behind him, he could picture Kummerlos inside flapping his fat flippers joyously.

February's brunch saw Goff inching closer to Christine. He taught her to make an egg cream and watched her own excited bubbling as the frothy creamy bubbles came foaming up, exactly to the rim, halting just short of overflow.

"That's the ticket, Mrs. Kummerlos," praised her fond instructor. "Getting that foam up to the edge, but not letting one drop flow over."

Her reserve was dropping. She was so beautiful in blond animation. Pity, her goyishe girlish delight prevented her from catching his deeper meaning: that she had contained her own bubbles, halting them before they overflowed.

"Ah," said Kummerlos on his way to the sturgeon to fill up his plate again. "You are teaching the missus how to make an egg cream. Ha, ha, ha. Don't let the bubbles overflow," he cautioned heartily as he waddled by.

Goff remembered how he had once so revered his doctor.

The brunch of March approached. Goff was still pouring it on about Alexandra. He was definitely waiting for something, something, he didn't know what; and then he'd make his move. He was beginning to see Epstein in a different light. The man had some bad traits.

"Like what, Arnold?"

"Well, he's sleazy."

"Meaning what?"

"Two-faced."

"Possibly a projection, Arnold?"

"So what? You don't project until you have a damn good reason."

Kummerlos smiled. "We must close now."

"My brunch of March in a week and a half."

"I'll be there."

A book arrived for Goff. An expensive-looking picture book titled, *Basque Country, an Ancient People Survive Intact.* He became delirious with joy as he read the accompanying perfumed note from Christine:

Dear Mr. Goff:

You have been so kind and gracious to us. I hope you enjoy this book as much as we have enjoyed your hospitality.

Sincerely,
CHRISTINE KUMMERLOS

Goff sniffed ecstatically at Christine's perfumed note and studied her calligraphic slant, reading it as slanted for his benefit. He momentarily forgot the silky Park Avenue manners he had been trying so assiduously to master and reverted to blunt Brooklyn vulgarity, rubbing the perfumed note up and down his expensively covered crotch, while sounding off rapid little triumphant yelps like a happy puppy.

She had accepted him as Basque. Well, whattaya know? She must have wanted to for her own reasons; telling her had been a gag more or less, because he almost assumed she would know, if not from Kummerlos (although it *was* possible he didn't speak about his patients, but Goff had another category too, host, and coming on strong, friend), then surely from his brunches which were really such heavily Jewish productions. Was it because she was a foreigner that she hadn't noticed? Like the gag about the Chinaman who jumps ship in New York and immediately gets a job as a waiter in a Jewish restaurant and learns to speak perfect Yiddish, thinking he's speaking English? No. Goff was inclined to reject these reasons. She had a need, he concluded.

The brunch of March: On the fourth Wednesday before the fourth Sunday, Ramona stiffly told Goff who had dropped in at his shul plant that morning that his psychiatrist's wife again wanted to talk to him.

"Good morning, Mrs. Kummerlos. Nothing wrong, I hope."

"Oh, no, Mr. Goff, except Dr. Kummerlos asked me to call you—his receptionist absented herself today—he wanted me to tell you he's sorry, but he had an emergency, well, it's not actually an emergency, but he had to leave town suddenly. It was so sudden, he didn't have time to make the call as he would have preferred. He must therefore cancel this afternoon's appointment, and also he won't be able to attend the group meeting tomorrow, and I'm also sorry, but your appointment for Friday afternoon he will also be unable to keep."

"Oh, that's all right. I only hope there's no trouble, Mrs. Kummerlos."

"Oh, no, no. Actually, he was summoned to California as a consultant on some film where a character has a psychotic episide. This was a long-standing arrangement; he didn't really expect to be called for several more weeks, but the director decided he wanted to film the sequence now instead of later because the actor had another commitment later, or something like that. He had to catch a plane at noon."

"Oh, that's OK. My appointments aren't vital, and he shouldn't feel bad about it. I'm sure going to Hollywood is a great honor and I'm very happy for him and for you. But does this mean he won't be back in time for my brunch Sunday?"

"Not at all. He expects to be back Saturday evening, possibly even Friday evening, if he's lucky. He wouldn't miss it for the world."

"Well, I'm flattered, and I hope you both do make it, but Hollywood can be . . ." He sought the right word. And playing way over his head, inspired by his psychiatrist's beautiful shiksa wife, he found it—"well, unpredictable."

"Yes, so I hear. But I'm sure he'll be back on schedule."

Goff, emboldened, advanced a little more. "Well, Mrs. Kummerlos, I hope he makes it, and I'd like to say, if by chance he doesn't, I would be honored if you dropped up yourself, seeing as you're practically my neighbor." Now! A risky probe! "Perhaps you'd care to have dinner tonight or perhaps tomorrow?"

"It would not be a good idea, Mr. Goff."

Goff palpitated, but tried to catch the precise tone and nuances in her anticipated rejection, for which he felt a peculiar relief. He would have been caught off guard by acceptance. He wasn't quite ready for that.

Her rejection had been mild. It wasn't a total rejection. "It would not be a good idea." That meant, with some modification, it might *become* a good idea. It wasn't an *absurd* idea, an *impossible* idea. Her tone also had a negotiable note to it. Once a very high-class broad had turned down his request for a date with "That's *quite* impossible." *There* was total rejection, absolutely. The chop-off blade of the guillotine slamming down for final severance. Yes, Christine's response was perfect, for a man not quite ready. But even though it was the answer he wanted, he still could not help a twinge of resentment at the turndown.

"Well, if you can't make it for dinner, please make it for brunch. I *do* want to thank you in person for that gorgeous volume you sent me. I really enjoyed it tremendously, so please try and come."

"I'm glad you enjoyed it. I thought you might."

"Indeed, indeed." So she thought he might, an excellent sign—thinking about him, weighing, considering. Great, great. Yes, his image had definitely entered her mind, and it was stirring around some; it was up to him to increase the stir to a churn.

"Again, I must remind you, Sunday, my spring brunch. To start the new season. I hope you will make it."

"We'll see. *Ciao.*"

"Chow," returned Goff.

He hung up, brimming with excitement. The significance of the "Chow" was not lost on Arnie Goff. "Chow," the code word; and he deciphered it.

"Chow" meant the continental approach; it meant jet-set morality, *La Dolce Vita*, the abandonment of middle-class values; it meant the ultra-sophisticated approach to relationships; it meant transcending the suffocating bonds of guilt and societal structures; it meant getting laid. Chow right back, you beautiful doll, you bet your ass! And Arnie Goff, the old chow hound, was going to win that bet.

What a TV show, he suddenly thought. Ladies and gentlemen, we bring you another week of that great family show: "You Bet Your Ass." Our first contestant is Merry Niederreiter, a lovely little lass from Punxsutawney, PA. Merry, are you ready (loud) TO BET YOUR ASS? She *is*, ladies and gentlemen (loud applause).

When Goff, munching a scallion, opened the door, there was Christine. He looked behind her to see if Kummerlos was with her. He wasn't.

The brunch was at its feverish height. The *fressers* mingling and mangling with orgiastic frenzy. It had already reached the peak of shrieking hysteria. All stops were out. Maybe because it was the first Sunday of spring. The consuming of new herring and sturgeon and whitefish was unrestrained. They were exploding with joyous spirits. Fleshy satyrs gleefully shpritzing seltzer. A Sabbatian *fresserei*.

Goff took her by the hand. He dared not go farther. In the context of his brunch, he night have got away with an exuberant little chow-chow hug or kiss—or he might not—but there was no question about getting away with a handhold. Leading her through the hordes, now like sharks in blood frenzy, he steered her around the heaped appetizer platters safely into a corner removed from the thrashings. He had caught a lot of the intoxicating effects of his surroundings. He was jubilant.

"So glad, so glad, so glad you could come! Don't move. Tell me what I can get for you. Don't even try to get through that mob scene." Christine gave him a brilliant blond smile. Goff soared. "What would you like to start with? Juice? Maybe a nice Bloody Mary? A screwdriver? What?" He didn't care, it could be anything. Christine could even start the day with a tablespoon of mineral oil with a prune juice chaser and it wouldn't tarnish her dazzling shiksa beauty; nothing could dim those shimmering northern lights.

"A Bloody Mary would be very nice."

"Great! Only yesterday I got a delivery of Wolfschmitt's best imported Russian vodka. The best. The best. Don't move." As he went off he could not resist turning back, still radiating his pleasure. "You don't know how happy I am you came!" It never entered his mind to ask where Kummerlos was.

Goff returned with the Bloody Mary. He still held the scallion. He was inspired. "Wait, don't drink." He tore the tubular leaf of the scallion and clipped off the point. "An old Basque custom. Sip your drink through a scallion, like a straw." Christine grinned and sipped. It worked!

"Ah, Mr. Goff. It imparts a delicate hint of onion to the flavor. Very tasty. How clever."

"Well, very clever, these Basques. A Basque never goes anywhere without his scallions. You know we're great smugglers. It's our pride. And often to escape from the border patrols we might suddenly have to hide in a river or bury ourselves in mud. We stick up our scallion stems and breathe through them. This trick is something we don't care to have get around, naturally, but I feel I can trust you." Goff saw her eyebrows, her eyes, her nose generate amusement at his whimsy. Time and time again a beautiful shiksa cunt could bring that out in him. "Oh, and that beautiful, beautiful book. What nostalgia it gave me. Not that I've ever been to northern Spain. But I still got nostalgia. Does that ever happen to you, getting nostalgia over a time and place you've never been to?"

"Yes, yes, I know what you mean. *Déjà vu*, of course."

Ah, she knows what I mean, thought Goff. *Déjà vu* means I fuck you. But what he meant was not bullshit. This was a real feeling. She was making him feel real, making a better man of him. This nostalgia *déjà vu* thing was not a bullshit line. It was bullshit in a way, but it wasn't a bullshit line.

It was more than half genuine. It was *true* bullshit—if one knew what he meant. Shit, he could be genuine with a broad. It wasn't the first time. And she was bringing it out in him.

Like a priest paying homage to his deity, proffering only the best and the purest, Goff laid before Christine platters of his choicest offerings. The belliest of his belly lox, the avatar of his caviar, the schmaltziest of his herring, the cream of his cream to his sex supreme (intended) and his shiksa Queen, his pure Christine.

"Simply delicious, Mr. Goff. It's amazing how you can supply yourself so consistently with such choice fish and everything else."

"Again, Mrs. Kummerlos, it must be the Basque in me. It is said that not a day goes by in which a true Basque doesn't eat fish at least once. So naturally a Basque should know his fish as well as his scallions."

"Really?"

"Uh-huh."

By two o'clock everyone had departed except Christine and Wandalee, who was cleaning up. Without rancor she followed her employer's directions to make up two large packages of the various delicacies.

Goff and Christine sat on a low Danish couch. "Wandalee, honey, could you please make a fresh pot of coffee? And then don't mind us, just work around us." He turned to Christine and felt that a transformation had taken place; he felt himself different from any time before. He was resolutely somber. He had never been somber before with any broad with whom he was trying to score. Somber after, maybe, but never before.

"You have a very somber expression, Mr. Goff."

"Ah, so you noticed, Christine." Christine, right out with it. No phony footsying. "If it makes you uneasy, I'm sorry, Christine, but any other expression would be untrue."

"And why do things have to be so true?" she asked lightly.

"Because for one thing, the party's over, and second, you stayed. Staying was, I feel, your attempt at truth, Christine. Why did you stay? I'd be interested to know."

"I stayed because your request seemed rather urgent."

"And my request to take you out to dinner, you didn't see that as urgent?"

"It didn't have the same quality."

"So when you detect urgency, you respond. A question: are you possibly doing this in some way as a duty to your husband's patient, because he isn't in town? Am I a patient to you?"

"No, you're not a patient to me, and I'm not acting as surrogate for my husband."

"But where the hell is he?"

"He was delayed in California. He arrives tonight, this evening. That is certain."

"Did he tell you to come here?"

"No, he told me I could come or not, as I liked."

"So why did you?"

Christine shrugged charmingly and reached for a bite of whitefish.

"Do you know how long I've been seeing your husband?"

"No."

"Doesn't he tell you anything about his patients?"

"No, of course not."

"I've been seeing him over nineteen years. I owe him something tremendous. But I've yet to make my final breakthrough." An even darker expression passed over his face. He reached for Christine's hand and clasped it to his in a grim damp clamp. She made no move to withdraw it. There was a distinct change in her demeanor. Her eyes closed, her face took on a sad resignation. A strained silence engulfed them for several moments as Wandalee busied herself unobtrusively doing her postbrunch cleanup around them.

Christine finally spoke. "Arnold, I'm sorry that you see your final breakthrough as accomplished only by possession of me."

"Why are you sorry?" asked Goff, noting with a thrill that he was now Arnold.

"Because it has happened similarly time and time again."

"What's happened, Christine?"

Christine shook her head, "Oh, the usual things. No need to go into detail. It shouldn't concern us."

"Can I guess?"

"If you like."

"My guess is that Jewish men have always gone *meshugge* over you. Let me continue. And that it has never ended well for either you or them. Am I on the right track?" Christine smiled remotely. Goff looked at her intently. Excitedly. On the verge of a discovery. "What do you take me for, Christine?"

"What do you mean?" she asked a little warily.

"I mean, do you still take me for a Basque?"

"Yes, you said you are Basque, so I accept you as that. What would you like me to take you for? Do you wish me now to accept you as—Jewish?''

"Could you?'' He gazed at her with the poetic intensity of a Byron and thought, take me for whatever will best speed me into your shimmering shiksa cunt, my beloved. And that's what I shall be.

"I can accept you as whatever you prefer.''

"Does not being Jewish make a difference?''

"I don't suppose so.''

"But you're not sure?'' He saw her smile turn enigmatic. He raced on. "For you I can be whatever you want. Tell me, what do you prefer?''

"Whatever you wish, Arnold.''

"Oh, I thought you would say, Just be yourself.''

"But you may prefer not to be yourself.''

"Then I can be anything?''

"Anything. Arnold, whatever is your preference.''

A sudden disquieting thought seized him. "Christine,'' he asked, "are you by any crazy chance Jewish?''

"No, Arnold. *You* can also take me at face value. I am just about what I seem. The blond Nordic Aryan type penultimate shiksa.''

"The reason I asked was because our conversation suddenly made me think of a story I once read about a fellow who finds his dream girl in Italy, but he hides the fact that he's Jewish and he loses the girl, because unexpectedly she turns out in the end to be Jewish also and cannot accept a goy.''

"This was a story by Malamud. I've read it,'' said Christine softly. "It was clever, but no more.''

"Yes, yes,'' he agreed excitedly, "because the story never takes up the question whether this man would have still regarded her as his dream girl if all along he had known she was Jewish. You see?''

Christine listened, still smiling her remote smile. The whole topic seemed to disturb her. Which role to emphasize, Jew or Basque? Which actually would hasten him into her cunt? He would let it rest for the nonce. She was a puzzle, this gorgeous girl. Ah, how defenseless she looked, how sad, how resigned! Goff was moved.

"Maybe I'm a Basque passing as a Jew,'' he offered, attempting lightness.

"It's not as implausible as you think. Would it not be to one's advantage living in New York to be taken as Jewish? Oh, I see I'm upsetting you. Forgive me.''

"There's nothing to forgive, Christine. You have not upset me. Actually, you have revitalized me." He drew her to him. She came. He kissed her. She permitted it. He placed his hand where he calculated her pale scant breast should be. He felt the merest, tenderest frailty of her womanhood. It was beautiful. Wandalee ignored it all, keeping to her work, scraping up onions in cream sauce ground into Goff's deep pile rug.

Trying not to jar him, Christine drew gently away. He sought no pursuit; dropped his hands. A never-before-felt sense of quiet exaltation settled over him. Christine rose, smiling in mingled sadness and tenderness. "Dr. Kummerlos is coming home today. He's probably at the airport already."

Goff looked at her northern blue eyes. "I have a thousand questions," he said.

"I'll answer all of them."

"You've made me very happy."

"I have to go now."

"Shall I call you or will you call me, Christine?"

"Let me call you."

"When?"

"Whenever you say."

"Tomorrow at eleven at my plant."

She nodded and put on her coat and started for the door. Goff suddenly jumped up and shouted, "Wait!" He ran to the kitchen and brought out two bulging bags which he pressed on her. She recoiled ever so slightly. He told her one was for her and one was for her husband; he wanted her to have one for her own, all for her very self. She smiled; she understood.

"You've made me very happy," repeated Goff with a deep quaver in his voice. And she was gone.

Ah, how to extend this rare delicate feeling!

He leaned against the door and thought about Christine. He knew Christine was different. For this beautifully different girl, he would discard the crude code which had so long governed him—Jesus, since he was nine! He had never had an innocence. He was entitled to it. He must rummage around for it, dig it out, polish it up. Christine was worthy of his sacrifice. He would cleanse and purify himself, like any good Jew preparing for a sanctified event. No, he would not besmirch her with the old Goff, but anoint her with the new. He would court her, be her swain. (He had never been that to any maid.) He would shower her with gifts and sweets, excite her, romp with her, share things with her. They would discover delicious secrets together, delight each other with recognition of their unique compatability, flow together like laughing waters. And after

all that—they would make love, but not before. And what a fuck that
would produce! A fuck worthy of a king, nay, a poet. A poet-king! That
was the right way.

One last troubling question. How could he best enchant her? As Jew or
Basque? He would watch and see, keep a foot in both camps.

The next day, precisely at eleven, the phone rang at Goff's shul plant.
Ramona answered and looked at him as he was looking at her. She gestured for him to pick up the phone. Goff was thrilled at Christine's punc-
tuality. For him it signaled the first important commitment.

"Christine. How glad I am you called. I've been thinking about you all
night, all morning. How are you? Did you enjoy the package? Did you eat
any of it? Did your husband ever get home? Can we meet? Perhaps for
lunch?"

"Your thousand questions. I think you've asked half of them. Yes, Arnold. I can meet you for lunch."

"When?"

"Right away."

"Wonderful. Where?"

"Oh, perhaps at your plant. I think I'm right in the vicinity."

"Where are you?"

"At my mother-in-law's apartment. She isn't feeling well again and I
thought that I would come down to see her this morning. I brought her
some of the smoked fish you gave me yesterday. She loves it. I hope you
don't mind."

"No, no, not at all. I would have given you a third package if I'd
known." He could advertise: By special appointment, A. Goff, purveyor
of appetizing delicacies to his shrink, the kink. He knew she had shared
her package, not Kummerlos'. Kummerlos would never have surrendered
a crumb, not even to his mother. How he had come to resent his psychiatrist!

They finally decided to meet on East Broadway and Essex Street at the
Paradise Cafeteria.

"Do you know it, Arnold?"

"Sure I know it. It's five minutes from my plant. Do you know it?"

"Yes, yes. I ate there once with my mother-in-law. I would love to
have lunch there with you."

"Christine, we could go any place we want. I don't think the Paradise
Cafeteria is the place for you."

"It's a beautiful place for me. You'll see. But we're wasting time. And you still have five hundred questions for me. See you in ten minutes?"

"Yes, yes, I'll be there."

A beautiful day was enveloping New York that morning. The Paradise Cafeteria, one of the last outposts of the old lower East Side, bustled even more than usual. It was the thaw. Old Jews who had been holed up for the winter were hobbling out of their suffocating tightly barricaded tenements, reviving and straightening up, straining tired lungs to take in the *fruscher luft,* filling up the few benches or sitting on steel-framed wooden milk boxes in the triangular swatch of a park across the street from the Paradise. Gossip and kvetchings were exchanged. Even the woes were clothed in a new liveliness. The few plane trees were starting to show the first fat buds, miraculously still alive in this battered polluted neighborhood.

Thick-bodied, graying, horse-playing Jewish taxi drivers barreled up with renewed vigor and vigorish, streaming in from all over lower Manhattan, converging on the Paradise for coffee and Danish and shootin' the shit and horse doping. The revolving doors spun briskly, the punch ticket machine clanged continuously.

Goff was at the corner in five minutes. Usually repelled by the scene, his attitude on this sunny morning was accepting and warm. Jews of assorted low types bustled by, including black-garbed bearded Chasidim, the burly taxi drivers, gaunt old-line Socialist types, heavy yentas, aimless abandoned parents, social workers from the still lively Educational Alliance, zesty gray-haired Yiddishist writers from the old Forward Building down the street; also plenty of assured Puerto Ricans zigzagging confidently among them. They actually had a friendly air, these spics. The day had a festive tone: thoughts of muggings had been temporarily suspended, among them at least, if not among the muggees.

Goff saw an ancient knish man bent to his cart at the curbside. He hadn't seen one in years. Goff smiled and felt brotherhood suffusing him. This must be the last knish man in the world.

A retarded Jewish shoeshine boy-man had set himself up near the curb. A taxi driver haggled with him good-naturedly about the price of a shine. "Maxie, thirty-five cents is too much. For a good shine, yeah, but not for your shine."

"I give good shines," Maxie spluttered.

Goff stared at Maxie. Could this be Maxie Cocktepel, the idiot delivery

boy of his pop's grocery store thirty years ago? God, it was! Goff decided
to get a shine from him. He sat down on the little stool Maxie provided.

While Maxie bent to his task, a brash Puerto Rican stud came up to the
old knish man and flashed him a big gold-toothed grin. "Hey, pop, gimme
a knish, make it a kashe."

The knish man absently reached for the potato drawer and reached in
with the tissue he used for handling and serving.

"No, no, pop," said the youth with cheerful patience. "Kashe, man."

The knish man nodded, returning the potato and pulling out another
drawer. Goff was amazed that a Puerto Rican could have acquired the
advanced tastes necessary to appreciate kashe. Yes, Goff had to grant
them, little by little, they were slowly becoming Americanized.

While the Puerto Rican youth vigorously salted down his knish from an
oversized tin salt shaker, a police car containing a sergeant and a patrolman suddenly pulled up, slamming insultingly to a halt barely a few inches
short of the knish man. The big beefy sergeant gave brusque orders to his
patrolman driver, who leaped out of the car and rapidly wrote out a ticket,
while the Puerto Rican grinned at him brashly. The patrolman thrust the
ticket at the dazed old knish man, then quickly piled back behind the
wheel. He then put the car in reverse, shot back, and was already jolting
forward even as he still went backward. He swerved, missing the knish
man by an indifferent hair, and screeched into an insolent careening as the
car U'd around the street. The law against peddling without a license had
been vigorously enforced.

The Puerto Rican gave the disappearing car the finger and said sympathetically to the knish man, "Eh, pop, don't let him scare you. He's full o'
shit, fuck'm." And he went jauntily on his way up East Broadway eating
his kashe knish.

Goff, witnessing all this next to the knish man, smiled sympathetically
also. The old man sighed and mumbled, "Yeah, the Puerto Rican says
fuck'm, fuck'm. That boy could fuck'm, his friends could fuck'm, all
New York could fuck'm—but *I* can't fuck'm, *I* gotta pay the ticket."

Goff said kindly, "How's *gescheft*?"

"*Gescheft* is in *d'rerd*. The same knish I once was selling for a nickel I
have to charge thirty-five cents now. And my Yiddishe customers don't
want to buy no more. They gimme an argument. If it wasn't for the *shvartzehs* and Puerto Ricans I'd be out of business. They a gentleman. They
don't give me no argument. You wanna buy a knish, mister?"

Maxie was spitting on Goff's shoe when Goff saw Christine hurrying
along East Broadway from the direction of the East River. "That's all,

Maxie," he said, removing his shoe in the middle of the final slap-slap of Maxie's shoerag.

"But I'm not finished, mister," said the retardate.

"It's OK," said Goff, taking out a five, because that's what he had wanted to give him all along for old times' sake.

"Keep your fuckin' five," blubbered the idiot angrily, his eyes and lips and face puffing up. "I don't take money if I don't finish the shine." Bubbles of saliva collected in the corners of his mouth. The thick-bodied taxi drivers and other East Broadway Jews were closing in on them. A burly spokesman threatened, "Mister, why don't you let Maxie finish givin' you a shine."

Goff was now pissed off. Regardless of how tough these guys looked, they were still only Jewish taxi drivers and he could take care of *them*. "Why don't you schmucks keep out of this. I want to give him this five, and if he doesn't want it, fuck'm—finished or not. I know Maxie Cocktepel for thirty years, so mind your own goddamn business."

Just then the circle gave way to make passage for Christine. All the taxi drivers stared in awe at this beautiful willowy long-haired blond shiksa. How did a broad like this get washed up on East Broadway? Something like this hadn't been in the neighborhood since Peter Stuyvesant. How did she get so *farblondjet*?

"Arnold," said Christine, "is there any trouble here?"

"Yeah, a holy war was about to start because I didn't want to wait to have this shoeshine boy finish polishing my shoes, but I was ready to give him five dollars for his trouble."

Maxie kept his eyes broodingly downcast, except for sneaking an upward move or two of his retarded eyeballs to look at the beautiful blond lady. Christine sized up the situation at once and spoke sweetly to Goff. "Arnold, it's such a beautiful day. There's no hurry. Why don't you let the man finish shining your shoes?"

Goff shrugged. "OK, Maxie, you want to finish?"

Maxie nodded dumbly. Goff resumed his seat, placed his foot on the shoe box. Maxie tapped it off. Wrong one. Goff replaced it with his other foot. Maxie spit on it and happily gave it the final couple of swipes. Then he sat up satisfied and tapped the shoe with his finger to signal all done. Goff smiled and handed Maxie the five. Maxie beamed and took it. Christine beamed. Goff beamed. His shoes beamed. The onlookers beamed. And suddenly there was a round of applause from all the taxi drivers. Maxie joined too. It was all meant for Christine, the *farblondjet* fairy princess.

"She must be that Swedish actress. Must be taping a TV special up on Second Avenue in one of the old theatres," said one of the knowledgeable taxi drivers. "But they never come as far down as here. Never get below Ratner's. How did she get so *farblondjet?*"

"What a doll. What a smile. What hair. A beautiful shiksa. A princess."

But one little boy with Chasidic sideburns, picking his nose, called out, "But look, she has no *tsitskis.*"

As they suddenly realized the truth of this observation, they all shrugged. Alas, the fatal flaw. Yeah, that's right, they conceded, no tits.

"That Jew boy with her doesn't seem to mind."

"Well, maybe that's the only way he could get a dish like that. Y'know, bargain basement. Dishes, seconds, which you can't tell unless you look very hard."

"With tits, he could never touch her," said a fat cigar conclusively.

Through the revolving door of the Paradise, clang, clang. Two punch tickets. Goff and Christine entered the vegetarian cafeteria. Except for living human flesh aplenty, no meat had ever crossed its threshold. Sturdy counter workers with assorted foreign accents dished out tons of vegetarian concoctions to the East Broadway masses, many of them still not unhuddled after forty or fifty years. The accents varied greatly; with the exception of Spanish you could detect nothing west of the Oder River. Czech, Polish, Hungarian, Rumanian, Serbian, Russian, Greek, Turkish, Cypriot, a kind of Balkan verbal goulash.

Christine looked around delightedly. "I love the ambience here, Arnold."

Goff smiled at her. He loved it too—what she loved, he loved. Although to tell the truth, he wasn't too crazy about the atmosphere. Never had been. Such a greaseball joint. Jesus, if you feel like eating this stuff, at least do it at Ratner's which had worked up a little class. He himself hardly ever came here. What was with this Christine anyway? Why was she such a Jew lover? What kind of peculiar hangup did she have?

Christine declined with a smile when Goff suggested they take a table in the more secluded section reserved for waiter service. No, she wanted to sit in the self-service section with the old frumpy saggy-fleshed shopping-bag Yiddenehs with their knotted stocking rolls on varicosed legs, soon to be widowed by their gaunt hollow-eyed consorts; sustained by their life-clinging gossip, bile and bitterness, and their tea and coffee in glasses. They were ten times worse than his old man.

It was among these that Christine wanted to mingle.

"Could you please move over one seat, lady, so I can sit down together with the missus?" Goff asked of a weary old safety-pinned Yiddeneh. She had never before been asked such an outrageous question, to shift her weary bulk for the benefit of the young and well dressed, and was trying to figure out an appropriate reply when she caught the blinding blondness that was Christine and her mouth froze. She lowered her head as one who fears being struck blind by a deity and moved submissively to the next seat to allow the *momzer* and the goddess space together at the table.

"Thank you, lady," said Goff with a sarcastic edge. "Christine, what would you like?"

"I'm not sure. Let's go up to the counter and pick something out."

"We'll lose our seats."

"Well, then, I'll go. I'll bring *you* something." She was so full of childish delight, here in this dump. Goff agreed.

"OK. I'd like an order of kashe varnishkes—it's what that guy is eating at the next table."

"Oh, I know what it is, Arnold. I think I'll get that too."

"Good. Make it a double order for me. I'm starved."

"Some dessert? A drink?"

"Oh, a cinnamon Danish and coffee."

"Would you like your coffee in a glass?" proposed Christine delightedly.

"Yes, sure. Why not. In a glass." Goff thought about old A.G. It would have warmed the cockeleh of his heart. An island of silence had settled around them, as the Paradise regulars strained to hear the historic conversation between the *momzer* and the blond shiksa princess. They were all taking her to their hearts, she who knew kashe varnishkes and drinking coffee from a glass.

When Christine reached the counter, the usual chaos where the *fressers* crowded and pushed and hollered to get the servers' attentions parted with a hush to allow the princess her swath of access to the sweaty counterman. His normal sour arrogance dissolved, replaced by smiling solicitous encouragement. Never before had the regulars seen such a change come over Gregory. They called him Gregory the gregor, for his harsh growling ways. No one ever remembered seeing him smile. And now miraculously, Gregory the gregor had astonishingly transformed himself to Gregory the groveler.

Christine asked sweetly for two orders of kashe varnishkes, one of them double.

"Kashe varnishkes, one double," echoed a jovial Slavic boom. With rare flare, Gregory positioned two plates precariously on one massive hand and with a long abandoned St. Petersburg flourish grandly scooped his ladle deeply into his steaming pans, neatly piling up mountains of varnishkes on each. His moon face and broad nose widening in smiles, he handed the plates over to Christine, who in turn handed him the two punch tickets with a smile, and with great élan he snapped neat round holes in them.

Christine proceeded to the coffee and cake section, where the stern stocky serving woman also melted into smiles. And when Christine asked for the two coffees in a glass, the woman almost swooned from the grace of the shiksa princess. And the mobs ordinarily shoving and pushing, never deterred by someone trying to make his way with a loaded tray, were suddenly stilled, and parted to allow her to pass unhindered, untouched, with not a drop spilled.

As Christine stopped to get the silver before returning to the table to lay out the dishes, a little old man with the *Forward* folded under his arm came up to her and handed her several paper napkins. "I see you forgot the napkins," he said respectfully.

She thanked him with a radiant smile. The little man nodded and walked away with a self-satisfied strut. His message was clear: "We welcome you here, O blond Shiksa Princess; please observe that we know the niceties and are not common people."

Kunt kisser, thought Goff disdainfully.

Eating at last, Goff asked Christine, "What is it about you—this love affair you have with Jews? And they're all crazy about you."

She smiled as she bit into her kashe varnishke with pearly teeth. "Eat, Arnold, eat." Goff, filled with excitement, ate, without tasting much. "It's true, Arnold, I love Jewish people."

"I don't."

"I know. I know."

"I'm crazy about you, Christine. I've never been so happy or relaxed in my life. I feel like a kid. I just know my breakthrough is right around the corner." He looked at her very seriously. "Christine?"

"Yes, Arnold."

"Christine, do you mind if we don't go to bed right away?" She looked at him earnestly for a moment. He thought he caught a quick shadow of sadness, an unexplainable sadness. But she broke once more into her dazzling smile. "I think that's a wise decision, Arnold," she agreed.

"Let me explain. I want to go to bed with you more than anything else in the world, and that's why I want to hold off. Do you understand?"

"I understand enough. I don't have to understand so clearly. Look, I'm all finished and you're not half done, and you were so hungry."

"The hell with the kashe varnishkes. Christine, you've got to tell me. What is this thing you have with Jews? Such a beautiful girl like you. Why?"

"Arnold, it is really quite personal."

"Please, Christine."

"Well, the main reason: when I was a little girl my family, very much like Anne Frank, hid a Jewish family in our house in Amsterdam. And one day the Gestapo—well—" Christine threw her hands out. "What's more to say, except—I suppose I made up my mind to—to compensate."

"Christine, didn't you say you're Danish?"

"Yes, I've said both. I later moved to Denmark. Arnold, please, I don't want to talk about it. Come, let's walk outside. It's so beautiful."

Goff chose not to press. It was immaterial to him. He would be delighted to walk with her. He would conduct her on a little tour. The cloud quickly passed from her face, and she was radiant again.

They walked north on Essex Street, passed Delancey's indoor market, the quiltmakers, the wholesale skeins of wool. Christine was eager to see everything. She made Goff stop in front of one of the shops selling religious articles. A beautiful silk Jewish prayer shawl was draped in the window. "My husband has one of those shawls," she told him.

He felt uncomfortable standing here, and urged her to move on because there was a great outdoor candy stall a few blocks up. And they continued up Delancey and on to Rivington. The Puerto Rican influence had now almost blotted out most of the old Jewish traces. They bought assorted candy and nuts from a huge spread of sacks and cartons arrayed outside the shop. The tubby Jewish owner waited on customers, helped by a lively wise guy whom Goff recognized as the Puerto Rican stud he had seen eating the kashe knish. He knew his nuts and candy, and worked with swift sureness and accuracy.

Carrying their brown paper bag of assorted nuts and chocolates, Goff guided her across Essex Street through the foul-fumed traffic, to an outdoor pickle stand. A hunched but energetic weather-beaten old man tended his pickle works behind a barricade of pungent barrels. Nothing could harm him, behind this pickle barreled fortress, neither the snows of winter nor the heat of summer. He was cheerfully filling up a jar of pickles for a customer, engineering two last pickles expertly into the jar to give full measure. His hands were briny, raw, red.

"Plenty good, plenty everything," he kept repeating in a Judeo-Slavic mumble-chant as he went about his task in a kind of pickled religious bliss.

Again Christine was delighted as Goff suddenly became a pickle mavin, carefully pointing out those he wanted.

They continued strolling, eating the pickles al fresco, starting with a pickle apiece and converging to one, bite on bite. He had never before enjoyed pickles so much as at this moment, with Christine sharing his pleasure.

What is so beautiful and rare as a man and his maid on the first bright day in spring, munching away on a tangy new pickle while walking together along Essex Street? It beats plenty, thought a Goff who had never before experienced such innocent and pure fun. He wanted to carry her books and do handsprings. Amazing—all his fucking around hadn't immunized him. He was a moony-faced kid in love. He guessed a man never forfeited his guaranteed one-time shot at it. The ripe bursting pickle juice ran down both their laughing faces, as hand in hand they frolicked through the old fast-fading ghetto.

# Chapter 6

*Hot pastrami*

At two-thirty Goff dropped Christine off at Bloomingdale's and continued on his way to Kummerlos' office for his regular Monday appointment.

He decided to look grim and troubled, completely contrary to his true feelings of elation. He had not only to fake out Kummerlos, but also the antagonistic, fat Hunter College receptionist, whom he suspected was on to him and Christine. As repulsive as she was, Goff figured she had to have brains at least to get into Hunter. Distressed-looking or not, she gave Goff her usual fat-faced disdainful look.

Why did she begrudge him? What had happened to traditional Jewish compassion, he wondered. An empty Tab bottle should only get stuck in your blubbery cunt, Fatty Arbuckle, he wished her without looking at her.

Despite his vehement dislike, he felt he should maintain his air of distressed preoccupation. But when she turned her back to get the phone to announce him, he snapped her a quick silent Sicilian arm.

Goff saw that Kummerlos was waiting for him to begin. The patient opens and the doctor closes. Man proposes and God disposes. Well, Goff was in no hurry to start. How content the doctor looked.

Kummerlos finally broke the ice. "What are you thinking about, Arnold?"

Goff scowled back from beneath his unibrow.

God, but Kummerlos was getting fat! He was becoming remote in his fat. The essence of him was becoming more and more buried in his flesh. He would soon disappear entirely within it.

It would give Goff a lot of satisfaction to feel that he had contributed even in a small way to his burial. He must find ways to hasten it along. Bigger and better brunches. But it was difficult to see how he could surpass them in their sumptuousness. Jesus, Kummerlos couldn't possibly eat more at these things than he did already.

Kummerlos smiled. Goff knew that smile was for himself, not for Goff. He was so fat-assed pleased with himself. And now he had also become a Hollywood consultant. All that fish shit he fed him; it made him fat, but even so, fish was supposed to be healthy. No cholesterol. Eskimos never had heard attacks. If only he could increase his cholesterol consumption.

Suddenly he was struck by the true essence of Kummerlos; he'd gotten to the root of it at last!

"Hot pastrami," Goff murmured intimately.

The doctor's eyes grew attentive. "Why hot pastrami?"

Goff knew why hot pastrami! "Hot pastrami," he repeated lovingly.

"Did you say 'hot pastrami'?"

"Yes."

"Why, Arnold?"

"Because hot pastrami is on my mind."

"Why? Are you hungry?"

"Only for Alexandra."

"Fine. But what has hot pastrami got to do with it?"

"She's crazy about it. There was a big first for me today. A preliminary one, though. For the first time we met, alone, deliberately. It was our first date. I asked her to meet me near my plant for lunch. We were like a couple of kids. I was so happy I didn't even want to go to bed with her. I just wanted to be with her, to show her around, to buy her treats, to please her. You know what I mean?"

Kummerlos, paying no attention, gave off a cover smile. Goff knew he had drifted easily three thousand miles away. Where the fuck was he, in Malibu?

"Hot pastrami," he murmured again. Kummerlos' piggy eyes snapped back to attention, scooting right back to New York. He was definitely a pastrami man, Goff knew it! In addition to the flesh, a greasy sheen had lately exuded from his doctor's face. Kummerlos was a pastrami man!

In New York there were thousands of them. They all had a distinctive look about them, never leaning to lean; always to fat—never quite ungreasy. Essentially they had no other commitments but to pastrami and its consumption. Hot pastrami claimed their prime loyalty. To an untrained eye, the fleshy lawyer, for instance, displayed extreme concern to his distressed client pouring out his anxieties. But Goff knew better; he could detect the pastramied glaze in his eyes behind which he barricaded himself; he knew that nothing really mattered much to him but his hot pastrami. In every walk of life you saw them. Everywhere.

He could picture Kummerlos wrapping his short thick legs around the legs of his chair to anchor himself in order to provide leverage to his jaws for the hippopotamus width they would have to attain in order to be able to tear into the mighty hot pastrami sandwich, double meat.

"I speak of hot pastrami because Alexandra is crazy about it. And I happen to know where they have the best hot pastrami in the world. It's in Brooklyn. So we hop into a cab on Delancy Street and in five minutes we're over the Williamsburgh Bridge and at this delicatessen on Roebling Street. It's called the Pastrami King. Do you know it?" Kummerlos wasn't drifting anymore, he was shaking his head in rapt attention, never so serious in his life. "Well, you never ate such pastrami as they have there. They make it themselves in their cellar or some place—an old family recipe from Rumania. And when we were finished . . ."

"Wait," interrupted his now avid doctor. "Tell me more about your lunch, the pastrami . . . and . . . whatever . . ."

Shit, Kummerlos couldn't fake him out. He didn't want no "whatever." The pig only wanted to hear about the hot pastrami. So he'd tell him about the hot pastrami. "First, when the taxi gets you there, the neighborhood stinks. I mean in both ways. It's run down. Once it was all Jewish with a little Polish, but now it's becoming all Puerto Rican" (as if that prick who grew up just across from the river didn't know). "So it stinks *that* way; and it also stinks from pollution and a lot of factories around there. But the minute you get out of the taxi on the corner where the delicatessen is, in that spot, there is no stink. The beautiful aroma of that hot pastrami takes over the whole corner. And even if you're not hungry, you begin to get an appetite. And then you go in, and you can imagine the aroma now inside. Right? It drives your salivary glands stark raving mad. Pastrami, big fat rich dark slabs of it, the glass-enclosed counter crammed full of it. And the counterman with his long fork deep in the steam heater, hooking those he's ready to slice. And then he slices it, and the meat inside—that rich burnished red color of that juicy delicious meat—as he slices, slices, slices, all thick slices. Because they give you a tremendous sandwich on the best rye bread with the crispest crust in town, or if you want, on club. You know what I mean, Doc, right? And then for those that are absolutely bananas about their pastrami, you can order your sandwich with double meat. The size of it is unbelievable. Double meat! Unbelievable. Can you just picture it?"

Yes, yes, he could, he could.

"And then that first bite. I'll tell you, the first time you sink your teeth into that hot pastrami and crusty rye bread, nothing in the world exists except you and the hot pastrami. You're actually making love to that juicy hot pastrami sandwich. And Alexandra, she's making love to her hot pastrami. It was like sharing a sexual experience"

Kummerlos was now mesmerized. He nodded in a daze. That telltale glazed pastramied look had come over him. He had succumbed to Goff's brilliantly rendered pastrami pornography.

Goff saw that Kummerlos was drained. He decided to avoid overkill and concluded, "Well, anyway, I highly recommend it. By the way, strangely, the delicatessen was recommended to me by my C.P.A., Addelson, you know."

Kummerlos had taken repossession of himself somewhat. "Yes, of course," he said. "Just quickly, Arnold, I don't get over to Brooklyn often, but I would like to make a note; where again is the location of this delicatessen?"

Goff gave it to him; Kummerlos would be closing soon. Goff wanted to get back on the track. "Doctor, about Alexandra. This platonic dry run we had today. As I said, it's what I wanted. But it is now inevitable; the next time we meet we will be lovers. And I'll hate myself for it—for Phil Epstein, you know?"

"Ha, ha," said Kummerlos, now completely recovered. "No, Arnold, I guarantee you you will not hate yourself. Do what you have to do, and if afterwards you tell me you still hate yourself, I will prescribe some anti-hate pills, guaranteed effective. Ha, ha. We must close now. Ha, ha."

Goff left, considerably outraged that this fat son-of-a-bitch shrink, this closet pastrami man, was actually becoming unprofessional. Laughing and making a joke out of Goff's practically telling him he was gonna screw his wife. Well, joke or not, Kummerlos had given him the go-ahead.

And now he knew how to put the double fix on Kummerlos. Aside from Christine, he had seen through his mask, knew he was secretly a pastrami man. At his next brunch he would see to it that heaping platters of hot pastrami would laden his tables. It would lure him away from cholesterol-free fish. He'd charge into the pastrami, get his arteries clogged up with the stuff, and would eat himself into a cholesteroled stroke. Ha, ha, we must close now, Goff thought with hot malice.

# Chapter 7

*C.P.A. drops dead, Ramona defects, Leon Finger gets*
*dumped, but Goff's sensational day moves inexorably on*

Goff was completely immersed in planning next Monday's tentative lunch date. If the timing were similar to last Monday, he would have about three hours with Christine before his appointment with Kummerlos at three. It never occurred to him to cancel his appointment. The appointments had become so ingrained in him. Actually, despite what he had told Kummerlos, it wasn't in the cards for their consummation to occur on Monday. It would mean a matinee. That wouldn't be right, not for Christine. After they were established, OK, but not for the first shot. Oh, he felt confident he could talk her into it, but he wouldn't. Their first time had to be a proper nighttime event. He had to go formal. On Monday they would again just do fun things. Maybe he'd take her to Chinatown for lunch. Also like Brooklyn, only five minutes away from his plant. Now, where would be the exact right place? Something a little dingy but with sensational food; where at least fifty percent of the customers would be chinks. Maybe he ought to consult with C.P.A.

Coming right into the heart of the tax season, it was hard to get hold of C.P.A. He'd call him at home Sunday. But before Goff could make the call, Cookie, C.P.A.'s wife, called *him* to give him the shocking news that C.P.A. had dropped dead of a heart attack that morning in their local schoolyard handball court. The funeral services on Coney Island Avenue would be at twelve noon sharp tomorrow, Monday. Would he come? Did he know where the funeral parlor was? Yes, he knew where it was. Yes, shit, he'd be there.

There went the lunch with Christine. And who the hell was going to complete his tax returns now? Jesus Christ, C.P.A. was only forty. And for an accountant, in great shape. That fuckin' treacherous pastrami must have done him in. Poor fuck. But, actually, what after all did he have to live for anyway? Trust nature.

Now he must take a chance and call Christine. If Kummerlos got on the phone he'd put on a thick Jewish accent and work it as a wrong number. It was Christine. "Thank God it's you, Christine. I'll be brief. I can't make it tomorrow. An old friend, who is also my accountant, died of a heart attack today. His funeral is tomorrow. Please call me Tuesday at eleven at my plant. If your husband is around you now, you can put him on if it's easier for you, and I'll invite him to the funeral also. This guy used to be a patient of his." Goff was talking very rapidly.

"Arnold, Dr. Kummerlos is not home."

"Oh."

"His brother drove down from Scarsdale today and they both went to visit my mother-in-law. And afterwards they're going to Brooklyn. It seems they heard of a wonderful delicatessen there, and they want to try it. Do you want me to tell him about his patient dying?"

"No, Christine. Actually he hasn't been his patient for many years. I'm sorry about not being able to see you tomorrow. I haven't been thinking about anything else but you."

A silence followed. Goff broke it. "I don't know when I enjoyed myself more than our lunch last Monday. You know, Christine, I'm going to get a complete physical checkup. I'm perfect, but I want it confirmed. This fellow was a very young man. But I don't think he really knew how to enjoy himself. If you have that capacity, I truly believe it keeps you healthy. It's as if nature wants you to survive. Nature is rooting for you."

"That sounds interesting, Arnold."

"Right. Look, call me Tuesday at eleven. Have you ever been to Chinatown?"

"No, I never have."

"Will you call?"

"Yes, Arnold, I will."

Tuesday morning Goff woke in a surly mood. The funeral of C.P.A. the day before had depressed him and deprived him of his date. Seeing Kummerlos after the funeral hadn't helped either. His doctor was turning into total blubber. The satisfaction he might get from cuckolding him was thereby diminishing. It was becoming no contest. It had been clear to Goff that Kummerlos had indeed run to the delicatessen Sunday. He seemed even heavier—his movements and breathing were more labored, and he was burping. Goff could swear he could smell the odor of pastrami garlic. But of course he couldn't ask Kummerlos about it. And Kummerlos didn't have the grace to tell him, to say, "Oh, Arnold, by the way, I tried that delicatessen Sunday. Very good, very good." No, his anal code wouldn't allow that. God, how he must have gorged himself. All double meat without a doubt.

But he must snap out of his mood, if for no other reason than today was Tuesday and tonight his kids would be coming to stay over. And more important, Christine would be phoning at eleven. He wondered how the kids would take to Christine. Ah, they'd love her. Christine wasn't an icy beauty, she had such warmth, such a smile.

At his shul-plant, the phone rang precisely at eleven. Ramona didn't pick it up until after several rings because to Goff's annoyance she was busy bullshitting animatedly with his shipping clerk, Malcolm Feiler. Finally answering, she pointed to her expectant boss, and mouthed the word "psychiatrist," accompanied with an impertinent rolling of her eyes.

Goff was ready to forego his usual announcement "Arnold Goff, here" and leap in with a vocal embracing of "Christine," when he heard Kummerlos' voice, "Mr. Goff, Dr. Kummerlos."

Goff stiffened apprehensively. "Yes, Doctor?" he muttered.

"Arnold, I wanted to get you as soon as possible. I just got another call from California. It is urgent that I go there immediately, but it was impossible for me to go today. I have my appointments. But I promised I'd catch a six o'clock plane tomorrow evening. So I'm sorry, but we'll have to cancel our three o'clock session tomorrow. Again, I expect to be back on the weekend. So the next session will have to be next Monday."

And now Ramona was signaling that another call was waiting for him. Again she rolled her eyes and mouthed the word "psychiatrist." Goff was greatly relieved and elated. A quick plan formed. He signaled Ramona to hold his other call, but he said to Kummerlos, summoning all his charms both as an old patient and now good neighbor and frequent host, "Doc, I have a very sound idea. Frankly, at this particular time, with these new developments I've been telling you about, I'm a little uneasy at having a whole week go by without a session. So is it possible for me to see you tomorrow, and we cut the session fifteen or twenty minutes, and I drive you out to the airport? I could get you there by five-fifteen or five-thirty the very latest, in plenty of time for your plane."

Kummerlos didn't hesitate a second. "Well, Arnold, your idea has a certain feasibility. But you are sure it won't be an inconvenience to you?"

"No, not at all. I'm free as a bird Wednesday. Actually, I hope it's not an inconvenience to you."

"But are you sure you can get me there in time?"

"Absolutely," he reassured. "And if you want to take the missus, well, by all means. I'll be coming straight back."

"Take the missus, eh? Ha, ha." Kummerlos was back to his old routine. "Well, maybe I will, maybe I will. That's very nice of you, Arnold."

"Don't give it another thought."

"OK, Arnold, see you tomorrow."

Arnold push-buttoned onto Christine. "Sorry to hold you. But you know who I was talking to on the other phone? Right. Christine, I'm driving your husband to the airport tomorrow afternoon right after my session, and I gave him permission to take you along."

Christine laughed. "That's very thoughtful of you, Arnold."

"Yes, it is. In case he forgets to bring it up, maybe you can find a way to remind him."

"I'll try."

"Please, because I'd hate to be making that long trip back from the airport all alone."

"You won't. See you tomorrow, Arnold."

Goff hung up. He stared at the phone with intense almost palpitating satisfaction. That's the way he wanted it. He wanted Kummerlos, his shrink for nineteen years, to hand over his beautiful wife, right into his arms.

When Goff left Dr. Abraham Levine's office, it was close to noon. He hurried over to Fifth Avenue to get a cab heading downtown. He had never figured his checkup to take over two hours, for such a cruddy nothing. A complete irritation, totally useless. More apt to bring on sickness than prevent it. What a schmuck that Levine had turned out to be. What a schmuck Kummerlos was turning out to be. Was that only with doctors? Wasn't that everyone's fate? A case could be made out for everyone he knew. What about him? Was that happening to him too? Well, maybe. But, anyway, once you start thinking about it, doesn't that automatically arrest the process? Well, he just thought about it. But he'd have to remember to think about it again, periodically. It was like his pop taking a physic. Another thing, very important, he might be a schmuck, but at least he was nobody's schmuck but his own, which all the others he knew weren't, because he at least wasn't on public display. That's what Yom

Kippur should be for. If they had it for a guy to spend one day once a year to get him to think about his schmucky behavior the past year and meditate on how to avoid making the same mistakes, teach himself to reduce his incidents of schmuckiness, get it out of his system, instead of worrying about his sins—*that* would have some value. It would make a lot more sense than sins. And you might even get him to go to shul that day.

Goff ran up the steps of his shul-plant. Malcolm Feiler and Ramona, in his office, looked like they had just separated from a smooch. He didn't give a shit. Leon hadn't come yet for their lunch appointment. It was too much to hope that he might have forgotten altogether.

He began to sign some checks and letters that Ramona had laid out on his desk, but through the corner of his eye he saw Malcolm and Ramona edging together, very stiff—and oh shit, they had developed clasped hands—and were now standing rigidly side by side in an each-giving-the-other-courage formation.

They were getting set to tell him something.

"Arnie," said Ramona defensively, "Malcolm" (she pronounced both l's) "and me are going to get married." She paused, dug in and fired again. "Tonight!"

Malcolm, shaking, threw up a sick grin.

Goff was ready to get pissed off. This could screw up his management problems. But he would not be small-minded today, for in a sense wasn't he going to be married tonight too? And on his marriage day he would be magnanimous. "Well, whattya know. Great, kids, great!"

Malcolm, relieved by Goff's acceptance, sputtered joyfully. "And you know what, Arnie? We're going to be married by a rabbi; Ramona has converted to Judaism. She knows how to say all the *broches*. Say the *broche* for vegetables for Arnie." Ramona declined.

Come to think of it, Goff hadn't seen her wearing her little gold crucifix in a long time.

"Great, great, congratulations, *mazel tov*," he said, maintaining a look of false joy. Actually, it annoyed him. Ramona handled the Puerto Rican crew like a whip. Because she was one of them. Would she be able to continue effectively in her new status? Oh, he supposed she would. Once a Puerto Rican, always a Puerto Rican. Blood runs thicker than Manischewitz.

He supposed it was none of his business, but where did a schmuck like Feiler take it on himself to recruit members for the club without asking permission of his betters? Jesus, anybody could nowadays become a Jew. Screening and controls had gone to the dogs. And even though he always thought he would have been happy not to have been one, he still was one—and old tribal embers still occasionally sputtered into flame.

Also, what had Feiler's psychiatrist to say about this? Since it was common knowledge that Feiler saw him every Wednesday night, Goff felt it would not be such an insult to explore a little. "So, Malcolm, I suppose you've canceled your appointment with your shrink tonight. Or is he giving the bride away?"

Malcolm laughed happily. "Giving the bride away? I'm giving *him* away. I dumped him months ago when he started telling me to try to analyze why I had chosen Ramona. I saw the guy was ruining me, and I finally dumped him. I've never been so happy. Right, Ramona?"

Ramona squeezed closer to him in a smug cuddle Goff felt was directed spitefully at him. The question hanging in the air was clearly: and what about you, schmuck? When already are you going to dump yours?

These two shits of his had a lot of nerve. But he'd be out ahead anyway. He'd put them in their place with magnanimity. And fuck it, let the quality of his magnanimity not be strained.

"Kids," he said, "this comes as a very pleasant surprise. But there's been no notice. What were you thinking about a honeymoon?"

"Well, Meester Goff," meestered Ramona, punishing him, "we will wait for the July vacation."

"I'll tell you what. Today is Wednesday. Why don't you go on a nice little trip for an extra long weekend? And whatever you do, I want it all to be on me."

Ramona immediately reverted to an exonerating "Arnie! Oh, Arnie, really?"

"Sure, really. The Concord, Grossinger's, whatever. All on me. And even if you don't come on in Monday, even if it's Tuesday, I'll understand. And again, it's all on me, and I don't want you to stint."

Oh, how happy they were. They would clear everything up this afternoon so no loose ends would be hanging. They would even skip lunch today. Thank you, thank you, thank you.

And so Goff resubdued them completely with his magnanimity. And actually it would cost him very little. He had no doubt that they would be back Monday, not Tuesday. And as for urging them not to stint, that cost him absolutely nothing, because he knew also that slobs like Ramona and Malcolm didn't even know how not to stint.

Leon Finger walked in. Goff thought he must have put on thirty pounds since he had seen him last two years ago. But that was his only change.

He was still insufferably overbearing with his heavy Jew jokes, still trying clumsily to show his easy separation from his more unfortunate brothers, who never had the wit or style to unencumber themselves from unattractive Jewish ways. More than thirty years had gone by, and nothing had changed with the guy, except he was now an unattractive overfleshed specimen himself.

"Arnie, so where's a nice piece of sponge cake and a glass of Mogen David? Do they still have services here?" Same old jokes, same old horse's ass delivery.

He turned to Malcolm and graced him with a "*Vuss macht a Yid?*" then turned to Ramona and started talking Spanish to her. And the horse's ass was doing it well. It seemed to Goff he had better command of Spanish than he ever had of German.

"Leon, you'll have to excuse yourself. I'm in a little hurry. Let's have lunch. Where do you want to eat?"

"I worked up an appetite for the Jew food here in your shul."

"Let's go to Ratner's."

"Is Ramona coming with us?" he said, eyeing her like a boulevardier from Linden Boulevard.

"Not today," said Goff wearily to the ballbreaker. This kind of horse's ass make-out man behavior used to drive him wild. But no more. He was just so tired of him. He determined this would be the last time he would see Leon. He was ready to make a mental note to bring it up with Kummerlos as was his custom, when he remembered he had better start learning not to.

At Ratner's Leon had to demonstrate his aggressive expertise of the dairy dishes with the Jewish waiter. He ordered pickled fish and a plate of blintzes. "Don't give me the *schvantz*. I want a center cut," he told the drooping waiter zestfully. The old waiter nodded listlessly and shuffled out. Leon turned to Goff. "These waiters have lost their fight. They're no more fun. Whatzamatter, Arnie, you so quiet?"

Goff gave a wan smile and said he guessed he was tired. Which he was, of Leon. He wasn't mad or anything at him anymore, just tired. He listened to Leon ramble on about his new girlfriend, a Bolivian named Rosalba. She was a great cook, knew some fabulous Inca recipes. Whenever they were in town, they moved in with his old Trotskyite father, now a rabid eighty-one-year-old Zionist, who got along famously with Rosalba. They collaborated mixing his old Jewish dishes with her Inca dishes, and got some terrific results. She didn't speak English too great but neither did his old man, so they understood each other fine. "He treats her like a princess; he doesn't let her lift a finger. He does the cleaning and washing."

Goff remembered from his early years how old man Finger had made a slave of Leon's mother; and how in turn Leon made a slave of his father whose name was Boris. So the former Trotskyite, now in bondage to his son and an Inca Indian. So now, naturally, he's a Zionist. He wants his freedom.

Leon's lifeline had routed him via the Andes and Indians. Once a proud Teuton, now a fat-stuff Inca-dinka-doo. He no longer sported his German, but had settled for pidgin Indian-Spanish.

Leon told him Rosalba suited him fine. She had inherited some land in Bolivia, and they might go there to live for a while. She was a very comfortable woman. Goff translated that as fat. Goff, who had anticipated with some pleasure eating Leon's heart out telling him about willowy Christine, no longer had the desire. It was really no contest anymore. The long, long rivalry was over. He had absolutely no need for Leon anymore. So he let him go on making his tired jokes about blintzes and sour cream. What a hasbeen he was.

When they finished their lunch, Goff, determined to be a gentleman, soberly told Leon to give his regards to his father. And as Leon drifted up Delancey Street, mingling with the chattering Puerto Ricans who now inundated the street, Goff figured Leon was in his right element now. And soon even his height no longer helped to keep him visible. Leon was lost in the Hispanic flow. Goff decided he would never see him again.

# Chapter 8

*Christine*

When Goff arrived at his apartment, he ruled out the lovely customary afternoon nap he enjoyed so much. That lunch with putzy Leon had killed it. He was too excited anyway. Tonight was the night! Everything! His final breakthrough, his sex supreme!

He sang in the shower as he sudsed his balls. Easy there, *baytzim*, he sang at them, don't get in an uproar yet. Gotta-get-you-clean, for-my-village-queen. . . . A guy could always work up a terrific lather in his crotch, which was as it should be.

Goff was out of the shower, toweling his entire body dry, brisk rub-a-dub but changing to pit-a-pat for his rich, plump, scoured balls. No, sir, these weren't the artificially puffed-up balls of long ago. He had finally earned his balls.

After dropping off Kummerlos, what? Well, it would be five-thirty or so. They'd drive back to Manhattan and find some place for cocktails and dinner. He had several very classy intimate spots in mind. But as to exactly where, he'd have to play it somewhat by ear. And after . . . ah, after . . . Flow gently sweet after . . . up at his place. She would consent; she wanted it as much as he did. And he wanted it at *his* place, nowhere else. It would be clean and straight. Because he was in love. For the first time, he was truly in love, and he would seize his dream.

Right now he'd rate himself as a three-and-a-half ball guy. After tonight, four balls. There was no higher rating. So Goff, the fast-fuck operator, virtuously imposed a fuckfast. At sundown the fast would be over. Yahoodie!

Goff had ordered the garage to deliver his Caddy. When he stepped out of the building shortly before three, it was waiting. He was surprised to see Stahrts instead of Fitz at the door.

"Your Caddy, Mr. Goff," said the nightman with a certain air of shared proprietary pride. In response to Goff's slightly quizzical expression, Stahrts told him, ja, Fitz had to go to a doctor so he was filling in for an extended shift. Goff nodded, figuring hernia.

Stahrts accompanied him out to the street and stood attentively by while the garageman stepped out, holding the door for Goff. It annoyed the ass off him to have that prick, Stahrts, nosing in also. What the hell did he think he was accomplishing? Standing by to open the door for him in case the garageman dropped dead or something?

Goff gave the garageman a buck and slipped into the driver's seat. All the while, Stahrts stood by, in alert attendance. Another thing that burned his ass was that he noticed that the Nazi prick was now sporting one of those little American flag pins on his doorman uniform. He always bristled at anyone who wore these pins. He didn't know exactly what the message was supposed to be, but he knew for sure it wasn't for his benefit. And wouldn't you know, a Nazi prick would be first on line to get one.

As Goff started off, Stahrts cheerfully bade him a pleasant trip. Goff responded with a patrician nod and a muttered fuck you.

Five minutes later, Goff was back, double parked in front of the building, honking.

"Stahrts, I have an appointment in a few minutes just two blocks away. No place to park there. Here are the keys. Look after the Caddy. I'll be back in a half hour."

He tossed the keys to Stahrts, who was very pleased with himself when he managed to catch them with two-handed ineptness, strictly greenhorn style. He practically heel-clicked an ecstatic *Zum Befehl* to Goff, who was already jogging his way down the two blocks to Kummerlos. He pictured Christine, her long, pale, man-wrapping legs loping in lyrical slow motion just ahead, and he jogged faster.

At precisely three he sat down cheerfully in his accustomed place opposite his doctor.

"Why are you smiling, Arnold?" Kummerlos began.

"I really shouldn't be."

"All right—why shouldn't you be?"

"Because tonight, excuse the expression, Doctor, I have to shit or get off the pot."

"Ah, before we go into that, are we ready to drive to the airport?" asked the worrier-psychiatrist.

Jews, always worriers.

Not too many warriors. All right. Israel was changing that, Goff thought. "All systems go, Doc, right on schedule. That's why I was smiling. I couldn't find a parking place for my Caddy, and I thought I might be a little late, but I was here on the dot."

"Good. Now what about the pot? What crisis confronts us?"

"Well, I'm glad I could see you today, Doctor, even if it's a minisession, because after I spoke to you, Alexandra, the Greek girl, called me. Her husband, Phil Epstein, is checking into Mount Sinai today. No emergency. Just for observation. His angina was acting up again. She wants to see me tonight." Goff saw a twitch of concern activate his doctor's face. "Oh, it won't interfere with my getting you to the airport," he reassured him. "We're not meeting till nine o'clock. She feels she should stay with Phil till eight-thirty when visiting hours end. And she's sincere. She really wants to be with him. She's a great human person. Well, I said fine, how about at my place. And she said O.K. She'll be there at nine." Goff paused. Kummerlos, whose usual policy was to sit out a pause, had no time to wait this time. He couldn't take a chance of being late for his California flight.

"So, what's the problem, Arnold?"

"Well, it's obvious that tonight must bring a decision. That's what I have to ask you about: should I shit or get off the pot?"

"Shit!" shot Kummerlos with a quick glance at his watch.

"I figured that," said Goff.

"Again and again and again. Here is yet again an opportunity to exercise an act of creative selfishness. It will serve the interests of all concerned. Give her a good bang, Arnold. It's what you want me to say; it happens to coincide with my studied opinion. Give her a yentz and get it out of your system already. She'll thank you, her husband'll thank you, and I'll thank you." He shrugged an impatient apology. "We have to close early now." He opened an inner door and called out "Chris, we are ready."

Goff, the old infallible sex appraiser, watched the two closely as boarding time neared, Kummerlos in his baggy pants, Christine in her shimmering northern lights beautifully molded blue silk suit. They would kiss soon. Would he give her a little grab on her ass? Would she do likewise? Would they sock it to each other up front in hard concave, or would they arch away down there in formal convex? He guessed he would see daylight between them. When the boarding announcement came, Kummerlos was obviously straining to get started. Christine gave his cheek a cheerful little kiss in exactly the same manner she'd used in reporting the baseball score the first time Goff had ever seen her. She looked happy to be seeing her husband off on a trip which would bring him so much pleasure. Also he saw they were clearly convex. Plenty of daylight showed. Great! A great girl! Way too good for the fat slob Kummerlos had become. Goff had been on the right track about them all along. In Kummerlos' own words, had they a joyous bed? Not a fuckin' chance.

There was no longer any question in Goff's mind that all this would be his soon. But how exactly would she give herself to him? He thought he would like it baseball-score style too. But maybe it would be better on a deeper level. Intense Scandinavian style. The swing from gay to brooding, from brooding to sudden violent passion. A great style. Very powerful. Yes, yes. Beneath Iceland are these steaming volcanic springs. Or love, sauna style, from ice to steam in one lunge and vice versa—could be very exciting. Somewhere in between would be very nice too. Like Brigitte Bardot's pussy pout would also be sensational. But no matter—any style that was comfortable for her would suit him fine.

Kummerlos is gone. Goff is giddy. She's all his—forever. She will announce baseball scores for him into the millenium. He will start graying soon. He will mature with dignity and grace. Remain lithe and limber and dance the marimba. And Christine will take long-legged golden Scandinavian strides beside him. And when people look at them ten, twenty years from now, they will still see how she worships him, and they will sense how sexually potent he still is. How nobody in the world can possibly satisfy her as he still does. Only *he* knows the volcanic depths beneath her cool blue surfaces. And she will whisper north country endearments to him—baseball scores—and he will nod, confident of her fealty and love.

Entree will be his in every fashionable spa, elegant hotel and restaurant. Even in Israel. Just flash his Christine and all doors open with sweeping bows. Teddy Kollek, the mayor of Jerusalem, will greet them. And Kollek would appreciate Christine, would appreciate her display of respect for Jewish sensitivities and rituals. Goff would donate handsomely to the Appeal.

And the jolliest thing of all: when introducing her around, the deadpan announcement that she used to be his psychiatrist's wife. Greater therapy hath no man.

Goff headed for New York but before long the Cadillac veered right onto an exit ramp and emerged on Queens Boulevard. He had an inspired flash, a strange one: he must buy her flowers. He soon spotted a florist and parked. "I've never bought flowers for anyone in my life. I never saw any sense in flowers before," he said, excited by this unexpected urge.

For his flattering thought, Christine took his face in her hands and gave him a soft lingering kiss. He ignited at once. She quickly responded to his excited, prying tongue, returning tongue for tongue. What a tongue she had when aroused. Never dreamed! Still tongues run deep. Darting, slithering, demanding, playful, searching, questing, restless, electric, straining—a tongue unhinged. Suddenly still, suddenly flapping with frenzy. A tongue of moods. How suppressed Kummerlos must have kept her. She was exploding through her tongue. He loved her, he loved her. And she him. With all due respect, what a blow job she could undoubtedly bestow. That fat ass Kummerlos had plainly never bought her flowers.

Her intensity made it plain that he could without much effort persuade her to enact her affection right then and there. His Cadillac, an island fortress in the midst of the rapids of Kew Gardeners swimming home from work, flooding out of the subways, upstream to their spawning grounds. All would be streaming by them in their instinctive surge: all the tumbling Bumble Bee salmons would steadfastly not notice the naughtiness in the Caddy. Wasn't this after all the locale of the Kitty Genovese unpleasantness? Which had ushered in the new era of *laissez faire* and noninvolvement? A new America uncovered by yet another Genovese?

Goff weighed the pros and cons. The desire to have Christine blow him was certainly excruciating. In their kisses and embraces his excitement had reached feverish pitch, almost to the point of seepage. His lost sureshot chance with Rhoda Lewin nearly thirty years ago still haunted him. He had promised himself never to allow such a repetition. Christine was throbbing with passion—moaning and gasping in a sexual frenzy. His hand found the waistband of her pants and slithered inside, down her silken belly and into her cunt. He had expected it to be sodden and juicy, but to his surprise it was dry. He fingered Christine's pussy with tenderness, gently probing to strike moisture and bring in the well. But what should he do about pursuing his blow job? She would do anything he wanted. Her moans clearly translated that. Oh, that bastard, Kummerlos. He had deprived her in some basic way. She was now groping with her hand for his cock trying to undo his zipper and moaning slippery sounds into his mouth. Using all his will, he made a sudden decision: he pulled his hand out of her pants and disengaged tongues. This was different!

No, for Christine he would relax the inflexible code he had adopted. She was no common plum for a Plum Beach backseat fuck, or an upfront blow job. No. Christine, the ultimate fruit of his labors, would have flowers and get fuckayed properly, with myrrh and minstrelsy, in his Park Avenue splendor.

Christine, palpitating heavily, accepted Goff's stalwart decision with a small resigned smile. Goff was surprised to hear himself reciting the girl's part, "Darling, let's wait. Later. It will be better." Christine nodded without changing expression. Gee, she had really wanted to blow him. He hoped he hadn't made that old mistake again.

They went into the florist, where he asked her to choose whatever pleased her. She said she would rather have him make the selection; she was sure it would be perfect.

What the hell did he know about flowers? Nothing! All he knew was daisies and roses. And orchids. Orchids from very fancy affairs, when the caterer's package included orchid corsages. None of these seemed exotic enough for Christine. Something special. But what? What? He looked around the shop, lost in the lush tropics behind glass doors. God, give him an idea! And for once God, realizing the importance of the occasion, came through. A distant recall materialized. He remembered the title of a mystery movie of those days of yesteryear (as the Lone Ranger announcer had put it) called *The Black Dahlia*. He knew it was a flower, but nothing more. What it looked like, smelled like, he had no idea. But the name had always intrigued him. He associated it vaguely with black lingerie and illicit sex. He would ask the Greek for them. "I'd like a dozen dahlias, please." The Greek, who was admiring the blond Christine, the kind of girl he too in his milder assimilationist fantasies had often dreamed of fucking, snapped over to Goff, "Yes, sir, what color?"

"Mix'm," said Goff, learning fast.

As the Greek finished assembling them, in purples, yellows, reds and whites, Goff's eyes were agog. Each of those fuckin' dahlias alone was a bush, a bouquet by itself. He thought they would have a cunty exotic look, with long tendrilly petals, excitingly malevolent, and here were these bushy things like the hats of Buckingham Palace Guards in technicolor. *Black Dahlia* my ass, he thought.

Anyway, Christine seemed to go for the gigantic bouquet in a big way. Oh beautiful, she murmured as the Greek handed it to her with greasy floorwalker elegance. Goff was pleased by the lecherous look he saw in the Greek's eye. Go make a circle, you prick, he thought. The best that guy could hope for was a black bushed Mediterranean olive-oiled twat like dumpy Alexandra. You have to go some to grab off a Christine. The way he saw it, even Onassis had never made it.

Where would Christine like to eat? Just name it, you got it. Chinese? Japanese? Polynesian bullshit? For her he'd eat bullshit. French? German? Jewish? What? What? You want to eat in Paris? Come, we'll go to Paris. London. Munich. Bangkok. Anything . . . but don't ask me to go to Harlem. I don't drive to Harlem.

Christine wanted none of these. Why not go to his place, she said. She had enjoyed his brunches so much. But it had always been so crowded and frenzied. She'd enjoy the same thing quietly, just the two of them. Would that be all right with him?

The staid Cadillac leaped forward, weaving from lane to lane, rakishly cutting off cars by the dozen. Streaked down Queens Boulevard, through grimy Long Island City, shot over the double-tiered girder-glutted hump of the Queensborough Bridge like a strike-bound bowling ball. Bullied and shouldered its way west through narrow traffic-jammed 60th Street. Opened up again on Central Park South and shot up north on Broadway. Reversed its field on 81st Street, lurched south for a moment and dashed headlong into a parking place smack right in front of Zabar's. From Kew Gardens to Zabar's, in heavy traffic, in the unheard of record time of twenty-one minutes. An Olympian dash.

While the garageman held the doors open, Goff clambered out clumsily laden with two bulging shopping bags from Zabar. Christine, burdened with the enormous bouquet of dahlias, emerged with difficulty from her side. The garageman drove off, but where was the doorman? Nobody there to let them in or give them help.

Wouldn't you know it, Goff thought about Stahrts, just like a German Nazi prick, when you need him, no one's home. When there's nothing he can do for you, he's sucking around like a snake at a fresh laid egg.

When he had finally managed to open the door by backing into it and holding it for Christine, he finally saw Stahrts clomping toward them. "Oh, Mr. Goff, please can I help you with your packages?"

Goff handed over the two shopping bags. Stahrts then turned to Christine whose face was hidden by her enormous flower bush bouquet, asking whether he might help her. Christine, lowering the bouquet, was about to decline graciously when she stopped in midsentence. Stahrts stiffened abruptly. Goff thought with satisfying malice that the sight of Christine's beauty had stunned him into Prussian paralysis. Yes, he practically clicked his heels as the shopping bags suddenly hung limp, grazing the floor, at the ends of his rigid arms.

But Christine was also standing at attention. Her face had flushed. Her startling blue eyes became even bluer. She finally managed to say to the rigid doorman, "Ah, Hans, how are you?" Stahrts nodded stiffly but remained speechless.

"You two seem to know each other," said Goff.

"Oh yes, Arnold, yes, from the old country."

What old country? thought Goff uneasily. "Look," he said, "I'll go up and start setting out the food. And when you finish catching up on old times, follow me up. I'll try to have everything ready. Let me have the bags, Stahrts."

"Oh no, Mr. Goff," sputtered the doorman from the old country. "I will take it up for you."

"That won't be necessary, thanks, just the same. I'll take them. You see we're having a late brunch," he said drily. Stahrts unclamped his rigid fingers as Goff slipped the shopping bags off them. Turning to Christine he asked, "Why don't you let me have the dahlias. I'll put them in water."

"Oh no, Arnold," said Christine, a little more collected now. "I'll bring them up in a few minutes."

"Right," said Goff as he turned, and balanced by the two bulging shopping bags shlumped into his elegant Park Avenue lobby to make his way to the elevator. He felt like a peddler.

Ascending, he became depressed. These were some openers to usher in his sex supreme. What the hell was going on? What was this between Christine and Stahrts?

He grew more agitated. Aggravation was starting to set in when the elevator reached his floor. Was this to be still another blow job shot down the drain? He dragged the shopping bags. They seemed much heavier than they had been in the lobby. He sighed.

He let himself into his apartment, put the bags down and went up to the closed circuit television screen which monitored the lobby. He switched it on and saw (but could not hear) Christine and Stahrts. She was speaking earnestly while he remained at respectful attention. He nodded and smiled. She also smiled, and then he was writing something down. What? Who knew? She started to edge away. She suddenly thrust her hand out. His response seemed to start out as a salute, but it was never completed; midway it changed its direction and he clasped her hand, shook it ardently. God, that salute that never made it! Would it have been the innocent

Boy-Scout type salute that Fitz, the day doorman, always threw at you, or would it have been the Nazi Heil-Hitler spasm? It wouldn't really have surprised him. He gritted his teeth.

What had fate served up for him this time? Was some ideologically spawned catastrophe about to befall him again? Another turn of the screw or some demonic-Jehovic punishment for his Jewhood? Or for his non-Jewhood? Oi, it's hard not to be a Jew! He didn't need another Friggan Columbus.

Who was Stahrts? Who was Christine? Some Nazi conspiracy? A cult maybe? Be careful, dress warm, stay out of drafts, you shouldn't catch a cult. Not heeding this ancient protective wisdom, had he caught one?

A wild theory: Just before Hitler committed suicide, he had ordered Bormann to cut off his genitals and pickle them in a jar of alcohol to give the lie to the scurrilous and embarrassing reports that he was deficient in cock and ball. A secret Nazi cult had arisen. The jar reposed on an altar shaped like a swastika in a cave in the Schwarzwald. They worshiped Hitler's pickled genitals and were preparing for the day when they would once again arise to jar the world. The pickled genitals had been stolen and since Goff was an art collector, he was suspected of possessing them. Stahrts, formerly an SS general, was a mole. Christine was a special agent of very high rank.

Another theory: Christine was not Danish. She was German. She had been the daughter of an extermination camp commandant. She lived on base as a little girl in a charming house surrounded by beautiful gardens growing extraordinarily bright and oversized blooms. Dahlias! Every Sunday the prisoners' band in striped pajama uniforms would perform, and little Christine with a big ribbon in her blond braids would accompany them, singing *The Lorelei*: "*Ich weiss nicht was soll es bedeuten, dass Ich so traurig bin . . .* " The SS audiences wept like babies. It really grabbed them. A big common grab. It brought down the casino. She was so cute; the darling of the SS troops assigned to the camp. They saw to it that she was completely sheltered and isolated from the crematory and bone pile pits; also huge fans had been installed and were turned on whenever wind shifts threatened to waft the noxious crematory aromas toward her. But one day, through the drunken laziness of an Estonian Nazi guard who qualified for the job only because of demonstrated super Jew hatred, she had slipped out through the garden gate and happily skipped over to the killing grounds. A little girl clinging to her mother in a line of sobbing women had given her a doll to hold until she came out of the shower-bath house. The shock had never left Christine. When she grew up, she was determined to devote the rest of her life to the benefit of the Jews. Stahrts was either Christine's father or some high-ranking SS banality. Had been in this country for thirty years under false papers and had become a door-man because of his military bearing. He always wore a little American flag pin on his doorman uniform. He had recognized her in the lobby instantly, had chokingly remembered her as a little girl with bows and braids singing with the band in the extermination camp's lush garden.

It must have been something like *that*—the last one! Goff could not conceive of Christine as anything but a loving person. Why should he? And if by some incredible chance she was evil . . . well . . . shouldn't the old Shamuses SAC motto take charge? "Never duck a fuck." And didn't he love her? Love forgives all. He must ignore as irrelevant what he had just witnessed on the closed-circuit television. It was vital. Every-thing he'd ever valued depended on it.

The door buzzes. Goff rushes. He's at the door prepared to forgive Christine for anything.

Enter Christine with her giant blooms. Goff glows his shiniest. He takes the blooms and places them in an urn. She is radiant. She fondly calls him Arnold. He fondly calls her Christine. He sees her only in purity. Pristine Christine; Schwester Christine; Mother Christine; Mamanÿu Christine. He will not be narrow. He has always brought to bear his capacity to learn whatever is needed for the occasion. For the Angel Christine, he must show himself at his best. He will now draw on everything he has ever pos-sessed, acquired, touched, absorbed. Everything will be utilized. So he wills better speech, usage, vocabulary, enunciation, articulation. He is in-spired. He can maintain it for extended periods. The triumph of the will. Of course, there will be lapses, but she will not notice in the splendor of his overall performance. He will suppress the unnecessary and the ugly. The hell with those thousand questions.

He escorts her to his art-filled living room. He pours her some Cherry Heering. They settle in deep-slanted Danish chairs. He notices for the first time the pale blue silk between the lapels of her exquisitely tailored jacket, the dainty blue silk collar around her darling neck. How charming. He wants to get that jacket off her.

"Ah, Cherry Heering. Your exquisite thoughtfulness, Arnold, is so warming. . . . "

What a darling she is! "Let me take your jacket, Christine. It's so warm in here." She smiles and allows him to slide the sleeves down her arms and off. He places the jacket on another chair.

"Dear Christine, do not fear to tell me everything. Do not fear to tell me nothing. My devotion to you, whichever you choose, is unalterable." He pulls a square Danish hassock across the room and seats himself at her feet. "So tell me or tell me not—what are you exactly? Nationality, I mean."

"I'm Danish," says Christine, who widens her eyes for openness. "During the war I helped spirit Jews out of Denmark. I proudly wore the Star of David."

"Weren't you too young?"

"You're never too young," she says with unflinching blue.

"I love Danish. The people, that is."

"Actually I'm not Danish; I'm Dutch." Christine cocks her head in candor. Her eyes remain steady. A hint of blue challenge.

"Dutch is good too." Goff attempts to ease her torments.

"Not as good as Danish. *They* were the best. I would rather be Danish . . .. " she pauses, deliberates, but now with lowered eyes, and lowered voice, "just as you would rather be Jewish."

"I would?"

"Well, I sometimes feel you would. It is really terribly important to be Jewish."

"Is it more important than being Presbyterian?"

"I couldn't say, Arnold."

"Is it more important than being Episcopalian?"

"I couldn't say, Arnold."

"Lutheran?" She shrugs. "What's the importance of being Jewish?"

Christine looks at him intently. "The importance of being Jewish? The Jews are the main threads in the weave of the West. Do you know my meaning?"

"Of course. Not that I necessarily agree."

"How truly noble are the Jews, truly a chosen people. What infinite sacrifice have they undergone to serve humanity. Down through the centuries they have selflessly lent themselves as outlets for the basest most primitive instincts of barbarians, and then in turn furnished them with objects for salvaging conscience. Ah, the glories and emotions they provide, the dizzying pendulum of love and hate, the ecstasy, the warmth of soul-cleansing penance, of the sensuality of remorse, of Dostoyevskian redemption, of expiation and reparation for a momentary extermination. The Jews are the world's only totally permissible pornography. The murderer thus renews his life. The Germans killed five million."

"Six."

"It is said the figure is exaggerated. We must be utterly scrupulous not to help perpetuate an injustice. One must be careful before bringing a charge of one million killings. Are you positive?"

"Positive."

"How can you be sure?"

"A careful inventory was taken. Jews are clannish; they keep track of one another. Witnesses interviewed, records and documents checked and rechecked. Pits undug."

"I'll buy that, Arnold. It is thoughtlessly charged that the victims went docilely to their deaths. How wrong to condemn the glorious submissive march of the Jews to the gas chambers. Execrable, say the critics, but I hold precisely to the contrary."

"*Au contraire.*"

"Yes. I say it is to their everlasting glory. It culminates to perfection the beautiful logic of their whole diasporic history. It is their mission. Do you know my meaning?"

"*Mais oui.* Why don't we move onto my low Danish couch together?"

"Of course." They settle down together. Christine talks on. Goff is strangely fascinated. Although he is intent on her words, her beautiful blue silk blouse also demands his attention. . . . She too has dressed with care. No bra; for him, no bra. Not much to tuck into a bra; still, she has decided well and graciously displays her darling nipples through the silk. Now that is class, he thinks with a happy glow in his groin. But back to her words. They continue to arrest him too.

"They disperse but never disappear. Throughout the centuries time and again, countless opportunities arose for the Jews to disappear, if they had merely said: 'I am no longer a Jew.' But they could never choke it out convincingly. So they rejected and in turn begot rejection."

"No loitering around the country club, please."

"It was willful, even arrogant, but divine, their chosen function to act as the target of the furies of the western world."

"The western world? Have you noticed who the less advanced peoples in Asia and Africa, seeking to modernize themselves, and emulating their technically advanced brothers, have designated as their enemy? Do you know the Chinese now hate the Jews? This is the great leap forward?"

"Exactly, Arnold. Ever available for all colors, races and creeds, God has placed them on earth as nature's balancer. Ah, how I pay homage to the Jew. I hold them above all other people. Arnold, what do you think of the Jew?"

"Dear Christine, I agree with a lot of what you say, but I tend to con-

clude otherwise. I think he clings with unreasonable tenacity to his identification. Pure *angeshpart*. Personally, I'm not so crazy about them. I
think they're crazy continuing to offer themsleves for nature's handy balancing act. Life may be a cabaret, but it's not a vaudeville act."

"But, Arnold, the Jew can't help taking on the role. Can the plant re-
fuse to take part in photosynthesis? Can the big fish decline the little fish?
Ah, nature is so exquisitely subtle; it assigns its roles so discreetly, with
such exquisite perfection. And it overlooks nothing. The plan is all en-
compassing, all purposeful. Do you know what Goethe said about nature?"

"For the moment it escapes me."

"He said, 'One obeys her even when one resists; one acts with her even
when one thinks he's defying her. . . . '"

"Ah, quite. So, the Jew then is not so much the chosen people as the
chosen scapegoat."

"Ah, you are beginning to know my meaning, although it is an oversim-
plification. Anyway, the Jew has no choice. The chosen have no choice.
This is the ultimate in balance; the perfect equation."

"*I* have a choice."

"No. One can have a preference, but not a choice."

There is quiet now between them. Christine's look is very soft, but penetrating. Goff takes her hand. He sees clearly now the direction he must
take. It is inevitable. It is what Christine wants. She wants him to be a
Jew. So be it!

Goff lets out a long-suppressed sigh. "Then I really have no choice, but
to be a Jew. Ah, Christine, for the first time it is not hard to be a Jew, once
you stop fighting it. You really never took me for anything else, did you?"

"Oh, Arnold, I didn't want to force it on you. You see, I wanted to hon-
or your preference, Basque."

"But I wasn't serious. It was just more a joke than anything else."

"I wasn't sure, Arnold. And you never actually came right out and said
it. I just wasn't sure. Even Stahrts wasn't sure. But he told me in the lobby that today he was finally convinced."

"Yeah? What did I do wrong?"

"You tipped him too much. When you picked up the car he was watching for you, you gave him ten dollars. The right amount, he said, was five.
It was typical Jewish generosity, he said, born, understandably of course,
of insecurity."

"Stahrts had that all figured out!"

"Yes, of course."

Goff thinks bitterly: the dumbest bastards become geniuses, brillant theoreticians, when it comes to Jews, figuring out why everything they do is no good. *Tayg nit.* "Well, Christine, does it please you that I have come out as a Jew?"

"I'm so happy," she says, snuggling in under his arm. "I was just waiting for you to settle down."

Again, settled by a cocksucker. Albeit, a beautiful, Gentile, blond, sweet-tongued one this time. Events had come full circle. He would have his ten sweet years of extra life after all.

"Oh, Arnold, I'm so happy that you of your own volition settled down to Jewishness."

"Oh, Christine. It was more your volition. I sensed you wanted me to be Jewish. I hope you want me more for myself, rather than for my Jewishness."

"Of course, of course, dear Arnold. And I hope you want me more for myself rather than for my Christianness."

Goff responds, "As it turns out, yes, of course. All my life I've sought the shimmering northern lights. You are they, Christine. You who know Jews so well, you've had Jewish lovers, yes?"

"*Only* Jewish, dear Arnold."

"Then you know what I mean. Conditioned as I was, I originally found it inconceivable that the shimmering northern lights could ever be attained by a Jew. So ever so long ago, with the incalculable support of my therapist, your husband, to whom—I must be fair—I owe so much, I succeeded in eliminating the debilitating effects of the Jewish ethos. I coached myself and couched myself, and groomed myself and bloomed myself into an individual with no particularly identifiable markings. If, however, somebody was vulgar and literal and insisted on an identity, I tossed them the Basque, which so many have hailed as an absolutely brilliant masquerade. I can say with a certain sense of pride I never resorted to Presbyterian, Unitarian, Episcopalian, Lutheran, Methodist. Although once in an emergency I had to resort to Turkish Moslem. And now, Christine, my dearest, I find, through you, that not only were these efforts foolish and in vain, but they were almost fatal to our beautiful relationship. No, no, Christine, it is not your Christianness, it is you. My Jewishness has been a lifelong conundrum to me. Rabbis and melameds, family, friends, enemies have all been unable to impress me with the importance of being Jewish. But *you, shayneh maydeleh*, have." Goff accompanied his Jewish endearment with a corresponding universal caress, brushing his hand over Christine's blue silk peek-a-boo nipples. It wouldn't be long before he would be at them—in hot nibble—but there are certain formalities to be observed. When you finally have your penultimate Jew-loving shiksa free and clear and waiting anxiously but showing such refinement, such class, you hold back and behave with refinement and class as well. It is all for the common good.

"I laid out a great spread in the kitchen; I'll bring it in. We'll have that great tête-à-tête dinner-brunch."

"No, Arnold. Please not now." She presses alongside of him putting her head on his shoulder and reaching for his hand. He buries his face in her shiksa neck breathing deeply of her shiksa scents. How like those gorgeous Irish teachers of yesteryear.

"Christine, do you sense how crazy I am about you?" Her response is to nuzzle closer, to squeeze his hand harder, to kiss his ear. "Christine, my sister, Blanche, and others consider I have keen powers of discernment about people's sex proclivities and sensitivities. They consider me a sex mavin. Do you know what I mean?" She orchestrates a cooing note into his ear. Yes, she knows.

"Christine, I've assessed you." Christine maintains her murmuring. Its source is very deep. Nothing can disturb it. "Christine, I've concluded you're a girl of fantastic inner passions, who has never been fulfilled. I've never seen such bottled-up sexuality. Is my evaluation correct?" Her response is a dart of tongue into his ear and an even deeper murmur. "Christine, fate has directed that I shall be the instrument to release the awesome passions imprisoned in you." Her murmur is turning into a moan. Again as in the Cadillac she reaches for his zipper. Goff stretches back to achieve a tautness of fly to make it easier for her. She succeeds in fishing out his cock. An astonished gasp of delight issues from her as straight, strong, stalwart soars his cock. Her gasp turns into a delighted gurgle as she pounces on it and captures it in her mouth, to swaddle it and caress it with feverish lips and cunning tongue and muted sweet crooning sounds.

Goff leans back in ecstatic sprawl. Among his other satisfactions is the one that his gamble paid off, and ten years of extra life is just around the corner.

But no, this is not what he wants. He wants to give, not to take. With a shudder of superhuman will, he suddenly detaches himself and sits up. He must make this sacrifice for her. The second time tonight! He is headed for something far beyond mere sex as he has always known it. He has

selected, wooed, pursued Christine for his sex supreme; he feels himself
being drawn upward into the celestial spheres of the shimmering northern
lights where dwells the soul. What awaits him? An exaltation always
dreamed of, never attained. He will even sacrifice his ten years. He must
be at the extreme ready for Christine, he must not risk failing to provide
her with the fulfillment he knows she's never had. Patience, strength of
will, she has earned it. He has earned it! He is made of firmer stuff. This
touching generous act. Christine senses it and she raises her head in sweet
apprehension. He kisses her feverishly.

It is his tongue that is now the benign aggressor. As she feels his approval she responds, and they hold each other in a long clinging kiss.

When they finally separate, Christine says, "You are a real man."

"Christine," he mutters, "it is true that you have never been fulfilled!"
She makes no reply, but resumes kissing him, little rapid puffs of kisses
on his face and ear.

"I mean, you've never had an orgasm."

"Yes, yes. It's true. Your reputation as a mavin is well deserved."

"Tell me, Christine, does your husband fuck you?" he whispers.

She nods.

"Often?"

She shakes her head.

"And your other Jewish lovers, did they?"

"Did they what?" she pants.

"Fuck you," he pants.

She nods.

"Often?"

She shakes her head again.

"But they were fulfilled, the bastards!"

She nods.

"Dear angel Christine! Have you no bitterness?" She shakes her head,
his earlobe between her lips shaking with it.

"Did they at least appreciate you?"

"They were grateful," she croons.

"Please accept my thanks on their behalf," Goff says with a bitter irony. "It has been written that when the sun shineth on the Jew in Tiberias,
the Jew in Fairbanks feeleth the warmth. But your sweet sacrifice shall
not have been in vain, darling Christine, I swear it!"

"Thank God, thank God! I believe you, Arnold! I have been burning
with fever for so long, so long!"

"Consider what drives me, Christine! I can't rest till I have ravished my psychiatrist's beautiful blond Nordic wife! A humble Jewish Brooklyn boy who has been going crazy in his longing for your shimmering northern lights!" She moans. "Fascinating, simply fascinating. How about a little food?"

"No, no," she moans.

Goff is the master and Christine the slave. A perfect combination! He rises from her arms, showing his command. She whimpers. But when he returns with his fly closed, bearing a tray laden with food and drink and puts it on a low table, she is sweetly composed and agreeable again, although slightly flushed. She joins him on her knees on the rug and they feed each other delicacies, sucking each other's fingers. He knows exactly what he is doing, where he is going, his nineteen years of psychoanalysis are coming in handy. Nineteen years, and all for Christine! It was worth it.

"Don't eat too much, Arnold." She smiles.

He knows. He knows soon he is going to fuck her within an inch of her life, and it's not good to fuck on a full stomach. Mama Christine is right.

He wipes his mouth on a napkin, pulls her to him, and kisses her as they topple over onto the rug. He is now irretrievably inflamed by the tiny breasts whose nipples, visible through the delicate blue silk, have never left his sight. He places his hand on her breasts and feels one through the silk. The slightness, the fresh delicate springiness, like the breasts of a very young girl, arouses him infinitely more than the buxom mass he usually favors. He *appreciates* them. He is sure his brethren with their gross appetites haven't. He is superior to them. And that's why he has this beautiful girl. Goff's face reaches down and he begins to suck at her nipple through the fine silk. He has never sucked through silk. It is sensational. But, he supposes, it can only work with the finest silk. Christine struggles to open her blouse. She cannot detach him, he is going crazy! He won't give, he ravishes it through the silk.

Finally he rises and lifts her to her feet. "Come," he says.

She nods avid little nods, opening all the buttons herself as he leads her to the bedroom. She stands waiting for his move. Slowly, reverently, he removes her tantalizing silk blouse. To his surprise and delight, her armpits are filled with golden tufts. Her breasts are small little handfuls. They would only fill a child's hands. Gorgeous miniatures, he convinces himself, with smooth pink shiksa nipples just as he'd expected. He kisses them as he eases her onto the bed. She is now writhing, too excited to remove her pants. He does it for her, removing them with trembling reverence like holy vestments. And they are off. And there is his shrine and altar, his holy grotto, haloed in golden curly fur. The shrine is in slight undulation. He stares transfixed for a moment, then kneels to it in obeisance and kisses it humbly.

He rises and undresses in measured movements. A high priest in ceremonial. She lies in continuous moaning undulation. He is standing above her in pure undress. His cock juts out over her in oaken strength. The worshiped gazes up at worshiper in awe. She reaches slowly up to touch his cock, and he sinks into bed beside her. She places her hand around his cock and holds it as she would a bird. He feels the tremble of worship in her hand.

She whispers to him, "Arnold, you are truly a man. Come to me! I love you. Is it always so big and hard with you? Never before have I seen one such."

Of course not, he thinks smugly. "I love you too, Christine, and strangely it seems to me also that I've never before known it to be this hard and this large."

"How do you account for it?" she shudders ecstatically.

"LOVE. I've never truly loved before." He feels impelled to continue his worship at the shrine and moves his head down to so address it, and Christine now writhes with such violence that he has to bury his head hard at his golden shrine to carry out his devotions.

Christine is in uncontained rapture. "Oh, darling, I know tonight is the most wonderful night of my life. Oh, oh, oh! You will . . . "

"Mmmm . . . "

". . . fulfill me!"

"Mmmm . . . "

"Orgasissimus," she pants.

"Whatever she wants," hymmmmns Goff. "Whatever those former petz of hers never gave her. I'll give her the big O, orgasissimus, orgasmanique. The best. She deserves it; she who rescued the Jews from the Nazis. She deserves everything." And he goes on with his silent devotions.

The services now require that he rise, and they engulf each other. His hand now reaches deep into the blond grotto and is anointed with holy water—at last! Real shiksa holy water! And his love swells within him, throughout his whole being, and he sends his love to his fingers and his fingers attain inspiration and they delve and caress and unfold with exquisite tenderness. His excitation approaches exaltation as Christine thrashes and moans. And his mouth and fingers leap and dance. His excitement is uncontained. He is bringing in a gusher.

Her legs spread wide, her body arched, the way is clear. He is TREE-MENDOUS and at perfect readiness. His cock crows. He aims it into her lubricious, thirsting cunt, and he sails right in, docking cock into a paradisaical enclosure. No sooner is he in, than Christine locks the gates of Eden, wrapping her beautiful long legs around his back. All is now ready. So locked and docked, they go into slow undulation. His cock in her nest has never before felt so good. His true nest. Christine is now blithering with spastic joy. Their tempo increases rock-in-dock, rock-in-dock, rock-in-dock, rock-in-dock. Christine's cries become shrieks. Her hands become claws. Her legs around him squeeze in python crush. They are one as a whip in a windstorm. But she is not ready. He holds back or he will be spent. More, more, she moans; I am almost there!

Goff cannot fail her. He steams up again and goes into locomotion. Faster, faster, faster, pound, pound, pound, pound of flesh, pound of flesh, pound of flesh! He can kill her! *Kill me, kill me!* He loves her, he loves her! *Don't stop, don't stop!*—her cry from her crazed cunt core.

"Don't worry, darling!" he assures, as he keeps walloping in. He has never been so good, so strong! But for Christine, he *must!* Again the same old story. Anyone else could get away with mediocrity, but a Jew had to excel. He must erase the deficiencies of Kummerlos and the others.

"Arnold, *Liebchen,* I have never had a man like you! *Heiliger Gott!*" This earns her another tattoo of deft thrusts. He applies olde English. He fucks with consummate mastery. "I feel it coming, *Liebchen,* I feel it coming! Don't stop! Or I will be undone!"

And the lightning struck. It struck in Goff's chest and burst out in jagged savage electrical bolts, turning him purple. He went stiff.

Except for his cock. The last sign of life in Goff was his cock contracting rapidly out of Christine's cunt into his scrotum. Goff's last thought was *that fuckin' Levine!*

Christine was aghast. She had been absolutely convinced she was finally about to have her climax. Now she was left with only Goff's dead weight on top of her. She wriggled out from under him and looked at him. He was motionless. Should she try some mouth-to-mouth resuscitation? Ach, no. It went against her. He was dead anyway.

She dressed quickly and left the apartment. In the lobby she spoke to Stahrts in German, telling him Goff had apparently died of a heart attack.

He had better call an ambulance. She would appreciate it if he did not disclose her name.

Stahrts snapped to attention. Of course! She could count on it. Unconditionally! She put out her hand to thank him. He took it and kissed it in stiff courtliness, snapped erect and held the door open as Christine walked out onto Park Avenue.